RILLA

BOOK ONE OF THE PARADISE SERIES

IVANA L. TRUGLIO

JONQUIL
PRESS

First published in Australia in 2014
by Jonquil Press
ABN: 99871403756
Reprinted by Jonquil Press 2017

National Library of Australia Cataloguing-in-Publication data:
Author: Truglio, Ivana L.
Title: Rilla/Ivana L. Truglio
ISBN: 9780992565442 (paperback)
Series: Truglio, Ivana L. Paradise series; bk One
Subjects: Fantasy fiction
Dewey Number: A823.4

Cover illustration by Les Petersen

Typeset in Minion Pro 9.1pt/10.2pt

For my sister,
who told me I was the little star in her story

ABOUT THE AUTHOR

Ivana lives in Sydney, Australia. She devotes most, if not all, of her spare time to writing the Paradise Series.

She studied aviation, archaeology and ancient history at university. During her studies, it was rumoured that she lived in the university library. She currently holds a private pilot licence and rides a motorbike.

Ivana is married and has two young children who reap the benefits of having a mother with a wild imagination. She has been writing since she was a child and the characters in the Paradise Series have been living in her head for over 15 years.

ACKNOWLEDGEMENTS

My first thanks goes to my high school English teacher, Mrs Milton, who told me that this "short story" was the beginning of a novel. If not for her, *Rilla* would never have come this far.

A very special thanks goes to my sister, who wrote the star story many years ago and allowed me to use it in *Rilla*.

Next, I'd like to thank all my family and friends who supported me through this project, especially my husband, who made me many teas during the long nights of writing, my friend Anicee, who edited the story for me and probably most importantly, my friend Patrick, who read every version of the story and only pouted a little when I changed it each time.

My final thanks goes to everyone involved in my Kickstarter Project. Firstly, to Les Petersen (yes, my illustrator) for doing such a fantastic job that people were drawn in simply by the cover. Secondly, to all of my backers. *Rilla* would not have been published if it weren't for your extraordinary generosity. Particular thanks go to my biggest supporters, Catherine, Graham, Kathrin, Keiran, Kylie and Nicole.

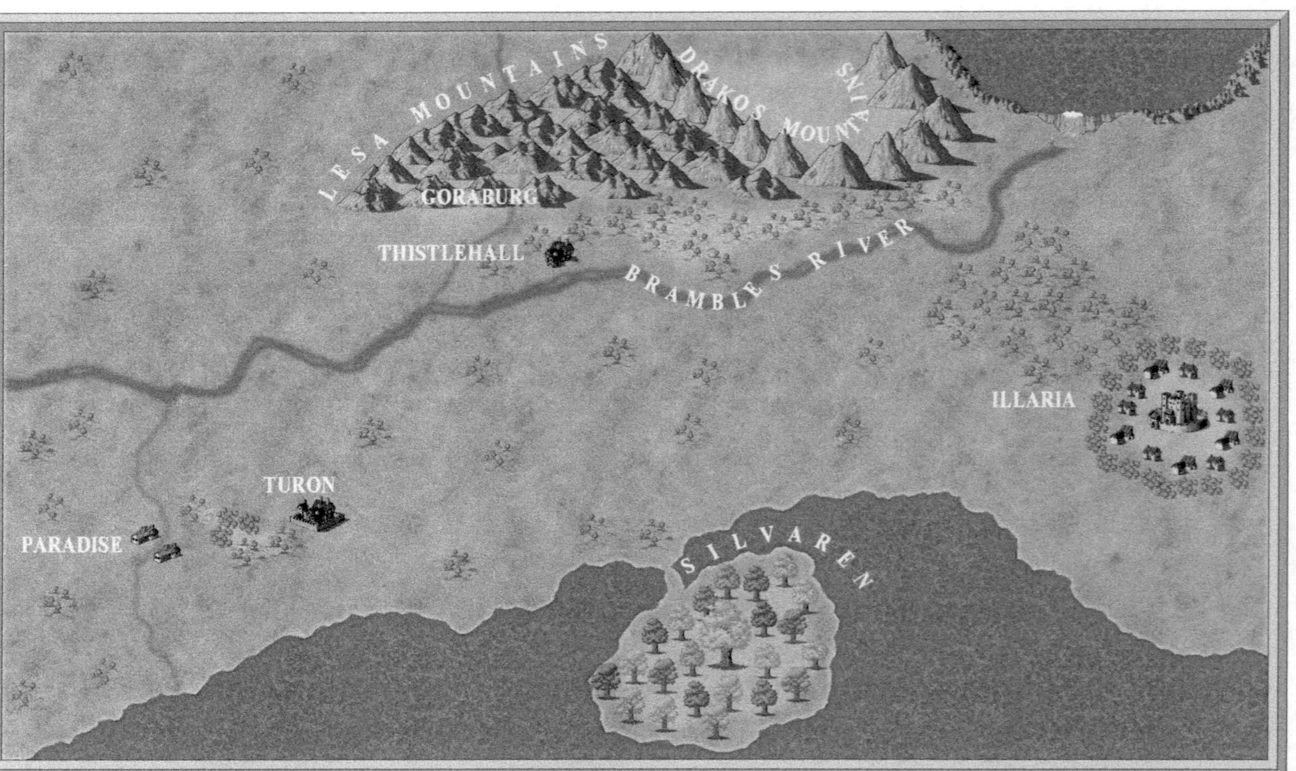
LESA MOUNTAINS
DRAKOS MOUNTAINS
GORABURG
THISTLEHALL
BRAMBLES RIVER
TURON
PARADISE
ILLARIA
SILVAREN

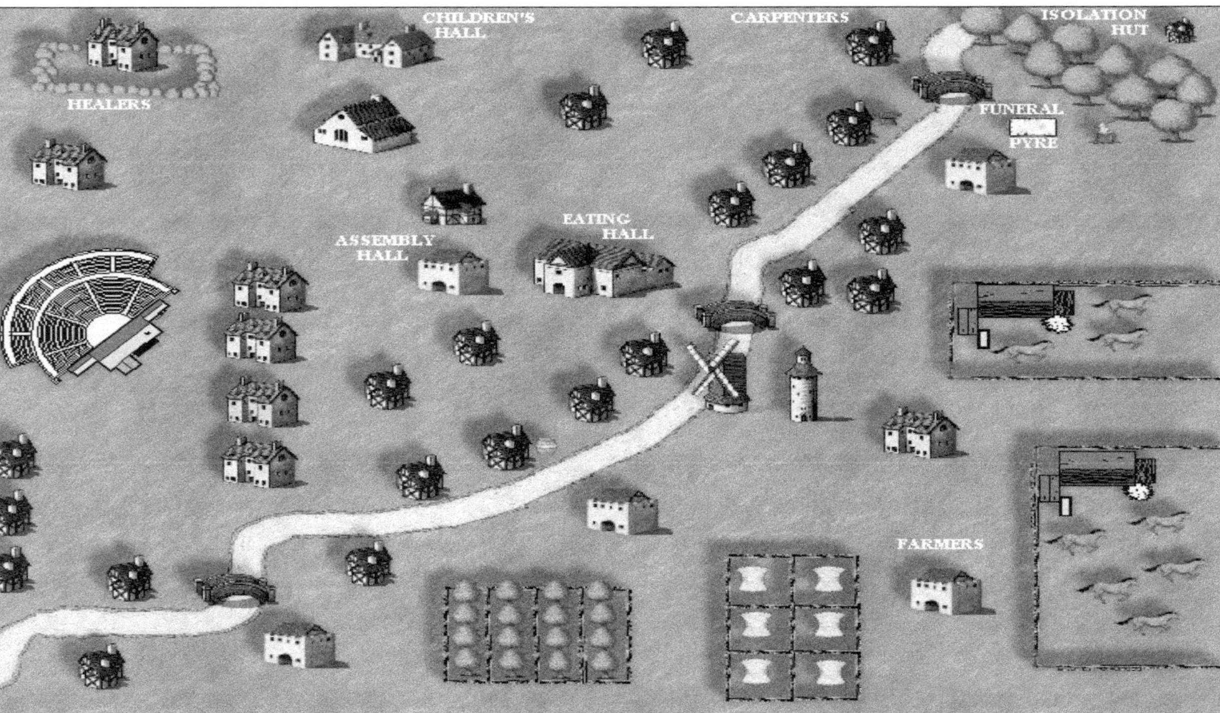

CHILDREN'S HALL
CARPENTERS
ISOLATION HUT
HEALERS
FUNERAL PYRE
ASSEMBLY HALL
EATING HALL
FARMERS

Chapter One – Rilla

Running across the northern bridge of the fast-flowing stream, Rilla felt her cheeks flush with anxiety. She had found a lady at the north-eastern edge of the boundary, in the forest. By her close-cropped hair and multiple weapons, Rilla assumed she was a banwep. She had been taught about them from a young age. They were dangerous people – people who didn't fit in. They lived by their wits and their weapons.

This banwep's body was bloodied and broken. Her wits and weapons clearly hadn't been enough this time. She needed help. Rilla had torn strips from the hem of her dress to bind the worst looking wounds, but the healers were the only people with a chance of saving her.

She knew it was taking her too long to run to the healers' building, but there was no other way. Damn these long skirts they made her wear – they only got in the way! The stranger was dying as she struggled with her clothes. *The healers will know what to do. The healers will know what to do.* It was all she could think to stop the image of the lady's bloodied body surfacing in her mind.

"Healers!" she yelled out as she neared their building. "Healers, help me!" To her surprise, no one came out. She felt panic rising to overcome her, then the sound of bells tolled in the air. It was time for the morning meal. Everyone would be in the eating hall. She turned instantly and ran towards the sound of the bells, cursing the foolishness of not leaving even one man behind for emergencies.

Rilla ran ever faster to the eating hall where she knew the healers would be. The red hair falling into her eyes triggered flashes of the lady. She wiped the hair from her face and felt the blood on her fingers smear across her face.

Please live. Please live.

It didn't take her long to reach the eating hall. Everyone was already assembled there, waiting for her before they broke their fast. Her sudden entrance caused a commotion. She didn't even glance towards the Paradise's leader, but headed straight for the healers.

"At the edge of the boundary ... a banwep ... she's hurt." Rilla gasped through the words, trying to catch her breath. The healers probed at the her forehead and turned over her bloody hands. "Don't waste your time on me. She's dying!"

The healers moved to follow her. She saw them glance apologetically at Erton, the Paradise leader.

"Torak, Belial, go with them," Erton ordered his enforcers.

Rilla groaned before rushing back out the way she had come. She hurried everyone along to the healers' building so they could collect basic supplies.

"You'll need a stretcher," she called out as the healers hurried into their building. As she caught her breath against the wall of the building, Rilla smirked at the discomfort she could feel cascading off Torak and Belial. It amused her to know how much she affected them.

Eventually two healers reappeared with supplies and a stretcher. They handed the latter to the enforcers. Wordlessly, Rilla led them all to the boundary of the Paradise.

A few moments after they arrived at the battered body, Ursher, the younger of the two healers, finally managed to catch his breath. "What were you doing all the way out here?"

Rilla clenched her jaw tightly. "It doesn't matter what I was doing here. If I hadn't come, she would be dead."

The older healer, Rhanya, looked between the two of them, the creases on his face sagging more so than usual. "The girl is right, Ursher. There is no point arguing over it. The lady needs our help." Looking over to Rilla, he added, "You did well to try and stop the bleeding."

Rilla started and blushed at the compliment. None of the other healers would have bothered to praise her for her actions. Rilla watched curiously as Rhanya sorted through his salves and unctions until he found the one he was looking for. She would not learn what they were all used for until she was officially an apprentice, although Rhanya has already secretly started her training.

She knew the first thing he would do was try to staunch the bleeding. For that he would need cayenne powder. Rilla remembered her surprise when the old healing master had first told her that cayenne pepper had powerful medicinal uses.

"That will do for now." Rhanya sat back on his haunches with a sigh. "Torak, Belial, please help Ursher get the patient on the stretcher. My old bones are too tired for such work these days. Take her back to the other healers. We'll follow you."

Rilla creased her brow as she helped the weary healer to his feet. She should have insisted one of the younger healers come with Ursher, but Rhanya was their master. He knew more than anyone else about the healing arts.

The other healers were waiting for them when they arrived. Rilla was forced to wait outside their building. She was not a healer so was not allowed to watch them at their work. It seemed a ridiculous rule to her. With each trade, only those apprenticed were allowed to see the masters at work. Knowledge was closely guarded here. She found herself wondering if all Paradises were the same and, if so, if they all had rebels like Rhanya who shared information on the sly.

Rilla waited outside for what seemed like hours, sitting cross-legged on the grass. No one came to keep her company. She had no friends her own age to speak of. Most people would probably have been happy to know that she was occupied for the morning, knowing that there was no chance she would find a way to bother them.

The bell tolled for the midday meal, but Rilla did not move. Nor did the healers come out of their rooms. The patient consumed all of their attention. Only on occasions such as this was it acceptable for the communal meal to be begun with part of the flock not in attendance.

"Little one." At the sound of Rhanya's concerned voice, Rilla raised her head. "Have you been waiting here all day?"

"Is she alive?" Her voice was strained with worry. Rhanya nodded, holding out his wrinkled hand to her as she stood up.

"You can see her if you like." He put his arm around her shoulders and guided her inside. "She isn't awake, but she survived."

The old healer led Rilla to the room housing the stranger. Her short-cropped hair gave her away as a banwep – the slyest and wittiest of people to roam the Outworld. They were feared in this Paradise. Night time stories were told of them to scare the youngsters away from straying too close to the boundary. Those stories had never worked on her.

"You were right to make us rush, little one. Another hour by herself and she would have bled to death." The other healers gave Rhanya a look of barely disguised disgust. Their discomfort at being in the same room as Rilla was plain. She shared a wry look with Rhanya. He suggested the other healers head towards the eating hall while he and the "little one" watched over the newcomer. Not needing a second nudge, the healers quickly and quietly filed out of the room and away from Rilla.

"Erton and his fools," Rhanya muttered under his breath, as he eased himself into a wicker chair by the window. "He really hasn't made this life very easy for you, has he Rilla?"

Rilla smiled at the sound of her name. Erton had forbidden everyone from using it soon after they had entered the Paradise. The edict had made most people avoid her, just so as not to accidentally speak it. The punishment was isolation which, in a Paradise as closely bound as this one, was a severe punishment. Rhanya was the only one who tempted this fate.

She still remembered the time, years ago, not long after her mother had disappeared – had left her in this Paradise with her father. Everyone had stopped calling her by name, most had stopped speaking to her at all. She was hurt and confused. But most of all, she was lonely.

One awful night, she couldn't sleep. She cried until the other children started to complain. Tugging her roughly by the arm, one of the dorm leaders had taken her to the healers. Rilla hadn't understood why, though now she realised it must have been to ask for a tonic to force her to sleep.

Rhanya had answered the furious knocking. He had already been old then. Rilla remembered looking up at him through teary eyes. There were wrinkles across his forehead like a tilled field. He placed a gentle hand on her shoulder as he nodded and spoke to the dorm leader. She soon released her tight grip on Rilla's arm, all but shoving her towards the old man.

Rilla would have fallen but for Rhanya's firm hand on her shoulder. He stood there for a moment looking down at Rilla. She shied away from him, expecting angry words shouted at her. Instead, he bent down closer to her.

"I was just about to make myself a cup of hot cocoa. Would you like some, Rilla?"

She looked at him in relief and gratitude. She tried to answer but all that came out was a little squeak accompanied by another rush of tears. Rhanya scooped her up into his arms and carried her into the kitchen as she clung to him tightly. She knew this old, wrinkled man was the kindest man in the Paradise. From that moment onwards, she stayed as close by his side as possible and he made a point to call her by name whenever he would not be overheard.

Shaking her thoughts from the past, Rilla squared her shoulders. "Let them avoid me if they want to. It gives me more time to explore."

She studied at the Outworlder. The woman's closed eyes were twitching oddly.

"She must have been in a vicious fight." Rhanya answered her unasked question. "If she hadn't strayed into the Paradise, I dare say she would have died. Her saving grace was that her attackers didn't make it through as well."

The two of them stayed silently watching the banwep until the other healers returned, Rhanya in his chair, Rilla on the reed floor beside him, her head on his knee.

"Erton is waiting for you," Ursher told Rilla as he entered the room. She did not reply, but stood up silently. Rhanya made to accompany her before Ursher spoke again. "Alone." He glared meaningfully at the older healer before turning towards the banwep. Rilla squeezed Rhanya's hand tightly before walking purposefully out of the door.

"What were you doing at the boundary?" Erton did not even deign to raise his head as Rilla walked through the door, continuing to write on a yellowing piece of parchment. "You have been told time and time again not to go there."

"Is there any point in answering your question?" The anger in Rilla's voice was barely disguised. The Paradise leader chose to ignore it.

"And you missed the midday meal. That's two meals in one day that you've disrupted." He carefully placed his pen in its holder before looking at her over his half-moon glasses.

"I apologise for putting you out, Father."

"Don't call me that, child." His honeyed voice did not disguise the threat behind his words.

"Do you think anyone has forgotten that three of us came to this Paradise together? Surely, they know you are my…" Erton's hands slammed the top of his desk, his black hair flicking forward. Rilla jumped involuntarily.

"I do not need to be reminded, by a child of fifteen years, that I once lived in the Outworld." The muscle beneath his right eye began to twitch uncontrollably. "You are ordered to the isolation hut. You will be given only bread and water. You will stay there until the day before the Choosing."

Gritting her teeth, Rilla took two deep breaths before walking back outside. Waiting for her were Erton's brainless followers, Torak and Belial. They escorted her to the isolation hut, ironically the building closest to the Paradise boundary, and shut the door. There were no locks in the Paradise. Everyone knew better than to stray where they did not belong.

Inside the hut, she found a dry husk of bread and a clay cup full of water. In the far corner was the bed she had come to think of as her own. It was still early afternoon, but the day's excitement had exhausted her. Rilla sank down into the woollen blankets and closed her eyes, falling almost immediately into a deep sleep.

Chapter Two – Arishen

"I know what you are," she whispered menacingly into his ear.

Arishen's eyes opened wide in fear. Parthak's face was too close to his – the furious blush on her cheeks a stark contrast to her pale skin. Her cold, dark eyes stared down at him.

"What are you talking about?" he asked her in a low voice, eyebrows arched in feigned surprise, as he scanned the room.

"Why would you need to check that no one else is here if you don't already know the answer to that?" He didn't answer, so she continued, "You had another dream last night."

That was all Parthak had to say and she knew it. Instantly, Arishen drew back from her, refusing to even meet her gaze. *Does she really know?* It wouldn't matter if she could prove it or not. All she would have to do was suggest the possibility to Erton and the problem would be taken care of.

"You wouldn't ..." the protest died on his lips.

"Wouldn't I?" Parthak lifted her chin defiantly. "People like *you* are not meant to live in Paradises. People like *you* should be taken care of or left to their own devices in the Outworld."

"You can't mean that!" he cried in a panic. "We're Partners." *Partners. We are bound together, even beyond death.*

"I was too young to know what you really were when that decision was made." Her disdainful manner left him little hope.

"Parthak, *please*." Arishen had nothing to bargain with and it was all too clear that she would not change her mind about him. She stood up gracefully. *How can someone as pure as her be so unsympathetic?*

"I will give you until the Choosing, Arishen. If you don't leave, you'll wish you had." Her words left little to the imagination as she walked from the room. It was death either way – one possibly slower than the other.

Arishen wanted to ask how she knew, when she had found out, who else she had told. He wanted to explain it all to her – that it wasn't his fault. No one could control the way they were born. In this Paradise, none of the children knew who their parents were. Perhaps this was so no blame could be attached to anyone else. A human seer in a Paradise, in the one place where no magic should be. The mere possibility was unthinkable and yet, there he was.

The bell tolled for the morning meal. Arishen got out of bed and dressed quickly. The children's hall was empty save for himself. He had slept late because of his dream and Parthak had left without him. People would notice that. People always noticed what was none of their business. He walked quickly to the eating hall.

It was four days until the Choosing. Four days to decide what he would do. He shook his head. There wasn't much choice. Parthak would betray him if he stayed. He knew he had to leave, but that didn't make the decision any easier. Leaving the Paradise for the Outworld was a death sentence.

Trying to banish these thoughts from his mind, he entered the eating hall and immediately located Parthak sitting in her usual seat. *Perhaps she didn't really mean it.* He pushed the thought away, knowing it to be wishful thinking. He sat down next to his Partner in silence.

Erton was standing at the front of the eating hall, making sure that everyone was present before breaking the fast. His eyes came to rest on an empty seat at the children's table. Arishen noticed the Paradise leader's face flush as he realised it was *the girl* who was absent yet again. It was the third time in the past week.

Suddenly, she burst into the hall yelling for the healers to help her with a banwep. Rhanya and Ursher hurriedly followed her out, looking apologetically towards Erton. The other healers left soon afterwards, begging the forgiveness of everyone gathered, to prepare their rooms for the new arrival.

It was all anyone could talk about during the meal. A new Outworlder come to the Paradise. She would be made welcome if she met all of Erton's requirements. Humans were meant to be welcomed into Paradises, if they ever found one but Arishen had noticed that the unskilled ones never stayed, even though only fools would dare brave the Outworld again after finding one of the rare safe havens.

The girl's hasty arrival and departure must have made Parthak reconsider her silent treatment of Arishen. He knew she did not want to be seen as an *independent*. *The girl* was an *independent* and was shunned by their entire community. She was a prime example of what life could be like if you didn't follow the rules of the Paradise.

"What do you think happened to the Outworlder?" It was the obvious question to ask, though Parthak need not have bothered. It was the same question half the people on their table had asked simultaneously.

"Perhaps she was attacked by a savage beast," one person guessed.

"Maybe her raid on an isolated farm house was expected and they fought her tooth and nail." Suggestions floated around the room from every table. Each person either had an answer or a question about the newcomer. Arishen tried to offer suggestions that could not later be remembered as being correct. He had dreamt of the stranger the night before and knew exactly what had happened to her, but not the reason why.

When the morning meal was over, Erton rose from his chair to make an announcement. As he raised his hands, the room fell silent. It did not do to make him wait.

"As I'm sure you are all aware, the Choosing will be held in four days." This sent a low murmur throughout the room. Arishen and Parthak were not the only ones who would be Choosing this year. *The girl*, along with Tika and Plyke, would also be making their choice. Raising his hands for silence a second time, he continued. "Should the newcomer choose to remain in our Paradise until that time, they will be made available as a mentor as is their right."

A sharp intake of breath went around the room. Arishen heard Parthak's tiny gasp in amongst them. He took a deep, steadying breath before daring to meet her eyes.

"Who in their right mind would choose a banwep?" Her snide comment was just what he had expected. He looked at her sorrowfully. She had changed. Erton had managed to truly make her one of his sheep. She had been growing more and more distant from him until the culmination of it all with her brutal revelation that morning.

"Perhaps the newcomer isn't a banwep," he said, as they left the eating hall together. "Perhaps she was just travelling by herself and got into a fight."

Parthak looked at him cruelly. "Do you really think anyone other than a banwep would be so foolish as to travel the Outworld alone? She has to be a banwep. Besides *the girl* called her one. She would know better than anyone."

"Even so," he persisted, "perhaps this one isn't all that bad. If she was born into it, it doesn't mean that she wanted to."

They were far enough away from the other Paradisians that Parthak obviously felt she could speak freely. "Don't for one moment think that you can sway me with talk of this banwep to change my mind about you. I know what you are and it disgusts me."

"Parthak, surely you don't mean that," he pleaded. "It isn't my fault that I was born this way."

"Oh, that much I know," she conceded. "But whoever your parents are, they should have been taken care of before they had the chance to bear you. If you don't leave this Paradise, I will make sure that mistake is not repeated with you."

Chapter Three – Plyke

Plyke and Tika watched in excitement as *the girl* ran from the eating hall with the healers. A banwep in *their* Paradise! Nothing like this had ever happened before.

"Do you think she's met the elves?" It was Tika's favourite question. Plyke smiled, knowing that their entire day would now be consumed with talk of the Outworld and the strange creatures that lived in it.

"Possibly. It depends if she ever found the way to Silvaren. Banwep might be as unwelcome there as they are everywhere else in the Outworld."

"Silvaren! Is that *really* what the elven stronghold is called?" There was sceptical wonder in his Partner's voice. Plyke shrugged.

"That's what Kora says. The older ones know more about the Outworld than we do. Some of them even lived there for a time."

They left the eating hall with the rest of the crowd, and walked to the stream, close to the windmill. There would be no one to tell them what to do until the midday meal. It was their last four days of freedom. With the Choosing, they would start their new lives.

"Have you decided yet?" Tika asked the same question he'd been asking for weeks.

Plyke shook his head. Not looking at his Partner, he navigated past the creaking sails of the windmill to the bank of the stream. From here, Plyke could see most of the Paradise. On this side of the stream were the farms and storage areas. Back across the bridges, the more refined trades had their workshops. He could not even decide which side of the stream he wanted to live.

"You know there are only four days left. What will you do if the Choosing comes and you haven't decided?"

"I don't know," replied Plyke. "I can't think of anything I want to do for the rest of my life. It seems like such a long time to be stuck doing just one thing."

"Better to be stuck doing one thing your whole long life than to be thrown into the Outworld."

"Is that what you believe?" Plyke looked up to see Kora approaching them. The slowly turning windmill had masked the sounds of her soft footsteps.

"Kora!" Tika stood up quickly and ran to hug her. Plyke smiled at his reaction. He knew the tall, brown haired lady was Tika's favourite adult in the whole Paradise.

"You didn't answer my question, Tika." She held the frail looking boy at arm's length and stared straight into his hazel eyes. "Do you really believe what you said?"

"I suppose so," he answered hesitantly. "You would know better than us. You lived in the Outworld for a while, didn't you?"

"For a little while, yes. But then I found this Paradise." Her voice was distant, almost sad. "Tika, do you mind if I have a quiet word with Plyke?"

Tika opened his mouth to protest, but Plyke waved him on. Plyke knew his Partner was confused by the request. The two of them shared everything together. Tika would only ask him about it later anyway.

"I'll meet you back at the stables." Tika turned slowly and walked away at an excruciatingly slow pace, no doubt hoping Kora would say something while he was still in hearing distance.

Plyke hid a smirk as Kora tapped her foot until Tika was well out of hearing distance. This was going to be another one of *those* conversations. One with dangerous consequences for both of them should anyone overhear. The fewer people involved, the better.

"Have you decided what you're going to do, Plyke?"

"You and Tika, both," he replied, looking up at Kora through the sweep of hair that obscured the left side of his face. "No, I haven't decided what I'm going to do yet."

Kora hesitated before continuing. "This banwep, dangerous as she may be, she could be of assistance to you if you choose to leave."

"Tika would never forgive me," Plyke replied instantly. "I couldn't do that to him."

"He will understand if you explain it to him. His fascination with elves is a favourable sign." Plyke looked away and unintentionally began biting his nails.

"The decision is yours, Plyke. But don't choose something just to appease your Partner."

"Oh, so you'd rather I choose something to appease *you* then?" he asked in all seriousness. "Isn't that just a little hypocritical?"

"I will say this once, and once only." Kora sat beside him, wrapping an arm around his shoulders. "If you decide to live here, I will support that decision, but you will never be free. You will have to hide your true self from everyone until the day you die. If anyone even *suspects* what you are, Erton will have you killed. You may think it safer to stay in the Paradise, but at least in the Outworld you'll have the chance to find happiness."

"If there are so many risks here, why did you ever decide to stay?"

A look of sorrow flashed across her face. "Because I fell pregnant. I couldn't leave my child behind."

She had never told him that before. Admittedly, he had never thought to ask. "Then why don't you leave now?" Plyke refused to feel guilty. It hadn't been *his* decision.

"I've been here too long. I would never be able to survive in the Outworld now." Plyke saw the resigned look on her face, which confused him. She was a strong and clever woman. Surely she would be able to survive out there again. "But you, you're still young. You can learn from the banwep. If she leaves, she can teach you how to survive. You can find a place where you belong. But you won't be able to do it on your own. Either you leave with this newcomer, or you try to survive in here."

Plyke walked to the stables where Tika was waiting for him. *I wonder if Tika would come with me.*

He knew Kora had good reason for wanting him to leave, but did she truly know what he would be leaving behind? Tika saw him coming and ran out to meet him.

"What did she want?" he asked. The thought that perhaps it was private didn't occur to him.

"Nothing much, just trying to get me to make a decision about the Choosing." Plyke smiled at his Partner, hiding his uncertainty. "Perhaps the two of you should get together to decide for me."

Tika did not respond well to the jibe.

"It's important, Plyke. I'm sure the rest of us have all chosen something already." He continued without being asked. "I'm going to work here, in the stables. Parthak will surely work with Erton's favoured scholars. Arishen will probably choose to go with the carpenters. And is there any doubt that *the girl* will stay with the healers? Rhanya is probably the only person who talks to her willingly."

"I know, Tika." Plyke was tired by the conversation. He knew it was important, but that didn't make his choice any easier. What would he do if the banwep decided to stay?

Chapter Four – Rhanya's secret

Rilla woke at the sound of the door opening. More bread was pushed through alongside a jug of water. She lay staring up at the ceiling in silence. Erton had forced her into a life of solitude. He couldn't understand it, but sentencing Rilla to the isolation hut was barely a punishment. The confinement was more of a chore than the distance from people. He had made sure that most Paradisians weren't comfortable talking to her. The only exception to that was Rhanya. He often made time to talk with Rilla. When they were completely alone, he even called her by name. In that, he was unique.

The bell tolled for the morning meal, signalling to Rilla that there were only three more days until the Choosing. She had long ago decided to join the healers and Rhanya supported her choice. It would not be an easy life for any of them – the other healers constantly trying to avoid her, Rilla simply wanting to learn from them.

* * *

Footsteps outside the hut brought Rilla out of her musings. Erton's muscle men did not stand guard all day. They came and went with her food and water. There was no need for a guard when all knew the punishment for speaking with someone in the isolation hut was to switch places with the person inside.

"Rilla, are you in there?"

"Rhanya, what are you doing here?" she asked her old friend in concern. "If Erton finds out that you've been here, he'll punish you."

"Never mind Erton, little one." He brushed the threat aside. "The banwep – the stranger from yesterday – she woke up. She spoke to me."

Rilla frowned. From what she had seen of the woman's injuries, she should not have recovered enough in one day to wake up, let alone speak coherently.

"What did she say?"

"The usual. She wanted to know where she was and who we were. But that isn't important," he continued hurriedly. "If any other healers had been there but myself, she would already be dead."

"What? Why?" A sliver of panic found its way to Rilla.

"Isn't it obvious? She isn't human." At her sharp intake of breath, Rhanya went on to explain. "At least, she isn't fully human. She must be at least part lintep."

Part lintep! Rilla didn't answer. The lintep were a race of people in the Outworld. Unlike dwarves and elves, there were no physical distinctions between these people and humans. It didn't matter to humans that the lintep mainly used their powers to heal people. It didn't matter that they were the most knowledgeable in all things to do with magic, and the most powerful. In fact, that only made matters worse. They looked like humans, but they weren't.

"Rilla, do you understand me?" The healer's voice was strained with quiet intensity. "She needs to leave before anyone else finds out. You need to make sure she leaves."

"How can I do that from in here, Rhanya?"

"You won't be in there for long. If I can keep her safe until the Choosing, you must choose her as your mentor. Together, you can leave this place." He spoke too rapidly for her to object. "Someone's coming." With that, he was gone.

The door to her hut opened. Rilla squinted in the sunlight. Torak and Belial motioned for her to follow them. They never spoke to her. It was almost as though they thought Erton would punish them if they exchanged a few words with her.

Rilla walked a few steps behind the two huge men as they headed towards the assembly hall. It seemed everyone was gathering for an announcement. For Erton to release her from the isolation hut, it must be important.

The three of them waited outside until everyone else had entered. Torak and Belial pointed to an empty corner of the room, and once she had taken her place stood guarding her so that she could see nothing but the raised platform at the front of the hall. Erton had designed the hall so that, at the same time every day, the sun hit the northern window and shone directly onto the platform.

He waited patiently for silence and the right time. The room quietened after a short time and the sun moved into position. Erton stood directly in the path of the light, assuring himself that he would be seen by one and all before addressing his flock.

"My children," his voice boomed in the silence, "it has come to my attention that our newcomer is a banwep. I stand by my statement yesterday. If she is awake, she *will* be available to be chosen as a mentor."

A gasp heaved through the crowd. So the newcomer *was* a banwep. She should not have the right to be a mentor.

"What if she wakes up and decides to leave?" A lone voice called out in the crowd. It was not difficult for Erton to pinpoint the speaker. A small circle had appeared around the tanner at his question.

Erton looked at him with acid eyes. "*If* she wakes up in time and decides she wants to leave, our young apprentices will be able to leave with her if she agrees to it." A low murmur went through the crowd at his words. His flock was not happy. "In this case, I would strongly suggest that the five children carefully consider the consequences of their choice. A life in the Outworld, as intriguing as it may sound, is one of danger. Remember all you have learnt of it before making such a disastrous choice."

So much for free will, Rilla thought to herself from her corner. The fact that Erton was considering the possibility that one of his sheep might choose to leave his flock was clear from his severe warning to them.

As people began to file out of the assembly hall, Rilla noticed a meaningful glance directed towards her guards. Torak nodded almost imperceptibly. Once the hall was empty, Rilla was led to the raised platform. Erton stared down his nose at her.

"I'm sure you know that the warning was meant for you. The banwep is *not* to be chosen as a mentor."

Rilla took a steadying breath to keep her temper. "Why would you assume *I* would be the one to choose her, if anyone does?"

The Paradise leader did not answer her. He took one final look at her before signalling his muscle men to remove her from his sight. They escorted her back to the isolation hut and left without so much as a word.

* * *

Rhanya hurried back to the healers' building. He did not like to leave the banwep alone. If any of the other healers discovered her true nature, she was as good as dead. Lintep, or humans with any sort of magic, did not survive long in Paradises. They had been specifically created to let humans live apart from magic. The old healer had been born into this Paradise. He'd never had a chance to experience the Outworld. In his heart, he couldn't deny that the thought of magic intrigued him.

He remembered the time before Erton came to his Paradise. Even then, Paradisians had been afraid of magic, but they did not hate it. Their new leader had made certain that this had swiftly changed among the more impressionable people. Any human who appeared to have any *strange* abilities was taken care of. There had been more and more occurrences in recent years. It made no sense to him.

As he walked into the room housing the invalid, his eyes came to rest upon an empty bed. Frantic, he spun around and he saw her standing in front of the herb cabinet.

"Get back into bed," he whispered urgently. "Don't say anything and close your eyes. Quickly!"

The banwep obeyed and not a moment too soon. A few of the other healers strode into the room to check on her. As Rhanya sat on the edge of her bed, they gave the patient a cursory inspection, checking her pulse and temperature.

Once they had left the room and Rhanya was certain they could not hear him, he spoke quietly to his patient.

"I know what you are."

Her grey eyes opened wide and she stiffened at his words. He shook his head. "I will not hurt you, but you have to pretend to still be ill. Your life depends upon it. Paradisians are not tolerant of magic. If anyone else suspects …"

The banwep said nothing, but simply nodded and closed her eyes again.

Chapter Five – A leaf falls

Tika was quieter than usual as they left the assembly hall. Plyke noticed the change in his mood immediately. Something Erton said seemed to have struck a chord in his Partner. Not wanting anyone to overhear them, Plyke waited until they were, once again, at the bank of the stream before speaking.

"What did he get you thinking about?"

Tika looked up at Plyke in astonishment. "How could you tell?"

"Something made you so quiet, I was afraid others would notice it," Plyke said, raising an eyebrow.

Tika remained silent for a few minutes, and Plyke did not press him for an answer. He knew his Partner well enough to understand when he needed some time to think.

"Ask me again tomorrow," Tika finally answered. He walked towards the healers' building, leaving Plyke confused and curious.

* * *

Tika walked to the healers' rooms. He didn't know what he would say when he got there, but he wanted a glimpse of the stranger. Ursher was standing at the outer doorway, drinking a cup of tea. Tika walked determinedly towards him.

"What can I do for you, young Tika?" the healer asked amiably. "Do you have an upset stomach? Perhaps you need something to calm your nerves before the Choosing?"

Tika stopped short of him in surprise. "Nothing is wrong with me, Ursher," he replied. "I ... was curious to see the Outworlder."

Ursher's eyes narrowed, and the middle-aged man was coldly silent as he led Tika to the banwep's room. Seeing Rhanya inside, Tika walked towards the older healer as Ursher left the room. Rhanya turned at the sound of his footsteps.

"Well, young Tika, I did not expect to see you here today." His voice was soft and inquisitive, but not reproachful. "What can I do for you?"

Tika hesitated. "I ... I was curious to see the newcomer." He made no attempt to move closer.

"Erton certainly knows how to shake the tree," the healer mumbled almost under his breath as he motioned Tika closer to the bed. In a louder voice, he spoke again. "She has not woken yet. Her wounds are healing well and I expect her to be available for the Choosing, though perhaps not as her complete self."

Tika took a close look at the banwep. Her light brown hair was cut short, as was the fashion of her kind. She was tanned more than any Paradisian, betraying her outdoor life. Even though she was slender, he could see well-defined muscles. Bandages were tightly bound around her ribcage and parts of her arms and legs.

"Rhanya," Tika asked timidly, "do you think she's ever seen an elf?"

"I'm not sure," Rhanya answered, placing a hand on his shoulder. "Perhaps you can ask her when she wakes."

"I would give *anything* to see an elf." Tika looked up into the healer's brown eyes and smiled sadly before walking away, taking with him the hope that the stranger could tell him some new stories of the Outworld, untainted by Paradisian lies.

After the assembly, Arishen headed off by himself. He was certain people would have noticed that he and Parthak were spending a lot of time away from one another. Preparing for the Choosing could come in handy as an excuse for it.

He walked over to the carpenters' work sheds. Kalid had spent many hours talking to him over the last few days. Together, they had been trying to sort out what role he would be best suited, and he had been quite keen to start working with the master carpenter. She was a single-minded woman with strong, steady hands and a good eye for wood. She could look at the grain and size of the log, imagine what it would turn into and, less than a week later, it would be done.

Kalid looked up as he approached but did not slow her work as she spoke. "Back again, young Arishen. Still haven't made up your mind?" The master carpenter had come from the Outworld when she was only a child. She didn't much speak about her life before the Paradise, but Arishen wanted to ask her a few questions.

"Actually, I was hoping we could talk about something else today." His hesitantly hopeful voice made Kalid look at him with something like irritation.

"Would this have anything to do with Erton's speech?" she asked in annoyance. Her tone surprised Arishen, but he nodded all the same. "Sometimes that man simply doesn't know when to keep his mouth shut. Come, we'll sit inside awhile." She motioned him through the door into her own private room where he sat on one edge of her bed. Kalid left him there while she made some spicy tea. Bringing the two wooden cups in with her, she pushed the door shut with her back. Arishen rose to take one of the cups from her and held it between his cold fingers.

"What I am about to tell you is important," she began in a low voice. "I have lived in this Paradise for the past forty years. For the first twelve years of my life, I lived in the Outworld with my parents. I did not find it to be as bad a place as they describe in here." At that admission, Arishen's eyes brightened. Studying his face, Kalid hastened to add, "Many years have passed since that time – things may have changed. The villages in the Outworld are not like the Paradise. There are no communal eating halls. Food is not provided by the leaders of the villages. You have to work to be able to feed, clothe and house yourself. There *are* roaming thieves who would rather take what they need from passing travellers than to work for it."

"It sounds ... different," Arishen mumbled into his tea, eyes downcast.

"Arishen, there is more to the Outworld than that." Kalid hastily looked through her window and cocked an ear towards the door. Once certain that no one was around, she leant in closer and whispered conspiratorially. "There are wondrous things beyond that boundary. Forests that stretch further than your eye can see. Mountains that rise above the clouds in the sky. Oceans, bodies of water that stretch on for miles and miles. Magic more magnificent than you can imagine. Elves, dragons, karliki and even lintep. There are more things to see than you could possibly fit into your lifetime. And the most wonderful thing of all, you have the freedom with which to do it."

Arishen looked up from his tea at Kalid in awe. He'd never heard anyone speak so lovingly about the Outworld. All the stories they had been told from childhood made their Paradise seem like the only place you would ever want to live. Leaving it for the Outworld had never even crossed his mind until yesterday.

"But, if the Outworld wasn't that bad, why did you stay here?"

"I was young," she replied with tears in her eyes. "My parents had died and there was no way for me to support myself. Finding this Paradise was a stroke of luck for me. I couldn't believe how easy it was to survive here. Food, shelter and clothing were provided. A few years after I arrived, I chose a trade and by the time I had trained in it, I had already been here so long that I would never have been able to survive in the Outworld again. There were so many sacrifices I had to make along the way, but it was worth it to the child I was then."

"Do you think the banwep will stay?" he whispered. He knew it was dangerous to speak about things like this openly.

"I can't tell you that, Arishen." Her reply was not encouraging. "It depends on so many things. Does she like being a banwep? Can she give up her freedom in exchange for some degree of safety? Does she have a trade to offer the Paradise? Is there a family that might miss her? There is no way to know the answer to any of these questions without talking to her. In any case, these conversations are pointless unless she wakes up in time for the Choosing."

Chapter Six – Will you stay?

Erton had seen the newcomer the day she had been found, and Rhanya had talked him through her injuries and provided his diagnosis. She would not die. After holding his assembly, the day before, doubts had crept into his mind. *What can this banwep possibly have to offer my Paradise? Does she even have a trade? Will she lead my sheep astray after I've spent so much time and energy on them?*

He swept these questions aside as he strode to the healers' building. According to Rhanya's prediction, she might awaken this morning. He did not want to miss the opportunity of talking to her. There were many things that needed to be discussed, mainly the Choosing and what she could expect her role in it to be.

Erton wasted no time on niceties. Ursher opened the door for him and led him to the Outworlder's room. The old healer was there, helping the banwep with her broth. Rhanya nodded amiably at him before turning back to his patient. Erton fought to keep the annoyance from his face, though it made his eye twitch to do so.

Seeing that the banwep was awake, Erton walked over to a wicker chair, pulled it closer to the bed and seated himself comfortably. He studied her silently as she ate her broth. She had not finished half of it before replacing the spoon in the bowl and sinking back down into her woollen blankets. It had given Erton all the time he needed. Her mind betrayed no fond thoughts of the Outworld, nor any inclination towards unnatural powers. These were always the first things he looked for in any newcomers. They had to pass this test to have any chance of being truly welcomed into his Paradise.

"My name is Erton." He spoke suddenly, forcing the banwep to sluggishly reopen her eyes. "I am the leader of the Paradise you find yourself in."

She did not reply for a moment, confusion clouding her eyes. "I'm in a Paradise?" she finally spoke, hope trickling into her voice. Above all others in the Paradise, his questions were undoubtedly more important than hers, and he did not answer her question.

"There will be an important ceremony held here in two days' time — the Choosing. It is a time when Paradisians of fifteen years choose a mentor to teach them a trade. I understand that most of the children this year have already decided who they will Choose. However, I am obliged to explain the procedure to you in the event that one should go against my wishes and Choose you."

"Erton, I'm not sure that she is up to this conversation. Perhaps it can wait until tomorrow?" Rhanya's interruption fell on angry ears. Erton did not even acknowledge that he'd heard the old healer before continuing.

"Generally, each child chooses a mentor who they will live and work with for the rest of the mentor's life. In the case that a child chooses a mentor who refuses to take them, the child is given the choice to either be executed or banished to the Outworld. In the case that a child refuses to choose a mentor, they are given the same choice."

The newcomer stared at him in confusion. "Would a child ever choose to be executed rather than banished to the Outworld?"

"All Paradisian are schooled during their childhood of the terrors that the Outworld contains. Unless a child is particularly wilful, they would rather choose execution than the uncertainty of a life of hardship and pain," he replied, eyebrows raised at her expression.

The banwep remained silent. Erton searched her mind for anything that would betray her true thoughts but found nothing. Her mind was strangely empty.

"I understand you need your rest, but I must ask you a few further questions before leaving you in the care of the healers." The newcomer merely nodded her head in acquiescence. He continued, "Do you have a trade to speak of?"

"I am capable of doing many things," she answered carefully, "but I have not specifically been trained in any one trade."

"Is there anything you can offer to the people of my Paradise?"

"I can teach them to fight," the banwep suggested. Erton stared at her icily as she fumbled for an explanation. "I mean to defend themselves in case of an attack."

"We are hardly likely to come under attack in the Paradise," he replied flatly. "It is one of the reasons the Paradises were built in the first place."

"I can fish, hunt, cook, patch clothing, track animals ..." her voice trailed off and Erton watched the banwep squirm as the realisation dawned on her that she would not be welcome in this Paradise.

"You must decide before the Choosing if you wish to remain here. Think carefully. We would not wish you to be *unhappy* with your choice." With that, he rose and swiftly left the room.

* * *

Rhanya silenced the banwep with a single look before returning his gaze to the window. He waited until Erton was out of sight before allowing her to speak.

"I won't be welcome here, will I?" the Outworlder asked quietly.

Rhanya sighed heavily. "Don't tell them you wish to leave until just before The Choosing. If you do so before that, your life really will be in danger."

"Wouldn't Erton be glad to know that I don't intend to stay?" There was genuine confusion in her voice.

Looking towards the door and back again, Rhanya spoke softly. "Erton does not like losing his sheep. If he thinks, for one second, that any of the children choosing a mentor wish to leave the Paradise, he will kill you to keep them here. It does not matter if you intend to accept them or not. In his eyes, they will be lost just the same." The banwep creased her forehead. "Rest now, I will explain to you more tomorrow. Perhaps we can take a tour of the Paradise to show you your new home?" She nodded her head silently and closed her eyes to the world around her.

Chapter Seven – This is your new home

Shuut was standing at the window, lost in thought, when a healer came into the room. Slowly, as though afraid to lose her balance, she turned to greet the middle-aged healer.

"You must be one of the healers responsible for saving my life." He merely inclined his head towards her. She smiled shyly at him. "Thank you."

"It is my trade," he replied shortly.

"Do you think it's possible for someone to take me for a walk around the Paradise? I'd like to see it, but don't think I can manage on my own." She made her voice as helpless as she thought would be believable. With any luck, he would suggest the old healer. She insinuated the thought into his mind and was rewarded by his immediate response.

"I will see if Rhanya is available. Wait here." He turned abruptly and left her alone in the room. She waited silently, looking out the window at what could have been her new home. Hearing footsteps approaching her, she turned her head to see Rhanya.

"I hear you'd like to see your new home," he said, as though it was the first he'd heard of it.

"Well, if I am to decide whether I shall stay or go, this would be the best way, would it not?" She smiled cheekily, and the old healer's eyes shined in response. He walked over to her and held out his arm, waiting for her hand to slip into place before leading her out of the door.

Once outside his domain, the old healer turned and gestured back at the small building. "These are the healers' rooms. If anyone has an ailment, or a stranger is found in a bad state within the boundary of the Paradise, they are brought here and we treat them. We tend them in these rooms until they are well enough to return to their trade or to the Outworld."

Shuut looked at the building. It was made of clay bricks with a thatched roof. There were few windows – none of them shielded with glass, but all had reed shutters to keep the worst of the weather out. Noticing the lack of security, she took a closer look at the wooden door, only to realise that there was no lock with the handle.

"Are you not afraid that someone will break in and steal something from you?" she asked in surprise. "Those reed shutters and wooden doors can't keep many thieves away."

Rhanya's forehead creased in bewilderment. "Why would anyone want to steal what they would be freely given?"

"You mean you don't charge them anything?" Shuut was incredulous. The mere thought of getting something for free, without stealing it, was astounding.

"Ahh." He nodded in understanding. "I forget myself sometimes. I've lived in this Paradise all my life, but others have told me stories of the Outworld. Everything is freely given in a Paradise. You are fed, clothed, sheltered and healed for free. The way you 'earn your keep' is by your trade. This is a utopian society. There is no greed, no hunger, no murder."

No unauthorised murders. Shuut distinctly heard the old healer's thought and stared at him until Rhanya continued.

"If anything strange is noticed about you, like you might have a smidgeon of magic in you or you don't accept everything the Paradise leader tells you ..." He left the sentence hanging.

"No murder?" she asked sceptically, eyebrow raised.

The healer motioned her into silence until they had walked away from the building.

"What happens to those who have no powers, but help those who do?" Her eyes briefly met Rhanya's before the healer smiled sadly and patted her arm. She wondered whether it was to reassure her or himself.

"You will see that there is a garden behind my home. There we grow the herbs used to heal our patients. We have a variety of plants from those that help you to sleep to those we used to stop your bleeding."

Shuut did not interrupt the old healer's chatter. She understood he was doing his best to help her and the only way was to be interested in the Paradise and not question anything.

Motioning to the south, he pointed out a somewhat larger building than the healers' rooms. "That is where the midwives and wet nurses live. It is strongly encouraged that parents do not raise their own children. It's meant to make the Choosing a less biased ceremony. Parents are discouraged from admitting any relationship to their child."

Shuut understood what Rhanya couldn't say aloud. Any parent who acknowledged their relationship to a child was executed. She wondered how many children chose a trade in which they thought their parents might be employed.

"Where do the children live when they are too old for wet nurses?" Shuut asked, hoping to lead them to another part of the Paradise. Rhanya motioned to another large building to the east of the healers' rooms.

"That is the children's hall. All children live there until they choose a trade. With them are dormitory leaders. Their main purpose is to look after the children when they are not attending classes or eating meals.

"The building you see next to that is the school. Most of the teachers are particular favourites of Erton's. They teach only what he wants Paradisians to know, whether it is truth or not." Rhanya had lowered his voice with this last statement. Shuut feared that she was placing the elderly healer in danger, with this excursion, but could not bring herself to insist that they return to her room. It might be the only chance she got to see the Paradise.

Walking past the wet nurses and midwives, Rhanya pointed out a small amphitheatre. "This is, by far, my most favourite part of our Paradise. Both the playhouse and the musicians' quarters are located here. Every full moon, a performance is held with the festivities lasting half the night. The musicians also play in the tavern most nights."

"You have a tavern?" Shuut asked in surprise. "But who would stay in the rooms there? Surely you don't get travellers."

Rhanya laughed. "No, no, the tavern is simply a place where people can go after their day of work to drink some honey mead and listen to music. As far as I've been told, our tavern is nothing like what Outworlders would expect."

"Can we go in for a drink then?" she asked hopefully.

"*You* are meant to be ill, my dear one," he said, patting her arm jovially. "Besides, they do not serve drinks until after the day's work is done. Perhaps we can go there after the Choosing, tomorrow night."

He led her further south, closer to the stream running through the Paradise. They walked past the tailors, spinners and weavers, dyers and painters as he explained that most of the trades that worked closely with each other were grouped together. The brick makers and stonemasons were just as close to the stream as the potters. Across the nearest bridge was a storage yard which held the clay from the clay-pit. Near this same storage yard was a plantation of reeds where the thatchers got their materials.

Walking upstream, past the thatchers, he pointed out the brewery, chandler, bakery and butcher. All of these were fairly close to bridges. Most of their supplies came from the other side of the stream, so easy access was important to all of them. Walking past them, Shuut noticed a few larger buildings to their left and pointed them out to Rhanya.

"Ah yes," he answered her, "they are the central buildings to the Paradise. There is the assembly hall, where everyone gathers to hear Erton's announcements. Next to that is the eating hall and, attached to it, the kitchen. And over there is the bell," he said as he pointed between the three buildings. "It is rung for the morning, midday and evening meals. Above those buildings, can you see another smaller house? That is Erton's place. Being the Paradise leader, he is the only one to have a place of his own."

They both stood silently for a moment, reliving the previous morning's meeting with Erton. Rhanya shivered, though it was not a cold day, and walked onwards forcing Shuut to follow closely behind.

"These are the only other buildings on this side of the stream. There you will find the cobbler, blacksmith and carpenter."

"Blacksmith?" Shuut asked. "How do you get metal for the blacksmith?"

"The Paradise began with a plentiful stock of metals. All the Paradisians needed was made from that. Now the only things the blacksmiths do is fix any broken or damaged items. If they are lucky enough to get more metal from any weapons that Outworlders bring in with them, they can make new items."

"But who would willingly give up their weapons? They are precious to Outworlders. We cannot survive without them."

"You forget, dear one, that once you live in a Paradise, you are a Paradisian. There is no violence here. One of the reasons is that there are no weapons. All Outworlders must give up their weapons if they choose to stay here."

Rhanya began to walk over the northernmost bridge in the Paradise. Shuut hurried to catch up with him. Knowing that he was probably the only person not hostile to her, she did not wish to be separated from him by any great distance.

"Is it all farmland on this side of the stream?" she asked, listening to the sounds of animals and men at work in the nearby fields. Rhanya pointed towards upstream.

"Up there is the funeral pyre. We don't have much room to spare, so the dead are cremated instead of buried, as I understand is the custom in the Outworld."

Shuut nodded as Rhanya proceeded to point downstream.

"Down that way, everything has to do with farming of some sort. There are the stables and cattle-herds. We have our beehives for honey mead and candle wax. The farms grow various grains and vegetables and the orchards supply all our fruits. Further downstream are a watermill, silo, tannery and olive press." Motioning towards the nearest building to them, he continued. "This is where the fishermen live. There aren't too many fish that swim down our stream, so they lend a hand on the farms whenever they are needed."

The banwep looked around her, taking everything in. The land was flat, as far as the eye could see, apart from the odd building scattered here and there. It looked much like any farming village she had ever visited, though possibly a little more organised. Looking over her shoulder to the north-east, she saw what could only be described as the narrowest forest she had ever seen.

"Does that *forest* stretch to the edge of the Paradise?" she asked, sarcasm thick on her tongue.

"It stretches as far as the isolation hut," he replied with a chuckle.

"The isolation hut?" *How can there be need of an isolation hut with no locks or violence in the Paradise?*

Rhanya led her to the edge of the forest and seated himself with his back against one of the larger trees. Shuut, making sure to seem grateful for the rest, joined him.

"Much as you may not believe me, most of the people living here are quite content with the situation. Erton has managed to *convince* most of his sheep that magic is evil and that the Outworld may as well be a death trap. He has made certain to let them know how wonderful this Paradise is, and almost everyone believes him. One of the things he encourages is unity. People do not like being by themselves – they don't like to be seen as individuals. The isolation hut is the only form of punishment here and, usually, it suffices to keep people in line."

"But why would anyone stay there if there are no locks?" Shuut interrupted him.

"Most people are too afraid to go against Erton's wishes. If he has put you in there, you can be sure the entire Paradise will soon know about it. If you are seen out and about when you shouldn't be, it will be reported to him. If anyone is seen trying to talk to someone in the isolation hut, they are made to switch places with the person inside. That is more than enough of a reason for people to keep away."

As he was explaining this to her, Shuut noticed two large men walking towards them. Rhanya immediately fell silent, nodding to them as they passed by, but not acknowledging them any further. She followed his lead and did not ask the obvious question until they were well out of hearing distance.

"Who were they?"

Rhanya only shook his head vigorously, white hair flying around his eyes. Shuut strained to hear his thoughts.

Torak and Belial! Please let this Outworlder hold her tongue around them. If Erton finds out ...

Shuut placed a hand on his arm and squeezed gently, her lips shut tightly. They remained in silence until Torak and Belial returned, walking with a quicker step than when they entered the forest. Watching them cross the bridge, Rhanya let out a long sigh. Shuut laughed lightly, almost masking the sound of approaching footsteps.

"Careful, Rhanya," a girlish voice called out from the forest. "Torak and Belial might start thinking you just don't like them."

Rhanya smiled. Shuut looked up in surprise as a girl stepped out from behind a tree, red hair pulled back into a long thick plait. She didn't bother lifting her muddied skirt as she walked towards them.

"You should know by now that you can't sneak up on me, little one." Rhanya greeted the girl as she sat by his side. "Whenever Torak and Belial emerge from that forest at such a rapid pace, you're never far behind them."

Shuut watched the exchange with interest. This was the first Paradisian she had met outside of the healers' building. The olive-skinned girl could not have been more than fourteen or fifteen years. Something about her did not sit well with Shuut, though she had learnt enough in the Outworld to mask such thoughts.

"Forgive me, my new friend." Rhanya finally looked back at her. "This is the girl who found you. Were it not for her, you would certainly have died before anyone noticed you."

"I owe you my thanks." Shuut looked straight into the girl's piercing green eyes, inclining her head slightly. "If there is anything I can do to repay you ..." She didn't know how to complete the offer. There was probably nothing she could do for this Paradisian. They had no money here and any other form of repayment was more than likely useless or forbidden.

"You may yet get the chance." It was not the girl who answered, but the old healer. Shuut frowned. The look that passed between the two Paradisians was not lost on Shuut – but she remained silent.

A bell tolled in the distance. It was time for the midday meal.

"You go on," the healer told the girl. "You've been in enough trouble over the last few days. Besides, I have the excuse of a healing Outworlder."

The girl smiled brightly and hugged the old man before running towards the eating hall. Rhanya got to his feet slowly. It was clear he was unaccustomed to sitting on the ground. Together, Shuut and the healer made their way slowly back towards the eating hall. It would be her first appearance in front of the Paradisians. Possibly too soon, but they could not possibly say she was ready for the Choosing if she was not at least *seen* today.

Their slightly late entrance caused everyone in the eating hall to look towards the doors. Shuut, at Rhanya's instruction, leaned heavily on his arm and walked with a shuffling step. It took quite a bit of effort to keep up the pretence, but he had warned her more than adequately of what the consequences would be if anyone realised what she was.

Rhanya pointed over to his usual place with the healers. As they realised they would have her seated with them, the men edged closer to one another, making space for one more. The cooks brought out a spare plate, cup and cutlery for Shuut.

As she sat down, she noticed all the plates already had food on them, including her own. *Too bad if you don't feel like chicken today*, she thought to herself as she looked at the meal in front of her. She moved to pick up her knife and fork when Rhanya placed a gentle hand over hers. Looking up uncertainly, she saw him turning to face the front of the eating hall. A chill ran down her spine as she saw Erton looking straight towards her.

"My people." His voice carried effortlessly through the large hall. "Joining us today is the banwep. It appears as though she will be available for the Choosing after all."

A low murmur surrounded Shuut, but she did not look around. There could be no doubt that all eyes were on her now, but she dared not look away from the Paradise leader into the frightened eyes of the Paradisians.

None of the healers spoke to her, but there was conversation amongst themselves. They said nothing to interest her. The health of the Paradisians was not her concern. She strained to hear the conversation at other tables, only to realise that they were all concerned about the fact that she would be allowed to participate in the Choosing. From what Erton had told her, these concerns were baseless. No Paradisian would even dream about choosing her, especially if they knew she intended to leave. She would have to remember to ask Rhanya when she could announce her intention.

* * *

Plyke waited until after the midday meal to resume the previous day's conversation with Tika. He'd noticed his Partner's face light up the second Rhanya entered the eating hall with the banwep. There was no doubt in his mind that the newcomer was the reason for his odd behaviour.

Together, the boys walked towards the stream. Plyke was surprised when they didn't stop on the west bank. He followed Tika to the water mill – the noisiest place in the entire Paradise. They stayed well away from any farmers, instead choosing to sit in the shadows between the water mill and the silo.

"Is there something I should be worried about?" Plyke finally asked his Partner under the cover of the sound of the water mill. Tika pursed his lips before raising his eyebrows almost apologetically.

"I've changed my mind."

"Changed your mind about what?"

"The Choosing." Tika's chin tilted, defiantly.

"So ... you're not going to work in the stables?" Plyke's Partner shook his head. "Then what *are* you going to do?"

"I'm not exactly sure."

"What do you mean you're not sure?" Exasperated, Plyke resorted to asking the same question Tika had been pestering him with for weeks. "Have you decided who you're going to choose?"

"Yes." The confident answer burst immediately from Tika's smiling lips. Throwing his hands up in the air, Plyke gave up.

"Who are you going to choose?"

"The Outworlder."

"What? When did you decide that?" Plyke managed to hide his astonished relief.

"Yesterday. But I couldn't be certain until I saw her in the eating hall." Tika could barely contain his excitement. "She'll be available for the Choosing."

"What if she's never met the elves before?"

Tika shrugged indifferently. "At least she'll be able to teach us to survive so that we can find them ourselves."

"Us? We?" Plyke leaned forward. "What are you getting at?"

"Well ... you're going to come with me, aren't you?" Plyke toyed with him for only a moment before smiling. Tika sighed with relief. "Don't do that to me!"

"You know I could never let you visit the elves by yourself. Who would be there to stop you from making a fool of yourself in front of them?" Plyke laughed with his Partner, amazed that he was going to leave after all. Tika had made the choice for him. Plyke hoped Kora would be happy about the decision.

* * *

"My dear little one," Rhanya called out to her as Rilla approached him in the fading light in his garden. "To what do I owe the pleasure of your company?"

She smiled at the old healer. If she'd had a grandfather that she knew, she always imagined he would be just like Rhanya. He had a way of making her feel like the most special person in the Paradise.

"I wanted one last talk with you before the Choosing." She scratched the side of her nose, signalling to him that she was just saying that for the benefit of any eavesdroppers.

"We are quite alone here, Rilla," he reassured her. "The others have all gone to the tavern tonight. Probably one last night of drunkenness before they get stuck with you." They both laughed at the thought. It had always amused them to think how the other healers would deal with Rilla in their midst. Now that day would never come. "Are you set for tomorrow?"

"Does she have any idea?" Rilla asked, not daring to name the banwep.

"I tried to warn her," replied Rhanya with a heavy voice. "I could not give away too much for fear that she might voice her intention to leave before it was time."

"Did anyone notice you helping her, Rhanya?" Rilla couldn't hide her concern.

"I can't be certain this time." He patted her hand gently, as she lowered her eyes at his admission. He hastened to reassure her. "If it works, then it will have been worth it for you and the others. Look after them, Rilla. I don't think any of them are as strong as you."

Slurred voices in the distance reached their ears. The other healers were on their way back. Rilla hugged Rhanya fiercely before running away towards the dormitory, eyes stinging with the threat of tears. She would be leaving her only friend behind. Would it be worthwhile?

Chapter Eight – Death in Paradise

"No!" The blood curdling scream echoed through the dormitory. Arishen still slept. Even his own scream had not woken him. Every other person in the children's hall was awake in an instant. No one knew where the scream had come from. There was panic in the air. The dormitory leaders were running around, hushing the younger children back to sleep.

Parthak lay silent, eyes wide open. Why was she cursed with such a Partner? It wasn't the first time Arishen had spoken in his sleep, but this was the loudest she had ever heard him. His scream could probably have been heard outside their building. Grinding her teeth, she got out of bed to wake him up. She would *not* be remembered as the one with the odd Partner.

"Arishen," she called his name, shaking him roughly. "Wake up." He jerked back from her in a panic.

"Don't touch me!" He yelled at her. Parthak felt her face flush with anger and embarrassment as others turned to look at the commotion.

"Be quiet," she whispered firmly. "You had another dream I take it?"

He nodded.

"Well *done*. You woke up the entire dormitory. Can't you learn to control yourself just for one night?" She knew her exasperated tone did not escape him, but noticed his eyes flicker to her side. Following his gaze, she saw *the girl* approaching them.

"What do *you* want?" Parthak asked icily. *The girl*, not at all taken aback by her tone of voice, ignored Parthak.

"Arishen, some of the younger ones are a bit distressed. Do you think you could help me put them back to sleep?" Arishen almost leapt at the chance to escape, and Parthak watched angrily as her Partner followed the quickly retreating figure.

* * *

True to her word, Rilla led Arishen to a group of younger children who were worriedly looking at the commotion around them. There were not nearly enough dormitory leaders to care for all the children if they were all upset at the same time. In Rilla's mind, it was yet another drawback of Erton's ridiculous notion that parents should not raise their own children.

Together, she and Arishen managed to quieten the small group they had approached. Children of this age were not afraid of Rilla. They weren't old enough to understand the consequences of associating with her. Not yet anyway.

"Who would like to hear a story?" Rilla asked the children in the calmest voice she could manage under the circumstances. A chorus of "me" went along with the raising of hands. Arishen seated himself on one of the beds nearest them, Rilla on another. The younger children sat around them excitedly, the previous commotion forgotten in the light of a proposed story.

Rilla chose a story that Rhanya had been telling her for years. She wondered if anyone else in the entire Paradise had heard it before.

"Said the little star to the big star, 'Tell me more Big Star. What about those ones over there?'

'Ah,' said the elder one. 'They are the learned ones. They spent many hours learning the histories, the tales, the ballads. See how together their shining lights form a scroll?'

The little star twinkled delightedly. 'And over there? What about that cluster?'

The big star dazzled as he spoke. 'They are the artists, the musicians. They understand the way of the soul; they painted and sang of the greatest souls.'

The little star shivered in awe.

'Big Star?'

'Yes, Little Star?'

'What about those ones? Why they don't group together like the others'

The big star smiled brightly. 'My little one, do you see how they shine more brightly? And how their light is as a beacon? Yet they are as gentle as fairy dust, as magic?'

'Yes,' whispered the younger one.

'Well, Little Star, they are the ones that the learned ones read about, that the artists paint and that the musicians play about.'

And the big star smiled in pleasant surprise as he noticed that the little star had shivered in awe and was quietly, unconsciously, glowing the light of the ones who inspire."

The children were all staring at Rilla in awe. Stories like that, that actually mentioned magic and inspiration, were not told in their Paradise. Even Arishen, who was too old for stories, had listened on in wonder. If any of the dormitory leaders had heard her telling the story on any other night, Rilla knew she would certainly be put back into the isolation hut.

Seeing that the younger children were getting sleepy again, Arishen and Rilla disentangled themselves from the ones nearest them, covering them with blankets. Arishen joined Rilla as she walked back towards her own bed. It was in the furthest corner of the dormitory, not surrounded by any others. The easiest solution, to keep everyone happy, was for no other child to be placed near her. It did not bother Rilla, but sometimes made her wonder why Erton bothered with punishing her with the isolation hut as she was isolated anyway.

"Thank you," Arishen said in a soft voice once they had reached Rilla's bed.

"It's nothing," she modestly shrugged the thanks aside. His brow creased as though he wanted to say more. "You'd better get back to sleep if you're going to stay awake through the Choosing."

"Oh, right," he replied listlessly, looking back at her as he walked towards his own bed. Rilla watched him. He'd barely reached Parthak before the girl pulled his arm roughly, turning him to face her.

"What did *she* want?"

"Are you becoming possessive of me all of a sudden?" he asked her mockingly. Rilla found herself smiling as Arishen lay on his bed, refusing to talk to his Partner.

* * *

The bell tolled for the morning meal. Everyone in the children's hall had slept in well past sunrise. The night's disruption had not been forgotten, but there was no time for the dormitory leaders to discover the cause of the commotion. Rilla knew Parthak was less than willing to place herself in a bad light by announcing what she knew.

Rilla felt an emptiness swelling inside of her. Today was the Choosing. She couldn't wait to leave this Paradise, but she didn't know how she was going to live without Rhanya. For the first time in years, she actively sought out companionship amongst some of the others her age. Once inside the eating hall, she located Arishen and quickly sat next to him, with Parthak on the boy's other side. Rilla did not meet Parthak's narrowed eyes for long, but the cruel look behind them was hard to miss.

The children were the last to enter the eating hall. Erton had been waiting for them to begin. Rilla's eyes scanned the hall in search of Rhanya. Perhaps she could ask him just a few questions about the banwep before the Choosing. Her heart beat faster as she found the healers' table and there was an empty place where Rhanya normally sat. Even the banwep hadn't appeared at the table.

"Does anyone see Rhanya?" Rilla heard her own voice asking the question. She did not even realise she had spoken until a few pairs of eyes turned on her. No one answered, but she noticed Arishen's head lowering. Turning to the boy, she asked him directly. "Arishen, do you see Rhanya?"

"He isn't here." His quiet voice was almost lost in the surrounding conversations. *They killed him.*

Rilla stared at him in confusion. She didn't know if it was his thought or hers but without another word, she stood up to find Rhanya herself. Ignoring Erton's order to sit down, she ran from the eating hall straight to the healers' building. Erton's henchmen were following her at a distance, she could hear the heavy thud of their feet. Time seemed to slow as she raced into Rhanya's room.

Her eyes went straight to the motionless body on the bed. He seemed to be sleeping peacefully, but somehow Rilla knew there was no life left in her friend. She stepped closer to Rhanya, hardly daring to breathe. Clutched tightly between his hands was a folded piece of parchment bearing her name on it. She gently prised it from his cold fingers and surreptitiously placed it in her pocket before Torak and Belial entered the room.

"He's dead," she told them in a detached voice. "Which one of you did this to him?" Neither of them answered her. A few moments later, the other healers entered the room.

"Child, what are you doing here?" Ursher asked her in a harsh voice.

"Did you not notice that death entered your home last night?" she asked angrily. "Did none of you hear these men coming in to *kill* him?"

She ran over to Torak and punched him relentlessly in his stomach, tears rolling down her face.

"How could you?" she screamed at him over and over, sobbing hysterically. Ursher pulled her away from the huge man and called for a chamomile tea. One of the other healers ran to do his bidding, while another ushered the pair out of their home.

"Ursher, did you not hear them?" Rilla asked him in a pleading tone, the tang of salt from her tears in her mouth. "Did you know they were going to do this?"

The healer did not answer her. He didn't have to. She knew the knowledge could not have escaped his attention. She *was* surprised to notice that she wasn't angry with him. The only feeling she had any room for now was sorrow. She'd known she was going to leave her friend behind after the Choosing, but she didn't realise he would be dead.

Crouching into a ball on the floor, Rilla sobbed into her arms. The world around her disappeared in her pain. Gently, she rocked herself back and forth on the cold floor, crying in short gasps.

It felt like hours had passed when she felt a light touch on her back. She didn't know how long ago she'd stopped crying, but could still feel the raw paths her tears had made down her cheeks. Looking up through her swollen eyes, she saw the banwep sitting beside her.

"Drink this." The banwep offered her a clay cup of tea. Rilla sat up stiffly, her eyes immediately noticing the emptiness of Rhanya's bed. She looked back at the banwep and the proffered tea with unseeing eyes.

"Where have they taken him?" The words felt heavy on her tongue.

"I pushed them to see if there was any foul play." The newcomer's words surprised her. "Drink the tea. It will calm you down a little, if nothing else."

Rilla took the cup in her cold fingers and sat with her back against the herb cabinet, looking around Rhanya's room. There were so many memories within these walls. Some of them the happiest she could remember. Without protesting any further, she slowly sipped at the lukewarm tea.

The Outworlder sat with her in silence until Ursher entered the room. Rilla did not look at him. She knew Rhanya had been murdered. She also knew Ursher couldn't admit that to her.

"I'm sorry, little one." Ursher looked down at the her. "Sometimes, it is just our time to go."

"You're right, Ursher," Rilla replied emotionlessly as she stood up to face him. "Sometimes it is our time to go."

Ursher hesitated momentarily before speaking. "Erton has requested that Rhanya's body be taken to the funeral pyre immediately. The Choosing will take place after the midday meal instead of this morning."

Rilla walked towards the funeral pyre. She knew the way there well. There had been many funerals in the last few years. More than she knew there should have been. Too many of them had Erton's stench on them. Her eyes watered again. Erton had killed Rhanya, not by his own hand, but that made no difference to her. Everyone knew it was his doing.

She stopped walking, her heart suddenly aching too much to keep going. Sinking down to her knees, she wept quietly into the grass. People were walking on either side of her. She could hear their footsteps hurrying to pass her. Normally, she wouldn't have cared. Today, it just accentuated the knowledge that Rhanya was the only one who would normally have stopped to lend a kind word to her.

Her body shook with the effort of silencing her tears. She did not want Erton to see how badly he'd managed to hurt her. Getting to her feet, she quickly ran to the stream, passing the last stragglers, and slid down the bank to the fast-flowing water. Cupping her hands, she splashed the cold water onto her face, hoping to wipe away any signs of sadness. She took a quiet moment to try to compose herself before climbing back up the bank.

Everyone was already gathered at the funeral pyre when she neared it. Even the Outworlder was standing there, at the back, away from everyone – but she was there nonetheless. Rilla wondered if this banwep had any idea that Rhanya was dead mostly because he tried to help her. She walked closer to the crowd, pushing her way past the first few people before the crowd gave way for her. It was no secret to anyone that Rilla had been closer to Rhanya than any other person in the

Paradise. The old man had always spared time for her. No doubt they would take that as a further warning to have as little to do with her as possible.

As she approached the funeral pyre, Rilla saw her old friend's body lying on top of the pile of wood, dressed in plain white robes. To her eyes, he still looked like he was sleeping, but there was something missing. It wasn't just the lack of movement. It was as though the person Rhanya was no longer existed in this wrinkled body.

Tears fell from Rilla's eyes as she looked at him. She caught a movement on the opposite side of the pyre. The healers were standing there, with their arms around some of the other Paradisians, lending them comfort. She shook her head in anger. No one would be there to offer her a shoulder to cry on, even her own father ... especially her father.

Erton stepped close to the funeral pyre with a flaming wooden torch in his left hand. "Today we witness the death of a dear old friend. Rhanya has been there for each, and every, one of us. Today, we are here for him. It is a great loss for the healers. We can never hope to replace him."

Rilla listened in disbelief. How could he stand there and say all of that, knowing full well that he had ordered the old man's death? Her raging scream echoed through the Paradise at the same time as Erton lit the bottom of the funeral pyre. She flung her head back, calling out Rhanya's name to the sky before collapsing in a trembling heap on the ground.

As though feeling with someone else's mind, she noticed someone lifting her. The intense heat of the flames lessened as she was moved away from the pyre. At some distance away, she was placed back on the ground, facing towards the flames. An arm remained around her as she stared into the fire. Rhanya's body was already alight. She couldn't bring herself to move away, even with the pungent smell of burning flesh and hair.

She stayed there and watched until the fire had burnt out. Rhanya was no more. Rilla hung her head in silence, barely noticing people starting to walk away from the scene. She couldn't move.

"Arishen, are you coming?" An impatient voice called out from a distance. Rilla heard no answer, but looked up through blurred eyes to see the blonde boy shaking his head. His pale blue eyes caught Rilla by surprise. She had forgotten that anyone was standing so close to her. Staring up at him in incomprehension, she let him gently raise her to her feet.

"He's gone," she told him. As if he didn't know. He didn't reply, but looking sadly down at her, placed his arm around her shoulders and carefully guided her back to the centre of the Paradise.

Chapter Nine – The Choosing

When they returned to the assembly hall that afternoon, it was as though Rhanya had never existed. His death seemed to mean nothing in the light of the Choosing. This ceremony could not be stopped for anything. As soon as Arishen and Rilla arrived, Belial closed the doors behind them. Torak signalled to Erton that everyone required was now present. The Paradise leader took his usual place on the stage and held his hands up for silence.

"My children, it is time for the Choosing." His cold black eyes scanned over his flock. "When you leave, everyone is required to go to their own private room. The five new apprentices will then go to the room of the person they wish to have as their mentor. If any of the five come to you, you are asked to wait in your room until I arrive. I will then ask if you accept the child. If you don't accept, the child will be given the choice of execution or banishment."

Everyone knew the rules of the Choosing, but this one clause always generated a murmur throughout the crowd. It was a grave responsibility to be a mentor, but there would have to be an extremely good reason for refusing any child.

The doors to the assembly hall were opened, allowing light to stream into the room. Slowly, people began to head for their homes. When the hall was empty, save for the five Choosing, Erton and his muscle men, the Paradise leader descended the platform. Arishen walked towards Parthak, Tika and Plyke, leaving Rilla to follow in a daze behind him.

"My children, this is an important day for you. I ask you all to carefully consider what you decide to do today as it will affect the rest of your life." He looked at each of them in turn. When his eyes met Parthak's, the young girl broke into an arrogant smile. Everyone knew what her choice would be. Erton had already applauded the decision. The only child he was concerned about was his own. He looked at Rilla without any affection.

"It is a great honour for you to choose first, my child. Choose well. Remember, your choice cannot be undone." When Rilla did not move, he continued, a hint of uncertainty catching in his voice. "Child, did you hear me?"

Rilla raised her head, defiance shining brightly in her eyes. "You have brought this day upon yourself, Erton." With that, she turned to go, leaving her father wondering what she could possibly have meant.

Rilla walked towards the healers. She could not help but think that it was not Rhanya's room to which she was walking. The old man had been her only friend in this false safe haven. It seemed strangely fitting that her departure coincided with his death.

The healers' building was quiet as she approached it. Each healer was in his own private room. It did not occur to Rilla that she would have been the only female healer in their Paradise had she decided to stay. Without thinking, she walked straight into Rhanya's room, temporarily confused by his absence. Looking over at his bed, she remembered his lifeless hands tightly holding a folded bit of parchment with her name on it. Her hand went straight to her pocket, feeling the stiff parchment. *There will be time to read it later,* she told herself.

Bringing herself back to the present moment, Rilla straightened her back and raised her head high in an attempt to leave the morning behind her. She walked to the room where she had helped Rhanya and Ursher lay the newcomer down. She was certain that the lady would be there.

The door was closed when she arrived. Rilla's hand paused on the handle. There was no turning back once she opened the door. The Outworlder would be forced to accept her or let her die. Even a banwep would understand a life debt. Rilla was risking her life on whether the banwep chose to honour that debt.

"Are you lost?" The tanned lady eyed Rilla curiously as she walked through the door. "Your healer's room is down the hall."

"What makes you think I was looking for Rhanya's room?" Rilla raised her eyebrows as she sat cross legged on the reed flooring.

"I wouldn't make myself comfortable if I were you, girl," the Outworlder cautioned. "Erton doesn't seem to have a sense of humour. Go and choose your mentor before he finds you here."

Taking no notice of the Outworlder, Rilla remained seated where she was. She hoped Rhanya had been right about this. If the other children chose Paradisian mentors, this could be the biggest mistake of her life.

It didn't take long for the old healer's words to prove truthful. Rilla spied Arishen walking through the halls of the healers' building, his golden hair a beacon in the darkness. As soon as he saw the open door, he headed towards them.

"I don't suppose this is a gathering of Erton's supporters, is it?" He smiled as he looked down to Rilla's sigh of relief and across to the Outworlder's panic stricken face. "No? Well, I suppose I'll stay anyway."

"Are you both mad?" The stranger raised her voice, more in fear than anger. "Get out of my room!"

"It doesn't work that way." A confident voice called down the hall. Tika poked his head into the Outworlder's room with Plyke close on his heels. "*We* get to choose whoever we want. Whether you accept us is your decision, but you can't tell us to leave before Erton gets here."

Rilla hid a smile as the Outworlder looked up at the two new entrants. Tika was the shortest of them all, his black hair and hazel eyes a stark contrast against his pale skin. Slightly behind him, Plyke stood taller, but less noticeable, his eyes obscured by his messy brown hair.

"I'm warning you, I have no desire to take four Paradisians back into the Outworld with me."

"So, you *are* leaving then?" Tika almost bounced with excitement. "I was hoping you'd say that."

"Did you not hear the part where I said you weren't coming with me?"

Tika ignored her question, turned to Plyke smiling happily. His partner tried to hold back his own smile, but failed miserably. Rilla watched the exchange with interest. They spoke with expressions. She'd never had that relationship with anyone her own age. It intrigued her.

At a movement by her side, Rilla's musings were interrupted by Arishen seating himself on the ground next to her. Instinctively, she frowned and drew ever so slightly away from him. She didn't trust many people in her Paradise. It had become a normal reaction for her to shy away from any contact.

"Your leader is coming." The banwep was looking out of her window, watching Erton approaching the healers' building. "I believe this is your last chance to get yourselves out of this mess."

"We've chosen you as our mentor." Rilla's steady voice carried forcefully through the room. "It's your turn to choose whether you will accept us or not."

"I already told you I'm not taking four Paradisians into the Outworld."

"It's your decision. Only remember that we will be executed if you decline to take us with you."

Everyone started at Rilla's words.

"What do you mean we'll be executed?" Tika's voice had lost some of its confidence. "Erton never said that."

"No, but then our chosen mentor *forgot* to tell Erton she has decided to leave." Her bright green eyes pierced the Outworlder. "I assure you, it will mean our death if you don't accept us."

They were still staring at each other when Erton walked through the door. His eyes opened wide when he saw not just one but *four* of his flock in the room.

"Explain yourselves." His barely contained rage was directed at Rilla. She did not reply, but only looked at him icily. Turning to the Outworlder, his glare was more than enough to make her speak.

"I didn't have time this morning to tell you of my decision to leave your Paradise."

"What was that?" Erton's calm voice did not disguise the danger they were in.

"I'm leaving, tomorrow morning."

"I see." He looked over the faces of his Paradisians, as though weighing his options. "Have you decided if you will accept these foolish children?"

"What will happen to them if I don't?" Curiosity got the better of her. The three Paradisian boys held their breath in anticipation of his answer.

"They will be executed – immediately." A cruel smiled appeared gradually on Erton's face at the sharp intake of breath. "Choose carefully, Outworlder, their lives are in your hands. I will expect your answer at the evening meal."

Chapter Ten – Decisions

Shocked silence filled the room. Shuut could not believe her ears. She had the power to sentence these children to death. Her only alternative was to take them with her. It was difficult enough to survive the Outworld alone, but with four young apprentices – she couldn't begin to imagine how they would all survive.

Tearing her eyes away from the empty doorway, she looked over the faces of the three boys. None of them could disguise their fear. They had not realised the consequences of their choice. She could almost feel herself sympathising with their plight. The only one in the room she could not understand was the girl. She had known what could happen and yet she tried her luck anyway. Massaging her forehead with her long, thin fingers, Shuut tried to think of a way out of the situation.

What have you done to me? She looked at the girl without saying a single word. Confusion flickered across the girl's face, but was gone before Shuut could truly say it was there.

"You're not going to let us die, are you?" It was the tall boy who voiced their concern, bringing Shuut out of her thoughts.

"What would you have me do? I cannot look after four Paradisians in the Outworld."

"You could at least *try*." It was a desperate plea. She could feel it in his voice.

"I don't have any choice."

"Yes, you do," the smallest boy answered defiantly. "You have the choice to let us be executed or not."

"Do they not tell you any stories of the Outworld in this cursed place? There is a reason these Paradises were created."

"It can't be that bad. *You'd* rather live there than here. There must be something worth leaving for." His hazel eyes stared pleadingly up at her.

"I don't have a say in this. I *must* leave."

"Rhanya risked his life to look after you until you could safely leave," the girl spoke up. "Are you telling me that his life was wasted trying to save the one person who could help us survive the Outworld? He believed you would help us to escape."

"It isn't that I don't appreciate what the old man did for me, but I can't help you."

"That *old man* was my only friend in here. Without him, I could never survive this place. The least you can do is tell Erton you'll accept us and then leave us once we reach another settlement."

"How would you survive? You don't even have weapons, let alone know how to use any." It was madness, pure madness. This girl, who was barely more than a child, was putting her between a rock and a hard place.

"I saved your life. If only for that reason, you should at least help us escape this place. Rhanya wasn't the only one with enemies here."

It took the better part of the afternoon for them to convince her, but Shuut finally gave in to their pleas. She had no idea how they were going to survive, but the red headed girl had assured her that they would not ask for help once they reached the nearest village. Her only hope was that the four of them weren't killed before then. She did not want their deaths on her conscience.

She heard a bell ringing out – it was time for the evening meal. This was it. The four new apprentices hesitantly got to their feet. They hadn't said a word since she'd reluctantly agreed to take them with her. The healers came out of their rooms at the sound of the evening bell. Doubtless they'd have heard at least some of what had been said that afternoon. It could not have escaped their attention that four of the Paradisians had chosen her as their mentor.

Ursher walked past the room as the green-eyed girl approached the door. "Little one, I am truly sorry for your loss, but do you really think leaving with this Outworlder will bring him back?"

"If you were truly sorry, Ursher, you would have done something about it when they came for him last night." Her words obviously stung the healer as he bit his lower lip and turned away from her. The tall, blond boy reached out a comforting hand, but the girl flinched and quickly walked away from him.

Shuut watched the entire exchange with growing interest. She remembered the young girl telling her that she had no friends in the Paradise, but it didn't look as though she was making much of an effort to kindle any sort of relationship with her fellow Paradisians.

The five of them entered the eating hall amidst a crowd of others. It seemed to Shuut that everyone knew her decision would be voiced at this meal.

She sat at the children's table alongside her new companions, noticing as she did so that the blond boy's eyes flicked around the hall in search of someone. Once he'd located that person, Shuut turned her head to see who he was looking at. It was the other girl who was meant to be choosing a mentor that day. She was sitting at a table of adults, actively keeping her eyes averted from the other children.

"Who did she choose?" It seemed the logical question for her to ask the boy. He was obviously attached to the girl in some way.

"The scholars. All of Erton's most loyal supporters choose that path." Saying so, he tore his gaze away from the apprentice scholar to look down at his plate. He didn't seem surprised by her choice, but it was plain to see that it disturbed him. Shuut meant to say something further to him but silence descended upon the hall. Looking up, she saw Erton hold up his hands in his usual gesture for quiet.

"I am pleased to announce that one of my children has been accepted by the scholars." A polite round of applause went around the hall as the apprentice scholar waved her hand, blushing as she did so. It was obvious that Erton approved of this decision. However, that was not the choice everyone was curious about. "I would ask the Outworlder to now please stand."

Grudgingly, Shuut got to her feet as all eyes focused on her. The choice had been made for her. She wasn't exactly pleased about it, but at least it meant that the Paradise leader would not win this battle.

"I have decided to take these four Paradisians with me into the Outworld. We will leave tomorrow." Silence followed her words as she sat back down. She noticed people shifting uncomfortably in their seats, not knowing what was to be done about her decision. Even Erton was speechless. His flock was lost without him. Looking across the table, she noticed a small smile creep onto the quiet boy's face. She could not catch his eye through his mop of brown hair, but she did not need to see them to know he was genuinely happy with the situation. Despite herself, she smiled back at him.

The five of them began to eat their beef steaks as though nothing out of the ordinary had happened. The younger children followed their cue, obviously not completely understanding what had just transpired. All they could think about was their stomachs.

* * *

Later that evening, Rilla stood alone in Rhanya's room. The boys were in the Outworlder's room, asking all sorts of questions about the next day. She did not want to be around them. In fact, the only person she did want to be around was the old healer – her only friend. She had left the banwep's room unnoticed, a short candle in her hand. Her silent footsteps along the reed hallway had been missed by all the healers. She pushed the wooden door open and stepped cautiously inside. The glow of her almost spent candle lit the room in soft yellow patches.

In its usual place on Rhanya's small table was his little leather travel bag. He kept his most useful herbs and potions in that bag in case of emergencies. It was the one thing he kept with him always, only taking it off at night before he went to bed. Rilla placed her candle down on the table and picked up the bag with hesitant fingers. Inside there were many compartments, designed specifically for keeping the medicines apart from each other. She doubted anyone would notice if she took it. Perhaps no one else had even noticed the bag when Rhanya was still alive.

Tying the leather straps around her waist, Rilla walked over to the herb cabinet. If she was going into the Outworld, she was going to be as prepared as she could be. She did not consider what she was doing stealing. If Rhanya had still been alive, she was certain the healer would have insisted she be well stocked with whatever he could give her.

The cabinet was full of tiny clay jars, sealed with wax. Each had a symbol etched into the side, describing what was contained within. She deftly sorted through the vessels, setting aside those that would be useless to them and carefully placing those she knew how to use in the leather bag at her waist.

Once she was done, Rilla looked around the room one last time. Her candle had gone out while she was working. Only the moonlight was now shining in through the window. It left a faint silvery glow on whatever it touched. Rilla closed her eyes, committing the image to her memory. She would never come back here again. Once they left this Paradise, they would never find it again. That was one of the wards on the boundary. *If* you managed to find a Paradise and left, you would never be able to enter another one again.

By the time she returned to the Outworlder's room, the boys were fast asleep. The banwep looked up as she came in.

"Get some sleep. I'll wake you when it's time to get ready."

Rilla needed no further encouragement. She walked over to the reed chair by the window, curled herself up, closed her eyes and fell into a deep sleep.

Chapter Eleven – Final preparations

Shuut woke them before dawn. There was much to be done before they left, most of it before the other Paradisians awoke. She doubted there would be much cooperation on their behalf when it came to supplying deserters.

"We need supplies before we leave. You will all need a rucksack. If there is anything resembling a weapon, try to take one of those. Any food that will last well should be taken, by force if need be." She looked the girl up and down with a critical eye. "Those skirts will only get in your way. See if you can find anything else to wear. All of you make sure you're wearing leather shoes. Soft fabric will be ruined within a day of hard walking. Even if the weather is warm now, bring your warmest cloaks with you."

Four faces stared at her eagerly. They were all anxious to get away from this place before Erton found a way to stop them. The tall boy looked at the others, brow creased in concentration.

"I may be able to get us some weapons," he told them. "Don't anyone follow me. I don't want them to get in trouble if they help me. Tika, Plyke, go to the kitchens and see if you can't get some food before the cooks arrive. On your way, see if you can pick up our things from the children's hall."

The three boys walked over to the open door together, not including the girl in their plans. She followed them out at a distance, going her own way.

* * *

Arishen headed between the children's hall and the school, straight towards the carpenters' rooms. He didn't know if Kalid would give him any tools, but she was probably the only one who *might* try to help him if she could. Hoping his footsteps across the grass were quiet enough not to be noticed, he ran as swiftly as he could past the huge school building. Parthak was sure to be inside there. If she saw him, there was no telling how much trouble she might cause.

As he neared Kalid's home, Arishen slowed down. There were no lights on in the building. No one was awake yet. He walked around to Kalid's window, carefully pulling open the reed shutters. She did not move from her bed. Scratching his head, he wondered whether it would be a good idea to climb into her room. He decided to try his luck. The base of the window only came to his waist, but it would take a small jump to get into the room.

With his hands spread across the window frame, he jumped and landed awkwardly on the wicker chair beneath the window. Struggling to keep his balance, he flailed his arms widely, knocking over the wooden cup on the small table and falling beside it. Kalid sat up instantly, pulling a chisel from under her pillow and looking wildly around the room.

"Kalid, it's only me," Arishen whispered, looking up at her from the floor. Once her eyes had adjusted to the early morning light, Kalid lowered her weapon and got out of her bed.

"Arishen, what are you doing climbing through my window?" she asked him sleepily. "Why didn't you just use the door?"

Arishen waved his hands, motioning her to silence. "I didn't want anyone to hear me." The carpenter raised her eyebrows cynically. "I need your help and didn't think you wanted the others to know about it."

"Does this have anything to do with leaving the Paradise?" He nodded sheepishly. "We'll have to go to the work shed. If anyone notices that all the missing tools are mine…" She looked at him meaningfully. "Let's just say I don't want to end up like Rhanya."

Together, they clambered out the window and walked around to the work shed. They were on the far side of the building, close to the stream. The running water masked their steps as they walked among the unfinished projects. Kalid stopped at random benches, finding tools that would not be missed immediately. Arishen took off his shirt and wrapped the tools in the wool so that they would not make any noise on his way back to the Outworlder's room.

Before they left the work shed, Kalid pulled Arishen's arm, holding him back. "I know this Outworlder has agreed to take you with her. I don't want to know what your arrangement with her is, but be careful. You may think she is a lady of her word, but she is a banwep. They cannot generally be trusted. If you have to use any of these on her, don't hesitate for even a second or your life will be forfeit."

"I'm sure she wouldn't…" he began but Kalid interrupted him. "That may be exactly what she is counting on. That you don't think she would do anything to hurt you because she has agreed to help you. Be always on your guard, Arishen."

The carpenter shook his hand in farewell before heading back to her room. Arishen was left staring after her, wondering whether she could possibly be right about the banwep.

* * *

Leaving the banwep's room, Tika and Plyke headed straight towards the children's hall. They had decided to get all four of their cloaks and rucksacks before going to the kitchens so they could carry as much food as possible between them. It wasn't difficult to enter unnoticed. The dormitory leaders were heavy sleepers, a useful trait when dealing with children. They parted ways when they walked through the door, Tika heading towards their beds and Plyke going to find Arishen's.

The blond boy's bed was easy to find. Parthak and Arishen had slept in beds beside each other, just as Tika and himself had. All he had to do was find the only other two vacant beds together. Once he'd located them, he found Arishen's cloak rolled up under the bed beside his rucksack. Crouching down to retrieve them, he noticed another, unusually heavy, cloth bundle hidden beneath the cloak. Thinking it might be important, he unrolled the cloak, wrapped the other bundle within it and placed both within the rucksack. Tika met him as he was shouldering the bag.

"Do you know where *the girl's* bed is?" Tika asked in a whisper. Plyke pointed over to an isolated, vacant bed in the far corner of the dormitory. Together, they walked over, not certain if the girl would approve of them going through her things. Under her bed they found her cloak and rucksack, its bottom lined with dead leaves. Padded by the surrounding leaves was a silver necklace with a tree pendant attached to it. Looking curiously at the contents, Tika placed the cloak within the rucksack, handing it to Plyke. He couldn't imagine why she had dead leaves in her rucksack or why she hadn't given up the precious piece of metal to the blacksmiths.

By this time, the sun had started to stream in through the northeast windows. Some of the children were groaning sleepily. They didn't have much time before one of them was bound to wake up and find them. As quickly and quietly as they could, the Partners left their dormitory for the last time and headed towards the kitchens.

It only took them a few minutes to reach the kitchens, but already they were bustling with cooks when they arrived. There was no way around it now. They would have to ask for the food they needed. Whether they would be given it was another matter altogether.

Tika opened the door, just wide enough to poke his head through. Candles were burning brightly in the growing sunlight. He walked inside, motioning behind him for Plyke to follow. They had never been inside the kitchen before. It was a forbidden area, just like all other places where a skill was practised. It didn't take long for one of the cooks to notice them.

"What are the two of you doing here? You know it's forbidden." A portly middle-aged man yelled at them over the sounds of the kitchen.

"We're leaving today and thought you might give us some food to help us on our way." Playing on their sympathies, Plyke thought he might have a better chance. That hope was soon shattered at the cook's laughter rumbled around them.

"You traitors thought we might help you. Is that what you're telling me?"

"We're not traitors. We just don't want to live here anymore," Plyke spoke more calmly than he felt.

"I'd say the only reason you wouldn't want to live here anymore is that you have something to hide." The cook leaned in dangerously close to the boys, but his words were heard by all the cooks. "So, is there something you want to tell us?"

Plyke did not back away. Doing so would only exacerbate the situation. "All we're asking for is some food so we don't starve out there."

"You should have thought of that before you decided to leave." With that, the cooks all returned to work, pointedly ignoring the two boys. Neither Tika nor Plyke were fooled by this display. They knew they were being watched. If they so much as leaned in towards the barrels of food, there would be more trouble than they had bargained for.

Outside once more, the Partners exchanged a silent glance. By this time, most people in the Paradise would be awake. They would receive much the same reception anywhere they went. Instinctively knowing what the other was thinking, they both turned to head back towards the healers' building.

* * *

Rilla silently followed the boys out of the healers' building. None of them spared her a glance as they went their separate ways. Not that she was expecting it – the act just drove home her isolation even further. She wondered whether living in the Outworld would change anything. Rhanya had made her promise to look after them, but had he even considered the fact that they might not let her?

She had heard their plans before leaving the banwep and resolved that the only thing left for her to do was go to the tailor to get some appropriate clothes. She couldn't deny that the thought of leaving her skirts behind brought a smile to her face. Her only hope was that the tailors had something already made that would fit her.

By the time she reached the small amphitheatre, the sun had started to tinge the sky a deep orange. It wouldn't be long now before people started to wake with the dawn. She quickened her step in an attempt to reach the tailors before anyone stirred within.

The building was still in darkness when she arrived, the sunlight barely touching the roof. Rilla headed straight for the main entrance. She knew she would not be heard entering – she never was. It seemed to be an added benefit of her forced isolation that people tried not to notice her. She could slip in unnoticed practically anywhere she wanted. All she had to do was think about blending in with the shadows and no one paid her any attention. Even an open doorway could be explained away by a forceful, if erratic, gust of wind.

She closed the door quietly behind her. There was no need to test her skills unnecessarily. Waiting for her eyes to adjust to the darkness, Rilla stood still for a few moments before locating the room for finished clothes. It was a room that everyone in the Paradise had used many times. Anything the tailors made was stored in that room until the owner came to retrieve it. Pants, shirts and overalls were folded in piles while skirts and dresses hung on thin pieces of wood along the walls of the room. There were few special orders. Rilla sorted through the piles of folded pants, holding possibilities up to her waist to see if they would fit. It didn't take long to find something. There were plenty of boys around her size constantly growing out of their clothes. She picked a few pairs for herself as well as some for the boys, certain that none of them would have thought far enough ahead to pack spare clothes into their rucksacks. Once she'd set aside the pants she intended to take with her, Rilla hastily took a handful of shirts, and wrapped the clothes all together under her arm.

She was just passing the tavern on her way back to the healers' building when she realised that Arishen had not allocated the cobbler to anyone. Rilla didn't know how much walking they were going to be doing in the Outworld, but she was fairly certain the soles of their shoes would wear out quickly. With a grimace, she turned towards the cobbler and started running, hoping to beat the sun there.

She was too late. As she arrived, she heard the lazy sounds of people beginning to stir. Hoping that she could avoid detection one last time, she hid her stash of clothes under a nearby bush and listened carefully. The stream masked most of the noise from within, but she could still hear people moving clumsily about inside. In the distance, a small flock of birds called out to each other in the dawn light. It felt to Rilla as though they were trying to alert the cobblers to her presence.

In an attempt to evade any wakeful inhabitants, Rilla skirted the building until she found the room that housed the materials already cut in preparation for sewing together. Taking care to make as little sound as possible, she climbed in through the window staying as much in the shadows as possible. It didn't take her long to find some leather soles. She picked them up just as the door to that room opened.

Heart pounding, Rilla immediately backed up to the nearest wall, thinking of nothing but the shadows. She watched as Kora walked into the room, looking around with sleepy eyes. Rubbing the morning sleep from her eyes, the cobbler searched the room intently. Noticing, after a cursory glance, that something was missing she looked around more intently. Her eyes passed over Rilla several times before she finally saw the young girl standing there.

"What are you doing here?" she asked in a hushed voice, looking over to the open doorway. Rilla's eyes widened at her discovery, but she said nothing. Kora saw the leather soles clenched tightly in the girl's fists. Rilla looked on in silent curiosity as the older lady gathered some thick needles and coarse thread.

"Here." The cobbler held out the extra supplies to her. "They won't be any use to you without these."

Not knowing what else to do, Rilla hesitantly took the offered items and fled through the window without a word. Too stunned at her discovery to think about anything else, her hands fumbled in the bushes where she'd hidden the clothes. Bundling everything together, she ran as fast as she could back to the banwep.

The sun had risen above the horizon by the time Rilla returned to the healers' building. Out of breath, she stopped when she saw the boys standing outside the banwep's room. They motioned her into silence before she could ask why they hadn't entered. Seeing her rucksack on the floor, she knelt and started to fill it with the items she had gathered, all the while listening to the conversation behind the closed door.

"Have you had time to reconsider your decision?" Erton's snide voice was difficult to mistake for anyone else's. "Surely you realise what a burden four young Paradisians will be in the Outworld. It will be far better to let them die here, in peace, rather than to risk the dangerous uncertainty out there."

"I think you underestimate these children." The Outworlder's voice was quietly confident. "They are still young enough to learn how to survive in the big bad world out there. The only way they will come to harm is if they listen to a single thing you've ever told them."

"I'm giving you one last chance…" Erton's angry response was cut short.

"I don't need anything else from you." Each word was enunciated carefully and loudly. "As soon as they return, we leave this place."

Rilla needed to hear no more than that. With the boys trying to hold her back, she shouldered her rucksack and pushed open the door. Erton turned to her in a rage.

"I know you're behind this," he practically screamed at her. She'd never seen him so angry with her.

"Think of it this way, Erton," she told him in a patronising voice. "You're sending me to the isolation hut for a *very* long time." Turning to the banwep, her tone changed completely. "We're ready when you are."

The Outworlder had been ready to step in once again when the Paradise leader raised his voice at her. Clearly surprised that she hadn't been needed, the banwep followed the four Paradisians out of the building, leaving Erton in a trembling rage behind them.

Chapter Twelve – Escape from Paradise

"How do we get out of here?" Arishen asked. Plyke and Tika both shrugged. The boys turned towards the Outworlder.

"What makes you think *I* know?" she held up her hands.

"I know how."

Everyone turned towards Rilla. She led them between the children's hall and the school. Small, dirt stained faces peered out of the windows of the dormitory as the five companions passed by. A few shy hands waved a silent farewell which the boys returned, almost sadly. Rilla searched the faces, trying to find any she knew. Only the younger children ever spoke to her, but she couldn't see any of them. More likely than not, they were all still asleep. She wondered how many of them would remember Rhanya's star story. It was the only one she'd ever told them and only ever when the dormitory leaders couldn't overhear.

Comforted by the thought that part of Rhanya might still live on in the Paradise, Rilla smiled and quickened her pace leading her new companions towards the northernmost bridge. Once across it, and purposely keeping her eyes averted from the funerary pyre, she walked straight through the tiny forest and emerged on the other side at the isolation hut.

"What are we doing here?" The discomfort in Tika's voice was easy to hear. Most children had, at one time or another, been the sole occupant of the isolation hut – none so frequently as Rilla. It was not an experience they had enjoyed.

"I just want to change before we leave. No one will bother us here. Just wait for me." Rilla disappeared inside the hut, leaving the others standing uncomfortably outside.

"What is this place?" the Outworlder asked, after a brief silence.

"The isolation hut," Tika answered quietly.

"A place to go when you're in trouble?" the banwep laughed through the question. When the boys' only answer was silence, she struggled to wipe the smile from her face.

"Erton's idea of punishment." Rilla answered as she emerged a changed person. The boys stared at her, wide eyed. Gone were her long skirts, replaced with long dark orange pants and a plain cotton shirt. The final touch was her long red curls, bundled up under a soft hat. If they hadn't looked closely, any of them would have taken her for a boy.

"It's just over here." Her statement broke the spell.

"What's over here?" Tika stumbled over the words.

"The boundary. Follow me." Rilla didn't wait to see if they would, but headed straight towards the edge of their Paradise. A shimmering wall of thick air blocked her way. She had been here many times, looking out at the blurred images beyond the barrier. Rilla stretched out her hand, savouring the feel of the magical barrier. Closing her eyes, she walked ahead through the almost solid fog. A shiver went through her body as the air pushed in around her.

It only took a few steps before she was on the other side. She walked a bit further before opening her eyes to the Outworld. The land was still as green, though not tended to as farms, the sky was just as blue with the same white clouds.

* * *

On the other side of the boundary, Shuut noticed each of the Paradisians looking around them, almost fearfully, to see what the Outworld held. None of them knew what to expect. But how could they? From what Erton had probably told them, creatures should have already detected their scent and be on the move to surround them.

"It…looks the same," Tika commented.

"Of course it looks the same," Shuut told them. "After all, Paradises *were* built from the Outworld."

The relief of being on the other side of the barrier washed over her new companions. Even if only for that one moment, Shuut was glad she had freed them from their misguided leader. She let them look around for as long it took her to find her bearings.

In a moment of confusion, she thought perhaps the past few days had been just in her imagination. She was standing in exactly the same place where she had tried to fight off five huge men. Her eyes darted around in panic, surprised to only be surrounded by four people at least ten years her junior.

"Is something wrong?" the red-headed girl asked with raised eyebrows.

"No…I just didn't expect to come out right at this place."

"I thought it might be easier for you to orient yourself if we emerged where you entered."

"That was quite clever of you."

Turning back to where they had just come from, Shuut led them through the now empty area where their Paradise had been just a few moments before. "This way."

Without waiting for a reply, she began to walk towards the stream whose double had flowed through the Paradise. The village of Turon lay to the east and slightly north. She had been on her way there when the unfortunate incident had occurred. It seemed as good a place as any to continue towards. Under normal circumstances it was two days' walk from where they were. She hoped the Paradisians were in good shape. If they weren't it could take much longer. Three sets of heavy footsteps, and one much softer pair, followed her. She fought the temptation to look behind her to make sure all her new companions were in tow. If they were to make it to Turon alive, she had to trust them right from the start.

There was a rotting bridge over the small stream. Not that it really mattered – the stream was quite small enough to swim across if the bridge broke beneath them. They crossed it without trouble, though Shuut could sense her companions' hesitation at using a structure as well-worn as this one.

After a few minutes of walking, the tall boy quickened his pace to catch up with her. "Why does everyone think the Outworld is so bad? The way they describe it, I'm surprised no one has ambushed us yet."

Shuut was silent for a while, trying to think of a short answer to a complicated question. "Well, boy…"

The blond boy interrupted in an almost arrogant voice. "I have a name, Outworlder. It's Arishen."

Shuut narrowed her eyes at his tone, conscious that the rest of their companions were listening intently to their conversation. "You would do well to remember that you're an Outworlder too now, Arishen. Out here, what you say can cost you your life. If people hear you calling me "Outworlder" they will know that you think of yourselves differently to me and will probably guess correctly that you're from a Paradise. When that happens, we will all become targets because they will think we are weak."

Arishen's eyes softened a little at the rebuke. "Forgive me." He inclined his head slightly down towards her. "What may we call you then?"

"My name is Shuut." It meant "shadow" in an ancient language. Her companions did not know it, but she had been well named. Her father had taught her to blend into the background so well that she could not be picked out from the shadows.

"Shuut." Arishen spoke her name with a small smile. "This is Tika and his Partner, Plyke. They had their ceremony when they were only five years old. The youngest ever in our Paradise." At the mention of their names, both Tika and Plyke inclined their heads in acknowledgement of the introduction. Shuut looked expectantly towards the young Paradisian girl, waiting for her name to be given. Arishen's extended silence made her curious.

"And you are?" she asked.

"Most people used to call me '*the girl*'." The girl shook her head with a strange smile.

"What did the rest call you?"

"The rest didn't speak to me."

In exasperation, Shuut raised her voice. "Well what can *we* call you?"

"I suppose any name will do. Why not Parthak?"

"No!" Anger flared up in Arishen. "Just call her Karinya."

"Karinya it is," the girl replied nonchalantly. Shuut shook her head at the absurdity of the conversation, glad that she would only have to deal with these Paradisians until they reached Turon. Without another word, she continued on towards the village.

It was a few hours after leaving the Paradise that a small forest came into view on the horizon. As the younger travellers noticed it, their reactions varied. Arishen stopped silently in his tracks, simply staring ahead. Tika missed a step then continued to walk open-mouthed. Plyke slowed his pace considerably, but did not stop moving. Karinya, alone, continued walking unfazed. A look of recognition flickered over her face, but it was gone so quickly that Shuut almost doubted she had seen it. Eventually, the boys caught up with the two girls.

"Are we going in there?" asked Tika, with a hint of mingled curiosity and concern.

"We need to go through there to reach the village of Turon," Shuut replied offhandedly.

"But ... won't anything try to ambush us in there?" The look on the others' faces mirrored his concern.

"The Outworld isn't as bad as Erton may have made you believe," Shuut told them in what she hoped was a reassuring voice. "It *is* dangerous, but there are not creatures waiting behind every turn to attack us. In any case, this forest is not a large or dense one. The sky will never completely disappear from sight and after a few hundred feet we'll be on the other side."

Shuut could see her words had done little to allay their fears. The boys looked worriedly at each other, none of them convinced that they would come to little harm.

"Tika, you can't seriously be scared. You *do* know that elves live in forests, don't you?" Karinya mocked the boy with a laugh. He nodded his head shyly, clearly not used to being spoken to directly by the girl. "So, won't this forest be good practice for you? You don't want to be scared of *their* forest if you ever visit them, do you?"

Shuut looked on in wonder as Tika's entire disposition changed. He was now as eager as he could be to enter the forest. She briefly wondered why Karinya didn't seem to react to the forest in the same way as her companions.

As they continued travelling, the forest drew slowly closer. Walking at this pace, the banwep knew they wouldn't reach the forest until at least the next day, but she doubted her companions had realised that.

They rested when the sun was high up over their heads. Tika and Plyke had been completely unsuccessful in obtaining any food for them, so Shuut had to share her dwindling supplies with her new charges.

By mid-afternoon, the pace of the new Outworlders had slowed considerably. Even the redheaded girl was showing signs of fatigue. It was still hours before dusk when Shuut made the decision to set up their campsite for the night. Exhausted by the day of walking, her young companions lay down on the soft green grass with their arms and legs wide spread, soaking in the heat of the sun.

Shuut paced restlessly for a few minutes before realising she did not have the patience to waste the rest of the day. Walking a few hundred paces away, she felt four pairs of eyes on her as she unsheathed her hidden daggers. Her father had drilled sparring practice into her as a child. The habit had not disappeared through her years of wandering the Outworld alone. Even if she did not have an opponent, she practiced every day.

As dusk approached, Shuut instructed them in lighting a hidden campfire. Old habits died hard. Even though she knew there would be someone keeping watch all night, Shuut did not want to build a fire high enough for the flames to be visible by anyone else in the area.

Once they had all laid out their cloaks around the fire, Shuut set the watches for the night, making sure to give each of them as much rest as possible. As soon as she turned her back, she heard the sound of their breathing deepen as they all fell into a well-deserved sleep.

It was mid-morning, two days later, before they eventually reached the boundary of the forest. The thick, roughly barked trees enveloped Karinya as she walked in unhesitatingly, seeming to welcome the feel of the forest. Shuut waited for the other three to follow before she brought up the rear.

The boys walked on slowly, looking up to see the canopy of leaves covering them, leaving patterns of blue sky visible. Shuut watched them turning circles to look at the trees, rocks and moss. The call of the birds was louder within the confines of the forest than they had been in the grasslands. At each sound, all four heads turned simultaneously to see if they could catch a glimpse of the creature responsible. Karinya, too, was absorbing her surroundings, but she did so without comment to the others. It seemed as though her exclusion in the Paradise had followed her into the Outworld.

As the day wore on, Shuut noticed her new companions grow irritable with hunger. The small store of food she had left would not last them to the end of that day. Feeling sorry for them, she called a halt to their journey in a small clearing where they could eat and rest. Thankfully, it hadn't rained recently, so the ground was dry enough to sit on. Apart from Karinya, none of the Paradisians seemed used to walking great distances. Shuut wondered why they were so different from this one strange girl.

During the meal, she began to explain how they were to survive in the Outworld. They were all shocked to learn they would need to hunt for their own food. In the Paradise, only the farmers, fishermen and butchers needed to deal with slaughtering animals. Unless they chose that field, none of them would ever have had blood on their hands. As such, Shuut decided to begin their hunting lessons.

"How would you like to play a game?" She waited for the curious nods before continuing. "The object of the game is to be as quiet as possible and hide from each other. If someone comes close to you, capture them. The one who remains undiscovered the longest, wins."

The game began. High above the contestants, Shuut hid in the treetops so that she could see the game. She watched as each of the opponents ran in opposite directions from each other for a count of ten. At the end of that time, Shuut watched with growing interest as she noticed Karinya was not hiding from the others, but studying their movements. She tested each of them to see what their giveaway signs were.

Arishen's heavy footsteps made too much noise when he thought he had to hide. He was her first target. When she was sure the other boys weren't around, she snapped a twig to scare the tall boy into hiding. Karinya heard exactly where he was and stepped out from a bush to catch him. Grudgingly, the boy accepted defeat and returned ahead of the young girl to the clearing they had used to rest and eat.

Shuut's attention was diverted from Karinya and Arishen by a movement directly below her. Plyke was silently wrapping a fallen vine around two trees. His Partner was nowhere in sight. After hurriedly disguising the thin vine with some leaves, he stood behind the thicker of the trees in wait for either of the remaining contestants.

It was not long before he was rewarded for his patience. Shuut had been watching Tika grow ill at ease being so far away from his companions. He rushed towards the clearing, not watching where his feet were landing. Unconsciously Shuut tensed, anxious to see the outcome. As soon as the small boy fell into the trap his Partner had set, he sprawled across the forest floor.

Instantly realising he may have hurt his Partner, Shuut watched in anger as Plyke let his guard down to assist his victim. As he helped Tika to his feet, a lassoed vine swept through the air to surround both boys. Karinya stepped into their sight with a satisfied grin on her face. Without saying a word to either boy, she led them to the clearing where she had left Arishen.

Shuut followed them in the treetops, dropping to the centre of the clearing once they had all sat down comfortable. Her new companions stared in surprise at her sudden entrance. She was furious with the boys, but they were oblivious to the reason.

"Not one of you took this game seriously!" she yelled at them. "Not one of you except Karinya." The three boys looked at her strangely. She could not understand why until she heard their thoughts.

Games are not meant to be taken seriously.

She had to teach them otherwise.

"The games you will play from now on will be exercises to help train you to stay alive in the Outworld. You will try to take them seriously and try your best to win. This is the only way you will learn the skills you need to survive. You need to step more lightly." She directed her suggestion to Arishen before looking over at the Partners. "Tika, you need to learn to be comfortable in solitude. And you, Plyke, need not to show weakness through sympathy."

"He's my Partner," the larger boy protested. "What was I meant to do? Not even ask if he was hurt?"

"That's exactly what you were meant to do. Anyone in the Outworld will see that as a sign of weakness that they can and will use to exploit you."

Disappointment flowed from all of them as they turned away from her. Even Karinya, the victor of the day, did not show any signs other than sympathy for her companions. The boys had tried their best, but Shuut knew that their best wasn't good enough yet.

As twilight fell, Shuut called a halt to their travel. They had long since left the forest behind them and had been walking through flat bushland for most of the afternoon. She ordered them to set up a campsite while she went to catch food for their evening meal. Tika and Plyke struggled to start a fire in the small pit they'd dug out. Arishen and Karinya set out everyone's cloaks as sleeping mats. It was the one thing all four Paradisians regretted not bringing with them to the Outworld.

Shuut returned shortly with four hares – enough food to last them until the next evening. They all watched on with interest as the banwep skinned and skewered the small animals. With Arishen on the other side of the fire from her, together they held up the two sticks, each with two hares on them, turning them slowly until the hares were cooked through.

When they had all eaten their fill, Shuut gave them their shifts for the night watch. She would be first, then Tika, Plyke, Arishen and, finally, Karinya. After they had been given their order, the four new Paradisians lay down to sleep. Shuut looked over them all momentarily before shifting her eyes to the darkness surrounding them.

Chapter Thirteen – Yoswen

It was raining when Rilla awoke. Arishen was sitting on a log at the edge of their camp, asleep on his watch. There were two strange creatures with their backs towards the her, in the ashes of the fire which should have been kept burning all night. Rilla thanked her lucky stars that the moonlight was shining brightly enough through the drizzle for her to see what was happening. Staring at the creatures through half closed eyes, her heartbeat quickened.

The animals had small leathery wings, probably useless for their short stocky bodies. They grunted while running their short, but effective, claws through the leftover hares before eating them in strips. Rilla knew there was no way that small meal could possibly satisfy the two beasts.

As silently as she could, she felt around in her sack for a weapon. Her hands closed around the sharp chisel Arishen had given her when they left the Paradise. Carefully drawing the tool out of her rucksack, Rilla scanned the rest of the camp only to notice that no one else was awake. She thought to slide over to Shuut and let her fix the problem, but worried the creatures would catch her before she got there.

As silently as her panicked mind would let her, she stood up. The creatures still had not noticed her. Slowly bending down, she picked up the lasso she'd made earlier that day and started to swing it around her head. The two animals instantly dropped the skewered hares to run heavily towards her. Before she had time to think, Rilla had thrown the lasso over the head of the nearest creature, pulling the rope back towards her as it tightened around the creature's arms. Hoping the creatures were even remotely loyal to each other, she immediately put the sharpened chisel to its throat. The other beast hesitated momentarily, but that was all she needed to kick her rucksack onto Shuut.

The banwep woke immediately and stood silently. These creatures were clearly not unknown to her. In a matter of moments, she had disappeared behind the nearest bushes and reappeared behind the advancing creature with her sword in her hand. Before the stocky beast could hear her, she cut off its head with one swift motion. Rilla watched in horror as it dropped, headless, to the ground. She stood, numbly, as Shuut took the other creature from her and killed it in the same way. When she was sure there were no others near the camp, she stormed over to Arishen, who had slept through the entire ordeal.

His eyes widened in fear as the banwep dragged him to the middle of the clearing, the bloodied sword in her other hand. Tika and Plyke awoke at his short cry. The moonlight shone off the rain sliding down her wraithlike form.

"Explain yourself!" The banwep's harsh voice cut through the sound of the increasingly heavy downpour. Arishen's eyes did not move from the sword point in front of his face. "Are you deaf boy? I said explain yourself."

"I don't know what you're talking about," he replied in confusion.

"Look around you, Arishen." Shuut motioned to the decapitated creatures. "These yoswen attacked while you were sleeping."

"No." He shook his head in disbelief. "It was only a dream."

"What are you talking about you, foolish boy?" Shuut asked tiredly. "What was a dream?"

"Everything," he replied, staring straight ahead. "Karinya was watching me on the log. I was sleeping. She looked over to the creatures…"

"Yoswen," the banwep corrected him.

"Yoswen, and swung a vine above her head. They attacked her. She used my chisel to defend herself. I could feel her hands tightly gripping the handle. I couldn't wake up. I wanted to, but I couldn't. Then you cut off both their heads."

"How can you possibly know all of that if you were sleeping?" The banwep moved her bloodied sword closer to his throat.

"It was a dream." Arishen shook his head as he repeated himself over and over again, his eyes never moving from the sword point.

"What is he talking about?" Shuut looked around at the other Paradisians, not lowering her sword.

"He has nightmares," Rilla tried to explain. "I didn't know they were anything more than that. He has nightmares all the time."

"How do you know that?" It was the first time Plyke had spoken since waking. "You know him less than we do."

"How do you explain that he was always the only one still sleeping after someone yelled out in the middle of the night? Parthak's angry blush as she shook him awake each time. Did you never notice?"

Rilla searched for some sort of acknowledgment they knew what she was talking about. Their blank stares surprised her. Surely, she couldn't have been the only person to notice other than Parthak.

Shuut lowered her sword as Arishen sank down to the muddied ground. "Is this true? Do your dreams become reality?" He did not answer but looked up at her with haunted eyes. "How long has it been happening?"

"I can't remember." His voice barely carried over the sound of the rain.

"At least ten years." All four of them stared at Rilla's answer. She rolled her eyes impatiently. "When nobody pays you any attention, you learn to see things like that."

Shuut took a deep breath. Rilla wondered if she'd ever travelled with a seer before. It didn't seem like it.

"Pack up camp," Shuut order them, tiredly, as she wiped the blood off her sword with her shirt. "There's no use trying to get back to sleep in this rain."

* * *

The rain continued the rest of the day, lightening to a drizzle at times. Shuut walked behind her apprentices. It was easier to keep an eye on them if they were ahead of her. With the events of the previous night fresh in her mind, she did not relish the thought of another encounter where she was taken by surprise. The memory played itself over and over in her mind. Karinya was the only one who woke up in time. Had she heard something the others had missed? Did the creatures step more closely to her than anyone else? Was she simply a light sleeper? Whatever the reason, the young girl had undoubtedly saved all their lives. Shuut wondered whether the girl realised that.

She could see that Arishen was also plagued by thoughts of the red-headed girl. His thoughts were so clear to her she wondered how the others couldn't hear them. He was in awe of the person who had not only recently saved his life, but had kept silent when she could have betrayed him in the Paradise. Had Erton even half suspected his gift, the seer would have been executed without warning.

Karinya was completely unaware of his attention on her. Her mind was closed to Shuut's probing. Had the girl not been so peculiar, the banwep would have disregarded this oddity but, as she had come to realise, this Paradisian needed to be watched. A person whose thoughts she couldn't read was always a threat to Shuut. She had learnt that from a very young age. They could betray her at any moment. The only way she had survived this long was because she was always aware when there was danger in store for her.

"Karinya, a word please," Shuut called out. The boys turned their heads inquisitively as they walked past her. Shuut slowed their pace until they were out of hearing distance from the boys.

"Your quick thinking saved us last night. I want to thank you for it." Karinya's eyebrows shot up at the comment. She was delighted at the praise. Her reaction made Shuut wonder if she'd ever been thanked for anything before.

"I need to ask you a ... rather delicate question." Shuut chose her words carefully. She couldn't be too cautious in this situation. Karinya waited silently for her to continue. "Why did you never say anything about Arishen to anyone else?"

"You mean, apart from the fact that no one ever spoke to me?" Karinya laughed. When she saw the look in Shuut's eyes, she rephrased her answer. "Why would I want to say something that would lead to anyone's death?"

Shuut shrugged her shoulders. "You would have power over them."

"I don't need power." The girl turned her green eyes away. "I've seen what it does to people."

"Power can be useful," Shuut persisted. "You can make things go your way."

The girl looked at her closely. "Would you have preferred that I had threatened you rather than reasoned with you to take us out of the Paradise?"

Shuut missed a step. "What could you possibly have threatened me with? Everyone already knew I was a banwep."

"That's true." Karinya nodded. "But I doubt anyone other than Rhanya and I knew that you are at least part lintep."

"He *told* you?"

* * *

Rilla did not answer. Her thoughts had moved back to Rhanya. At times, she thought his death was just a bad dream. Other times, all she had to do was close her eyes to see his lifeless form clutching a parchment with her name on it. Instinctively, she felt inside her left pocket to make sure it was still there. She still hadn't read his message. For some reason, she couldn't bring herself to do so. No one else knew about it. Somehow it seemed to her that as long as she didn't read it, there would always be something more he could say to her. The moment she read the message – that was it – there would never be another message from him.

"Karinya! Are you listening to me?" Shuut's agitated voice called Rilla back from her musings. "What do you intend to do with your knowledge?"

Staring blankly at the banwep for a moment, Rilla shook her head to clear her mind. "Nothing. What do you expect me to do with it? Do you think I would betray the person who helped me escape from the Paradise and survive in the Outworld?"

"Only until we reach the first village," the Outworlder hastened to clarify.

Tired of the same argument they'd had days ago, Rilla rolled her eyes before walking away from her saviour. She did not attempt to walk closer to any of the boys. With the previous night's events, she had little doubt that they would view her with even more caution than usual. As it was, Tika and Plyke were eyeing Arishen with suspicion. She imagined she could hear their thoughts. The paranoia that perhaps this boy had, or would, at some point have a dream about either one of them. It was not a baseless fear, but one they would never have any control over. If Arishen's dream had helped him avoid last night's near-disastrous encounter, it may have been a different story. But as things stood, the Partners would keep an eye on the seer for as long as it took to trust him again.

Chapter Fourteen – Fringa

"Why is *he* being rewarded?" Tika was indignant. "He messes things up and you let him sleep longer than the rest of us. That's hardly fair."

It was the conversation Shuut had been dreading all day – how to let the children see she didn't quite trust Arishen without telling the seer himself.

"It's not a reward, Tika. We're not sure why Arishen fell asleep on his watch. If he was tired, that's something we can deal with. If it had to do with his powers ... well, it's just safer for now to remove the possibility for anything to go wrong."

Seemingly mollified somewhat, Tika backed down.

"It won't happen again," Arishen spoke up in his own defence.

"Can you be certain of that?" Shuut asked, already knowing the answer. The seer didn't reply. "Then until you can be certain about it, you will not take a night watch."

Shuut felt her skin start to tingle. It was the same feeling she got every time lintep communicated with each other. Each time she felt it, she remembered her mother telling her that a full lintep would be able to hear the high-pitched whistling as well as get goose bumps. Each time she felt it, she stopped in her tracks, straining to hear what she knew she never would.

She was vaguely away of four sets of eyes on her and heard their voices in the back of her mind.

"Shuut?" Tika called her name hesitantly.

"Shuut?" All four of them called out simultaneously, the noise startling her.

"What is it?" Annoyed that they had broken her concentration, Shuut rubbed the raised flesh on her arms absentmindedly.

"What were you concentrating on?" Plyke asked.

"I ... thought I heard something. That's all." It was bad enough that Karinya knew her secret. There was no need for the others to know as well.

"What was it?"

"Nothing. Now get to sleep. If we start out early enough, we should reach Turon tomorrow." She knew they were not satisfied with her answer, but it didn't matter. By the end of the next day, they wouldn't be her problem anymore. She would be free to travel wherever and whenever she wanted.

* * *

A sharp sound woke Rilla in the middle of Plyke's watch. It sounded similar to the whistling she'd heard the night before, when Shuut had been focussed on something. She had little doubt that the banwep had been listening to the sound, but the others hadn't mentioned hearing anything.

"Is something wrong?"

Rilla turned towards the sound of Plyke's voice. His brow was creased with worry.

"Do you hear another yoswen?"

"No. It must have just been a bad dream." Rilla wondered why he hadn't asked her about the whistling. She found it odd that he wasn't at all curious about it. Surely he recognised it as the sound from the previous day.

A rustle in some nearby bushes drove the thoughts from her mind. She eyed the bushes cautiously. They were too low to conceal any yoswen, not that those massive creatures felt the need to hide before. She spied a small bright purple bird the same time as Plyke. They approached the frightened creature slowly. Its left wing was bent at an awkward angle, obviously broken. A shiny black beak pecked viciously at Plyke's fingers as he bent down to pick up the injured bird.

"Come here, little one."

Rilla and Plyke turned in surprise at Tika's soft voice. The small bird eyed him suspiciously. Tika knelt beside them and continued to coax the shivering mass of feathers until it hopped over to him. As though he had done it every day of his life, Tika placed his hand flat on the dirt, waiting expectantly for the bird to climb onto it. The shivering bird hopped over to his outstretched hand, jumping on after a cursory taste with its leathery tongue. The boy gently caressed the bright purple feathered back, carefully avoiding the injured wing.

"How did you do that?" asked Plyke, and Rilla heard more annoyance than curiosity in his voice.

"There, there, little one," Tika cooed at the bird, shrugging his shoulders. "I don't know. Guess I've always been good with animals. I *was* going to work in the stables back in the Paradise, remember?"

"Tika, what are you doing to that bird?" Shuut's icy voice made all three of them turn towards her. "If you've hurt it in any way, I will *not* save you."

"Save me from what?"

"The kryti who was meant to protect it."

Rilla and the Partners stared at the banwep in confusion.

"That bird is a fringa. It, along with its flock, lives under the protection of a creature more dangerous than the yoswen. If you've hurt that bird, and its kryti finds out, your life will be forfeit."

"He didn't hurt the bird." Arishen's tired voice came from where he was huddled in his cloak. "It was hurt in a fight with a flock of yellow-crested white birds. They were a lot bigger than that little one. And the kryti won't come looking for you for a long while yet. It's lying face down in a puddle of blood."

"You have to help him."

They all looked at the tiny purple bird in Tika's hand. Rilla could have sworn it had just spoken.

"Don't look so stupid, boy. You have to save my kryti. If you don't, my entire flock will die."

"We can't." It was Shuut who replied. She seemed not at all surprised to hear the bird talking, and Rilla thought they must be quite common in the Outworld. "We don't even know where he is or how to save him."

"That tall boy can tell you. He obviously knows." All eyes turned to Arishen, as the seer rubbed the sleep from his eyes.

"All I remember seeing is the kryti in a puddle of blood."

"Is there nothing else you remember?" Shuut asked. Rilla could feel her impatience. This task would delay their journey to Turon, but the fringa were obviously not to be angered.

Arishen closed his eyes, trying to recall his recent dream.

"There was the sound of water nearby. He was lying on something that looked like yellow grass." Shaking his head, the seer opened his eyes once more as Rilla saw the look of frustration cross over Shuut's face.

"Water and yellow grass? That's the best you can do?"

"I don't choose what the dreams show me, Shuut. I'm telling you all I can remember."

"That's good enough for me." The fringa's high-pitched voice broke the rising tension. "We were heading towards a small stream to the north of here when we were attacked. He must have fallen there."

Shuut didn't need to give them any instructions. The four of them had already learnt, in the few days they had been with her, how to break camp and douse the fire before they left. In a matter of minutes, they were ready to follow her to the fringa's injured protector.

The detour was not long at all. Led by the sound of the stream, they found the kryti a few miles north. He was lying exactly as Arishen had described, face down in a puddle of blood. Rilla was surprised that his blood was not flowing freely, but oozing out of a wound they could not see.

Rilla walked cautiously towards the injured beast. Golden brown fur covered his entire muscular body. Blood soaked the fur of his left shoulder, creating a sticky pool under his arm. Hoping that Rhanya had taught her enough by occasionally letting her watch him at work, Rilla ripped off a long strip from the bottom of her shirt and began wiping at the blood, trying to find the wound.

It was no use. Every time she cleared away some blood, more came out seemingly from the very pores of his skin. She hurriedly wiped her now bloodied hands on the grass before opening Rhanya's medicine bag. She scanned over each label, trying to find anything that might be useful. Eventually, she came across a white balm she had seen the old healer use under bandages when an apprentice butcher had cut his arm a few seasons ago. Ripping the left sleeve off her shirt, Rilla scooped some of the contents of the little clay jar onto the makeshift bandage. Hoping that she had found the actual wound, she carefully wrapped the cloth around the kryti's shoulder, with the balm over the bloodiest section.

"I don't know if it will work, but it's the best I can do with what I have." She got to her feet and turned towards her companions, noticing their silence for the first time since she'd begun her work. It made her uncomfortable. It wasn't that she was unused to people not talking to her, but she was rarely the centre of their silent attention. "Is there anything else we can do for him?"

"We wait." The fringa bobbed its head in her direction appreciatively. "This time, I must be *his* protector."

The waiting went on until late morning. Shuut used the time to practice her sword skills with the others watching on for a time. Things felt strange for Rilla. The Partners were distrustful of Arishen, so only traded cautious words with him, leaving the seer to seek her company.

He approached her with only slightly less confidence than he had the previous few times. As he sat next to her, Rilla flinched away.

"I'm not going to bite, you know."

"I know that," she replied, hugging herself in an attempt to cover her bare stomach. "I just don't like people touching me, that's all."

"You didn't seem to mind it with Rhanya."

She looked at him with daggers in her eyes.

"I mean…"

"You mean to say what exactly?"

"Karinya, you don't have to be so cold towards the rest of us."

"Karinya, huh?" Rilla raised her eyebrows at his words. "What reason do I have to be warm to people who never even bothered to remember my name?"

She knew she was being unfair. The Paradisians had been told her name when they were so young and then forbidden from using it for so many years that they simply couldn't remember it anymore.

Rilla turned at a sound behind her. The fringa was hopping excitedly around its kryti. Its high-pitched chirping aroused everyone's curiosity. They cautiously gathered around, staying well behind Shuut and the small bird, not wanting to test their luck against an Outworld creature again so soon.

Standing a decent distance away from the kryti, Shuut spoke in a low voice. "If the kryti, for one moment, looks as though it's going to attack – run. Don't hesitate or you won't live to regret it."

Rilla took a step back as the huge creature rolled over onto its back. She watched in silence as the fringa hopped out of the way, chirping as loudly as it could. Hearing the noise in the nick of time, the kryti stopped rolling just before he would have squashed his charge. They looked on in unmasked interest as a brown leathery hand reached out towards the fringa. The little bird hopped onto it without hesitation, chirping the entire time.

"Why isn't it talking to the beast, letting it know we helped it?" Tika asked.

"What makes you think he isn't?" Shuut turned to face him. "The kryti can understand every sound its flock makes. They live together all their lives. How did you think they'd communicate?"

Tika did not get a chance to respond. The massive creature had loped silently over to them without anyone noticing and reached out snatching up Rilla in one huge hand and Tika in the other. The kryti raised them over his head and cried out loudly in his guttural voice. Rilla struggled vainly to get out of his grip. Below her, she saw Plyke run to the kryti's side to punch its leg ineffectually while Shuut unsheathed her sword in one swift motion.

"Fringa, you'd better tell that beast of yours to let them go or he won't be around much longer to protect you."

"Oh, do put that sword away," the purple bird chided her from the kryti's shoulder. "He's only showing his thanks to these two children for bringing me to him and healing him."

Plyke looked up to the fringa, his hand paused mid-punch. "What do you mean?"

"I mean, boy, he's honouring your friends. He will now stay with you until he has saved their lives." As the bird spoke, the kryti gently lowered Rilla and Tika back to the ground.

"We appreciate the offer, but tell him it is unnecessary," the banwep said.

"No." The bird shook its head. "I need time to heal before I can find the rest of my flock. He will stay with you either until he saves your lives or I am healed. He will not be satisfied with any other alternative."

Sheathing her sword, Shuut did not look at any of them but began walking towards Turon, leaving the rest to follow behind her.

Chapter Fifteen – Half-caste

Shuut was angry enough with the detour, but what annoyed her most was the fact that she was now forced to travel with a kryti and a fringa. The people of Turon were a fairly conservative lot. It was bad enough coming in to town when everyone there knew she was a banwep, but she had no idea whether they would stop her from entering with her newest companions. She had no thoughts for the future other than to rid herself of her apprentices. That was supposed to have happened already. She knew there was no way they would reach Turon before the next morning now.

Paying no heed to the fact that her companions were struggling to keep up with her rapid pace, Shuut strode along furiously, leaving the kryti to bring up the rear. If he was meant to be their protector, she would use him to her full advantage.

"Shuut, wait up." Shuut heard Karinya calling from not too far behind, but she did not let it slow her pace or soften her resolve to distance herself from the situation.

"What do you want?"

"What are you going to do once we reach Turon?"

The question took Shuut by surprise. Karinya was the one who had finally convinced her to take them into the Outworld. The only condition had been that she would take them safely to the first town they reached. After that, they were on their own.

"Leave you to your own devices. Change your shirt, girl."

In the thick of the moment, Karinya had apparently forgotten about her ripped sleeve and hem. She could hear the girl rummaging around in her rucksack, trying to find a replacement.

"I didn't ask where you're going to leave us. I asked what you're going to do once we get there." Karinya's voice had a sharp edge to it, and the girl's mind was even more clouded that she had felt before which made it difficult to hear her thoughts.

"I'm going to visit an old friend and then leave."

"Is there any way that we could find you if we needed to?"

Shuut looked into the green eyes closely, trying to discern if there was a hidden message behind her words. "Why would you need to find me?"

"You're the only person we know out here. What if we run into trouble?"

"That's none of my business. Our deal was only for me to take you to a town. You promised that was all you'd ask."

"I also promised Rhanya that I'd look after the boys. What if we can't survive in Turon?" Shuut knew the girl could not have noticed, but her promise to Rhanya was a curiosity for her.

"Why would Rhanya think you any more capable than the boys?"

Karinya was silent a long while before answering. Speaking of her old friend was obviously painful, Shuut could see that, but she needed to find out as much about this girl as she could.

"I don't know. Maybe he knew me better than the others. Maybe he thought they were too trusting for the Outworld. Whatever his reasons, he gave me this task. As it turns out, it was his dying wish. I have no choice but to try my best to keep my promise."

"You said only a few people spoke to you and those that did called you 'the girl." She waited for Karinya to nod before continuing. "I heard Rhanya call you 'little one' the day we first met. Would he have called you something different if I wasn't there?"

The girl's silence unsettled Shuut. If she had left the Paradise to escape everything associated with it, why would she not say something that could not possibly make a difference now?

"Either he called you 'little one' all the time or he didn't. It can't be that important either way – it's just a name after all."

"How can you say that when your name suits you perfectly? In an ancient language, it means shadow."

"Not every name is so fitting. Most of them are just nice sounds."

"What about the name Nyssa – it means beginning."

"Fine." She conceded just to stop the conversation. It disturbed Shuut to find that, of all the names Karinya could have picked out, the girl had unknowingly used that of own her mother. "Names are important. What's your point?"

"I just wanted to know, does everyone in the Outworld do that? It isn't something they did in my Paradise."

"In the Outworld, when people give their children names with meanings, usually they've spoken to a seer and know the vague future of the child, or they have their own hopes for how their children will grow up, and so name them accordingly. My mother knew she would train me to be a shadow, to blend into anything. To fade away, like a shadow. She had no other hopes for me than to just fade away into nothingness. Why do you ask?"

"What about names that don't mean anything but to a few particular people? Why would anyone name their child like that?"

"I wouldn't know." Shuut shook her head, almost apologetically. This was the most she had heard Karinya speak at one time. It was the most insight she'd gained to the mind she couldn't read and, with her simple answer, she may have ended her opportunity to learn more.

"There was a girl I met before entering the Paradise. Her name was Rilla. I can't remember much about it. My father told me it was a very special name but wouldn't say why. Do you know?"

That's the second time she's pulled an important name out of thin air. Shuut was taken aback by the coincidence. "That's not a common name. Where did you meet this girl?"

"I told you, it was before I entered the Paradise. I couldn't have been more than three years old. It was so long ago I can barely even remember my father's reaction."

"Well, it might mean different things to different people." She pursed her lips, trying to decide whether to say any more. "I doubt it means anything at all to humans."

"But you're not quite human. What does it mean to *you*?"

"To any race other than humans, it means hope. Rilla was a lintep princess. She was to save her people in a great war."

Karinya looked at her in confusion. "What war?"

"I thought you had a school in that Paradise of yours." Shuut raised an eyebrow in Karinya's direction.

"If you'd stayed long enough, you would have realised that only Erton's staunchest followers were allowed to become teachers. We were only taught what he didn't mind us knowing. All he told us of the lintep were that they were dangerous magicians who caused humans to find refuge in Paradises."

"That's true – from a certain point of view. What was meant to be a great war ended sooner than expected with the death of Rilla. She was the only lintep with enough power and compassion to fight humans."

"How can you say she had enough *compassion* to fight humans? What does that even mean?"

"It means she was only fighting the humans who wouldn't tolerate the lintep and their magic. She wanted to create some sort of unity, or at least a little peace, in what you now call the Outworld. Most other lintep would not have bothered wasting their time on people they considered less important than themselves in every way. Once Rilla died, the war ended. Those lintep with enough kindness banded together to create the Paradises. They really *were* meant to be safe havens from the Outworld, as well as a place to live away from magic."

"I don't see why that means anything to anyone now. That war must have been hundreds of years ago. I'd bet most people have even forgotten why it ended."

"As I told you, Karinya, it isn't a name that would mean anything to humans. But to lintep it still means hope. There is a prophecy of another Rilla to come."

Her curiosity seemingly aroused, Karinya pressed for more information. "Do you know the prophecy then?"

This was an awkward situation for Shuut. She'd never told any human that she was part lintep. Those who had figured it out themselves had come after her and ended up as food for vultures. Anyone she ventured to call a friend already knew the prophecy. It had been drummed into her from a young age, but she doubted any human alive had heard it. Doubting that it would make any difference if one did, she recited it as easily as a bard would a poem.

"*When a crystal heart beats in the body of another,*
Their song will destroy that which was created.
Every being will bow down to the child of Paradise,
All will hail Rilla."

Karinya held her breath for a moment. "Shuut, do you think it means that the next Rilla will be from a Paradise? How would that even work? If the next Rilla is meant to be a lintep, how would she ever find herself in a Paradise in the first place?"

"I ..." Shuut stumbled over her words. "I don't know. I mean, of course Rilla has to be a lintep. There are no two ways about it."

"Just pretend then, that when it all happens, Rilla is a lintep and she does live in a Paradise. At some point, she'd need to find other lintep, wouldn't she? I mean, what would be the point of it all if she just lives in a Paradise and doesn't know anything about this prophecy."

"Well, at some point, assuming she *does* live in a Paradise, Rilla would leave and find the lintep."

"And just how is she supposed to do that?" Karinya laughed. "The only way the four of us are even finding a human village is because we have you guiding us. How is she meant to find a race that sets itself apart from humans with no help at all?"

"Ah, there I have your answer." Shuut smiled knowingly. "All full blooded lintep can communicate without humans hearing them. They whistle. It's a special kind of whistle that makes your skin come up with goose bumps. If you listen to it closely, there's a meaning behind it."

"They whistle?" Karinya shook her head in disbelief. "A race, as powerful as you're saying they are, *whistles* to communicate?"

Not knowing why, Shuut felt the need to explain herself to the young Paradisian. It was as though she had nothing left to hide from her now that Karinya knew her secret.

"What do you think I was trying to listen to last night?"

"I don't understand. If you could hear them whistling and you don't have any friends or family, why wouldn't you just find the lintep and stay with them? Surely it would be an easier life than being a banwep, and not nearly as dangerous or boring as our Paradise."

"I'm only *part* lintep. I'm a half-caste. Only a full lintep can hear the whistle. All that happens with me is the goose bumps. I can strain to listen as much as I like, but in the end, I'll never hear it."

Karinya stopped talking, and Shuut was glad of the girl's silence. Her questions had stirred up too many painful memories. Nyssa had taken her to the crystal dragons when she was still very young. It was possibly the happiest time of her life. But, as with all good things, it didn't last long. Soon enough, her father came to take her away from everything she loved. It still broke her heart to remember the little dirty-faced girl she had been pulling against the hand that led her away, tears streaming from her eyes, screaming at the top of her lungs for her mother. The rare times that her father brought her back to the Drakos Mountains were her only reason to live. He was a banwep. Taking care of a child had never been part of his life plan. She learnt whatever she could by watching him like a hawk. He barely ever spoke to her.

It was after nine harsh years travelling in the Outworld that the crystal dragons gave her the worst news she would ever hear. *Your mother is dead.* She could still hear Celtan's deep voice as he apologised to her.

Soon after that, she gave up hope of ever finding happiness. Alone in a world of hatred, she looked to the crystal dragons for comfort – for some sort of purpose. They had given it to her.

* * *

Rilla walked on in silence. Shuut had told her more than she could cope with, the least of which was that her name was more important than she could possibly have imagined. She let all that the banwep had said sift through her mind. If she could hear the whistling, it meant that both of her parents were lintep. *She* was a lintep. She'd always known she was different, but this was just too much to take in.

Everyone in the Paradise knew Erton was Rilla's father, though they could not acknowledge it, but who her mother was had remain a mystery. According to Erton, she come in from the Outworld with him when Rilla was only three years old. On seeing what the Paradise was like, she left. He had only told her because she had constantly asked him about her mother. It was the only thing he had ever said about her.

Thoughts raced through Rilla's mind. If she was a lintep, that might mean she was capable of magic. *Magic* – the dream of every child. She smiled at the thought. What would Erton say if he knew she'd discovered the truth? Would he have trained her if she had stayed in the Paradise or would he have let her live her entire life not knowing her own capabilities?

Chapter Sixteen – Little Star

"There it is!" Tika called out excitedly. "We made it!" The sky had already turned a deep orange by the time they saw the village.

Shuut shook her head angrily. "Can't you see how far away it is? They won't let us in after nightfall. They never do."

"But we have no food left," Tika pointed out.

"Then we'll just have to hunt, won't we?"

Before the rest of them could move, the kryti was already running with a heavy tread towards a nearby cluster of trees with the fringa on his shoulder.

"Arishen and Karinya set up camp for the night. Tika, Plyke, you two come with me."

Arishen's stomach knotted at the thought of being left alone with the nameless girl. He watched anxiously as the other two boys left with Shuut.

Turning, he saw Karinya laying out her cloak. He hastened to lay out his own cloak before helping the silent girl with the others. When they had finished laying them all out in a wide circle, Karinya wordlessly helped him dig a small pit for the fire.

She'd barely said two words to him all afternoon. Even though he understood she was annoyed with him for not knowing her name, it was hard for him to accept her anger. His own Partner had practically disowned him when she realised what he was. Parthak had bluntly told him that he would regret it if he didn't leave the Paradise. Karinya, on the other hand, who had no reason to save him, had kept silent for ten years.

"Are you going to be angry at me forever just because I don't remember your name?" He regretted the words as soon as they were out of his mouth. It had only been half a day since she'd stopped talking to him. He was sure she just needed some time to cool off but, for some reason he had no control over, he couldn't give it to her.

"No, I'm thinking up new reasons by the hour," Karinya replied tartly.

Arishen was shocked that she'd said anything at all, but this new information was not what he'd been hoping for.

"What did I ever do to you to? It wasn't as if any of us had the choice to call you by name."

"Well, in actual fact, you did."

"Erton would have punished us!" he fumed at her.

She stopped placing twigs in the small hole they'd dug and stared up at him, her bright green eyes piercing.

"You're right. Rhanya paid for it with his life, although planning to help the four of us escape Erton's Paradise with a banwep probably didn't help matters."

Arishen cringed. Rhanya's death had affected him more than he had dared let on. The old healer had been the kindest person he'd known in the Paradise. Dreaming of his death had been torture. Watching Belial climb in through the open window, not being able to call out to warn the healer – it weighed him down. He remembered screaming in his dream, trying to stop Erton's henchman from smothering the old man with his own pillow. If he closed his eyes, he could still see Rhanya's arms struggling with the pillow over his face, and his legs flailing, trying to fend off his attacker. Even as healthy as he was, a man his age stood no chance against the muscular bulk of Belial. Unable to stop focussing on the images, Arishen remembered seeing a piece of paper scrunched up in Rhanya's hand. There was writing on it, but his long bony fingers were in the way, and he couldn't read it.

"You were the first one there."

"What are you talking about?" Karinya looked away from whatever she could see on his face.

"You were the first one in Rhanya's room after his death. What was in his hand?" She gasped, and Arishen knew he'd hit on something important.

"How could you possibly even know ..." She closed her eyes, shook her head and turned away from him.

Taking a deep breath, he tried to explain. "I don't get to choose what I dream about. Most of the time I'd rather not see all the things that I'm forced to remember forever." He tried to catch her eyes, but looked down when he saw her eyes glazed over with tears. For all his effort in trying to talk to her, he'd almost made her cry. It felt like, instead of moving closer, he kept pushing her away.

He'd was about to turn away from Karinya when he saw the tight fist which showed plainly through the pocket of her loose-fitting pants.

"You've got it in your pocket, haven't you?"

She didn't respond.

"What does it say?" he persisted.

Her only reply was a shrug. As though nothing had happened, she wiped her eyes with both of her hands and fetched her chisel and a stone out of her rucksack. Arishen guessed he'd get nothing more out of her that night. He simply sat back and watched as she lit the fire.

* * *

By the time her companions returned to their campsite, Rilla had started the fire and found a long enough stick to roast whatever animals the rest of them had managed to catch. Try as she might, she just couldn't stop thinking about Rhanya and the note he'd left for her. Perhaps it was time she finally read it – but not now, not with everyone around her. He'd written her name plainly on the front of the parchment. Knowing what she now did about the prophecy, there was no chance she wanted any of them finding out who she might be.

Together with the others Rilla skinned the hares and plucked the feathers from the quails. Shuut retrieved some salt and spices from her rucksack with which they seasoned the meats. She waited until Arishen and Shuut were slowly roasting the hares over the fire before making an excuse to be by herself.

"If you don't need me for a little while, I might try to find some berries or fruit." Arishen looked up at her sharply. The cursed seer probably knew she just wanted to get away from them all for a while. He probably knew everything, but she wouldn't let that change her plans.

"Take the kryti with you," Shuut answered almost absently. "You might find something further down the hill towards Turon. There were some farms around last time I was here. Just be careful no one sees you taking anything."

Rilla smiled her thanks to the banwep before turning to go. She wasn't annoyed that the kryti was coming with her. In fact, she was glad for the company of its fringa. The small purple bird intrigued her and might keep her mind occupied for a little while.

"I thought you might object to the quails that Shuut caught," she said to the fringa. She hadn't quite meant it to come out as bluntly as it did, but Rilla was still not used to speaking to anyone other than Rhanya.

"Quails are not very intelligent birds. If they are stupid enough to be caught, they deserve to be eaten," the fringa replied unfazed. "Why do you feel the need to run away?"

"I beg your pardon?" Rilla stared at the bird in surprise.

"A question for a question. It's my turn now. What did that boy say to you?"

Rilla weighed up her options. Even though the huge beast walking beside her had promised to save her life, she thought he would be more inclined to listen to the fringa than herself. "He reminded me of something I'd rather he hadn't brought up."

"You don't get off that easily, girl. What was it?"

"I have a note in my pocket that I've been carrying around since an old friend died."

"Well, what does the note say?" When Rilla didn't reply, the fringa pushed a little further. "You haven't read it yet, have you?"

Rilla shook her head without looking at the bird. "It's stupid, but I don't want the others to see it."

"They're not around now."

"What if I don't want *you* to read it?"

"Have no fear of that, girl. I can't read. Let's find some food and then you can see what this note says."

Suddenly too afraid to answer, Rilla simply nodded and walked on in silence until they reached an orchard full of fruit trees. She cursed herself for not bringing her rucksack along. Holding out her shirt so that it could hold as many apples as possible, she picked some from the lowest branches. The kryti, understanding what she was doing, picked some of the higher fruits, effortlessly dropping them into her shirt.

When they'd picked as many as Rilla's shirt could hold, she turned to head back towards the campsite. Half way up the hillside, the fringa stopped her.

"Any closer and they'll see you reading your precious note."

"I don't think I want to read it."

"This will probably be your only chance to be away from them in a long time. Don't be a coward."

Rilla hesitated only a moment before she sat on the grass, being careful not to spill the apples. She tentatively reached into her left pocket and felt the folded parchment. Taking a deep breath, she pulled it out and stared at her name on the front. She flinched as the fringa hopped from the kryti's shoulder to her own. Looking the bird in the eye, Rilla opened the parchment.

"Sooner or later, you'll have to look," the fringa said in such a gentle voice that Rilla found herself reading the note before she could stop herself.

My dear girl,

Do you remember the star story – big star and little star? Well, you, my dear, are the little star. On occasion, I overheard you telling the story to some of the younger children in our Paradise. I always wondered whether you knew.

I feel certain they are coming for me tonight. Don't be sad for me. I've lived a long life. The past twelve years have been the best by far.

When I was born, this Paradise wasn't the place it is now. Were I in your position, I would be trying to leave as well. Remember, Rilla, the others aren't as strong as you. Keep them safe.

Goodbye, my little star.

Rilla read the note over and over again. Her eyes welled up with tears and her breathing came in short, erratic bursts. The stars above looked like they were spinning around her. She didn't even remember the fringa was sitting on her shoulder until it spoke again.

"That bad, is it?"

"He said I am the little star."

She couldn't hold back any longer. Tears streamed freely down her face. Before they could touch the parchment, she quickly folded it and put it back in her pocket.

"I suppose that means something to you."

"In his story, the little star is one who inspires people. He said *I* am the little star. He thinks I inspire people. I inspired *him*. How can I be the one to inspire him when I always looked up to him? He was my favourite person. He was the only one who still remembered my name *and* called me by it. He silently stood up to Erton and his people. He did all of that for me because I inspired him."

"That doesn't sound like bad news. Why are you crying?"

"He died to give us all a chance of freedom. I promised him I would look after them. He reminded me of it in the letter."

"Then don't break your promise, child. It isn't that difficult to work out."

"You don't understand. As soon as Shuut leaves us in Turon, I've broken my promise. We won't survive in the Outworld without her. Try as I might, I can't learn to be a banwep in little over a week. I can't keep the boys and myself safe without her."

The fringa was silent for a while, mulling over what she had said. "Leave it to me. I will make sure she does not leave you in Turon. She may not have much of a choice in any case, but I will make certain that she cannot leave you behind. Will you agree that we are even after that?"

Rilla vigorously nodded her head. At that point, she knew she would have agreed to anything if it meant Shuut would not abandon them. Wiping her eyes on the sleeve of her shirt, she carefully stood up, making sure the apples in the folds of her shirt did not roll away. Together, the three of them made their way back to the campsite where the scent of roasted meat wafted through the air.

Chapter Seventeen – Turon

The walk down to Turon took only a few hours. By mid-morning they were taking the final steps towards the high wooden fence surrounding the small town. Plyke, more observant than he let on to anyone, was watching Shuut from behind his mop of hair. Kora had often given himself and Tika gentle words of advice. She was adamant that they should think for themselves and notice as much as possible. Whereas Tika took her words literally and wore his thoughts on his sleeve, Plyke himself was more cautious by nature. He took in as much information as he could from his surroundings, safely staying undetected while doing so. Along with his quiet nature, he understood most people saw him as uninteresting. It suited him well. He remained invisible while seeing everything.

For a time, he listened as Tika excitedly commented on the steady line of farmers trickling through the gate, heading into the town with their produce. This was going to be their new home. Here, Tika would find work as a stable hand and work his way up to stable master. Eventually, he might even get to visit the elves which he held in such high esteem.

With Tika so thoroughly occupied, Plyke took the opportunity to observe their companions more closely. He got the feeling that Shuut was arguing with the fringa. The tiny purple bird shook its head, its entire body trembling with the violent motion. His kryti growled lowly, coinciding with a look from the banwep in the direction of Karinya and Tika. It didn't take much effort to understand what was happening. Shuut, understandably, did not want the kryti to accompany them into the town but could not stop Karinya and Tika's protector from following them wherever they went. Plyke turned his head back to the slow-moving line as three Outworlders came to join the Paradisians.

As they patiently waited for the farmers to pass through the gate, Plyke took in everything. The gatekeeper was a stout man, at least forty years old. His unshaven face made him appear even gruffer than Plyke suspected he might be. The gatekeeper openly eyed them in between each of the farmers. Plyke doubted the suspicious man would allow them entry into their town. If it worked anything like a Paradise, this man would be the equivalent of Erton's muscle men. Even if they were let in, there was a very real possibility that, sooner or later, they would be forced back out again – just as Erton had done with Shuut.

"Here, you lot, what's your business here?" The gatekeeper's voice betrayed the uneasiness within him far more than the expression in his dark eyes. Plyke didn't blame him. Even he, as inexperienced in the Outworld as it was possible to be, could understand that their travelling party must seem an odd group. Even without the fringa and his kryti, four apprentice-aged people with a banwep could not have been a common sight.

"We're here to visit an old friend." Shuut spoke calmly and to the point. It was obvious she had dealt with men like this gatekeeper before.

"I suppose you'll all be leaving together after this visit."

"But of course." The banwep smiled, but Plyke though it was through clenched teeth. Plyke had little doubt that Shuut could easily leave them behind without the gatekeeper noticing. But before long, people would start to wonder what a group of four unskilled people were doing in their midst. He doubted it was as easy to begin an apprenticeship in this small town as it was in their old home.

"You be sure of that. I won't let you be leaving these children and that beast in our town."

"I'm sure you won't," Shuut muttered softly as the gatekeeper moved aside to let them enter the town. Her annoyance worried Plyke. If she did leave them behind, they'd be in almost as much strife as if they'd stayed in the Paradise. Only here, the reason to fear for their lives would be because they couldn't look after themselves. Kora had taught both him and Tika enough to know that they had to work for their food in the Outworld. They had to be good enough at a trade for someone to hire them in the first place. The four of them stood no chance if Shuut left them behind. He wondered if Arishen and Karinya knew that.

Plyke's eyes darted in every direction once they were past the gate. Turon was a small town by Outworld standards, Shuut had said, but as for him it was the largest community he had ever seen. It wasn't necessarily larger in land than their Paradise, but it certainly had more buildings in close quarters. So close together, in fact, that there were only narrow stretches of space between them for people to walk down. Plyke started to feel hemmed in by the lack of space. Oddly, it reminded him of being confined in the isolation hut. One time in that prison had been enough to deter him from every stepping out of line again in the Paradise.

As they neared a more open area, the town seemed to buzz with activity. There were people everywhere with food and other goods surrounding them, shouting out to passers-by. The array of smells assaulted his nose. Paradises were fertile places to live in, but did not offer the variety of a marketplace.

Shuut knew where they were going. He followed her closely, eager to get away from the sudden increase in noise and crowds. Too interested in their own affairs, he saw that most of the people barely even turned an eye to the strange company.

Shuut led them to a tall building. The only thing that set it apart from the others in the same area was a wooden sign with faded paint naming it as Dell's Inn. Plyke had no idea what an inn was. Certain his companions were in the same state of ignorance as he was, he resolved to find out as soon as they were alone with Shuut.

Dust smeared the glass windows, obscuring the view to a darkened room within. Glass windows were a luxury that only Erton enjoyed in their Paradise. Plyke saw that the upper windows were covered with wooden shutters.

A small bronze bell sang at their arrival. As one, he and the others looked up to see what had made the noise, before Plyke lowered his gaze to study the interior of the inn.

They were standing near one of the largest tables in the room. There were smaller wooden tables around the edges of the room, most of them in the poorest lighting the room had to offer. There were candles hanging randomly from the ceiling in groups of three. None were lit at this time of day, and the only light was a dirty yellow seeping in through the dusty windows. Against one wall was a long counter, with two thickset men behind it serving drinks to the patrons seated alongside. Doors led away in every direction, presumably to the kitchen and other serving rooms. To one side, there was a wooden staircase leading up to another level.

A few moments after their entrance, Shuut eyed one of the men behind the bar. With a simple nod of her head, they seemed to understand each other. He disappeared through a door leading to the back of the inn. They didn't have to wait for long before a plump, unattractive woman waddled through the kitchen door towards them. Wiping her hands on an already dirty apron, a warm smile lit her face as she noticed Shuut though her eyes narrowed quickly when she took a second look at the company she kept.

"Ah, Laila, so good to see you again, and with so many companions. What can I do for you this morning?" The lady had a rich voice, not what Plyke expected from a woman her size.

"Ratchin, my friend, I've been away too long."

"It's been three years, child. You've been greatly missed." Her voice carried a strong sense of sorrow as she gathered the banwep up in a bone-crushing hug. "How long will you be staying this time? A month? A week?"

"A single night, two at the most." Ratchin obviously knew better than to ask too many questions out in the open. Without needing any further information, the cook nodded her head sadly and motioned for them to follow her up the stairs. Once they reached the landing, she took them down a narrow hall. Her pudgy fingers fetched a set of keys from her apron pocket with which she opened the two doors as the end of the hall.

"I'll run a bath for you and your companions. I'm sure you could use it." Shuut thanked her with a smile. "Don't give me that look, girl. You'll be telling me everything once you're settled."

"Thank you Ratchin. I always could count on you."

With a cocked eyebrow, the large lady squeezed herself back out of the doorway, and down the hall to the bathroom. Once the door was closed, the questions flowed freely.

"Why did she call you a different name?"

"Is she your mother?"

"What's an inn?"

"Are we going to explore the town?"

Shuut quieted them with hands upheld.

"We have two rooms here. One for myself and Rilla, the other for the three of you." Looking over at the kryti and his fringa she added, "You two can stay where you please. Once everyone has had a bath, I'll answer all your questions. For now, just leave me in peace. I need to go out for a while." At the panicked looks on their faces, she hastened to reassure them. "I'll just be gone a short time. I have to bargain with ... someone I'd prefer you don't meet. As soon as I'm back, you can ask me anything you like. I promise."

Plyke, along with the others, watched in interest as she began to transform herself. Concealing her face in the hood of her cowl, she took some short hair out of her pocket and stuck it with a sticky substance to the area under her nose. The banwep picked up most of the hares and quails they'd caught the night before and left. Once she was out of sight, Plyke turned towards the kryti and his fringa.

"What did she say to you outside the gate?" he asked.

"She asked us to stay behind," said the fringa.

"Why would she do that?"

"It would have been much easier for the banwep to leave the four of you here if she hadn't been seen coming to town with a kryti."

"Then why didn't you stay behind? Wouldn't you prefer to be out there looking for the rest of your flock than here with us?" Plyke noticed a look pass between the fringa and Karinya.

"My kryti and I have made a promise to protect those who saved our lives. We will not leave them until that promise is fulfilled."

Plyke saw Arishen's curiosity at Karinya's reaction to the fringa's statement. Looking over at the red-headed girl himself, he saw a sad smile on her face. He watched her as she walked over to the window. She struggled with the metal contraption which kept the wooden shutters closed. After a moment, Arishen walked over to her, almost as though determined to make the girl notice him.

"Let me help you with that."

She didn't turn at the sound of his voice but flinched away at the touch of his hand on hers. "What makes you think you can open it any faster than I can?"

"I don't know. I just thought ..."

"That *I* need your help after I saved your life?"

Arishen tried to speak calmly, but Plyke could hear his anger at her easy dismissal of him. "Kalid showed me a thing or two in her workshop. She didn't always live in the Paradise."

It surprised Plyke that Karinya had no idea how infatuated the seer was with her. He looked over at Tika to see if his Partner had noticed it too. Seeing the smaller boy roll his eyes with a silent sigh almost made him laugh. Turning back towards the window, Plyke saw Arishen unlock the simple contraption with no trouble whatsoever. Barely hiding his satisfied smile from the quick-tempered girl, Arishen pushed the shutters open to reveal the town below.

"There she is." Karinya said, her voice low as she pointed out Shuut walking down the street. Plyke went to the window with Tika and looked out, realising that none of the them were standing too close to the strange girl.

The entire town was small enough that they could see to the other end with very few obstructions. Every now and then, Shuut would walk down a street and out of their view but, very soon afterwards, she would appear again a street or two away. They watched their saviour walk into ever shadier areas until, at last, she found the door she was looking for. She didn't look over her shoulder, but Plyke could tell that she was making sure no one noticed as she went through the door.

"The baths are ready." Ratchin's rich voice carried through the door. They all turned towards her. Pointing to Tika and Arishen, the large lady waved a hand to follow her. "There is enough water for two at a time. Come on boys, this way, down the hall."

Tika's eyebrows shot up at the idea that he would have to be alone with the seer. Plyke wished he could somehow keep those sorts of thoughts better hidden, but knew his Partner had no training in that department.

Arishen, too, had noticed the look on Tika's face. "I can wait. Why don't you go first?" Plyke said nothing in reply, but nodded and followed his Partner down the hall towards the bathroom.

"Why are you so afraid of him?" Plyke only spoke once Ratchin had left the room. She and Shuut may be friends, but he wouldn't trust her so soon after meeting her.

"You're saying you're not?" Tika was already undressed and dipping his toes into the warm water. He only looked at Plyke once he was almost completely submerged in the bath.

"Well, it's not as though he's dangerous just because of his dreams." Plyke was still undecided on the matter. He knew Arishen wouldn't purposely betray him, but his dreams might do that for him, unintentionally. Not knowing how the seer's gift worked was the biggest part of the problem. Did Arishen only dream of people he knew well, or those who he was close to? He dreamt of the yoswen attacking their campsite, but that could have been because it was something that would affect him. It was possible that he would never dream about those he knew little about. If Plyke was careful, and continued to distance himself from everyone around him, he might remain safe.

"What if he finds things out about us that we'd rather he didn't know?"

Plyke was surprised by the question. He knew Tika better than anyone else in their Paradise. There was nothing his Partner would ever need to hide from anyone. The idea that there was something Tika didn't want anyone else to know intrigued Plyke.

"And what dark secrets do you hold Tika?" Plyke dunked his head under the water. When he came back, he pushed his wet hair back from his face revealing both his eyes for the first time in months. It was the reason he grew his hair long. Having one brown eye and one green eye was more than enough to make people notice him. Attention was something he usually avoided at all costs. When he looked over, Tika's face was stormy.

"Don't think that you know everything about me just because I'm your Partner. I may have secrets that even *you* don't want to hear." Tika refused to say anything further, so Plyke concentrated on enjoying the warmth of a well-deserved bath. It was the first time they'd bathed since leaving their Paradise.

* * *

Arishen waited for Tika and Plyke to leave before he spoke. "Do you think they'll ever talk to me normally again now that they know what I am?"

"At least they have a good reason to avoid you. Most people simply avoided me because of my father – not because of who or what I am."

Arishen was caught by indecision. He wanted to talk to her, but hadn't had much success in the last few days. Everything he'd said to Karinya had come out so badly it had made things worse between the two of them. He was desperate to end the cycle.

"Well, I'm not avoiding you *now*. I think we'd all stop avoiding you so much if you would just tell us your real name. Or at least explain why Erton was so adamant about keeping it silent. Do you even know the reason for it?"

She stayed silent for so long that he thought she wouldn't answer. Just as he was turning away, she faced him.

"I have come to understand why Erton forbade anyone from using my name. I'm not certain if I agree with him, so until I figure that out ... let's just leave it at that. I'm sorry I snapped at you the other day. You didn't deserve it. I shouldn't have expected anyone as young as we were to remember my name if they were too scared to use it in the first place."

"Then you forgive me?" He couldn't help the smile that spread over his face. Karinya smiled back at him, shaking her head.

"I forgive you." Karinya turned her eyes towards the window once more. Arishen joined her, standing close near the wooden frame. "You don't have to stand so close to me, you know."

He looked at her in confusion. "I didn't realise I was. This is how close I always stand to people."

"No one ever stood that close to me in the Paradise. I guess I'm just not used to it."

Sensing the change in her mood, Arishen thought to move further away while still being able to see out of the window. He did not need another reason for Karinya to be angry with him.

"What do you suppose she's doing?" He changed the subject to something he thought they could not possibly get into an argument over.

"Did you notice she took the food we caught last night with her? Perhaps she's going to bargain with it – although I'm sure she's more than capable of taking what she wants without anyone noticing."

"Maybe she's going to find somewhere for us to be apprenticed. I'm sure she knows where the healer lives. She could ask them to take you in."

Karinya shook her head adamantly. "I'm not staying in this town. When Shuut leaves, I'm going with her. We all are."

"That wasn't part of our agreement with her. A banwep can't be expected to take four unskilled Paradisians around with her for the rest of her life," Arishen reasoned.

"If she comes back without asking anyone to take us in as apprentices, we'll ask her to tomorrow. I can almost guarantee you that we will have no luck."

"How can you be so certain? We've barely been here an hour." Arishen felt his frustration bubbling up. Karinya's attitude was starting to bring him down.

"Did you not notice the gatekeeper's reaction to us? He would be one of the more tolerant people in town, especially as he would meet more people than anyone else. The only reason he even let us pass was because Shuut promised him we would be leaving with her. Do you think that we would have had any chance of entering if she wasn't with us?"

"That doesn't mean she should take us with her," Arishen persisted.

Karinya didn't reply. Together, they watched the banwep leaving the building she had entered. She no longer had the hares and quails that had been caught the night before. Was Karinya right?

Arishen made a few more attempts to speak to Karinya before turning around in annoyance. The fringa and his kryti were standing quietly in a corner of the room. As he looked at them, the small purple bird avoided his gaze. He knew there was no loyalty there for him. Tika and Karinya were the ones who saved the kryti's life. If it came down to a decision of who to protect, the choice was obvious.

Walking over to one of the wooden beds, he sat down discontentedly on the feathered mattress. It was lumpy, but did not smell as bad as he'd imagined it would. Making use of the silence, he took in their room. The entire frame of the building must have been made from wood, with mud bricks being used only for the exterior walls. Ratchin had given them two rooms. This one had two beds in it, both against the same wall. On the other side of the room was a door leading, he assumed, to their other room. There was also a small wooden closet, doors open and standing empty.

Knowing that there would be no more conversation until the others returned, he stood up once more and walked over to the door opposite him. Karinya did not turn at his movement. This annoyed him more than he let show. He was tired of being avoided by some and simply ignored by others. The only time they paid him any attention was when he had dreams. It was the kind of attention he could do without — Shuut's probing questions and Karinya's offhanded answers.

The other room was larger, with four beds set out two against each wall. Between them were another two wooden closets. He opened a larger window, letting in more light than that in the other room. Sitting cross-legged on one of the beds against the further wall, he opened his rucksack and emptied the contents onto the mattress. There was his cloak that Tika and Plyke had packed for him, the change of clothes and spare leather soles that Karinya had taken from the tailors back in their Paradise and the heavy screwdriver that he'd been given by Kalid. Sighing deeply, he thought of his dream parchments that he normally kept under his bed. He wished, not for the first time, that he'd remembered to get them before leaving the Paradise.

Lifting his cloak from the mattress, he noticed a small green bundle under it. He stared at the package, silent and open mouthed. It was the cloth he used to conceal his dream parchments. Tika and Plyke must have put it in with his other belongings without knowing what was inside. With uncharacteristic gentleness, he fingered the soft green cloth, pulling slowly at the leather straps around it. It had rained continuously for over a day while they had been travelling. Would his parchments be ruined? He held his breath as he pulled the top folds of the bundle aside.

His hands moved over the parchments, writing scrawled on every available area. It was all still legible. His other clothing must have kept this precious bundle dry. He searched for the piece of charcoal he always kept in a pocket of the green cloth. Before he knew what he was doing, in full view of anyone who might enter the room, he began to furiously write down the dreams he'd had since leaving the Paradise. He hadn't noticed how much he'd missed the daily ritual. It was something he tended to do in the late hours of the evening, when everyone else had already gone to sleep. The moon generally provided more than enough light for his purposes.

Forgetting Karinya for the first time since leaving the Paradise, he was completely absorbed in his own world. It was a world that no one else could enter – a world that no one else could even understand. Even though it was this gift which put his life in danger, he loved it and loathed it at the same time.

* * *

Shuut walked in through the entrance of Dell's Inn for the second time that day. She was unsurprised to find Ratchin waiting for her. Doubtless her old friend had many questions to ask. There was no need for Shuut to ask where the patrons and owners of the inn had gone. Ratchin had a certain way with people that allowed her to clear a room with a single glance.

It was no secret to anyone who lived in Turon that Ratchin was a lintep. Her particular skill lay in healing. The town already had a healer, but for anyone who needed more than herbs and teas they sought out Ratchin. Dell did not begrudge her the time she needed to work with any desperate patients. In fact, his tavern was frequented by many people in the small town from a sense of gratitude they felt towards the large lintep woman.

Shuut had been a patient herself on more than one occasion. Ratchin was the only person Shuut had ever willingly told that she was a half-caste. Her secret was safe here. Ratchin would die before betraying her trust.

"Interesting company you've chosen to keep lately." Ratchin's comment was her polite way of interrogating Shuut without delving into her mind, as she was more than capable of doing.

"Don't worry, Ratchin. It isn't a permanent situation. I found myself in their Paradise and was persuaded to take them out of it."

A raised eyebrow from the lintep was all it took for Shuut to take a seat and relate the entire story up until that point.

"So, your intention is to leave them here, in this town, alone?" Shuut merely nodded before Ratchin spoke again. "No."

Shuut cocked her head to one side, leaning closer to her old friend. "What do you mean, 'no'? I can't possibly keep them with me."

"You can't leave them here, Shuut. Putting aside the fringa and his kryti, these Paradisians are barely more than children. From what you've told me, none of them have even begun to learn a trade. How can you possibly expect them to survive in such a small town as this?"

"That was our agreement, Ratchin. I took them to a town. Now I can leave without them." Shuut was firm.

"Don't make me rummage through that twisted mind of yours. You will not leave these children here. For one thing, you have a seer with you. For another, at least one of them knows you're a half-caste. How long do you think it will take the people in this town to turn on your little dreamer? How long before the girl tells your secret to gain asylum for her friend?"

"I don't care what happens to the boy once I leave. As for the girl, she had her chance to tell people when we were still in her Paradise. She could have threatened me with that knowledge and forced me to take them out of there, but she didn't. I doubt she would change her mind to save a boy she barely speaks to."

"She is very interested in lintep powers, as I discovered when I warmed her bath water with my own heat. What would you do if she accidentally let it slip?"

Shuut remained tight lipped.

"They are all far too trusting, Shuut. They will not survive more than a month in this place. If nothing else happens to them, they will starve. I will not allow that to happen. You cannot leave them here."

The finality in Ratchin's voice persuaded Shuut not to pursue the argument any further. She would still leave the Paradisians behind, even if she had to do it behind Ratchin's back. She looked into her friend's eyes, trying not to give away her plans.

Without another word, Shuut got up from her chair and treaded softly up the wooden stairs and headed straight for the bathroom. She couldn't remember the last time she'd had a bath. The healers, or at least Rhanya, would have cleaned her up as best they could while they worked on her in the Paradise, but she hadn't felt warm water surrounding her.

Much to her annoyance, she discovered Karinya already bathing in one of the large tubs. The girl settled her green eyes on the Shuut as she walked through the door. Shuut barely acknowledged her presence. She would enjoy this bath if it was the last thing she did.

The banwep took off her clothes and dropped them carelessly on the floor beside the steaming tub. Without even bothering to dip her toes in to test the water, she stepped straight into the bath and submerged herself completely for a few moments. She listened to her heartbeat through the water and let her problems float away from her. When she felt calm enough, she raised her head above the water, keeping her eyes closed. If she couldn't see the girl, perhaps she could forget all about her.

"Why can Ratchin show herself to be a lintep? Is it more acceptable to be a full breed than a half-caste?"

Shuut took a deep breath before slowly opening her eyes. Karinya held her gaze unwaveringly. There would be no way out of this conversation. If she didn't tell the girl, things would only get worse. If she did tell her, she would just have to hope that the Paradisian would continue to keep her secret.

"Full lintep have enough power to make humans be wary of them. A half-caste is only so powerful, most of them only in certain areas of lintep magic. There is still a great amount of resentment felt for lintep, but no sane human would ever attack one. On the other hand, a half-caste cannot possibly defend themselves as well as a full breed. They make slightly easier targets for cowardly humans. If a person is revealed to be a half-caste, they are automatically at risk of being attacked just for who they are."

"But surely even a full lintep can't reveal what they are until they have mastered every skill they possess."

It was going to be one of *those* conversations, Shuut sighed inwardly. The girl was insatiable when it came to a topic that interested her.

"All lintep living in the Outworld are taught by their parents to master their skills from when they are children. If they are living in Illaria, they are taught by the lintep masters. A human would never attack a lintep child, even one whose powers aren't fully developed, for fear of what their parents could do in revenge."

Shuut watched the girl carefully. There were thoughts running around in her mind, but she could not catch on to any of them quickly enough to read them. It irked her that this girl, who was not even fifteen years, could evade her probing so easily.

"Who taught you to be a banwep?"

The question surprised Shuut so much that she answered before thinking what Karinya's next question was bound to be.

"My father."

"So, he was a lintep then?"

"That is none of your concern." She knew the answer would not satisfy the girl, but it was worth a try.

"What would a half-caste do if their only surviving parent was a human? Or if a full lintep became an orphan, who would teach them?"

"Can't you just let me enjoy my bath?"

Shuut closed her eyes once more and ducked her head under the water. It did not help to relax her this time. She could feel the girl's eyes watching her. There was no way out of this conversation. She did not want to talk about her past. It was painful enough to think about it – talking only brought the pain closer to the surface. Perhaps she could ask Ratchin to talk to the girl.

"Who taught you? What happens if a lintep grows up not knowing what they are?"

Shuut's head was barely out of the water before Karinya was asking questions again. The bathroom door opened just as Shuut was about to yell at the girl for silence. Ratchin eyed both of them as she came in.

"I taught Shuut and many others like her." Shuut tried not to breathe a sigh of relief as Karinya turned immediately towards the lintep. "Now if you would only stop pestering my friend, I may agree to answer those questions you've already asked her."

"How could you even hear those questions? You only just walked in."

Karinya was obviously impressed and curious at the same time. It reminded Shuut of the first time she'd met the lintep. Ratchin wasn't afraid to freely use her powers. No one in their right mind would ever attack her. Apart from what she could do to them herself, most of the inhabitants of Turon would rally against anyone who tried to harm her. She had saved so many lives in this small town that it was difficult to find a single person who hadn't benefited from her skills in some way.

"We lintep have more powers than you can possibly imagine. I do not profess to be a master in all of them, but I am quite capable in more than a few ways. I can quite easily project my mind to somewhere I've been before, or follow a person who is leaving me." Shuut didn't have to look at Karinya to recognise the stunned silence. She had felt quite the same way the first time she'd realised exactly what Ratchin could do. "Perhaps it was impolite to eavesdrop, but I couldn't help myself."

Waddling slowly over to a chair, Ratchin settled herself down for a chat with the curious Paradisian. With any luck, the lintep could sate the girl's appetite for knowledge. Shuut sank as deeply as she could in the warm bath, leaving only her eyes, ears and nose exposed. She resolved to relax as much as she could while keeping an ear on the conversation between her most troublesome companion and her old friend.

"Is there really no way to tell the difference between a human and a lintep? Surely after hundreds of years, someone must have come up with a way." It was the first question that all humans asked, their insecurities showing themselves immediately.

"Unless a lintep chooses to reveal their powers, or loses control of them, then there is no way to separate them. Even a lintep cannot pick out a fellow lintep from a crowd. They look as human as Shuut or I. For all we know, you could be a lintep, but unless we witness you doing something with your powers, then we will never know."

"Does that mean an orphan lintep might not ever know what they are? I mean, if no one ever told them or taught them to control their powers, could they live their entire life just not knowing?"

"No." Shuut knew this was a sore spot for Ratchin. "A child may grow to fifteen years before realising who they are. After that, their powers need to be harnessed or they will be lost forever. If the lintep in question has no idea what they are, they will mistake their sudden attack of headaches as nothing more than that. Depending on their power, the headaches will continue until their power has left them and then they will no longer be a lintep.

"If they are too powerful, when their power deserts them, they will die. Too many children have come to me only when their headaches were too painful to bear but, by that time, it was too late for me to help them. If it ever gets to that stage, only the lintep masters in Illaria can help them."

"How many people have you seen that happen to?" Karinya's voice was soft, almost scared.

"Too many to want to remember, child, far too many."

"But that doesn't happen with all of them, does it? I mean, you said you helped Shuut but her father wasn't a lintep."

"I would ask you to keep me out of your conversation." Shuut had kept silent up until now, but she would not have Ratchin accidentally tell this girl any more than she needed to know.

"Perhaps that is enough for now. You may come and find me any time you like to continue this discussion. But I do believe Shuut will slaughter us both if she doesn't have a peaceful bath."

Ratchin got up from her chair and waddled back to her chores. Shuut was pleased to notice Karinya drying herself off from her bath. For at least a little while, she would be alone. She needed this time to figure out exactly how she was going to leave these Paradisians behind with so many people keeping an eye out to make sure they left with her.

Chapter Eighteen – Rilla's discovery

"What's an inn?"

"Is Ratchin your mother?"

"Why did she call you a different name?"

"When are we going to explore the town?"

"Where did you take our food?"

Shuut was bombarded with questions as she entered their room for the second time that day. From her perch on the windowsill, Rilla didn't turn her head to acknowledge the banwep, though from the corner of her eye, she could see everything. She knew Arishen was still sitting on his chosen bed in the other room poring over pieces of parchment, surrounded by the contents of his rucksack, unaware of the commotion around him. The kryti and fringa were sitting quietly in a corner of the room where they had been for the better part of the day. Tika and Plyke looked at Shuut expectantly for answers.

"There's never a moment of rest with you around, is there?" Shuut took a deep breath before seating herself on one of the vacant beds. "Arishen," she called out loudly to the seer. He stopped his scratchy scribbling immediately, hurriedly stuffing the items on his bed back into his rucksack and came to join the others.

"So, what's an inn?" Tika asked impatiently. "Is it your home?"

"Well, an inn is a bit like the tavern, back in your Paradise. Downstairs, people come for a drink or a meal. Depending on the type of inn, musicians might come to play or people may simply talk or play games with each other. Upstairs is full of rooms like these two and the bathroom down the hall."

"How long do people stay?"

"It's up to the individual people and their purses." Shuut's explanation was met with blank faces from the boys. Rilla smiled to herself at the difficulty Shuut was going to have explaining the Outworld to her companions.

"Why would their purse determine how long they stay?" Arishen asked.

Rilla heard a conversation playing in her mind that she never had. Shuut talking with Rhanya – there was no money in the Paradise. Everyone was fed, clothed and housed without payment. Their society worked together to provide everything they needed.

Rilla recalled other Outworlders coming in to their Paradise giving up all metal that they'd called money with tears.

"One of the main differences between your Paradise and the Outworld is money. If you don't have money, you don't survive out here. When I said it depends on a person's purse, what I meant was it depends how much money you have to spend at an inn."

"Why did we come if you knew we didn't have money?" Tika asked in obvious perplexity.

"For one thing, you do have money." Shuut smiled and tossed a coin pouch to him. "For another, Ratchin never allows me to pay."

"Is she your mother?" Plyke asked as Tika emptied the coins onto the floor.

"Who? Ratchin?" Plyke nodded his head and Tika looked up inquisitively. "No. She's just an old friend."

"An old friend who doesn't know your name." Arishen's voice hardened at the question. "Or perhaps it's us who don't know your name."

Rilla could see that Shuut's humour was not going to last much longer.

"She knows my name full well. The only reason she doesn't use it is because she knows I use different names in different towns. You have no right to insinuate otherwise. Who do you think you are?"

The boys had fallen silent. Arishen was glaring at Shuut. Tika and Plyke occupied themselves with the coins in front of them. Rilla turned towards them.

"You must excuse Arishen. He was the only person in the Paradise who openly knew who his father was. Erton had him executed. He's a bit touchy on the subject of parents."

Shuut's anger subsided at this unexpected piece of information. She expected the seer to reprimand Rilla for telling her, but he didn't even turn his eyes to the girl.

"I'm sorry Arishen."

"Forget it. It's not your fault. I shouldn't have been so suspicious of you. After all, you kept your promise and brought us this far."

Rilla looked at the seer only to see him purposely avoiding her gaze. It wasn't as if she was the only person in the Paradise to have noticed what happened. Whether they called it execution or murder made little difference. Everyone knew what happened.

"No. To be suspicious of everyone in the Outworld is good."

"You're saying we should be suspicious of you. Then tell us, did you go anywhere other than to barter our food away?" Rilla knew the answer to this question would prove either herself or Arishen right in their assumption of her.

"No. I *sold* your food for these coins which, I might add, are yours to share amongst yourselves. After that, I came straight back. Where would you have had me go when there was a warm bath awaiting me?"

"Perhaps to a healer, or a carpenter, or even the stables," Rilla replied with a shrug.

"And exactly what would I have done with these people?" Shuut asked through clenched teeth.

"If you plan on leaving us in this village, it would be only fair to see us set up with apprenticeships before you leave. Don't you think so?" Rilla raised her eyebrows innocently as Arishen turned to face her, his eyes narrowed in anger.

"I don't believe that was part of our agreement."

"It's a good idea, however," the fringa noted, without the slightest betraying glance towards Rilla. The small purple bird hopped its way over to Shuut's knee. "You promised the gatekeeper that we would all leave together. I assure you that he will not be in a good mood if he sees you leaving by yourself, unless he knows they will not be a burden to this village."

"There is no way to find a master tradesman in Turon who is willing to take on an apprentice, much less four such masters. It is too small and not welcoming to strangers."

"Then you'll take us with you when you leave." Rilla knew it was a long shot, but she had to try. If Shuut left them there, they would die. There was no question about that. Sooner or later her powers would reveal themselves accidentally. Arishen would dream and people would start to realise no matter how much he tried to hide it. All four of them would starve to death if nothing else.

"No. I will leave you here. That was our agreement. I stuck to my end of it. Now it's your turn."

"But the gatekeeper..."

"Is of no concern to me. Do you think I would have lasted as long as I have in the Outworld if I couldn't slip past a man like him?" Shuut smiled smugly. Rilla turned her head back towards the town. The three boys had been listening to their conversation in silence.

"How long will you stay?" the seer asked.

"I'll leave tomorrow morning. There is no reason for me to stay any longer. I have other places I need to be."

"Would you mind taking us for a walk around the town?" Tika pleaded with the banwep. "At least to show us what you know of it. Perhaps there is a chance, however slight, that someone might agree to take one of us as an apprentice."

"It's doubtful, but if it will make you feel any better..." she trailed off as the three boys bounced up to their feet. Rilla kept her eyes on the streets below. No one asked her to come with them. She waited silently while they left and watched them walk down the street below her. She wouldn't stay in this town. There was no point wasting time getting to know her way around when there were better things to be doing.

Finally turning away from the window, Rilla saw the small purple bird hopping over to her.

"What now?" she asked him desperately.

"We find a better reason for her not to leave you behind."

Rilla closed her eyes. How could she possibly find a reason to make Shuut *want* to take them with her? The easiest way would be to reveal her real name, but that was not something she was prepared to do. She didn't know what the consequences of that might be.

What is Shuut's weak spot? Does she even have one? Think, Rilla! What's the one thing you know about her that ... That was it! Shuut was a half-caste. If Rilla somehow managed to show her that she was at least part lintep, then the banwep would be less likely to leave her behind. The only thing she knew about lintep magic was what Ratchin had told her in the bathroom.

"I have an idea." She opened her eyes to find the fringa sitting on the windowsill, waiting expectantly for her suggestion. "Ratchin mentioned earlier that lintep can sort of follow people with their minds, or just move their minds into other rooms or places where they have been before."

"Is there something you're not telling me, girl?" Rilla simply raised an eyebrow at the bird. "I see. Have you tried this before?"

"No. But I can try it now, if you don't mind helping me." She smiled sweetly at him.

"What do you need me to do?"

"I think we could try a short distance, perhaps to the bathroom and back again. Say something softly when you are there and we'll see if I heard it or not."

The fringa hopped over to his kryti, who had been watching patiently, and chirped at him in instruction. Rilla assumed that the massive beast would watch over her as she concentrated on using her power rather than on her surroundings.

Rilla took a deep breath. She watched as the fringa hopped out of the door. When he was no longer in her field of vision, she imagined she saw him hopping slowly towards the bathroom door. She could see, even from this distance that the door was closed.

It was slow going. His wing was still injured. All he could do was hop with his scrawny legs. Not knowing if she was really seeing him or just imagining it, Rilla tried to concentrate harder. It was beginning to give her a headache, but she refused to stop.

Every now and then, the fringa would stop to rest or turn his head, presumably in an attempt to make sure she was not physically following him. Eventually he reached the door at the end of the hallway where the bathroom was located. He nudged the door with his small head but to no avail. It was closed and there was no possible way he could enter it. He muttered in annoyance under his breath before turning to start the return trip.

"It was a wasted trip." His high-pitched voice called out to her as he entered their room once more.

"Foolish humans feel the need to lock everything." Rilla, her eyes watching him from the moment he appeared in her sight, smiled. The fringa stared at her intensely. "Isn't that what you muttered after trying to push the door open with your head?"

Instantly, the fringa chirped agitatedly to his kryti. His guttural response went some way to appease the fringa's anxious excitement.

"He says you didn't follow me."

"Well, not physically, but I think it may have worked. Was the door closed? Did you try to nudge it open with your head?"

"I don't trust this. You've been to the bathroom. You may have simply guessed that it was closed. For all I know, your hearing is sharp enough to have heard what I said. It's not unheard of. Mind you, my kryti will be watching you. If your try to leave this room, he *will* tell me."

Rilla said nothing, but nodded her acquiescence. Again, she watched as the small purple bird left the room. Once more, she imagined herself following him, not as though she was walking, but as though she was a fly on the wall, following his every move.

She followed as he hopped down the stairs. It was a painfully slow process for the two of them. She could feel pain shooting through his wing with each landing on a stair that was lower than he expected. Her own pain was more noticeable. It felt as though her brain was trying to leave her head. The conscious part of herself was no longer present in her body and she ached to be reunited with it. But if this was the only way to ensure their safe exit from Turon, then she would do it. For Rhanya, she would do anything.

The fringa finally reached the bottom of the staircase. He looked around at the grim and dusty patrons of the bar. Dell and his brother were behind the bar, as they had been when Rilla and her companions had first entered the inn. No one noticed the tiny purple bird. If they had, they probably wouldn't have cared anyway.

A door swung open to the side of the bar. Behind it, Rilla could smell the kitchen through the small bird's nose. She recognised some of the scents, but it was too painful to concentrate hard enough to work out what they were. Rilla, wanting to find Ratchin, tried to go through that door. She stopped immediately. She'd never been there before. She had no idea how to make her mind go somewhere she hadn't been to herself.

As though he could understand her intention, the fringa obliged her by hopping towards the swinging door. He waited until a serving girl was on her way to the back room and hopped onto her dull brown shoe. It was the easiest way for him to get through the door without getting squashed. He hitched a ride with her until they came to the kitchen. Not wanting to be caught out near pots of boiling water and flaming ovens, he refused to go any further.

Luck was on their side. Ratchin's rich voice came through another door, further down the hall. It looked to be one of the back rooms of the inn. Perhaps it was Ratchin's own bedroom. Neither of them knew whether she lived there or not. All they could do was follow her voice. Rilla wondered, not without some anxiety, how she would get her mind back to her body if something happened to the fringa.

Her musings were halted when her companion squeezed his way through the tiny open slit of the door behind which they could hear Ratchin's voice. She wasn't alone. On a stone step leading from the inn to a back garden, she sat talking to a sobbing old man. He was trying to hold back his tears, but couldn't help himself. Rilla felt his pain as her own — his only son had been gored by their prize bull. The boy was alive, but might not last out the night without Ratchin's help.

Suddenly, without warning, Ratchin turned and snatched at the fringa. Pain shot through his wing even as it shot down Rilla's arm. They simultaneously cried out. Ratchin assured the old man that she would come to his home before nightfall. The man dried his tears with his sleeve, nodded his head gratefully and turned to go.

Without even waiting for him to leave, Ratchin heaved herself up and stormed through the inn. No one tried to stop her – they all knew she was not someone to be trifled with. Rilla struggled to keep up with them, after being used to the fringa's slow pace. Ratchin practically flew up the stairs in her urgency. Their eyes met as she stepped through the door.

"You?" Ratchin's surprise was mirrored her face. "What do you think you're doing?"

The kryti growled, threateningly, before he was quietened by his fringa. Rilla rubbed her arm, where the bird's pain had so recently been her own.

"I wanted to see if I could do it."

"Do what exactly?"

"You said you could project your mind to different places. I just wanted to see if I could do it too." She shrugged her shoulders and frowned, pressing her free hand against her forehead. "You didn't tell me it hurts."

"You stupid girl! This was your first time? What made you think you could travel through an entire inn that you've never visited before?"

"How was I meant to know that I couldn't?" Rilla blushed in anger. "It's not as though you were very elaborate in your explanations."

"Oh." Ratchin closed her eyes. "She doesn't know, does she?"

Rilla didn't answer, but looked down instead. She hadn't really thought through what she was doing.

"Tell me you're just a half-caste. I can almost believe a half-caste to have those powers."

"You tell me. I heard the lintep whistling when Shuut could only feel a shiver with goose bumps." She raised her head, needing to see some sort of reassurance in Ratchin's eyes.

"And your parents?"

"I haven't seen my mother since I was three years old. As for my father ... he barely spoke to me. I doubt he would ever have told me."

Ratchin sat down on the bed closest to the windowsill. She beckoned Rilla to join her, but the girl remained seated where she could easily see out the window. She did not want to be caught unawares by her companions.

"I don't understand. How did you even know what to do?"

"She didn't know what she was doing." It was the fringa who answered. "It was the only way we could think of to get them out of this town. If Shuut knows the truth, then she'll have no choice but to take them."

"You don't know her the way I do." Ratchin shook her head. "If she is set on something, nothing short of lintep manipulation will change her mind."

"No. That isn't true." Rilla's eyes clouded over as she remembered their conversation in the Paradise. "She didn't want to even bring us here, to Turon. But we changed her mind. I helped to save her life and my best friend died to protect her while she was in our Paradise. She felt some sort of obligation to at least get us out of there."

"Listen child, this is something we can talk about later. For now, I need to find out what you know of your powers."

Rilla looked at her blankly. A few weeks ago, she hadn't even known that she was a lintep. Up until now, she hadn't ever tried to use her powers. She had no idea what she was or wasn't capable of.

Ratchin spent the next hour interrogating Rilla on her life in the Paradise. It appeared that Rilla had been subconsciously using her power her entire life. No one had ever taught her what to do, but she instinctively knew how to fade into the background, to go unnoticed if she wished it. It was an eye-opening experience for her. All her life she had assumed that people were just ignoring her, which suited her just fine. But to realise that half the time, people truly didn't know she was there almost scared her.

"But the day that we left, someone did see me when I didn't want to be seen. Does that mean it doesn't always work?" Rilla remembered Kora seeing her in the cobbler's house. She'd looked over Rilla several times before finally realising that she was there.

"There could be many reasons for that happening. You could have lost your concentration. This person may also have been a lintep. You may not be quite as good as you think you are at it. The possibilities are endless."

At that moment, Rilla saw a movement below her. She turned in time to see her companions returning. The sun had lowered in the western sky without their notice.

"They're back." Her voice was flat and emotionless. She did not want to give anything away to her companions. It was one thing to know that Arishen was a seer, but at least he was still human. None of the boys even suspected that Shuut might be a half-caste. She was the only one. For all she knew, they would not react well to discovering what she really was. It was not a risk she was willing to take when they were still in this town.

"Did you hear the man, the one I was talking to before your fringa arrived?" Rilla nodded, turning to face the door that would soon be full of her companions. "Would you like to come along? It may be useful for you to see how I help people."

Rilla looked at her with hope. No one other than Rhanya had ever offered to let her be part of something so important or special. Oddly enough, she wasn't even remotely suspicious of Ratchin's intentions. In Rilla's eyes, she had already proved to be a friend of sorts.

Shuut and the boys entered the room, the latter talking loudly and jovially. They did not even bother to greet Ratchin and Rilla before heading to their own room. Not that Rilla had expected them to. Arishen was annoyed with her and the Partners had never been among the first to talk to her, even in the Paradise.

The half-caste barely spared them a glance before dropping to her bed. Ratchin cast a reassuring glance at Rilla before patting Shuut lightly on the arm.

"Laila, dear, you know I never ask for any payment when you stay, but I would request a favour from you this time." Shuut opened her eyes and raised a questioning eyebrow. "My skills have been requested in a nearby farmhouse. I would appreciate this girl's company on the walk there. Also, there is a slight chance that her assistance may be required."

"If you need her energy, she has more than enough to spare. The longer you can keep her tonight, the better. After that, I'll be done with her."

Rilla had expected Ratchin to protest that last sentence, but she did nothing of the sort.

"Come along child. We must hurry to be there and back before sunset." Once they were in the hall, Ratchin lowered her voice. "I want you to see if you can make it out of this town undetected. The townsfolk will be easy enough to pass by. The real test will be the gatekeeper. See if you can exit by my side without him noticing you there."

Rilla smiled at the challenge and willed herself to blend into the background. She knew she was easier to miss if she stood still, but she had, on many occasion, walked straight past people in the Paradise without being detected. It was nothing she had ever consciously tried to do, but just willing it made it happen.

Together with Ratchin, she walked down the staircase, making sure to walk precisely by her side so that she wouldn't accidentally step on a creaky stair without the rotund woman. Ratchin stopped to speak with Dell for a moment. Rilla had been unprepared for the conversation. Nonetheless, she concentrated on blending into the shadows with all her might.

In the Paradise, it had been much easier. People had been prepared to ignore her. They would never have purposely sought her out. Here, in Turon, everyone was used to living in the Outworld. While they wouldn't be as suspicious as Shuut, they would no doubt be less trusting than the Paradisians she was used to.

Rilla waited patiently for Ratchin to open the door to the inn. Sunlight streamed in through the door, landing on her. Her shadow fell on the ground, but she was not visible in any other way. As soon as she realised her error, she hastened to the shaded side of the street, being careful not to walk too far away from Ratchin.

They passed through the rest of the town without incident. Rilla's heart quickened as they approached the gatekeeper. His keen eyes were sure to notice her. It was this self-doubt that was almost her undoing. Ratchin stopped to advise him that even if she was back after dusk, she expected to be allowed re-entry to the town. He argued with her for a few moments, peering behind her from time to time. Rilla was certain that he could tell something was amiss, but she concentrated as hard as she could on blending into the shadows around her that she somehow managed to stay hidden.

Eventually, he agreed to let Ratchin pass with the promise of her return to the town even after nightfall. She thanked him curtly and proceeded on her way, with Rilla hastily in tow.

"Well done, child. You may reveal yourself now. There is no point frightening old Cheyenne. He is worried enough about his son as it is."

"What did Shuut mean by you needing my energy? Is there something I have to do?" The question had been puzzling her for a while. How could Ratchin possibly use her energy? How was she even going to heal this boy? She instinctively reached down to her medicine pack and showed Ratchin. "Is there anything in here that you may need?"

Ratchin barely looked at her pouch. "Stop your fussing, child. If I need your help, I'll tell you. All I really want you to do is watch."

Rilla didn't have a chance to respond. They were already approaching a farmhouse. A frail old woman was standing in the doorway, handkerchief to her eyes. She stood a fraction taller when she saw the two of them coming and turned her head towards the house. A few moments later, Cheyenne was there, motioning her inside while he waited alone for Ratchin.

"Thank you for coming, Ratchin. He's inside with Gavryle. I'll be waiting right here if you need anything." His eyes strayed to Rilla, but he only acknowledged her with a nod of his head. She nodded back, not knowing what else to do.

Following Ratchin inside, Rilla's eyes widened at how sparsely furnished the place was. It was almost as bad as the isolation hut back in the Paradise. There was a table and four chairs in one corner and three pallets along another wall. One chest stood in the furthest corner. Rilla could only guess it held all their clothes and other belongings. Along the last wall was a fireplace with a small fire and a pot of boiling water. It looked as though it had been boiling most of the afternoon with no one thinking to take it off.

As Gavryle showed Ratchin to their son, Muyr, Rilla walked over to the fireplace. No one noticed her as she took the pot from the flames. She carried it over to the table, where there were three cups and plates laid out. Carefully, she filled two of the cups with water before returning the pot to the fireplace. She listened closely to Gavryle as she explained Muyr's accident to Ratchin, all the while looking through her medicine pouch to find the chamomile that had so recently been used for her own tea. She placed a pinch of the dried flowers in each mug and swirled them around to mix it well.

Not wanting Cheyenne and Gavryle to burn themselves through carelessness, she attempted another trick she'd seen Ratchin do that day. Placing one hand around each mug, she drew out as much heat as she could handle. It left her sweating, but she thought it for the best. With a mug in each hand, she went first to Cheyenne who stood, nervously, in the doorway. She offered him the mug without a word. He glanced down at her with unseeing eyes. She recognised that look. It was the same one she'd left on her own at Rhanya's death. She bit back her tears and took the old man's hand, placing the warm mug in it. Automatically, he raised it to his lips without blowing on it. Rilla was grateful that she'd thought to take some of the heat out of the water first.

She walked slowly over to where Gavryle was now standing, a ways back from Muyr's sleeping pallet. Again, she offered the calming tea. Gavryle looked down at her and took the cup without a smile, her eyes almost immediately going back to her son.

Not having anything left to do, she sat against the wall at Muyr's side, looking on in wonder at Ratchin's work. The man could not have been more than twenty odd years old. His face was pale with blood loss, making him look closer to death than life. He was holding a bloody rag over his side. The bull must have missed all major organs of his body, only going through muscle and skin. That was the only way he could have lasted as long as he already had.

Ratchin asked Rilla to bring her a bowl of water. Not knowing where else to get the water from, Rilla once again went to the pot of boiling water and cooled it by draining as much heat as she could take. The older lintep saw what she'd done and simply shook her head. Ratchin took the bloody rag from Muyr and rinsed it clean in the bowl. Trying to clear away as much blood as she could, the old lintep was investigating how serious the wound was. Even Rilla, as inexperienced as she was, could see that, without some magic, he would not last the night.

She watched in fascination as Ratchin placed one hand over the man's wound. The woman's face creased in pain as the wound became ever so slightly smaller. Fascination turned to horror as Rilla realised that Ratchin was taking on his pain to mend his wound. Rilla could barely stand to watch the process. It terrified her that Ratchin might need her help. She knew the lintep couldn't possibly ask Muyr's parents for help. They both looked like they would fall over with a gust of wind.

Her fears were never realised. Eventually, when the wound was half its original size, and blood had stopped freely flowing from it, Muyr opened his eyes. He did not seem surprised to see Ratchin, but relieved.

"Thank you," he strained to whisper to his saviour. She patted his head softly with her clean hand before rinsing his blood from her other one.

Rilla helped the healer to her feet, staring in wide-eyed wonder at her. Both Gavryle and Cheyenne, empty mugs still in their hands, stood over their son's peacefully sleeping form.

"How can we ever repay you, Ratchin? You've saved our son's life. You've saved *our* lives." The last words almost choked Cheyenne. Ratchin openly smiled at him.

"Cheyenne, when have I ever asked for payment? Your son's health and your happiness are enough for me." At her words, Gavryle burst into happy tears. Both Cheyenne and his wife shook Rilla's hand and hugged Ratchin in thanks.

They walked back towards the town in silence. Rilla could feel Ratchin's eyes on her, but kept her own eyes firmly averted from the older woman.

"We're going to have to talk about it sooner or later."

"I'd rather it be later than sooner." Rilla increased her speed, her hair falling in loose tendrils around her face.

"Really? You'd rather it be in Turon, surrounded by humans and people you've kept this secret from?"

Rilla stopped walking and waited for Ratchin to catch up with her. "Exactly what is it you want to talk about?"

"Who taught you to draw heat from water? I don't recall that in our previous conversation."

"I believe it was you, when you warmed the bath water at the inn."

"Don't be daft, girl. I didn't teach you how to do that and besides, what you did was the complete opposite of that."

Rilla tapped her teeth together in indecision. How could she explain what she didn't exactly understand herself? Ratchin didn't know her. She had no reason to trust her. If, instead, she was explaining it to Rhanya, Rilla knew he would have understood her and trusted her. She had nothing to lose. If she didn't try to explain, Ratchin would never leave her in peace.

"You explained that you used your own body heat to warm the water in the bath. I simply assumed that it might work the other way around. I tried to draw the warmth out of the water. The only thing was, I could only draw out so much heat before it made me sweat. I don't know enough to understand how to get rid of the heat once it's inside me." She watched Ratchin's face change from annoyance to incredulity to some semblance of understanding.

"What you're saying is, you did the same thing as with blending into shadows and projecting your mind. You simply thought of it and made it happen?" Rilla nodded, unsure whether Ratchin actually believed her or not. The lintep woman began to laugh.

"Oh, child, there is no way you can stay in Turon. I can't possibly teach you everything you'll need to know. Nor do I have time to constantly save you from the terrible mistakes I'm certain you'll make without even realising what you're doing. I'll talk to Shuut tonight. She will not leave without you. You have my word."

"I won't leave without the boys." Rilla made certain to be clear on that point. "I made a promise to an old friend to keep them safe. You and I both know that the moment Shuut and I leave them, that promise will be broken. They *must* leave with us." Ratchin said nothing more, but simply nodded her head.

As they approached the gates of Turon, Rilla automatically blended into the night. The gatekeeper had not seen her leave with Ratchin. If she tried to enter visibly by her side, they were sure to attract more attention than she wanted.

Chapter Nineteen – Shuut's decision

"Shuut, I'm not giving you a choice here. If you do not willingly agree to take these Paradisians away from this town, I will do something I've never wanted to do to you."

"You wouldn't dare," Shuut answered vehemently.

"I wouldn't try me on that." Ratchin was unflinching on the point. "I know the children somehow managed to persuade or guilt you into it, but I have neither the time nor the will to do that myself. You will take them with you one way or another."

"Why do you care so much about what happens to them? They're not half-castes stuck with the wrong parent or orphaned lintep. In fact, they're nothing very special at all."

"If there was nothing else, one of them is a seer. That should be enough for you. Can you imagine what will happen to him once the humans in Turon discover this? It's probably the very reason he fled his Paradise." Ratchin didn't pause long enough for Shuut to retort. "But that's not the only thing. The girl knows your secret. I know she didn't stoop to it last time, but what would you do if the next time you came here, she'd told your secret all over town and someone from Turon had mentioned it to someone from another town and word got around to every place you've ever been. What would you do then? Hide out with the elves or the crystal dragons for the rest of your life? Or do you think the lintep or the karliki would take you in?"

Shuut narrowed her eyes. "You make your point abundantly clear, old friend. But if I take them, where do you suggest I take them? As you've so brilliantly pointed out yourself, practically no place in the Outworld is safe for them. You can't possibly suggest that the elves would be willing to let humans live among them? As for the crystal dragons, they would have no use for these, perhaps other than the seer. I'll never find the way to Illaria and you've never been there yourself. The karliki are even less fond of humans than the other races."

Ratchin sat back on her chair and sipped her cup of tea with satisfaction. "You should have thought of that before you agreed to take them out of their Paradise. In the absolute worst case scenario, you could always teach them to be banwep. After all, that's what you're best at, isn't it?"

"Good night, Ratchin." Shuut got up from her chair in Ratchin's room and walked through the now silent inn. They had stayed talking into the early hours of the morning. The regular patrons had disappeared hours ago. Shuut walked silently up the stairs, even the noisiest ones barely making a sound beneath her soft tread.

She silently opened her door and slumped onto her bed. It would be her only night at the inn. She resolved to enjoy the soft down bed for as many hours as she could.

The night didn't last long for Shuut. She woke to the sound of strangled screaming. Her eyes opened wide instantly. She looked around the room in momentary confusion. The scream wasn't coming from her room. She followed the kryti to the boys' room through their adjoining door, Karinya only a few steps behind.

Both Tika and Plyke were sitting up in bed, staring straight at Arishen. The seer was curled up in a ball, screaming for people to stop, screaming out for someone to help him. Shuut had never seen a seer dreaming before. She hadn't the slightest idea of what to do. She turned helplessly to Karinya who quickly walked past her to the boy.

"Arishen," she called the seer's name, leaning in towards him. He didn't respond. In an effort to ease his pain by waking him, Karinya gently shook his shoulder. Before she could move back, his fist had struck her in the face. He woke as the punch connected. The young girl stared at him in surprise, which quickly turned to anger. She was on her feet an instant later, staring Shuut down with her bright green eyes. Blood poured from her nose. Her cheek was already starting to bruise.

"Next time, *you* wake him."

Shuut watched the furious girl walk out of the room in shock. She had not expected Arishen to react so violently. The seer went to get up off the bed but thought better of it when he heard the kryti growling at him.

"Call him off," Shuut instructed the fringa. "We already have enough problems here." After a few hasty chirps, the kryti moved back to a corner of the room, keeping a wary eye on Arishen. Shuut looked over at the Partners. They hadn't taken their eyes off Arishen since she'd entered the room. How long had they heard his cries before the rest of them came along?

"Well, what happened?" she directed her question towards the seer.

"It was just a bad dream." He shook his head as though attempting to erase the images from his mind. "Nothing to worry about."

"Nothing to worry about, huh?" Shuut's disapproval was plain to the boy's eye. "If there was nothing to worry about, you wouldn't have screamed out loud. I've had bad dreams before, boy, that one must have been particularly intense for such a reaction. You do realise you just punched Karinya in the face, don't you?"

"I didn't mean to do that. She must be so angry with me."

"Her anger is nothing compared to what mine will be if you don't tell me what you were dreaming of." Her tone of voice convinced the boy to speak.

"The four of us were here, in Turon, just walking down the street, the one with the bakery. You weren't there. You'd already left us behind." Here he cast his gaze down, refusing to look her in the eye. "Somehow, the townspeople found out what I was, what my dreams could show me. They were afraid and angry all at the same time. One of them, the gatekeeper, he told us to get out of the town, that we weren't welcome anymore.

"I told them that this was our new home and we weren't going to leave it. He bent down and picked up a large stone. He threw it up and caught it twice, then he threw it straight at my head. The others in the crowd all bent down to pick up anything that came to hand. All four of us were being pelted with whatever they could find. We couldn't fight back against so many of them and their circle was so tight that we couldn't run. I curled up into a ball on the ground, trying to protect myself from them. I was crying and screaming out for them to stop – for someone to come and help us. But no one was coming." He looked up with fearful eyes. "That's when she woke me."

Shuut patiently listened to his story before storming out of the room. She could feel the Partners' eyes on her, but she didn't turn to face them. Karinya had to be behind this. The girl was determined to leave with her. It had to have been her idea. They ran into each other in the hallway. Karinya's left cheekbone was a deeper shade of purple than it had been only a few minutes beforehand.

"You put him up to it, didn't you?" she snarled at the girl. "You told him to tell that story just to make me take you out of this town. Well it won't work. You're not coming with me."

The confusion in Karinya's face was barely masked by her anger. "You think I would go so far as to let him break my nose, just so that we get to leave with you? I haven't ever let a single person get close enough to me for that to happen. How can you be so self-absorbed to think that I would plan this just to make your life a misery?"

* * *

Ratchin hurried up the stairs as the arguing grew louder. "What's all this noise? You're going to wake all of our *paying* customers." One look at Karinya's bruised and bloodied face told her more than enough. "Both of you go back to your room now." Her voice was low and menacing. Neither of them dared object. They both walked silently into their room, Ratchin only a few steps behind them. She closed the door before either of them could speak and ushered them in to where the boys were still silently sitting on their beds, barely even daring to look at each other. The kryti growled softly at the sudden intrusion, but was silenced once more by his fringa.

"What is the meaning of this ruckus? You'll have woken the entire inn up." She looked around at each of them in turn. The two smaller boys gazed at the taller one in confusion, the latter trying hard not to tremble. Shuut was furious and Karinya's bruised face plainly told that some sort of fight had broken out. "Someone had better explain before I lose my temper."

"They organised for *him* to pretend he was having a dream ..." Shuut began, pointing over at Arishen.

"Oh, that's right," Karinya interrupted sardonically. "And I told him to punch me as hard as he could in the face as I bent down to *pretend* to wake him up."

"That's enough, you two." Ratchin silenced them with a wave of her hand, looking directly at Arishen, her eyes unfocused slightly as she gazed into the boy's mind. It was a skill she had tried to impart to Shuut on many occasions, but the banwep was not adept at it.

"He told you the truth," Ratchin sighed heavily, turning to face her friend. "Do you agree with me now? Can you honestly say you don't care what happens to these children now that you know what awaits them if you leave them behind?"

"That was never part of our agreement, Ratchin," Shuut insisted.

"I'm sure that would have been of great comfort to you when your father brought you to this town if I hadn't found you."

It was something Shuut rarely spoke about. When her father had had enough of her, she begged and pleaded for him to take her to the nearest town before he left her. That town was Turon. It was then that Ratchin had met her for the first time. Shuut's father left her behind with barely a backwards glance. If Ratchin hadn't agreed to help her, she would have died alone and hungry in this cold town.

"You don't get to ask this favour of me," Shuut warned her coldly.

"I'm not the one asking it – they are. But if you don't do it for them, I may just see my way to making sure you regret it."

Shuut ground her teeth together. "We leave in five minutes. Get your things together now. Ratchin will fix you up. Meet us outside." Her last words were for Karinya.

* * *

Rilla quickly picked up her rucksack before following Ratchin down the stairs to the tavern area, through the door where the fringa had gone and into another room. The lintep's bedroom was full of trinkets, almost like offerings.

Ratchin noticed her attention on these items. "Small gifts, tokens of appreciation from those who can afford no more."

Rilla estimated the gifts numbered into the hundreds. It must have taken years for Ratchin to accumulate so many tokens of appreciation, more than Rilla could believe possible.

"You would do well to hide your thoughts a little better, child. As a fully trained lintep, I can see them easily. For Shuut, it would be more of a struggle, though in your case she may be willing to put enough effort to see them too."

Rilla cringed as Ratchin laid a hand over her face. She was not used to human contact. Even though the lintep's work-roughened hands were gentle, it did not make her any less wary of their capacity to hurt her. Ratchin spoke as she healed her.

"We don't have much time. I had thought to teach you some control over your powers before you left, but that was obviously never to be. Be careful with what you have learnt from me. Do not overstep your boundaries or try anything extravagant. If you must, practice what you have already done, but do not try anything new. The thing that may seem small and insignificant to you could end up costing you your life. If you only remember one thing, let it be this – *the key to everything is balance.*"

In less than a minute, the pain in Rilla's face had subsided. She reached up to press the bruise that had so recently marked her face, but instead found herself completely healed.

"You would have healed quickly without my aid. But as you've avoided telling your companions about yourself, I assumed you wouldn't have wanted them to notice your lintep healing abilities." Her face broke into a sad smile. "Take care of my Shuut. I fear, after what I said, she won't come back to visit me for many a year."

"Thank you." The two words seemed too insignificant for what Ratchin had done for her, but it was all she could find to say. She didn't even have a token to give her. *One day I will repay you, Ratchin.* The old lintep patted her shoulder and led her back to where the others were waiting.

It wasn't difficult to tell that Shuut was more than a little irritated with Ratchin. She barely said a word of farewell to her old friend before turning towards the town gate. The gatekeeper warily watched their party leave, counting heads to make sure none of them had been left behind.

Arishen shuddered at the sight of the man. Had they stayed, he would have been the one to throw the first stone. Rilla felt a stab of pity for the seer but it soon disappeared as she raised a hand to feel where he had punched her.

Chapter Twenty – Favours

They left Turon with barely a backwards glance. Plyke had expected it to take much longer for the others to realise the town would not be safe for them. Of the four of them, his Partner seemed to be the only one who was somewhat upset to be going. This was to be their new home – a second chance of life. Instead, they had only lasted a single night. No one knew if Arishen's dream would have come to pass or how long they may have lived safely in Turon before it did. It didn't matter now. They had moved on, but Plyke was certain now that all five of them were thinking the same thing. *Where would they ever be able to live in safely while Arishen was among them?*

The seer had not said a word since relating his dream. Plyke could see that he was lost in dark thoughts. It must have been so difficult for him in their Paradise. Could Karinya really have been the only one to notice his dreams weren't just ordinary nightmares? What else had she noticed and kept silent about? He was certain she remained ignorant of his secret. He had taken steps to ensure that everyone was in the dark when it came to him. In fact, if Plyke hadn't left with the others, he doubted anyone in their Paradise would ever have noticed him.

"Where are we going?" Plyke's musings were interrupted by Tika's question.

"Silvaren," Shuut answered, without hesitation. "I was on my way there before I found your Paradise. We may as well continue on."

"Silvaren," Tika whispered to Plyke so that no one else could hear him. "Isn't that where Kora said the elves live?" Plyke nodded and smiled at his Partner's awe. Ever since he could remember, Tika had been talking about elves. He wasn't nearly so interested in lintep, karliki or even dragons. If they really were on their way to visit the elves, he wondered if there was any chance they would stay for any great length of time. Did elves usually allow humans to enter their forest? The lintep were very strict on that account – no humans were ever allowed to set foot in Illaria.

"How long will it take us to get there?" Tika always was the one to ask the most questions. Plyke realised it was probably best that way. Shuut would be less inclined to answer Karinya or Arishen's questions at the moment. He was certain she blamed both of them as much as Ratchin for their hasty departure from Turon.

Tika quickened his pace to trot alongside Shuut as she answered his questions. Plyke turned to see Karinya and Arishen walking as far away from each other as possible, with the kryti and fringa bringing up the rear. He began to slow his pace to walk alongside Arishen, but quickly thought better of it and kept his own pace.

"If I didn't have you slowing me down, I could be there in under a week. As it is, I doubt we'll get there in less than two."

"Do you think the elves will mind that we're with you?" Plyke smiled at the hesitant hope that was obvious in his entire demeanour.

"I very much doubt it. Elves are quite curious about humans. They are fascinated by the way we live our lives. Their longer lifespan makes them see things in a different light to us."

Plyke's mind wandered as Tika asked question after question about the elves. He absently started rubbing his arm when he felt goose bumps. Ahead of him, Shuut was doing the same, but his Partner wasn't. Turning around, he saw Arishen walking, eyes downcast, both arms unmoving by his side. Further behind him, Karinya surreptitiously looked in all directions, her hands twitching, but not rubbing her arms.

In an instant, his goose bumps disappeared, Karinya visibly calmed and Shuut stopped rubbing her arms. Puzzled, Plyke looked once more towards Arishen and Tika to reconfirm that they hadn't noticed anything out of the ordinary. When he turned back to Karinya, he saw the small purple bird was now sitting on her shoulder, talking agitatedly in her ear. Her eyes shot to the fringa and then instantly over to him. Even from such a distance, he could feel her green eyes burning into him. His stomach tightened as he realised she had already walked past Arishen and was heading straight for him.

"Why were you rubbing your arm?"

"Are you always so abrupt in your conversations?" Slightly taken aback by her directness, Plyke attempted to avoid the question. A puzzled look came over the red-headed girl as she shrugged.

"I guess so. Why were you rubbing your arm?"

"I had goose bumps. What difference does it make?"

"Were you cold?" Her intense stare unsettled him.

"No. I just had goose bumps. Haven't you ever had them before?"

"Of course. I'm sure everyone gets them when it's cold, but it's actually quite a hot day. In fact, I'm sweating. I don't think I've ever had goose bumps when it's been so hot."

"So I had goose bumps. What difference does it make?"

She stared at him in silence for a moment before shaking her head. "No difference."

"You're one strange girl, you know. I'd say this is the first time you've ever come to talk to me and what do you decide to talk about? Goose bumps. What kind of person has a whole conversation about goose bumps?" He watched her brow crease.

"Just me, I suppose. Sorry to have bothered you." With one last puzzled look, Karinya turned to walk back to the kryti. She didn't acknowledge Arishen as she passed him by. Perhaps she didn't even see him raise his head to greet her.

Karinya confused Plyke. He knew she didn't have many friends in their Paradise, but surely she'd heard other people carry on conversations. Could it be possible that she honestly didn't know what was considered polite or normal conversation? She hadn't been hurt or angry at his remarks, only confused. "Strange" barely even began to describe her.

* * *

The sun had begun to set by the time Shuut decided they should stop for the night. She asked the kryti to hunt for them, but he flatly refused to leave his charges behind. Having half expected such a response, she told him instead to watch over her companions as she went hunting. She hadn't gone more than a few hundred feet before she heard Karinya running after her.

"How did you manage to evade the kryti?"

"It wasn't *me* he refused to leave behind." Something in her voice made Shuut stop walking and stare straight at the young girl.

"You mean to say you aren't under his protection anymore?" Karinya nodded. "So, I could kill you now and he wouldn't make a move to stop me."

"You'd have to try it to find out."

It surprised Shuut that her threat had not even raised an eyebrow from the strange Paradisian.

"So, he thinks he saved your life. When did that happen?"

Karinya met her question with silence. There was no use in trying to continue the conversation. Shuut had come to understand how stubborn the girl could be and knew she'd get no further on the matter. Instead she turned her mind to the task at hand.

The Paradisian asked for no instruction in their hunt. She simply watched Shuut's movements and sensed where she needed to be to help her. As Shuut moved to corner some quails, Karinya did likewise from the opposite side. Once she saw Shuut was ready to throw her net over them, Karinya quickly moved forward and waved her arms at the birds, making them fly straight towards the net. They managed to catch ten quails in this way. It wasn't much, but the pickings were scarce in such open areas.

Before they were within hearing distance of their campsite, they saw the flicker of the cooking fire. Shuut was determined to reprimand whoever was responsible for that. In the fields, they were more exposed than any other place they had travelled together so far. Occupied by these thoughts, she didn't realise until she was already rubbing her arm that goose bumps had appeared on her flesh.

"How often does that happen?"

"How often does *what* happen?" she asked, distractedly, trying to listen to something she would never be able to hear.

"The lintep communicating. How often do you get those goose bumps?"

"What made me ever tell you about that?" Shuut muttered under her breath. Karinya watched her in silence until she answered. "It varies. I suppose it depends on if there are any lintep around where I'm travelling."

"Yes, but does it usually happen as often as this? Twice in one day is more than it ever happened before we reached Turon."

"How do you know it's been twice today?" Shuut raised her eyebrows inquisitively. She tried to read Karinya's thoughts. This girl was so strange that she simply had to know how she'd garnered that information. As usual, on the surface, the Paradisian showed nothing, not even her memories from the day. It irked Shuut that she could never get any further than the surface.

"You rubbed your arms like that when Tika was asking all those questions earlier today. Both times, it wasn't cold. I assume the lintep call is the only thing that would give you goose bumps on such a warm day as today. All I want to know is if that's normal."

"I don't usually notice it so much as I have lately. Though, that could simply be because you've been drawing my attention to it. How is it that you've noticed when the others haven't?"

Karinya shrugged. "I suppose it comes down to observation skills. The boys don't seem to notice as much as I do. Or perhaps they purposely try not to see things that disturb or puzzle them."

By the time they reached the campsite, Shuut could see the boys had settled in comfortably. Their cloaks were all laid out around the fire and a spit had been set up above the flames.

"Who lit the fire?"

"I did." Tika stood up with his chest puffed out.

"Then you get to pluck the feathers." Shuut threw the quails at his feet unceremoniously. "Next time, dig a deeper hole. It stands out like a beacon in these fields."

The small boy was crestfallen. Shuut knew he'd done a good job in lighting the fire, but they all needed to learn caution in the Outworld. Silently, Plyke sat down beside Tika to help him pluck the feathers. Their Partnership intrigued Shuut. She hadn't come across many Partners in the Outworld. Those she had were not nearly so close as these two boys. It seemed as though they could almost read each other's thoughts.

* * *

Rilla stayed silent long after she thought everyone had fallen asleep. Shuut had given her the first watch of the night and she intended to use her free time to her advantage. It had only been a day since she'd first actively tried to use her powers but, since then, she'd been itching to try it again. There was no way she wanted any of her human, or even half-caste, companions to know what she was.

She walked around the campsite in widening circles until she was far enough away not to wake anyone, but still be within a safe distance to alert the sleepers of any danger. The fringa on her left shoulder looked back towards the camp and the kryti's bulky form. Knowing that the others would be safe from all harm, he turned his beady-eyed gaze back to her.

"What exactly are you intending to do tonight?" he asked. Rilla turned her head in surprise. "You can't think I can be this close to your racing heart and not know that something is making you excited, or at least nervous."

For a moment, Rilla hesitated. She might only get one chance at this. If it failed, she didn't know how bad the situation could become. Ratchin had warned her not to overestimate her abilities – not to try too much. Even though she knew it was going against the lintep's wishes, Rilla couldn't help herself. She had to try. It had never been in her nature to take the safe option when the other choice was so much more exciting.

"You helped me test my powers yesterday. Would you be willing to do that again?"

"Yesterday it was to get you out of that town – to save your life. We've repaid our debt to you. I have no need to further help you," replied the fringa.

"Do you remember the man who was talking to Ratchin when you hopped over to her? The one I saw through your eyes?" The fringa's head bobbed up and down. "She took me to his house when the others returned. I watched as she healed his son. He was hanging to life by sheer will power. His skin was deathly white. He wasn't even conscious. Ratchin placed her hand over his wound and took away some of his pain. What she took from him, she gave to herself. That's how it seems to work. Ratchin said there has to be a balance. The pain doesn't just disappear, it gets spread out.

"I tried the same sort of thing with water. I drew out the heat from some water. It didn't just go away. It went into me. I could only take out as much heat as my body could handle."

She watched the fringa for some sort of reaction. He remained silent. Rilla could hear his thoughts, but saw that he was too afraid to voice them.

"I want to try healing you." At this, the fringa flapped his good wing in a huff. "Hear me out. You're tiny in comparison to me. The pain in your wing can't be more than I can handle. It isn't even life threatening. And imagine if it works! You could be back with your flock as soon as Tika's life has been saved." Rilla could barely contain her excitement as she waited for the fringa to decide one way or the other.

"In your eyes, would this put me in your debt again?"

"Of course not," she answered readily. "We'd be doing each other a favour. I heal you and you let me practice my magic."

Without waiting for his approval, Rilla took in her surroundings once more, making certain that there was no immediate danger and then sat on the grass. She lifted the fringa from her shoulder and held him on her outstretched hand. With her other hand, she lay two fingers over his broken wing. The touch by itself wasn't going to do anything. She needed to actively think about what she wanted, just as she had done with the water.

She closed her eyes and pictured the fringa in her mind — his glossy black beak and bright purple feathers. She recalled the way he flapped his good wing and felt for the pain of his broken one. A dull throbbing started in her shoulder. His wing had been broken where it attached to his body.

Instead of instinctively drawing back, she moved her fingers over the source of his pain. As though it was a stream, she drew his pain from his shoulder through her fingers. Pain shot down her arm – more pain than she had anticipated in a creature so small. She spread it throughout her entire body so as not to have an unbearable ache in one place.

When she had taken out as much pain as she dared, she placed the fringa on the grass beside her, keeping her fingers over his broken shoulder. With her free hand, she placed two fingers on his good shoulder. In her mind, she saw how the bones were meant to look. Carefully, she put the broken bones together in the same way and she willed the bones to fuse together.

Not knowing if it had worked, or if it had just been in her head, Rilla opened her eyes and drew her hands away from the small bird. The pain she had drawn out of him was only noticeable if she concentrated on it. She silently praised herself for thinking to spread it throughout her entire body.

"Did it work?" she asked excitedly. In her mind, she had pictured everything merging together perfectly. She waited expectantly for the fringa to answer her. Without a word to spare for his healer, he was already stretching his wing out with a claw. Chirping in delight, he flapped his wings and was airborne. He flew a few circles over Rilla's head before heading straight over to his kryti.

Rilla smiled at the sight. *She* had done that. She had healed his broken wing. Without guidance from another lintep, she'd managed to figure it out herself, just as she had with the water. By simply watching Ratchin perform these wonders, she seemed to have absorbed the knowledge herself.

How easily would other skills come to her once she was properly trained? Would the subtler uses of her power be more difficult to master? How would she be able to test her limits without another fully trained lintep to help if she overstepped her boundaries? These thoughts and more plagued her while she watched the fringa's joyful flight.

"You *do* understand that you can't let the others know you're healed, don't you?" Rilla felt a moment of pure panic. If the fringa told the others what she was, everything she was trying to do for the boys, for Rhanya, would be over. The small purple bird turned her way.

"I do not repay favours by betraying those who have helped me. Your companions will learn nothing of your powers from me. However, I would suggest that you tell them all sooner rather than later. I'm sure your half-caste friend would be most sympathetic to your plight." Having voiced his thoughts, the fringa perched himself on his kryti's shoulder and tucked his head under his wing, ready for the night ahead.

At the end of her watch, Rilla woke Tika. She waited until the sleepy boy had walked around the camp a few times before allowing herself to relax her guard enough to fall asleep.

Chapter Twenty-One – Secrets revealed

They travelled for the better part of a week through fields, which turned into hills and hills that gave way to rocky outcrops. Throughout this time, Arishen had increasingly vivid dreams of Shuut. They made no sense to him. He wrote them down in his dream book every morning, but that wasn't enough. If only he could talk to someone about them.

Trying to talk to the banwep herself was not an option. Shuut still hadn't forgiven him for the morning in Turon. Plyke and Tika were out of the question. The Partners barely spoke to him under normal circumstances. Besides, even if he wanted to get close to Tika, the kryti's overbearing protectiveness was too much to endure. That left Karinya.

He'd apologised for punching her a hundred times the day they left Turon. She had not forgiven him. They both knew it had been a reflex reaction to his dream, but that didn't seem to appease the fiery girl. She held him responsible for her argument with Shuut – as though they had never argued before that day.

It was already late afternoon by the time he found the courage to try talking with her. He waited until she was far enough behind the others that their conversation wouldn't be overheard. She looked up as he came closer, not saying a word. He took a deep breath, trying to dismiss everything that had passed between them since they'd left their Paradise.

"I've been having more dreams." He had come to realise there was no point in preamble with the strange girl. "I need to talk to someone about them and I don't think the others will listen to me."

"What makes you think *I* will?" Her green eyes were impassive. Not even a trace of anger was to be found in them.

"You were the only one in the Paradise who knew what I was and said nothing. You were the one to explain what was happening to Shuut. You were the one who woke me from one of my worst dreams." Karinya remained silent. Arishen hoped that was his cue to continue. "I've been dreaming about Shuut lately. It always starts with her rubbing goose bumps on her arms. Sometimes, she stops to listen to something the rest of us can't hear. Other times, she is distracted by conversation and does nothing."

"Do you have any idea what the dreams are about?"

"No. I was hoping you might be able to help me there."

Karinya shrugged. "It's just a dream about goose bumps, Arishen. I doubt it's all that important. But, if you really want to know what it means, why don't you just talk to Shuut?"

"And say what?" Arishen asked in exasperation. "I've been dreaming about you having goose bumps. Have you been cold lately? Honestly, Karinya, I thought you'd have a better suggestion than that."

The girl simply raised an eyebrow at him and turned away. So much for *that* suggestion. He'd have to solve this dream puzzle by himself. He was certain there was more to it than simply goose bumps. They had to mean something. He'd never had recurring dreams before. Normal people – people whose dreams didn't reveal anything – had recurring dreams. But Arishen was certain this wasn't one of those.

Arishen waited until they'd stopped for their midday meal before bringing it up with Shuut. He wanted to talk to her within hearing of the others. The insistence of the dreams told him it was something which would affect all of them. If he was dreaming about it, the others had a right to know. The last dream he'd told them all had caused their departure from Turon. Surely, they would be more inclined to at least *listen* to what he had to say after that.

He made certain to sit next to Shuut as they ate their cold food. There was never any time to light a fire for the midday meal. It was more just an excuse to give their weary legs a chance to recover before the afternoon journey. Arishen kept silent until he was certain *all* of his companions would be seated for a while.

"I've been dreaming about you Shuut." Though he kept his eyes firmly on his apple as he spoke, he could feel the tension in the air and the banwep's eyes on him.

"Arishen, I'm much too old for you."

He looked up at her, first in confusion, then embarrassment. Bright red, he stumbled out a reply. "It…it's not *that* kind of dream." The Partners laughed as he attempted to rectify the situation. Karinya tried, unsuccessfully, to hide her smirk.

"Out with it, boy. What was your dream about?"

Trying to recover from her previous comment, he struggled to find the right words. "You get goose bumps."

"Goose bumps?" Shuut raised an eyebrow. "You want to tell me that you dream about goose bumps?"

"It's not just goose bumps," he retaliated angrily. They were all going to listen to him this time, without laughing. "You get goose bumps and rub your arms. No one else is even cold in the dreams. Then you listen to something the rest of us can't hear. The only times you don't do that is if someone is already talking to you, so you don't notice yourself rubbing your arms. You never hear whatever it is unless you notice the goose bumps first."

Shuut's face turned to stone as he told her the dream. Once he was finished, the banwep immediately turned to Karinya and started yelling at her.

"You little back-stabber! You told him, didn't you? I should have left the lot of you …"

"How dare you accuse me? I saved your life …"

It barely took a moment for Karinya to yell back at the banwep, as loudly and vehemently. Arishen stared back and forth between the two of them, barely understanding a word either was saying to the other. He glanced over to the Partners only to find them experiencing the same difficulty as himself.

Their fight eventually died down. Angry glares replaced loud voices. Both stood with clenched fists and red faces. Shuut pointed a finger towards Arishen, without averting her gaze from Karinya's green eyes.

"You told him!" Her voice was low and threatening.

"I didn't."

"How could he possibly have noticed if you didn't tell him?"

"I noticed it. Why shouldn't he?"

Hoping to help out in some way, Arishen spoke up. "She didn't tell me anything. I told her about my dream earlier today and she said to ask you about it."

"Oh, that was a fine idea," Shuut replied sarcastically. "You just brushed him off in the hope that he'd actually have the courage to ask me about it."

"It would have come up sooner or later." Karinya's voice had lost its bitter edge.

"It may never have come up at all. I could have taken you to the elves and left you there without ever having this conversation."

"I don't understand what all the fuss is about goose bumps." It was Tika's timid voice that broke the tension. "You just get them more often than the rest of us. Who cares?"

"Why don't you just tell them?" Shuut glared at Karinya. "I know you're aching to."

The girl looked, almost pityingly, at Shuut. "You never did believe me when I said I wouldn't tell anyone, did you?" Without another word, she went to sit down next to the kryti. Arishen watched the fringa hop onto the girl's shoulder and nuzzle her cheek with his beak.

"We don't have time for this." Shuut tried to change the topic. "I'm not going to waste time explaining this to you when we should be walking. As it is, your stupid dream may have placed us in danger."

"How could my dream possibly do that?" Arishen refused to be blamed for yet another thing gone wrong.

"We don't have time for this," Shuut repeated, icily. She walked south without looking to see if they followed or not. Arishen looked worriedly at the others, shrugging shoulders and blank faces reflecting his own confusion. As one, the Paradisians shouldered their rucksacks to follow their explosive banwep.

* * *

Shuut kept her distance from the Paradisians. No matter how long she travelled with them, she doubted she would ever see them as anything other than Paradisians. Even trying to blend in, they would stand out in a crowded village square. How had they ever convinced her to take them out of their sheltered little world? Arishen seemed to have the only real reason to leave, although she doubted he was any better off in this world than that. Unless he learned to control his ability, he would constantly be a danger to himself and his companions. And how in the Outworld had he dreamt about her lintep heritage? Unknowingly, he had managed to discover her most closely guarded secret.

How could she possibly tell them that she was a half-caste? What would they do? Would she even be able to sleep again in their company without a paralysing fear that they would try to murder her, as anyone else in the Outworld would do in a heartbeat?

The sun had set while they were still walking. Without realising what she was doing, Shuut had reverted to her old ways, walking long past the time when anyone following her could possibly follow without needing to rest. It was the only way to keep safe. She was fit and needed little sleep. Somehow, lintep never needed as much sleep as humans. She could out-walk any human without breaking a sweat.

It wasn't until the whistling started that she stopped. She couldn't hear it. She could never hear it. But she knew what was happening. Goose bumps had formed within a few seconds.

"We stop here for the night." Her companions stopped walking, but did not drop their rucksacks. They were all staring at the visibly raised hairs on her arms. She had goose bumps on a muggy night. If anything, she should have been sweating, not rubbing her arms.

"Your arms ..." Arishen pointed, his voice faltering.

"Can the two of you stand watch while we talk?" Shuut's attention was on the fringa and his kryti. "I'm sure you've figured it out yourselves. It would be best if we weren't overheard tonight." She waited until the bulky creature had walked an uneventful wide circle around them before settling down.

"You don't have to tell them, you know." The suggestion came from Karinya. Shuut ignored her.

"We won't be lighting a fire tonight. The moon is more than bright enough for our purposes. Better to avoid any unwanted attention for this."

She paced for a bit before sitting down with her arms wrapped around her waist. Not since she was a little girl had she been so nervous. The only person she had ever told about being a half-caste was Ratchin. Anyone else who had found out about her had tried to kill her. Most of them had been unsuccessful in even harming her. But all too recently, a few had almost ended her life. Karinya had been right. If the girl hadn't found her at the edge of the Paradise, she would not have survived.

"What I have to tell you is something that few humans know," she began warily. "When you know what it is, you may wish that you had never asked. So, I want to be certain that you are prepared to accept it, no matter what it is." She looked at the boys in turn, gaining their agreement.

"As you may have guessed, Karinya already knows part of what I'm about to tell you. She has given her word never to tell anyone about it. Have any of you ever heard of the lintep?"

"Only what they told us in the Paradise," Arishen answered her, cautiously. "They're dangerous magicians who caused humans to find refuge in Paradises."

Shuut nodded her head with a cynical smile. "Did you ever wonder how Paradises were made?"

The Paradisians shook their heads, the boys not understanding what she was trying to tell them.

"Your Paradise was built by the lintep," she told them. "They all were."

"You mean they created those prisons?" Arishen raised his voice in a sudden bout of fury.

"No, Arishen," Shuut replied in a calm voice, almost expecting the outburst. "The lintep *lost* a war against humans and went into refuge. The ones who created these Paradises did so as a favour to the humans who wanted to live in them."

"Why would they do that for a people they were at war with?" Tika asked Shuut, with less anger than the seer. "And besides, what does any of this have to do with why you kept stopping today?"

"Well, my mother always spoke kindly of the lintep to me," Shuut answered, smiling slightly as she recalled her past.

"They are a race of people, similar to elves in their magical abilities, though closer to humans in their appearance. The lintep were shunned many centuries ago because humans were afraid of them. No humans had magical powers, so they were afraid of any who did because they didn't understand how magic worked. The lintep were particularly feared because they looked human. By appearance alone, you can never tell if someone is a lintep or human. That is why humans accept elves more than they do the lintep.

"My mother told me they whistle to each other so that no others can hear. If you aren't used to it, it makes your skin prickle." She paused to look at them closely. "I've been trying to find them my whole life, so when I feel goose bumps, or even a strange sensation, I stop to see if this time I can hear them."

"Are you trying to tell us that you're a lintep?" Arishen rose to his feet, staring accusingly at her. It was the reaction Shuut was expecting. Any Outworlder wouldn't have even waited for confirmation before attacking her. At least she had his hesitation to be thankful for.

"I'm only half lintep," Shuut replied, quickly and calmly. Tika was smiling at the news. His Partner, as usual, was completely impassive. Arishen alone was the problem.

"Why didn't you tell us before you took us out of our Paradise?" he asked in a stormy voice. "We had every right to know."

"You would have followed her anyway," Karinya rose to Shuut's defence immediately. "Hadn't Parthak already threatened you by that stage? She knew what you were. How much longer would you have survived in our Paradise? What difference would it have made to you that a half-lintep was taking you away from a lintep creation? Where would you have preferred to live had you known everything?" The silence which followed was deafening.

"How do we know the lintep didn't purposely imprison us in the Paradise?" asked Arishen sulkily.

"Because most of what we were told in the Paradise was a lie," Tika replied, easily. "Besides, why would so many people hope to find a Paradise and readily agree to their customs rather than return to the Outworld?"

"What about the terrible things they told us the lintep could do?" Arishen spoke up again. "They can control your mind, make you do things you don't want to do."

"That's *not* actually true." Shuut finally found a gap in the conversation where she might be able to turn the tables. "Lintep are only telepathic to a certain point. They can hear your thoughts and project their thoughts into your mind. They can influence the weak-minded, but they can't completely control your thoughts or actions. Besides, not all lintep are telepathic, some are empathetic. They can feel the emotions of people around them. Both skills depend on the strength of the person. Half-castes, like myself, struggle with even the simpler task of reading thoughts."

"Have you been reading our thoughts?" It was the first time Plyke had spoken. He fixed her with an unwavering stare.

"Once or twice," she admitted, rushing to justify her actions. "But only surface glances, to make sure you could be trusted."

"You have no right to do that!" Arishen yelled at her, angrily. "Stay out of our minds."

Shuut wasn't used to travelling with people. She had grown up doing whatever she had to, to stay alive. Reading people's minds had always been an advantage under those circumstances. She conceded to herself that perhaps it was something she should only do with potential enemies. Nodding, she promised not to try reading their minds in the future.

"What else can you do?" Tika asked her curiously.

"Well, actually, that's all, apart from the goose bumps," Shuut replied, suddenly almost ashamed at her lack of power. "My mother told me that full lintep get that feeling as well as being able to hear the whistling, but when they learn to understand the meaning behind it, the goose bumps don't appear anymore."

"So, that's it?" Tika asked in disappointment. "You can read minds and you get goose bumps?"

Shuut nodded her head sheepishly. When he put it that way, it didn't really sound like there was much of an advantage for her being a half-caste.

"That's not all," Karinya spoke up, reluctantly. "She heals abnormally quickly."

"How do you know that?" asked Arishen. "You've only known her as long as we have."

"Do I really have to remind you who died to give us our freedom?" Arishen looked down, shamefaced. Rhanya had been one of the healers working on Shuut. In fact, he had barely left her side. If Karinya knew Shuut was a half-caste before they left the Paradise, it only made sense that Rhanya had been the one to point it out to her.

"You've known she was different all this time and you didn't tell us?" Tika asked in a hurt voice.

"I didn't really know what it meant until now, Tika." The green-eyed girl tried to placate him. "I barely knew what a lintep was at the time."

"Will we see the lintep stronghold on our travels, Shuut?" he asked in excitement, his annoyance at Karinya already forgotten.

"It's doubtful," she replied, sadly. "The only ones who can find it are lintep themselves. I've been trying to find it half my life, with no success. I doubt it will be any easier with the four of you along."

Their conversation eventually died away, with Plyke moving to the opposite side of their campsite from Shuut. He was apparently not willing to sleep next to a half-caste. She knew her surface glances at his mind worried him. Even if she had made a promise not to do so anymore, she had to admit they had no reason to believe her.

Shuut looked over at Karinya and saw a strange look on her face, one of approval. It was something she was not used to seeing when people looked at her. Even her own father had never shown it when she succeeded in something he was teaching her. It was one of many harsh memories from her childhood. She wondered how her life compared to what she had seen of life in the Paradise and who may have had the stranger childhood.

Chapter Twenty-Two – Debts repaid

The last watch of the night found Tika cooking breakfast for everyone over a tiny fire he'd lit towards dawn. He'd been careful to dig a deep enough hole so that no flames would rise above the ground to give away their position to any enemies. His last attempt had been embarrassing enough that he did not want a repeat occurrence of it. The sweet smell of roasting meat reminded him of the quieter times in the Paradise, before the silent executions began to occur, before he knew anyone who had met elves and was part lintep.

Musing over these thoughts, he heard a faint whistling. His eyes followed the tiny fringa, which flew past him to land on the kryti's sleeping body. Over the last few days, the tiny purple bird's wing had healed sufficiently for him to attempt short flights.

Preoccupied with thoughts of his Paradise and the fringa, Tika turned the hares over the small fire. He did not notice the sudden silence of animals around him. The fringa chirruped as loudly as he could, rousing his kryti protector. Tika, alerted to the danger, looked behind him to see three humans crawling quietly towards the campsite.

In seconds, they realised they'd been spotted and were on their feet, running towards him. Tika ran towards his rucksack, where his only weapon lay. With three steps, the largest man was upon him, closing his calloused hand around Tika's throat, pushing him to the ground. Terrified, Tika kicked his legs and arms out, trying to free himself from the grip — it only tightened. He tried to scream, but to no avail. His attacker was well practiced in his trade. Tika watched as the other two closed in on the campsite.

Anger flared up inside him. The kryti was supposed to be his protector. He owed Tika a debt of honour for saving his life. Where was he? The grip around Tika's throat tightened as he continued to fight against it. He could feel each breath searing his throat, his vision darkening around the edges. Panic ran through his veins. It wouldn't be much longer before the man decided to be done with him.

Tika watched in confusion as the bandit looked up and slackened his hold. He took the opportunity to twist his head to look behind him. Shuut was standing between the two fallen bodies of the other bandits, her bloodied sword in hand. Before he knew it, the last bandit was lifted from the ground by the massive kryti. Tika watched in revulsion, gasping for breath, as the beast ripped the man's head off. The decapitated body was thrown over his slain companions, along with his severed head.

Tika momentarily closed his eyes against the horrific scene as the kryti cried out triumphantly in his guttural voice. He stood on weak legs, looking around the campsite. Karinya was standing defensively with her chisel, her only weapon. Plyke, waking at the sound of the kryti, sleepily scanned the campsite until his eyes came to rest on the slain bodies. Only Arishen remained tossing and moaning in his sleep.

"Don't look at me to wake him." Karinya broke the silence.

"We'll let him dream it out," Shuut replied. "Help me move them."

The kryti growled as Shuut knelt down to take hold of a body.

"If you don't mind, my kryti will take care of those himself," a high-pitched voice called out above them. The small fringa was circling around the bodies like a vulture. Shuut shrugged, dropping the dead man's legs, and cleaned her sword on the bandit's clothes.

"You don't mean to say ..." Tika left the unfinished sentence hanging.

"It's all food to him, boy. He's not been eating much in your company – too difficult to hunt for large creatures with you humans around. Now that we'll be parting ways, I believe he will enjoy this meal."

Tika dry retched, running for the water bottle in his rucksack. The thought of his protector eating humans was more than he could bear. If he and Karinya hadn't saved the beast's life, they could have suffered the same fate. The ease with which the kryti had ripped off the man's head kept playing itself over in Tika's mind.

"He *did* save your life." His Partner wrapped an arm around Tika's shoulders. "Would you have rather he let them kill you instead?" Tika shook his head silently, trying to calm himself with small sips of water and long, deep breaths. The fringa swooped down to land on Tika's bended knee.

"He will not eat until you are out of sight boy. Take heart in the fact that he will never try to harm you. Even though his debt has been paid, you will never be in any danger from him." Tika nodded, staring silently at the small purple bird. "Now, if you have enough wits about you, let me teach you a tune to whistle if you are ever in need again. If my flock and I are not near enough to hear it, another flock will certainly alert us to the sound."

Tika practised the tune over and over again, with the occasional correction from the little bird. The exercise took his mind off the decapitation. He whistled until the sound finally woke Arishen. The five of them ate the hares Tika had cooked before they broke camp.

Short farewells were said all around and the five original companions resumed their journey to the elves. Tika looked back one last time, to reconfirm that it hadn't just been a nightmare. He saw the kryti salivating over the bloodied bodies, but not making any move towards them. He would not eat until they were out of sight. Turning his head back in the direction he was walking, Tika noticed the fringa sitting on Karinya's shoulder, whispering in her ear. The girl nodded and the bird flew back to his protector. Her green eyes pierced his own until he turned away. He was certain he'd just witnessed a conversation that was meant to have remained secret, but he said nothing to the girl. She still scared him.

* * *

The fringa came to rest on Rilla's shoulder when they were already a hundred paces or so from their campsite. She turned to look at him with a sinking feeling.

"I realise there is no need to tell you, because you already know what I will say, but child, be careful. I know you see it as your duty to protect them, even more so now that we will be parted. Don't forget that there is no one to protect *you*, especially not from yourself. Don't be foolish with your powers. I understand you are excited by the possibilities of what you can do, but bear in mind that Shuut cannot help you if you overstep your boundaries. She is less powerful than you. I doubt she has ever even dreamed about doing what you have already achieved."

Rilla nodded. There was no need to say anything. They both knew the risks she would take if she practiced her newfound magic without the fringa and kryti to keep watch over her. She watched him fly back to his protector before turning to see Tika's gaze on her. Staring unflinchingly, she waited until he turned away before letting herself wonder if he had heard the fringa's whispered words.

They did not stop at midday. Shuut was afraid of another attack. Should anyone have been following the bandits as a second group, they would know that the travellers were now unprotected by the kryti. The banwep reverted to her old habits of rotating her position throughout the group to keep a watch on everyone.

Rilla studied her movements and committed them to memory. She had resolved to take in everything she could from Shuut while they were still travelling with the banwep. The next time she tried to abandon them somewhere, Rilla would be prepared and better able to keep the boys safe, as she had promised Rhanya.

By late afternoon, Shuut was back at Rilla's side. They had not spoken all day. Rilla was still smouldering over the half-caste's accusation. She had never given Shuut her word that she wouldn't tell her secret, but she *had* made it perfectly clear that she never intended to tell anyone. It made no sense to her that the banwep would automatically assume she had done so.

They walked silently for minutes that stretched over an hour — Rilla silently debating with herself whether she should reveal her heritage. On the one hand, it would allow her to freely practice her magic on a daily basis. On the other, Arishen's, and even Plyke's, reaction to Shuut's revelation weighed heavily on her. It would simply be another reason for the boys to disassociate themselves from her. Shuut would be even less likely to continue travelling with them. Rhanya's request would be more difficult to comply with. She shook her head, resigning herself to the fact that she would not be able to practice magic until she had left them all behind, no matter how long that might take.

"Are you shaking your head at me?" Rilla turned absentmindedly towards Shuut. She'd forgotten the half-caste was walking beside her.

"Not everything is about you."

"Yesterday's conversation would seem to prove otherwise."

"You have no idea what is going on in our minds. Whatever surface glimpses you've gotten have quite obviously done you no good. I had enough of people not trusting me in the Paradise. Do you really think I would try to start my life in the Outworld in the same way, by betraying the trust of the one person who has any chance of keeping me alive?"

"I honestly don't know what to think of you, Karinya. The four of us don't even know your real name."

"We're back to that again, are we?" Rilla rolled her eyes and turned away.

"It does tend to create a rift between people when they don't trust each other with their names."

"And accusing people of doing something they haven't done; how does that affect the issue of trust?"

"I'm not apologising for that." Shuut walked away, over to the far left of their company.

"I never expected you to," Rilla said softly to herself, closing her eyes against the insanity surrounding her. When she reopened them, Plyke was only a few steps away from her, leaving Tika by himself. Her creased her forehead. *What will he accuse me of?* It seemed to be the only reason any of them came to talk to her.

"Thank you." Rilla looked uncertainly into his eyes. There was no hint that he was being sarcastic.

"I don't know what you're talking about."

"I don't know why you keep everyone else's secrets, but thank you for mine. You've known Shuut was a half-caste since before we left the Paradise. When did she tell you about the goose bumps?"

"Oh, I see." The young lintep found herself avoiding Plyke's eye. He had put the pieces together. "Does Tika know?"

"There are things I would prefer to keep to myself."

Rilla nodded. Her decision to keep her own secrets to herself weighed heavily on her. She had never asked to be told their secrets. Most people had never observed her long enough, or with the required dedication, to discover her secrets. Even Rhanya, who knew her name, had never pried any further when he noticed what others didn't.

Plyke walked with her in silence until they stopped for the night. Tika made no move to stop him or join them.

Chapter Twenty-Three – Accusations

Since he'd discovered Tika and Plyke had packed his dream book, Arishen had been reading over his old dreams. Most of them had been pleasant enough to begin with. They just told him of events in the Paradise, some more significant than others — a foal's birth, a broken pot in the kitchen. Most of the time, he never heard about those events. It had taken him months to understand what was happening.

When things became more serious in their Paradise, the dreams were more intense, like he was living them in his sleep. Some were secret trysts between forbidden lovers. Unauthorised relationships were dangerous in their Paradise. Some of them ended tragically — a bad meal, a farming accident, a difficult birth. Arishen had started dreaming these years ago. At first, he thought it was his fault. It took him a while to realise that Erton had spies all over the place. They discovered secrets and made sure no one else ever knew.

Sometimes, he would simply dream about the person for a week, without any incident to foretell anything was amiss. But without fail, those people were secretly executed. He never dreamt about anyone without a reason.

It had been a few days since Shuut's stunning revelation. Arishen had thought of nothing else since then. His dreams about her had ended that same night. Why it was important for them to find out about her right then was still a mystery to him, but his dreams had brought that about. He stared into their campfire, trying to understand it all.

Karinya knew about it. Why hadn't she told them? Why had she kept this secret? She had kept silent, just as she had done in the Paradise. It was now obvious that she had noticed everything. Not once had she made a move to stop Erton. Surely the Paradise leader's daughter must have been the only person in the entire place who could have stood up to him and not be punished. She could have ended the secret executions, or at least made them public knowledge. There was no way Arishen could have done that. It would have drawn far too much attention to the fact that he knew more than he should. He may well have been executed himself. Erton would never have done that to his own daughter.

"Is there something on your mind, Arishen?" Shuut asked, looking at him through the fire. He wondered how often she had tried to read his mind before.

"Why don't you just read my mind and see?" He couldn't believe that Karinya knew what this banwep was before they left, before she put their lives in *her* hands. A half-caste who could read their minds whenever she wanted to! What was stopping her from seeing his dreams? They were his dreams. Not hers. *His.*

The half-caste glanced across to Karinya.

"Don't look at *her* for help." Arishen looked icily between them. The Partners looked up at his comment, but he took no notice of them. "She never helped anyone in our Paradise. Why would she do so now?"

"She saved my life there. From what I hear, she probably saved yours as well." The banwep was confused, and well she might be. She had no idea what had been happening in their Paradise before she got there.

"That's only two." Arishen got to his feet and pointed at the red-headed secret keeper. "Do you have any idea how many times she just stood by and let people die?"

"What are you talking about, boy?"

"Erton was murdering people. She knew about it. How could she not? She noticed everything." Karinya's silence infuriated him. He spoke to her directly. "How could you let so many of them die?"

"What makes you think she could have stopped that man?" the banwep asked.

"Erton's her father." Shuut's eyes widened. "Did she fail to mention that? If there was anyone in the Paradise who could have stopped him, it had to have been her."

"What do you mean 'Erton was murdering people'?" Tika captured the seer's attention. "I never saw him do that."

"Of course you never saw him!" Arishen answered furiously. "He never did it himself. But he arranged for accidents to happen. How do you think Rhanya died? Or your mother, once she admitted you were her son?"

"How do *you* know that? She never told anyone but me." Arishen cursed himself for his stupidity. Karinya was making him thoughtless. He never meant to reveal his dreams to them.

"It doesn't matter," he told the boy firmly. "What matters is that Karinya could have said something and she never did."

"I don't think that's very fair, Arishen." Plyke looked up at him through his mop of thick brown hair. "You can't accuse Karinya of keeping silent when you obviously knew what was happening as well. Even *I* didn't know about Tika's mother. He didn't tell anyone about that. Unless you were dreaming about these murders, then how did you know? And if you were dreaming about them, that makes you just as responsible as Karinya."

"She's his daughter!" Arishen stamped his foot. "She was the only one he would listen to."

"Didn't you ever notice how much time she spent in the isolation hut?" Plyke asked, shaking his head. "If any of us were put in there for a few hours, more usually than not, Karinya was taken out first. Erton had no trouble in punishing her more than anyone else. What makes you think he would have listened to a word she said against these secret murders you seem to know so much about?"

Silence descended on the camp. Arishen looked from one face to another, finding no sympathy among them. He pointed to the girl. "She is the murderer's daughter. It was her responsibility to stop him!"

Karinya stood up, never once looking at him. She walked over to her rucksack and pulled out the wide-faced chisel he had stolen for her. Handle first, she held it out to him. "You decide what happens to the murderer's daughter then."

He took the chisel from her loose grip amidst protests from the other three. Her blank, unfeeling eyes reminded him of Erton's cold, calculated look. She was just as responsible for all those senseless murders as her father was. Before the others could react, he stabbed her. The chisel went straight through the thin layer of skin and struck bone. She groaned as she fell to the ground, chisel in her ribs. He saw pity in her eyes. That's not what she was supposed to feel. Shame, anger, despair – those were the feelings that had plagued him. Why didn't they plague her?

"Arishen, what have you done?" Tika whispered in shock.

"Get him away from her." He heard Shuut's shouted order from a distance. Tika and Plyke led him to the far side of the camp as Shuut ripped a spare shirt into long strips. The bloodied chisel now lay on the ground beside the pair. Shuut tightly wound the ripped shirt around Karinya's ribs as she gasped for air. Blood seeped through almost immediately.

"Plyke, get me another shirt."

Plyke ran to his own rucksack and pulled out a heavier cloth. Together, the two of them worked to slow the bleeding in Karinya's side. She lay there apathetically, making no move to either stop or help them.

Arishen tried to rise once to get a closer look. A surprisingly firm grip held him in place. He looked with unseeing eyes at Tika. All he could see was Karinya's blood. It mingled with the blood in his dreams. All those executions – had he added to them?

* * *

Tika woke the next morning after dreaming of his mother. He hadn't ever told anyone about her. The only way Arishen could have possibly known about her was if he dreamt it. She'd died less than a week after acknowledging him, in a farming accident. A spooked horse had thrown her off and trampled her. Tika had always believed it to be an accident. He hadn't known she died because of him.

Every child in the Paradise guessed who their parents were. It was part of growing up. The constant question of where you came from. Most of them were content to simply wonder. Those who questioned were never answered. Tika's mother had been different. She had smiled and held him close. He could still remember the acrid smell of manure on her skin as she praised him for his keen detection.

He'd been so happy to finally know who his mother was. Plyke had noticed the change in him, he knew, but they'd never spoken about it. This was one of the secrets Tika kept from him — his most precious piece of information. He remembered searching his mother's face for traces of himself and watched her at work in the stables. He was determined to follow in her footsteps, until she was taken away from him.

How could Arishen possibly have known about it? He had to have dreamt about it. Did he know she was going to die before it happened or did he dream as it was happening? Had he dreamt about their secret conversation? Did he know *then* that she would be killed?

"Tika, it's time to get up." Plyke's gentle intrusion snapped him out of his trance.

"How could he accuse Karinya of doing nothing when he knew exactly what was happening?" Hot, angry tears fell from Tika's eyes. "If he knew Sen was my mother, he had to have known she would be murdered. If he'd already dreamt about others, why didn't he say something himself?"

Plyke shook his head, sadly. "I don't know." The two of them got up and walked over to Karinya. Shuut had not left her side all night. The banwep looked up at their approach through tired red eyes.

"How is she?" Tika heard the worry in his Partner's voice. He rarely displayed enough emotion for others to notice it, but this morning, it was hard to miss.

"He's cracked at least one of her ribs, but she didn't lose as much blood as I would have expected last night. We can only hope it doesn't stop her from walking today. It will be slow going until she recovers."

"How far are we from Silvaren?" Tika asked, less interested now in seeing the elves than in ending their journey.

"We would probably have reached it tonight had this not happened. But I just don't know now."

"Is she all right?" Arishen had walked over to them, unnoticed and unwanted.

"She'll survive." Shuut's voice could have cut through stone. "No thanks to you."

"I didn't mean to hurt her so badly." The seer tried to defend himself.

"You shouldn't have tried to hurt her at all!" Tika stood up to face him. "How dare you accuse her of not standing up to Erton when you knew all along what was happening and said nothing?"

"Erton would have killed me if he knew what I was." The protest fell on deaf ears. Shuut and the Partners delicately began to unwrap the ripped cloth from around Karinya's ribs. She awoke with a start.

"What are you doing?" Her eyes darted franticly between the three of them.

"We just wanted to check your wound," Shuut said more gently than she'd ever spoken before.

"I'll do it myself." The panic-stricken girl pushed their helping hands away. As they stood up and away from her, her eyes landed on Arishen. Immediately, a cold calm descended over her face. He made a move to apologise, but she turned away. Shuut walked over to her rucksack and returned with her water skin.

"Wash the wound and wrap it up tightly. That rib will need to be kept in place while it mends. We'll wait for you a hundred paces that way." She pointed southeast, towards the elves. Karinya nodded and waited for them to walk away from her.

* * *

Rilla waited until they had walked a decent distance from her. Even then, she still turned away before carefully unwrapping the cloth around her ribs. In the Paradise, she had never been injured so badly. For smaller things, she had always run straight to Rhanya. He was the only one she trusted. She frown with the memory of it. There had been so few occasions when she had visited the healers for herself. When she had, it had always been for single visits.

Rhanya had told her that she was a quick healer. Had he figured out what she was? He'd always been careful to take her straight to his room whenever she visited him. Had he been hiding her from the others? In his own way, had he been protecting Erton? Her thoughts ran to wild conclusions. Rhanya's silent execution held so many more secrets than she had ever suspected. Had Erton known that he would tell her about him, and by default, herself? It would have caused upheaval in their entire society. The reason Paradises were created was to have a place away from the Outworld and magic. To realise they were being ruled by a lintep would have caused a riot.

She pushed the questions away as she concentrated on cleaning what was left of her flesh wound. It had practically healed overnight. If her companions had seen it, there would have been little doubt in their minds that she was a lintep. They may not have even have the mistake of thinking her a half-caste at the rate she was healing. Pushing at the broken rib, she pressed to see if it was still broken. Gasping in pain, she realised her bones did not mend as quickly as her flesh.

Working slowly and methodically, she cleaned away the dried blood on the wound and winced as she pulled the scab apart. It created fresh bloodstains on the cloth she rewrapped around herself. There was no need to draw any extra attention to herself than necessary. The absence of blood would be an oddity she could not explain away. As she got up to join the others, she wondered how slowly she ought to walk with such an injury. She slouched over her left side, where Arishen had driven the chisel in, not having to pretend too much with her rib.

Once she reached the others, Shuut turned to her. "Let me know if you need to rest." It was the first time Shuut had offered such a concession to anyone in their company. Rilla felt a pang of guilt for deceiving them all but, considering Arishen's reaction to Shuut's heritage, she decided it was best to keep her secret as well as Plyke's. She wasn't certain if Plyke was only a half-caste, but either way, Arishen would feel outnumbered and even more threatened than he already did.

When she caught up to the group, Plyke and Tika slowed down to walk with her. They barely left her side all day. If Arishen so much as looked back at her, they drew closer to her. It was a strange feeling for Rilla. People were standing up for her. She wasn't used to it. In fact, she had expected the Partners to take Arishen's side in the matter. Most people in the Paradise had probably thought that she could get away with more than anyone else because she was Erton's daughter. It didn't occur to her that anyone would realise that that wasn't the case. The fact that she had anyone take her side meant more to her than she could possibly express. She hoped her gratitude was visible on her face. She had no idea how to express it any other way.

"Did you really know about the murders?" It was late at night. The others had been asleep for hours. Shuut had changed the watch, yet again, so that Karinya could rest. Arishen was still denied a turn at night watch because of his dreams, though in reality, there was no chance any of them wanted the volatile seer watching over them.

Tika's watch had been and gone. It was now Plyke's turn. He had walked around the camp numerous times, keeping a keen eye out for any danger. Having assured himself they were safe, he moved over to talk with the sleepless girl.

"I had my suspicions." She sat up, wincing at the pain in her side. "Even though they weren't allowed to let me watch, Rhanya turned a blind eye when I was around most of the time. I saw the increased *accidental* injuries, the sudden deaths of healthy old people. It wasn't until Rhanya died that I was absolutely certain of it."

"How do you know his death wasn't natural?" He watched as she closed her eyes tightly. If he thought hard enough, he imagined he could feel her pain at the memory. Instead of tears, when her eyes reopened, there was only numbness.

"He told me about Shuut. He *knew* she was at least part lintep. When Erton had me put in the isolation chamber, Rhanya sought me out to tell me. It was his idea that I leave the Paradise with her. Even if Erton's spies hadn't told him about that conversation, there were other things that pointed to his guilt that week. There was no way Erton could let him live after that, not if he thought Rhanya could have started an uprising against him."

Plyke listened in silence. It was the most he'd ever heard Karinya speak. He got a glimpse at the strange life she'd been forced to lead in their Paradise. But it wasn't nearly enough to understand her actions from the night before.

"Is that really all you want to ask me?" she asked, her voice full of resignation.

"I'm almost afraid to ask you anything else," he answered with a sigh. "You seem to have noticed so much more than anyone else about everything and everyone. I don't know if I want to know the secrets you keep. Maybe it's better simply not to ask anything else."

"You mean you're too afraid to ask what else I know about you." She smiled at him briefly before settling herself back down on her sleeping mat. "I don't blame you. I'd probably feel the same way if I were you. I think that's one of the reasons people preferred to avoid me in the Paradise, not that it seems to be much different out here."

"I didn't mean…" he began to protest.

"It doesn't matter." She closed her eyes, shutting him out. "I'm used to it."

Plyke looked at her for only a moment longer before continuing his vigilant circles around their campsite. He wondered how many of his secrets she knew about — the abilities he had, the knowledge he'd been given. He doubted she had ever overheard his conversations with Kora, but she may have noticed his abilities. After all, she had noticed Arishen's dreams when no one but Parthak had and *she* was his Partner. She was meant to know everything about him. They were meant to share everything. It was one of the things Partners were known for. They shared every part of their life with each other. If their relationship was strong enough, even death could not part them.

With that thought, the usual guilt began to consume Plyke. By mutual understanding, Partners would choose each other. In their case, Tika had chosen Plyke without the latter ever having thought about it himself. He'd never intended to take a Partner. For as long as he could remember, he'd known about his heritage. It was difficult for him to act as human as everyone else in their Paradise when he knew he wasn't. Tika had given him an easy way out. No one would suspect anyone other than a human to take a Partner. After all, it was a tradition unique to humans.

Kora had encouraged him to accept the offer. Had she known the guilt that would wrack him forever after that decision was made? Had she given any thought to poor Tika – when he died and found himself without a Partner to call on him or, worse, if he survived and found he couldn't contact Plyke? It would make no difference now to tell Tika. The damage had already been done. Partnerships were forged in childhood. He was past the stage where he could revoke his decision and find another Partner.

"You shouldn't think such deep thoughts, young one. It makes you less wary of your surroundings." A raspy, high-pitched voice came from right in front of him. Plyke rubbed his eyes in the hopes of seeing better. The sliver of moonlight that shone down made anything more than a few feet away difficult to see, but he could have sworn he saw a pair of golden eyes staring down at him from the darkness. "I suppose I should tell you that I mean you and your companions no harm. If you wouldn't mind waking Shadow, I would be much obliged."

Dumbstruck, Plyke ran back to where his companions slept. The tiny pit fire they'd lit for the night was only visible when he'd practically reached the campsite. Shuut woke as his heavy footsteps approached. Before he'd reached her, she was standing at the ready, sword gleaming in what little moonlight there was.

"Someone's out there!" he blurted out in a panic. "I couldn't see him properly, but he has gold eyes. He asked for you – well, he asked for Shadow, but I assume he meant you."

"You're sure they were golden eyes?" she asked him, as the others began to wake from the commotion. He simply nodded, not knowing what else to do. Shuut called out into the night, lowering the point of her sword as she curtseyed. "Good eve to you, Farrow of the Elves."

The slender elf walked soundlessly into the light of their small campfire, golden eyes glowing slightly, his large pointed ears partly covered by a mop of thick black hair.

"Well met, Shadow of the Crystal Dragons," he answered as he returned her curtsey with a short bow. "We have been expecting you for many weeks now. Has the journey been difficult?"

Replying with a formality Plyke had not heard before, Shuut answered. "The journey has been a trying one. My new companions do not yet know enough of the Outworld to make good time across the lands."

At this, Plyke was about to protest but Shuut proceeded to formally introduce them, being careful not to give any one person more importance than the others in the golden eyes of the elf.

"I am Farrow, personal messenger of the Elf Queen. Shadow and her companions are welcome in Silvaren." Plyke stared in wonder at the first elf he'd ever seen in their life. He watched in wide-eyed confusion as Farrow held out his arm. Suddenly a bird came swooping out of the night sky to land on his outstretched arm. It made a low repetitive oom-oom-oom noise softly into the elf's ear. The queen's messenger stroked the tuft of feathers above the bird's beak a few times before lifting his arm. In one swift movement, it flew off.

"Tawny frogmouth, my favourite of all birds." He gestured to the disappearing bird. "He will send word that you have been found. They will be expecting us tomorrow."

"But you didn't even speak to him," Tika stammered. "Is the tawny frogmouth something like a fringa?"

"No, young one. They are nothing like that small purple bird." He cocked his head to one side. "I assume you've never met an elf before. We are able to communicate with all intelligent creatures."

"You must forgive them, Farrow," Shuut interrupted. "They have not been taught much of the Outworld. What they have been taught is tainted by Paradisian narrow mindedness."

Farrow simply raised his already arched eyebrows at the excuse. Plyke, annoyed by the elf's easy superiority over them, went to pack his rucksack. He doubted they would be sleeping any more that night. The others followed his lead, Karinya dousing the fire with dirt. The sun had slowly begun to tinge the sky a vibrant orange during their conversation with Farrow. Within the next few hours, there would be daylight. There was no reason to stay when Silvaren was so close at hand.

* * *

Rilla walked with a slight slouch over to her rucksack. She could feel her rib had healed dramatically. It was still a little painful, but the flesh wound had healed completely during the night. Had anyone bothered to try to inspect her injury that morning, they would have discovered the truth about her. She silently thanked her lucky stars for the distraction of an elf.

His appearance disturbed her in an odd way. She felt strangely compelled to take out the silver necklace and tree pendant that she knew were among her belongings. As she packed her sleeping pallet and chisel away, her fingers brushed the dead leaves lining the bottom of her rucksack. For the first time that she could remember, they didn't rustle as she touched them. While the boys were busy with their own rucksacks, Rilla fastened the clasp of the necklace around her throat and hid it away under her shirt. A soft sense of relief swept over her, as though a part of her that was missing had finally returned.

Within minutes, the four of them were standing behind Shuut, ready to follow Farrow to Silvaren. The Partners stood together, Tika barely being able to contain his excitement at finally meeting an elf. As Arishen neared them, Plyke's glare warned him off getting too close to Rilla. She understood his reluctance to let the seer near her, but inwardly sighed at the effect. Arishen had already been shunned by his Partner, now his companions were doing the same thing. It was something Rilla knew would drive them all apart if it continued. She couldn't let that happen. Rhanya had entrusted her with the safety of the boys, *all* of them.

"Arishen, will you give me a hand?" The seer looked over at her in surprise, as did the Partners. "I can't quite get my rucksack on." It was a lie. But he didn't know that and neither did the others. He walked over, head held defiantly high as he passed Tika and Plyke. Rilla held her arms back a bit, forcing a wince for effect, as Arishen pulled the rucksack up onto her shoulders, being careful not to touch her.

Farrow and Shuut had already begun walking by the time the rest of them were ready to set off. Rilla noticed the banwep slow the elf down. There was no doubt in her mind that she was the reason for the change in pace. She had stopped feeling guilty over her deceit. All she was doing was keeping another secret.

The fact that it was *her* secret this time shouldn't make a difference. She'd been keeping everyone else's secrets for as long as she could remember.

Plyke looked back a few times to make sure she was safe with the seer. Her smile seemed to disperse his fear. She knew Arishen had noticed the exchange. It was just a matter of time now before he spoke to her. She only hoped he would do so before they reached Silvaren. It would be difficult to meet the elves with an argument hanging over their heads.

They did not stop for a break at midday, though Shuut frequently looked back to make sure Rilla was keeping up. Everyone knew they would be safer in Silvaren than out here in the open. The fewer rests they took, the faster they would arrive.

"I'm not apologising for getting angry." It was early in the afternoon when Arishen finally broke his silence. "I regret hurting you as badly as I did, but I'm not sorry that I got angry."

Rilla looked straight ahead as she continued walking in a semi-slouch.

"Aren't you going to say something?" he asked, ready to explode once more.

"You're not apologising," she replied calmly. "I heard you. What else is there to say?"

"I stabbed you with a chisel. I broke your ribs. Aren't you going to yell at me?" His response surprised her.

"Would that make you feel better?" She turned slightly to face him, an eyebrow raised.

"What? No! Damn you. I know you can get angry. Why aren't you angry at me? I practically called you a murderer and I stabbed you!"

"I remember, thank you." She paused for a short breath. "I'm not angry with you because I know you didn't really mean what you said. I know you're simply angry with yourself for not having the courage or the means to confront Erton yourself about the murders. You know I was just as helpless as anyone else in that Paradise. I was just the easiest person to lash out at. What good would it do for me to be angry with you?"

Her answer silenced him. She could almost feel him reflecting on her words. If she tried, she was certain that his mind was only a step away. But she had promised herself to never do that without first asking. She didn't want the boys to treat her as they had treated Shuut when she admitted to reading their surface thoughts.

"Why didn't you ever say anything?" he asked her more calmly than she thought he must feel.

"Erton never listened to me. The only time he even spoke to me was to reprimand me. If I had tried to talk to him about it, he would have realised how much I noticed. How long do you think it would have been before he tried to force me to reveal everything I knew about everyone?" She saw his eyes widen in realisation.

"Wasn't there anyone else you could tell?"

"Rhanya suspected as much as I did, possibly even more. There was nothing the two of us could do. An old man and an invisible girl – how much notice do you think people would have taken of us?" Rilla shook her head. She and Rhanya had been up against impossible odds. Even if Erton hadn't managed to get rid of them both, there was little they could have done.

Chapter Twenty-Five – Liessa

It was late in the afternoon when they crested the final, highest hill in a small series. In front of them stretched a vast expanse of water, interrupted only by a nearby island off the coast. The sound of the waves crashing over the rocky shore travelled all the way up to the weary travellers. The Paradisians stood mesmerised by the sight. They'd lived all their lives in a tiny section of the world. Oceans hadn't been a part of their reality.

Rilla was the first to realise Shuut and Farrow were already half way down the hill, heading towards the water. As quickly as she dared, she followed in their footsteps, the boys trailing slowly behind her. By the time the four of them had reached Shuut and Farrow, a thin stretch of sand had begun to appear between the coast and the forested island.

"What now?" Arishen asked.

"Now, we wait," Farrow answered.

"Is there no other way to reach the island?" The seer was incredulous. The elf turned a condescending eye on him.

"If you would prefer to take a boat and ruin it when the low tide catches you, be my guest. As for me, *I* will wait."

Grinding his teeth, Arishen remained silent and waited. They all did.

In the silence, Rilla watched Farrow. He was the first elf she had ever seen, and yet, the sight of him was oddly familiar. She was thankful that no one took much notice of her. If they did, they would have noticed her sense of unease. To comfort herself, she clutched at the silver tree pendant clasped around her neck. It was almost uncomfortably warm to the touch, as though it had been lying in the sun all day rather than hiding beneath her shirt. Rilla was too distracted to wonder why.

As they walked across the narrow stretch of land, Rilla felt her rucksack suddenly lighten. She put a hand back to feel what was happening, only to realise it had lifted slightly off her back. Trying not to alert her companions, she tightened the straps in an effort to stop the bag from leaving her back. Her stomach tensed and she fought to keep herself under control. There had to be a logical reason for her rucksack's behaviour. She would find out as soon as she was alone. For now, she would play the invisible Paradisian girl as she had done most of her life. It was a role she slipped into more comfortably than she cared to admit.

Once they reached the shore, it was a brief walk to the forest. Ancient dazzling trees towered over them, into the high reaches of the sky. The trees were like no other Rilla had ever seen before. Each had a smooth glossy black trunk and branches, though no two were alike in shape. The differences didn't stop there – no two trees had the same colour or shape of leaves and flowers. They were all unique, each just as beautiful as the next.

The power emanating from the black forest was tremendous. Never before in their lives had the Paradisians been able to *feel* magic in the air. Like gentle streams of water, it swirled towards and around them. For Rilla, it was as if the magic wanted to become part of her. The magic had a life of its own, fluttering like a butterfly on a warm summer's night.

It did not take them long to reach the very heart of the Elven stronghold, though night had fallen in the meantime. As Rilla looked closer, she saw some trees were occupied by elves. The elves lived inside the trees, not just in treehouse creations, but actually *inside* the trees. Elves looked out of the window holes to catch a glimpse of the party below them. The Paradisians were overawed by these dwellings, but even this could not have prepared them for the sight of the treetop palace in which the royal family resided.

A multitude of enormous ancient trees stood surrounding a crystal blue lake. The high black branches created level upon level of sealed floors, doming their way to the throne room in the uppermost reaches of the sky. Farrow explained they had grown together for so many years that they had somehow fused to become one — Silva.

With the help of Farrow's tawny frogmouth, word had spread that the company had arrived. The palace workers were hurrying all over the lower levels to prepare a feast for the newcomers. Small flameless lights were lit in various positions around the inner walls of the trunks. It seemed to Rilla that these lights were the very souls of the stars she had watched go by each night. Anyone who had ever seen them had left a piece of themselves in those lights. Rilla looked at her companions, and similar feelings to her own wonderment were plainly shown on their faces. The knowing smiles on the faces of the elves that made way for them showed they had seen this kind of wonder many times before.

The lowest platform of Silva was a common room. Music surrounded them as musician with wooden flutes played unearthly tunes well known to the dancers. Voices rose in song and lifted the spirits of the travellers with the sound. Rilla had never been very fond of the music in their Paradise. She was surprised how much she enjoyed this elven music. It became her whole world and she thought of nothing else. So entranced was she by the notes floating around the room that her companions had to return to collect her and drag her away. Her ears strained to hear the fading notes as they climbed higher and higher through the many levels of the palace. Their guide was taking them to the throne room, where his queen awaited their arrival.

Rilla and the Paradisians were excited and could not control the looks of wonder on their faces. They had met a few different creatures in the Outworld, but none as magnificent as these elves. Elvish features were somewhat different to their own, but their way of life was extraordinary. They could see that at a glance. Apart from everything else, they had a *queen*. They'd heard stories about human kings and queens from ages past, but they were long gone.

As they ascended and the levels became smaller, the travellers grew increasingly quiet. No matter what Shuut and Farrow told them about the royal throne room and the elves they would find within, they were still convinced that it would be an ordeal. Rilla clutched at her pendant even more tightly. It provided her a comfort that she couldn't understand.

The opening to the throne room was little more than an empty spot amidst tree branches with thin, glittering silver vines blocking the way. These vines were pulled aside for them as Farrow led the way to his queen. Shuut ushered them in behind the queen's messenger, for they were too mesmerised to do so themselves.

Under a domed ceiling sparsely lit with same small lights which had lit their path to the magnificent room, the young queen sat on a small wooden throne, which appeared to be woven by black branches of the ancient trees. They stood in awe of the elegant elf. Rilla released her deathly tight grip on her pendant, concentrating instead on the queen. She was rather pretty with her glossy black hair and vibrant silver eyes, but something was wrong. She didn't seem to have that regal air about her which Rilla expected to see in a queen. Nor, on a second glance, did she look at all comfortable with the situation she was in.

"Queen Liessa, may I present to you the long-expected Shadow of the Crystal Dragons." Farrow stepped aside as Shuut moved forward to curtsey in front of the Queen. Rilla shared curious glances with the boys at the introduction. It was the same one that Farrow had used when they first met, but Shuut had never mentioned anything about the crystal dragons to them before.

"It is a pleasure to see you again, Shadow. We have long been anticipating your arrival. Was your journey a difficult one?"

"It has been delayed, your highness, by my unexpected companions," Shuut answered with that same unusual touch of formality she used when greeting Farrow. The Queen nodded in understanding as Farrow stepped forward to resume his introductions.

"May I present to your majesty, Arishen of Paradise." The tall slender boy stepped forward, imitating Farrow's earlier bows, his usual arrogance hidden for the time being.

"Your majesty, I'm pleased to make your acquaintance." Arishen confidently greeted the young queen, before standing aside for Farrow once more. She slightly inclined her head towards the blond boy.

"Tika of Paradise." He stepped aside to make way for the timid black-haired boy. Tika bowed to the young elf.

"Queen Liessa, it's a pleasure to make your acquaintance. Long have I wanted to meet the elves."

"Master Tika, I do hope that we meet your expectations," she answered with good humour.

"Indeed, you exceed my expectations. I am overawed by the sight of you." Blushing at the importance the queen placed upon him, the small boy stepped aside for Farrow.

"Plyke of Paradise." Plyke bowed to the queen without letting his eyes drop from hers.

"It is an honour to meet you, your majesty."

Queen Liessa smiled at this. "My young boy, it is *I* who am honoured to make your acquaintance. It isn't often we meet Paradisians."

Rilla had been looking about the room as Farrow introduced her companions to his queen. Just as the messenger introduced her as Karinya, her gaze came to rest on an older elf. She was standing a little way back from the rest, as though trying to evade observation, but staying close enough to see what was happening. This did not, however, detract from the regal air that surrounded her. Rilla saw that this lady was the only one in the audience who seemed bemused by her introduction.

Shuut coughed to get her attention. Everyone was looking at Rilla now.

"I beg your pardon, Queen Liessa." She turned back towards the throne. "Very pleased to meet you."

"Karinya, you are most welcome in our home."

"Her name isn't Karinya." The lady from the shadows walked gracefully into the light. "It's Rilla and, whether you found her in a Paradise or not, she is of the lintep."

Rilla froze at the sound of her name. It was all she could do to remain standing, her heartbeat pounding in her ears.

"I think you will find you are mistaken, Lady Eléna." Shuut's voice found its way to Rilla's ears. "This girl doesn't have a name as such, so Arishen named her Karinya. And, let me assure you, she is quite human."

The tall elf, her jet-black hair peppered with strands of silver, glided towards the new arrivals. "I think not, Shadow. I would know her without ever having met her before. She is the exact image of the Rilla I once knew. There is no mistaking those deep green eyes and those fiery red curls. As for her lintep heritage, any elf here, within a few more moments, would have been able to tell you she is not human. Her power so emanates from her that Silva has been buzzing with energy since her entrance."

As the elf walked closer to Rilla, a flurry of leaves leapt out of her now floating rucksack, swirling around her in a sea of colour. Rilla stepped back, trying to evade the charmed leaves but they followed her movements.

"Do you believe me now?" Lady Eléna spoke again. "These leaves were a gift to her when she last visited me here. If I'm not mistaken, there is a silver pendant hiding somewhere among your belongings."

Rilla immediately put her hand up to clutch at the hidden tree. As she held it, the leaves slowed their dizzying pace and fell to the floor around her, leaving Rilla staring wildly at Lady Eléna. She was too terrified at the abrupt unveiling of her entire identity to face anyone else.

"Is that really your name? Rilla?"

She closed her eyes and bit her bottom lip as Arishen's angry voice broke the silence. Rilla nodded. The only people she remembered ever saying her name were Erton and Rhanya. Erton had stopped calling her by name over ten years ago. It sounded strange to hear the name in other people's voices.

"Why didn't you just tell us?"

"Who cares about her name?" Plyke interrupted before Arishen had time to speak again. "How long have you known you're a lintep?"

"Long enough," Rilla answered. She didn't like the attention she was receiving.

"I would assume it was around the same time you asked me about your name," Shuut said bitterly, as she put the pieces together. "That was a nice way to find out what you wanted without actually telling me anything."

Rilla lifted her head defiantly. She had no reason to be ashamed of what she had done. For years, she had been keeping secrets for other people. Why should she not have been allowed to protect herself?

"Have you been reading our minds or tried projecting your thoughts on us?" Arishen lashed out again.

"Of course I haven't." Rilla shook her head in frustration. This was exactly the sort of reaction she had been hoping to avoid by simply not telling them.

"Why didn't you just tell us?" Plyke demanded of her.

"Why do you think Rilla should have been so open about herself? It's not as if any of us have been so forthcoming ourselves." Rilla turned to stare at Tika. "The three of us barely said a word to her before we left the Paradise because we weren't allowed to say her name. It's not her fault that we didn't remember it – we never even tried.

"And as for being a lintep, look at the reaction Shuut received when we found out she was a half-caste. Can you imagine how scared she would have been to tell us the truth about herself? How do you think you would have treated her if you'd found out earlier?"

Rilla couldn't help the confused gratitude she felt spilling into her eyes, as, red in the face from practically yelling at the others, Tika moved to stand close to her.

"Well said, Master Tika," Queen Liessa finally spoke with an air of hesitation. Rilla thought that Lady Eléna's words seemed to have created a situation that the Queen was finding difficult to command.

"My Queen," Lady Eléna addressed Liessa in a calm and even voice. "May I take a short walk with this young lady as you get better acquainted with her companions?"

As though having no choice, the Queen nodded her assent to the proposition. Rilla was led away by the elf lady as the others looked on in shock.

When they had exited through the silver vines and walked a way beyond that, Rilla instinctively reached up to clutch at her tree pendant. Her betrayer and saviour simply sat on a nearby branch and beckoned her to join her.

"I apologise for disrupting your introduction, little one."

Rilla sat by the elf in silence. *How does she know my name? Or, for that matter, that I'm a lintep.* Rilla, herself, had not known for so long.

"The disruption isn't quite what I think you should be apologising for. Do you have any idea how difficult it was to keep those two secrets which you managed to reveal in a single sentence?"

"Had I known you were purposely trying to keep it a secret, I would not have revealed your identity so readily. Though why you felt the need to hide these things from your friends is a mystery to me." Her voice was compassionate, but Rilla could also see confusion in her face.

"I have no friends." Rilla thought back to Rhanya. "The only one I ever had was murdered in our Paradise."

"I'm sorry, child." A soft hand covered Rilla's tight fist. She gently pulled her hand away. They sat together in silence until the elf could not contain her curiosity any further. "I think, perhaps, you do not remember me."

"I've never met you before," Rilla mumbled, not looking up.

"Ah, but you have. I gave you that pendant you seem to be clutching for dear life, and the leaves that flew out of your bag."

Rilla closed her eyes, remembering the familiarity of Farrow. "But I've never been here before. How could you have given me those things?"

"Your parents brought you here on their way to your Paradise. Did you not wonder where your pendant and leaves came from? I'm surprised you never asked your parents about them."

Bitter memories threatened to overcome her. Rilla was saved from answering by the approach of an elf child. She inwardly thanked him for the interruption, welcoming any excuse to not think about her parents.

"My Lady Eléna, Queen Liessa requests the presence of her guests at the festivities this evening." The elf child, who was already almost as tall as Rilla herself, bowed and held out his hand signalling Rilla to walk beside him. Their conversation forcibly halted, Eléna smiled amiably and bid Rilla farewell.

Chapter Twenty-Six – The Queen's Guests

As the elf child led Rilla through the maze that was Silva, she reflected on all that had happened since she'd arrived in Silvaren. It was almost too much to take in. Queen Liessa hadn't seemed to mind when the elf with silver-streaked hair had interrupted the introductions, nor when she had requested to speak with Rilla alone.

"Who is Lady Eléna?" It was an obvious question to ask, but one she desperately needed answered.

"You don't know?" His large orange eyes stared at her in shock. She merely shrugged in response.

"Lady Eléna was our queen until only two days ago. She abdicated and her daughter, Queen Liessa, was crowned. It was a most unusual occurrence. In all our long history, it has only happened once before."

"When was that?" Rilla wanted to know as much as she could about Lady Eléna and the other elves. Her sheltered life in Erton's Paradise had left much to be desired in the way of Outworld knowledge.

"Thousands of years ago. Our King, Daelan, had two children who were bitter rivals. It was long thought that when it was time for one of them to inherit the throne, they would fight to the death. King Daelan was devastated by this idea. It is the main reason that there is only ever one heir to the throne. In an effort to avoid the deadly fight, he chose the son he thought most capable to rule after him and abdicated the throne in his favour. He lived only until his chosen son was truly accepted by his people. When he died, the elves were so secure with their king that they refused to aid his brother in rising up against him."

Rilla understood the implications of the boy's story. But why was Lady Eléna afraid people wouldn't trust her daughter? Did she fear Liessa was not worthy to rule them?

"Does Lady Eléna have another child?"

The elf child shook his head with a smile. "No. We do not understand her reasons in abdicating for Queen Liessa, but we do not question her actions."

When they had descended a few levels, the elf child halted in front of another doorway covered with vines, though these were a darker shade of silver than those obscuring the throne room.

"There is a water basin for you to refresh yourself. I will wait here to bring you to the festivities."

"Thank you, ah … I'm sorry, I don't know your name."

"My name is Gioshué, Rilla of the lintep." Rilla looked away from him. At her sudden change in demeanour, the elf child looked confused. "Have I upset you?"

"No, Gioshué," Rilla replied, unclenching her teeth. "You just reminded me of something. I'll be out shortly."

She pushed aside the vines and entered a multi-chambered room. The first chamber was not very large, but led off sideways to another, larger chamber. In this second chamber, Rilla found the water basin. She undressed and bathed hastily with the water, washing away the worst of the dirt. Beside the basin was a bed with a soft towel. She rummaged around in her rucksack to find the least travel worn of her clothes. There wasn't much choice, but she did her best to look presentable for the festivities.

As Gioshué led her down to the common room, Rilla struggled to keep calm. In a room full of elves who knew who she was, there was no chance to become invisible, or to pretend to be Karinya, or even to be just Rilla – not of the lintep. Aside from that, there was the issue of her companions. Arishen and Plyke were annoyed with her for keeping her lintep heritage to herself. But none of the boys knew why she had hidden her name. It was bound to come up at some point. As long as the elves simply called her Rilla of the lintep, the boys might not understand that the title held more significance than they could imagine.

Shuut had to be more than a little angry at the fact that she hadn't mentioned her name was Rilla. The half-caste had been right. Rilla *had* asked about her name, trying to find out all she could without revealing the reason why. Could she really be the person named in the prophecy? What did it even mean? She hadn't bothered asking Shuut before. She had wanted to forget about it and simply try not to reveal her name. In fact, had they not come to Silvaren, she may have succeeded in that venture.

Gioshué, seeming to sense her distress, took her to the common room through a small side entrance and led her to the quietest area he could find. His duty done, he bid her farewell and ran to find his friends.

Rilla sat well apart from everyone, watching as elves glanced her way before approaching and introducing themselves to the girl of the prophecy. Not wanting to appear rude, she spoke to them all with a frozen smile, repeating herself again and again when asked questions of her powers.

"I only realised a few weeks ago that I was lintep. I've barely had time to experiment and I have no one to teach me." They all nodded knowingly, assuring her that guidance was to be found in Illaria. Not wanting to disappoint them further, she neglected to point out the fact that she had no idea exactly how to reach the lintep stronghold.

After a while, Tika, in too much of a gay mood to ruin the evening, ran up to Rilla and pulled her arm until she had no choice but to follow him. Leaving his Partner to one side, Tika insisted they imitate the elven dancers until they collapsed in a laughing, tangled heap on the floor. Rilla found herself having so much fun, she barely noticed Arishen's flushed face, which he made no effort to hide while watching the two of them. They danced together for what felt like hours.

She loved the music. It entered her mind, danced through her thoughts, and took her to a world where she was safe. The music became a part of her. Any idle moment she had, Rilla spent it watching the musicians intensely. Their eyes glowed as they played their instruments, some more brightly than others. A dull blue or pale red would suddenly glimmer, evoking a stronger feeling through the music.

Rilla's gaze was often drawn to an elf whose eyes shone like the silver lining of a cloud. The elf, who looked no older than the Paradisian boys, played one of the wooden flutes that sounded so graceful and alive.

He took particular interest in her attention on him. When she and Tika were taking a break from dancing, the elf walked over to talk to her. She rolled her eyes and lifted her chin as he approached, ready to answer the same questions she'd been asked all night.

"My name is Eliséo."

"Rilla," she replied uncertainly.

"Rilla, would you care to dance with me?" He held out an open hand to her. She took it gingerly, following Eliséo to the middle of the room where other elves were still dancing. He showed her some of the more traditional elven dances, politely correcting her movements. Every moment, she expected him to ask her about her powers or her lack of training. Every moment, she was more and more surprised that he only asked if she was enjoying the dancing.

Eliséo spent the better part of the evening with her, aside from the times he played with the musicians. Rilla would have been content to listen to the ethereal music and dance the rest of her life, but the night's festivities soon came to an end. Gioshué came to find her when the music stopped and showed her back to her room. She and her companions all had separate rooms, though all on the same level of Silva. Aside from the isolation hut, this was the first time Rilla had ever spent the night in a room by herself.

She walked in half asleep, and went straight to the room with the basin. Against a wall of the room was a window, seemingly carved from the trunk of the tree. Exhausted, she stumbled over to the bed and threw herself onto it. She leaped off almost immediately as she touched the leaves covering the soft blankets. Those were *her* leaves. The leaves she'd had in her rucksack as far back as she could remember. The leaves that had come back to life as she walked through Silvaren. The leaves that had betrayed her as being Rilla. How had they found their way to her room? She had left them in the throne room when she'd hurriedly left with Lady Eléna.

Rilla stood staring at them for a few moments. What was she going to do with them? She could think of nothing better than placing them back in her rucksack, where they had stayed for most of her life. The leaves rustled, almost discontentedly, as she swept them unceremoniously into her rucksack. She tied the laces as tightly as she could and placed her shoes on top of the bulky bag. Too tired to think any further, she again collapsed on her bed, this time undisturbed by anything.

Chapter Twenty-Seven – Elessa

The next morning, Tika awoke with a smile on his face. He had just spent the night in Silvaren – home of the elves. It was like a dream come true. Only a few weeks after leaving his Paradise behind, he had come to the most beautiful place in the Outworld. There was little doubt in his mind that no other place could possibly compare with this treetop stronghold. He lay happily in his bed for a few minutes before opening his eyes. He didn't want the happiness to leave him.

An insistent knocking in the outer room soon brought him back to reality. It was Plyke's hand, rapping on Silva's trunk. They had barely spoken since the episode in the throne room. Tika was aghast at Plyke and Arishen's anger at Rilla. She had saved both their lives, yet they treated her so badly. Even when Arishen had stabbed her, she'd made no complaint. In fact, when she handed him the chisel, it had seemed as though she expected him to do that. He shook his head to clear his thoughts, but to no avail.

"Hold your horses."

Plyke ceased his knocking only long enough for Tika to splash some water on his face and then began again.

"Just give me a minute!" He pulled on a fresh shirt while walking out to greet his Partner.

"What took you so long?" Plyke stood, impatiently tapping his foot.

"Well, aren't we in a fine mood today?" Tika goaded him. "What do you want?"

"The queen has invited us to join her for breakfast. Your room was on the way. Hurry up."

"You go ahead without me. I'll be there soon." Plyke raised a questioning eyebrow but said nothing as he walked away.

Tika waited until his Partner was out of hearing before leaving his room. His guide, Tameo, was standing just past the vines, waiting for him.

"Good morning, Tameo."

"Good morning, Master Tika," the young elf greeted him with a nod. "Are you ready to join the others for breakfast?"

"Tameo, just call me Tika. Do you know the way to Karinya ... ah, Rilla's room?"

"Certainly Tika. It's on the way to the dining hall."

* * *

Rilla woke and instantly remembered the entire night before. Rhanya had been the only one to call her Rilla, and only ever when there was no one around to hear him. It had been their little secret. Since last night, her name held more meaning. It wasn't simply a shared moment between friends anymore. It wasn't even just a name people called her. It was a title – a supposition of who she was. The only person who hadn't instantly treated her as Rilla of the lintep was Eliséo. She had simply been Rilla to him. She smiled at the memory of dancing freely, without any thought of the responsibility that had been imposed on her by a name.

"Rilla, are you in there?" A familiar voice called from the other side of the vines. She looked at the rucksack, which now held the leaves, and left it behind as she walked out. The sight of Tika reminded her of Plyke and Arishen's reactions to her name in the throne room. She retreated within herself, almost involuntarily.

"Are you all right?" he asked as she emerged.

"Sorry, I was in a different world," Rilla mumbled apologetically, shaking her head. "Was there something you wanted?" A wave of sadness passed over her.

"Is everything alright? You look ..." he paused uncertainly, "... lost."

"I'm fine, Tika." Rilla quickly replied with a reassuring smile. "What was it you wanted?"

Lost, himself, for a moment, Tika hesitated. "We all ... uh ... breakfast. The queen has invited us to join her for breakfast." He paused again and Rilla could tell he was trying to understand what the problem was. "Are you coming?"

"Yes – yes, I'm coming." She looked beyond the human boy. "Good morning, Gioshué."

"Good morning, Rilla of the lintep." He and the elf beside him both inclined their heads to her. She ground her teeth through a forced smile. If only they understood how much she hated that title.

The only ones in the dining hall when they arrived were Plyke and the newly crowned queen. Rilla ignored Tika's Partner and walked hesitantly up to the queen. "Queen Liessa." She curtsied before her. "I'm truly sorry about last night. I didn't mean to disrupt our introduction."

"Don't think on it, Rilla of the lintep," replied the young queen, humility showing through her grey eyes. "My mother has a way of focusing everyone's attention where she wishes it to be. Do you not agree, Shadow?"

Rilla turned to find Shuut and Lady Eléna behind her. There was a confirming nod for the queen, but not even a glance towards Rilla. She felt a crushing weight on her chest as she sat down the far end of the table. Everyone else placed themselves around the table, Arishen and Shuut sitting as far away from her as possible.

It began as a quiet breakfast, with cautious pleasantries exchanged. The Paradisians, still in awe of the Royal family, remained silent unless asked a direct question. Queen Liessa, Shuut and Lady Eléna spoke guardedly amongst themselves. Rilla could see they had business to attend to, but would rather do it in private than in front of the Paradisians.

When they had all eaten their fill, the queen advised them that they were free to explore Silvaren while she and her mother caught up with Shadow. As she was explaining this to them Rilla noticed, with her first genuine smile of the morning, Eliséo and Farrow entering the dining hall.

The golden-eyed messenger introduced the musician. "My Queen, I bring before you, Eliséo, Ambassador of the Elves."

At his title, Rilla started in surprise. *Ambassador? He didn't mention that last night. Why didn't he tell me?*

"Your Majesty." The ambassador bowed to the queen. "With your permission, I would like to show your guests the wonders of Silvaren." Liessa nodded her head in dismissive approval and glided away with Shuut and the former queen. Farrow followed them out at a short distance.

Rilla stood back a few paces as Arishen introduced himself and the rest of them to Eliséo. When he turned to her, Rilla spoke in a cold voice. "We've met." The boys were taken aback by her tone, but said nothing.

"Indeed, we have," replied Eliséo softly, inclining his head courteously towards her, before turning to the boys. "Shall we begin our tour?" The others nodded their heads enthusiastically. "I believe you have already been through Silva, this most ancient of our trees, housing the royal family. We will then move along to the rest of Silvaren. There is much more to see."

As they made their way down through the many levels of Silva, Eliséo pointed out small details which they may have missed the previous evening. Rilla followed at a distance the entire way down. Tika quickly dropped back to her side.

"What's wrong?" he asked in undisguised confusion. "Why were you so cold to him?"

"*When* we met, he didn't tell me he was the Ambassador of the Elves. That title was conveniently omitted from our conversation."

"Why is that a problem, Rilla?" Tika queried, insistently. "What difference does it make that he is an ambassador?"

"You wouldn't understand, Tika." She shook her head in frustration. "My name means something to these Elves. He was probably sent to befriend me last night so that he could report on me later."

"Don't you think you might be overreacting a little?" He cocked an eyebrow.

"Just forget it," sighed Rilla. "Let's just get on with this tour." She hurriedly caught up to the others in an attempt to disguise her anger with their guide.

When they reached the root system of Silva, the real tour began. Eliséo took them back to the thin strip of sand they had crossed the night before, which was now covered over with water. He then led them around the coast of the island to parts of the forest they'd missed the day before, pointing out all the trees housing the elves. There was not a tree that looked under a hundred years old. He explained that the trees in Silvaren took their shape from the dreams and energy of the elves who lived in them. Each tree was alive, with its own magic, and bound to the elf residing in it.

Silva, he explained, was slightly different. She had been shaped through the minds of every royal elf in Queen Liessa's ancestry. Where most trees in Silvaren had only a single elf bound to them, Silva often had an entire family bound to her. Unlike other trees, those in Silvaren had a prolonged lifespan because of the magic in them.

The Paradisians stood in awe of the trees. Now they understood why it seemed as though they were surrounded by magic as they had entered the forest the previous evening. Rilla looked around at the forest, drinking in the sight and letting her mind flow through the magic encircling her. *This feels familiar*, she thought.

"It's magnificent," Tika exclaimed. "You mean the lives of the trees are intertwined with those of the elves?" Eliséo nodded. "Does that mean that the trees die if one of the elves it houses dies? Or the other way around?"

"For the tree to die, it is true that the elf, or in Silva's case elves, must be dead. As for the other way around, it is technically possible for a tree to die, killing the elf with it, but that would take an even greater amount of magic than the queen has. No mere axe could cleave its way through these trunks," explained Eliséo.

While he was speaking, the elf affectionately caressed the smooth black trunk of a nearby tree, his eyes shining brightly as he did so. At his attention, the tree suddenly grew slate buds on its branches. The boys laughed in delight. Even Rilla smiled at the beauty of it. Eliséo noticed this and beckoned her forward.

"Touch the tree," he instructed her.

"What?" she replied in surprise. "Why?"

Eliséo smiled at her. "Because if she likes you, she may show you." He moved aside to make room for her. "Just rest your hand on her trunk and introduce yourself with your mind."

Rilla was caught with indecision. She didn't know whether to trust the ambassador or not and she certainly didn't want the boys to look on while she attempted to introduce herself to a tree.

Plyke, unknowingly, saved her from the awkward situation by asking if they were all allowed to touch a tree. Eliséo nodded his head and pointed the boys to a group of nearby trees, leaving Rilla next to the tree he had chosen for her. She looked at him suspiciously, then hesitantly put her hand out and gently touched the smooth trunk with her fingertips. Her eyes went wide as a voice filled her mind.

Who are you to touch me?

I am Rilla of the lintep, she answered automatically. That was the way the elves had been introducing her to one another, it only made sense that she should introduce herself that way to the tree.

Let me into your mind. It wasn't a request. Instantly, Rilla felt the life force of the tree swelling through her, judging her, living through her memories. Rilla could only see what the tree was seeing, she no longer saw herself in Silvaren with her companions, but back in the Paradise with Rhanya and in the Outworld with Ratchin and the fringa. She closed her eyes to steady herself.

When the tree had seen all it wanted, its magic retreated from Rilla, leaving her slightly weaker than before. She took her hand away from the tree and glared accusingly at Eliséo, only to find that both he and the boys were staring at the tree behind her. She lifted her gaze to where the others were focused. Just above where her fingers had touched the trunk, there was an extra branch as smooth as the rest of the tree, but the black bark was tinged with red. Buds as fiery red as her hair and leaves the deep green of her eyes decorated the branch. The sight of it made her feel faint. There was no mistaking she that was responsible.

"What happened with your trees?" She turned back to the boys, hoping they'd had similar experiences. Eliséo stood back, looking thoughtfully at the tree before him, as the boys showed Rilla their trees. At the most, they could only point out a leaf or two that hadn't been there before.

When they were done, the elf resumed their tour. He showed them the different birds that lived in the trees, the other small creatures that made their homes in the forest and the rivulets and tiny lakes dotted throughout Silvaren.

Along the way, various elves begged them to enter their homes, offering them unfamiliar food and drink. By the end of the afternoon, the Paradisians were happily weary and quite full. They met Shuut on the return to their rooms and spent the evening discussing their day with her.

Rilla slipped out of Shuut's room, unnoticed by the others. She hadn't spoken much since their return. With only her companions around her, she found it easier to fade into the background and slip away from their attention. Rilla needed to be alone, to try to make sense of what had happened with *that* tree. Every time she closed her eyes, no matter how briefly, the image of the tree with its new branch, buds and leaves, was in her mind.

She didn't take note of where she was walking so was surprised to find herself at the small lake between the roots of Silva. Happy to be secluded from everyone else, she sat by the edge, watching the ripples her feet created in the water. Lying back, she closed her eyes knowing what she would see.

She saw how the tree was before she touched it – a strong old tree with sturdy black branches. The leaves were pale silver with intricate patterns upon them. Slowly, the image changed to show the dark slate buds that had appeared as Eliséo caressed its trunk.

Rilla considered this. When *she* spoke with the tree, an entire branch, complete with buds and leaves, had appeared. She tried making sense of the significance of this when she heard a cough beside her. In an instant, she opened her eyes to find the newly arrived elf and recognised her as the grey-eyed Eléna.

"Your Majesty!" Rilla cried in astonishment, quickly sitting up.

"I'm not 'your Majesty' any longer, Rilla." The former queen smiled.

"My lady Eléna." Rilla addressed her, slightly less formally. "Uh, may I help you at all?"

It was, by now, well into the evening. All the other elves must have already been asleep by that time as, she was certain, her companions were.

"I wanted to talk to you about what happened today," said the regal lady.

"So, the spy has reported back to you, has he?" Rilla asked with a bitter edge to her voice. Eléna smiled and nodded, knowingly, to herself.

"Now I understand. Eliséo was wondering why you were so angry when he was introduced as the ambassador." Rilla looked up at her curiously. "He isn't *that* kind of elf, child. Don't you think it would be a bit obvious to make a spy of an ambassador?"

"Then, he wasn't reporting back to you?" Rilla blushed hotly.

Eléna shook her head. "He came to ask my opinion on a certain incident in which you were involved. It confused him and he didn't know who else to ask such a delicate question."

"Oh," Rilla replied softly. "I thought…"

"I understand, child, but enough of that. Tell me what happened with the tree this morning." Eléna sat by Rilla's side, watching her intently.

Unsettled to find out just how wrong she had been about Eliséo, Rilla recounted her encounter with the tree. Eléna asked a few questions, to confirm that Eliséo had asked *her* specifically to introduce herself to *that* tree in particular.

"Why is that important?" asked Rilla in confusion.

"That is not something I can tell you, child." Rilla sagged at the denial of knowledge. "That is not something *I* can tell you," the elf repeated, lifting Rilla's chin with her delicately strong fingers. "Only Eliséo can."

"Do you know where I can find him?" Rilla asked eagerly.

"Stay here. I will make certain he finds you."

Eléna's eyes clouded over momentarily and she walked away. Rilla watched until she was out of sight before laying down and closing her eyes. As she waited for Eliséo, the tree forced itself to the forefront of her thoughts. She looked at the branch she had created, noticing again that the colour of the leaves wasn't merely similar to her eyes, it perfectly matched them, down to the different hues. Next, she focused on the buds – they were as fiery and twisted as her own red curls. She kept concentrating on the differences between her buds and the small slate ones until she was interrupted again by a cough behind her.

"Good evening, Rilla, Lady Eléna told me that I might find you here." The young elf waited for her reply before moving any closer.

"Eliséo, I have something to ask you." Rilla sat up, her feet still moving slowly through the water. Eliséo sat on a nearby stone and waited for her to continue.

"I apologise for ... well, for being angry with you this morning," she began agitatedly. "I should not have expected you to tell me that you were the Ambassador of the Elves."

The tall elf took a moment to answer. "In truth, Rilla, I had no idea why that angered you until Lady Eléna explained you thought I was a spy." He smiled mischievously. "That would have been a fun occupation, but not one that I'd say suited me. Out of curiosity though, what made you think I was a spy?"

"Why else wouldn't you tell me who you were?" asked Rilla.

"Why didn't you tell me who *you* were then?" replied Eliséo.

Rilla's eyes widened. "You mean, you didn't know?"

"I only knew who you were because I was in the throne room, but you didn't know that. You wouldn't have noticed me there with the havoc you wreaked." A cheeky gleam danced in his slate eyes.

Rilla grimaced. "You saw that, did you?"

"Even if I hadn't seen it for myself, news of it spread to every elf in Silvaren by the end of the evening. I understand you had tried to keep your identity a secret from your companions. It was wrong of Lady Eléna to expose you so completely."

Rilla turned from him with a silent sigh, watching the ripples around her feet as she moved them slowly through the water.

"Why did you ask to see me?" Eliséo swiftly switched topics.

"It doesn't matter," replied Rilla in a quiet voice, shaking her head.

"Of course it matters, Rilla. Lady Eléna sent me down here immediately to talk to you. What was it?"

"Nothing really, I just asked her why she found it an important detail that you asked me, in particular, to introduce myself to that tree out of all the trees in Silvaren. She said she couldn't tell me, but you could." She finally found the courage to look into the eyes that were now a dull grey compared to the bright silver she had first seen the previous night.

"Oh." Eliséo grew quiet. "That *is* something she wouldn't be able to tell you."

"Why is that?" Rilla asked curiously.

"It isn't her tree."

"Well, whose tree is it then?"

Eliséo looked at her closely. "Did you notice the colour of the leaves and buds that you created?" She nodded.

"They were the colour of my hair and eyes."

"What about the branch?"

"It was black, with a bit of red streaked through it."

"And did you notice the colour of the leaves and buds that were there before?"

"They were bright silver and a duller, slate colour." She looked closely at the elf's eyes and gasped in realisation. "It was *your* tree?!"

"Yes," he replied, turning his eyes away from hers. "It was my tree."

"What about the trees that the others touched?" she asked, anxiously, "Were they yours as well?"

"In a way," he replied, staring out over the lake. "However, that is only because no one resides in those trees and they surround mine. They belong as much to me as to the other elves whose trees surround them. Almost anyone could create a leaf or bud on *those* trees. But leaves and buds are fleeting – eventually they will die and not be a part of the tree anymore." He turned to look directly into Rilla's eyes. "The one *you* touched is the tree I reside in, Elessa. She has shaped herself completely through my dreams and thoughts. You should not have been able to make such an impression on her. At the most, a few leaves or buds like the others. But an entire branch, complete with hundreds of leaves and dozens of buds ..."

Rilla watch the elf intently as he explained this all to her. She began to understand the significance of it all. The change she had made to the tree had not been a simple leaf or bud that would die and fall off at some point. She had somehow created an entire branch – a branch which would not die unless the tree itself died.

"I'm sorry, Eliséo," she tried to apologise. "I didn't mean to change Elessa. I didn't even know what happened until I saw everyone looking up at her."

Eliséo looked at her sharply. "You mean to say you didn't ask her to grow a branch for you? Or have an image in your mind of what you wanted to create?"

Puzzled, Rilla simply shook her head.

"Then what did you say to my tree to make her react like that?"

"She asked me who I was, then searched through my mind. I didn't have time to think of anything but what she was making me recall from my past. Then she let me go and, well, you saw the rest." Rilla shrugged helplessly.

"Rilla, I regret I must bid you farewell." Eliséo announced abruptly.

"Wait," she called as he rose to go. "You didn't tell me why you asked me to touch your tree."

His cheeks flushed as he shook his head. "You were angry with me. I didn't know why. I wanted to show you that you could trust me and to see if I could trust you."

"I know now that *I* can trust you," she said. "What did *you* find out?"

He pursed his lips. "I don't know, Rilla. Nothing like this has ever happened before. I have to talk to Elessa. Perhaps she will be able to explain it to me."

"Was it so very wrong that I created a branch?" Rilla asked him sadly. It seemed as though anything she tried to do right always turned itself around on her.

"You don't understand what this means, Rilla," Eliséo looked at her with haunted eyes. "You are now connected to my tree forever."

"Do you wish you hadn't asked me to touch her now?" she asked, not quite understanding what he meant.

"I need to find out what happened. This could affect you more than you realise."

"Can I come with you, then? To see what she says?" Rilla suddenly realised she didn't want to be left alone.

Eliséo hesitated. "It's a long walk, Rilla. You should go to sleep. We'll talk tomorrow. Speak of this to no one. It could have more consequences than we can fathom."

Rilla stayed at the lake a little while longer before returning to her room. Her way was lit by the strange fireless lights inside Silva's trunk. By the time she reached her room, she was exhausted. She barely had the energy left to take off her shoes before snuggling under the warm blankets. She fell into a deep sleep and in her sleep, she dreamed.

Elessa was in her dream. Rilla watched as Eliséo approached her and ascended to his bed. He placed his hand lovingly on the inside of Elessa's trunk. The tree's thoughts were clear to Rilla. *I understood the importance you place on being accepted by this lintep. I glimpsed Rilla's past and saw she would need my strength to succeed. It was my decision to bind the girl to myself.*

Rilla sensed Eliséo's thoughts through Elessa. *You should have asked me before doing that. It could be dangerous to have a lintep bound to an elf's tree. Did that thought even cross your mind?*

Elessa answered her elf. *It was* my *choice to bind her to me. You do not control me, Eliséo, or have you forgotten that? We live together, you and I, making separate choices that affect us both. If you did not want me to bind her, you should not have given me the chance by asking her to touch me. It was not dangerous to bind her just because she is a lintep. The dangers may lie elsewhere.*

Eliséo's final thought was his most intent one. *What has it done to her?*

I'm not exactly certain how much it will affect her. I only grew her a branch, Elessa answered him carefully.

Eliséo drew his hand away from his tree at that point. Rilla could sense his thoughts no more, but Elessa spoke to her still. *It was important for you to hear that, child. Your life has changed. You will no longer age the same as other lintep. You will age as an elf. Take your thoughts away from me now and rest well.*

Chapter Twenty-Eight – Repercussions

Dawn approached as Eliséo awoke. He lay in bed listening to the waves breaking on the rocky shore. It was going to be an interesting day. He had lived through many interesting times, but he had never encountered this situation before. No tree from Silvaren had ever bound itself to anyone other than an elf, not even a lintep, as revered as they were.

It becomes us, Eliséo, Elessa spoke gently in his mind. *We never did follow the trends of the elves. After all, I was already an old tree when you came to Silvaren. By all rights, you should have chosen a much younger tree than I to bond with.*

He smiled despite himself. Elessa was right. He had never been the most conventional of elves. Perhaps that was one of the reasons they had made him the ambassador – he understood other races' view of the elves a little better for being an outsider in his own home.

You have a guest, Elessa alerted him while he freshened himself with the wash basin in his room. At the base of his tree, Farrow was waiting patiently for him. He walked down the few levels to the forest floor to greet him.

"Your Queen's mother would like a word with you," he told Eliséo in a raspy, high-pitched voice when the younger elf descended.

"I was just on my way to find her," Eliséo replied.

"She knew you were," he answered, knowingly. "Which is why she sent me to tell you she is at the eastern edge of Silvaren."

Eliséo thanked Farrow and hastened to his destination. The eastern edge of Silvaren was a code of sorts between the former queen and her chosen ambassador. It referred to a certain cave, part way down a cliff face. No one other than Eléna, Farrow and Eliséo knew of its existence – even Liessa had not been told.

He only ever met Lady Eléna here when complete secrecy was required. As he neared the cave, he saw the former queen looking out towards the amber ocean. The silver strands, peppered through her black hair, were the only sign that she was ageing. Her face looked just as young as her daughter's, though less innocent by far.

"My lady Eléna," he bowed low in greeting, "you wanted to see me?"

"No, Eliséo," she replied, lifting his chin up to look into his eyes. "I believe it was you who wished to seek my counsel."

"Exactly how far away can you be and still read thoughts?" he asked curiously. It was something that he had never quite been able to figure out himself. She smiled, evasively, as she always did.

"Tell me exactly what happened with Rilla and Elessa. All I got last night was a lintep's view – a child's at that. She has lived a sheltered life and knows less of the Outworld than you can possibly imagine."

Eliséo didn't hold back anything. He described rexpectly what had happened the previous day, watching Eléna's face grow more sombre with each detail. "Elessa told me that Rilla is now part of her at least as long as that branch survives. Though, I confess, I don't know the extent of the situation."

"That's all she told you?" the Queen's mother asked with a hint of anger. Eliséo nodded, confused by her tone. "When did you talk to her about it?"

"Last night, after I left Rilla," he replied. "The girl told me she didn't ask Elessa to grow her even a single bud, it was all my tree's doing."

"I see," she replied, her cheeks flushed angrily. "When you spoke with Elessa last night, did everything seem normal to you?"

"In comparison with her actions that morning it was normal," he replied, still not understanding Eléna's sudden change in demeanour.

"That simply means the young lintep doesn't understand the full extent of the powers Elessa has bestowed upon her."

"What do you mean?" Eliséo cocked his head to one side, "What powers other than prolonged life can she have been given?"

"I believe that is something you will soon discover."

Eliséo heard footsteps and turned to see Rilla following Farrow down the winding cliff path. He cursed under his breath. Bringing an outsider to their secret place was unheard of. Upon delivering the young lintep to his former queen, Farrow departed the small gathering with a curt nod.

"Good morning, my lady Eléna," Rilla greeted the Queen's mother in her smooth strong voice. "Good morning, Eliséo."

"Did you sleep well, little one?" Eléna asked without returning the greeting.

"Actually, I had an odd dream," Rilla seemed reluctant to go on. Eliséo hid his confusion at the question.

"What did you dream of?" Eléna persisted.

"I dreamt of Elessa. She was speaking with Eliséo about me." Her eyes remained firmly averted from Eliséo. If she had seen the fury he could feel rising in them, she would have fled in fear. Eléna placed a hand on his shoulder, her touch calming him as it always did.

The queen's mother spoke gently. "That wasn't exactly a dream you had. You are now bound to Elessa in more ways than you can fathom. There will be many repercussions of her actions, the least of which is the prolonging of your life.

"You will be able to hear her thoughts and the thoughts of anyone connected to her at the time. She will be able to lend you strength when you need it and, similarly, may ask strength from you if she is ever in need. In time, you may learn to contact her yourself, when you are not sleeping."

Rilla turned her deep green eyes towards Eliséo. "I'm sorry," she half whispered. "I didn't know it was real. I thought it was just a dream. I won't listen in again, I promise."

"You won't have a choice," Eléna told her, matter of factly. "If Elessa wants you to be a part of the conversation, you will be."

"Is there no way we can reverse this, my lady?" Eliséo asked, barely masking his fury. "Perhaps Elessa does not understand the repercussions of her actions."

Eléna smiled sadly at him. "The trees are wise, dear boy. They know what they do and will not have their will bent by ours. You've had Elessa all to yourself for many years. It is now time for you to learn to share her." Beyond the words she said out loud, Eliséo heard the thoughts she projected into his mind. *You are hurting her, my boy. You're making the girl think she is to blame. Put your anger with Elessa aside and explain things to her.* Aloud, she continued to speak. "I must return to Silva now. The Queen has requested that you and your companions meet her at the lake below Silva. I wish to see what she has planned for you. Take your time here. Eliséo will lead you back there himself."

Eléna looked at him meaningfully, then took her leave. Rilla watched the queen's mother disappear between the trees. Her anguish at being left alone with Eliséo was clear to his mind. Eléna had been right. Focusing on Elessa, he found the link to Rilla's mind. Without any intention, the frightened girl was shielding her thoughts, but her fears were clear to Eliséo.

"Rilla." She turned at the sound of her name. "I'm sorry for my reaction. It is not you with whom I am angry."

"But now you wish you hadn't asked me to touch your tree," she replied dejectedly, staring past him at the calm ocean beyond.

"It's not as simple as that," he tried to explain. "It isn't just for myself that I'm angry with Elessa – it's for you. She has changed your life."

"I know. Last night she told me I would no longer age as a lintep, but as an elf." Her answer came monotonously, belying the turmoil Eliséo could feel within her.

"Don't you care that your life has changed so much without having a say in the matter?" He asked her incredulously. *She mustn't understand what it means to age as an elf.*

"Eliséo, my entire life changed the day I left the Paradise. It was my choice to do that, so whatever follows can only happen because I took that first step. What's the point in getting angry over the gifts which Elessa has given me?" She hesitated momentarily. "I'm more concerned at the effect her actions have had on you."

These last words surprised Eliséo. He had misread her. That rarely happened to him.

"Elessa and I have grown together. I have always known that she is unpredictable. In time, I'm certain I will accept what she has done but, for now, I will simply warn you not to mention this to anyone. Your friends, of course, saw that you grew a branch but they don't know what that means and, more importantly, they don't know it was my tree. Even if they did know that, they could not possibly understand the extent to which this has affected you. You would be wise not to tell them. It may prove dangerous in the future. People can try to harm Elessa and I through you."

"I understand, Eliséo," she replied, quietly. "I've been keeping secrets from people my entire life. What's one more?"

The elf nodded, secure in the knowledge that she wouldn't betray them. "We should follow Lady Eléna's lead. The less suspicious we make the others, the better."

As they walked back to Silva, Eliséo withdrew himself from his connection with Rilla through Elessa. She didn't know enough about what was happening to keep her feelings and thoughts private from him.

* * *

"If you will all follow me." Tika looked up to see Farrow standing in the doorway. "The queen has requested that you join her at the lake below Silva."

As they rose from their seats, Tika hesitantly addressed the Queen's messenger. "Do you know where Rilla is? I passed her room on the way here and she wasn't there."

"Lady Eléna summoned her. She will join you on the forest floor." He replied aloofly. Shuut had explained to them that Farrow had been extremely loyal to Queen Eléna. There was no reason to assume that he had stopped being loyal to her just because she'd abdicated in favour of her daughter.

As they followed the golden-eyed elf down the many levels of Silva, Plyke held Tika back behind the others. "Don't tell me *you've* developed a fascination with that girl as well."

"What?" Tika's eyebrows shot up indignantly.

"It was bad enough Arishen obsessing over her when we didn't know anything about her. At least *he* has come to his senses now."

"So you think that just because we've discovered she's a lintep, we shouldn't talk to her anymore? That's a convenient excuse for you, isn't it? You've never been comfortable around her. Leaving the Paradise forced you to actually interact with her when you didn't want to. Now, at the first opportunity, you shun her again." He'd gone red in the face again. Plyke had never been so unreasonable in his entire life as in the last few days.

"Have you forgotten that she saved our lives? Do you think skills like that come without a cost? Can you possibly imagine what she's going through right now? And you and Arishen just seem to want to punish her all the more for it. It's all I can do to try to keep the peace between us."

"You seem to be getting along so well with her. Perhaps you should have become *her* Partner." Tika glared at his Partner angrily. Plyke hadn't been joking. The thought of his Partner so easily dismissing their bond was terrifying to him. He had no idea how to deal with it, so he simply walked faster to catch up with the others once more.

They found Queen Liessa, Lady Eléna, Eliséo and Rilla waiting for them under one of Silva's lower branches. As Tika and his companions reached the waiting party, the Queen rose gracefully to speak with them.

"I am certain you have all become aware of the dangers that await you in the Outworld. Yet, there are even more dangers to come. You have come to me as guests, with open hearts. I feel it is within my duty to arm you as best I can for your journey. Please follow me."

"What does she mean, our 'journey'?" Plyke whispered to Arishen. "I thought Shuut was going to leave us here."

"Doesn't sound like they're keen on keeping us either," the seer replied, almost sullenly. Neither of them noticed Lady Eléna's sideways glance towards them. Tika did, but kept his silence.

* * *

From the shadows of his gnarled tree, Ensil watched as *Queen* Liessa led her guests through the aboveground root system of Silva. The stumbling Paradisians cursed their way towards him. He wondered how much he could possibly teach them in the short time they were to stay.

"Queen Liessa." He inclined his head, but did not bow to her.

"Ensil, is everything prepared?" she asked, pointedly ignoring his lack of respect.

"Everything is as you requested, my Queen." The words escaped his mouth a little stiffly. He was firm friends with the former Queen Eléna and was not pleased with her recent decision to crown her daughter.

The new Queen turned to face her guests. "At my request, Ensil has agreed to find a suitable weapon for each of you to arm yourselves with in the Outworld. In

133

addition to this, he will give you guidance on how to use them well. If you will now excuse me, I have other matters to attend to."

She departed, leaving the Paradisians eager to receive their gifts. Ensil noticed that Eléna and Eliséo remained with the honoured guests so, smiling, he motioned for them to be seated on a nearby rock. He then turned first to the banwep.

"Shadow, it is the queen's wish that, if you so desire, you may leave your own sword here and replace it with one of your choosing."

She was already shaking her head before he had finished the offer. "I thank the Queen for her offer, Master Ensil, but my sword and I have been through many fights together. I would no sooner discard it for another than I would cut off my own hand."

Her answer did not surprise him – he had expected her refusal, though his Queen had not agreed with him on the matter. She had so much still to learn.

Ensil turned his attention to the Paradisians. "With your permission, I would like to examine each of you to see which weapon will suit you best." His young audience had no idea exactly how he intended to examine them, but they all agreed to it.

* * *

Arishen stepped forward first in his eagerness to be armed. He felt something like a light breeze pass through his body. Shivering, he rubbed his arms to distract himself from the strange feeling. The knobbly old elf looked at him for a moment. His eyes had changed from almost translucent to a deep blue. He turned to the assortment of weapons behind him and chose two long daggers. Arishen payed close attention as the elf tied their sheaths to the belt around his waist and slipped the blades in. He couldn't help but notice how similar they were to the chisel he had stabbed Rilla with. Had the elf sensed this somehow and so chosen the daggers to torment him?

* * *

Tika stepped forward in happy anticipation of the weapon to be given to him. He felt a light breeze pass through his body and shivered as it left. Ensil immediately turned to his weapons and rummaged around until he'd found what he was looking for. Tika was delighted when the ancient elf returned with not one, but two weapons. The first was a bow and quiver full of arrows.

"These will be useful from afar," Ensil told him. "However, in the case that the fight is brought closer, this may be needed."

The second weapon was a short dagger. Tika stood in place as the bow and quiver were strapped to his back, and the sheath for the dagger was placed on the outside of his right boot. Tika smiled as he stepped back to allow the next person.

* * *

Plyke stepped forward hesitantly. Both Arishen and Tika had looked uncomfortable and shivered when Ensil examined them. *What is the elf doing?*

Plyke pushed out a light breeze flowing in and around his body as he watched Ensil's eyes glimmer brighter than they had since they'd met.

The grumpy looking elf turned to his store of weapons. Plyke's eyes widened at the sight of the double axe being carried to him. It felt as though he was being reprimanded for having double standards with Rilla. He had thanked her for keeping his secret, when it was clear that she knew what he was. Then he'd had the audacity to be angry with her for keeping a similar secret herself. It hadn't even occurred to him until the weight of the axe was strapped to his back that she still had not said anything about his lintep heritage to anyone. Downhearted, he went to stand over with Tika.

* * *

Rilla had been watching as Ensil distributed his weapons amongst her companions. His eyes had changed colour the same way the musicians' eyes had the first night they'd arrived.

She knew each of her companions had been given a weapon that Ensil thought suited their personality. As her mind swam with ideas of which weapon he would choose for her, she felt a light breeze try to pass through her body. Instinctively, she resisted it with full force. Ensil took a step back and stared at her in open amazement.

"Rilla of the lintep, you must let me examine you to find the weapon best suited to you," the weapons master told her. "Just try to relax."

"I'm sorry, Master Ensil," Rilla apologised. She tried to relax as the breeze passed through her. Even so, she could feel herself resisting without meaning to. Sweat beaded on the elf's face, his eyes glow more brightly than before, as he tried to force the breeze through. Once the task was over, he sagged and took a deep breath before turning to his array of weapons. He stood there for a long while, indecisively. Finally, he took two slightly curved sheathed swords and brought them over to the Rilla.

"Be extremely careful with these swords, young Rilla. Once they are unsheathed, they must take blood, whether your enemy's or your own, otherwise they will be cursed." He proceeded to strap the sheaths to her waist as he explained further. "The longer sword always goes on your left side and the shorter sword on your right. They are sheathed with the sharp side of the blades facing upwards so that you can unsheathe and strike in one movement."

Rilla nodded as she felt the weight of the swords drop into place at her sides. She stepped back to Tika's side, sharing his delight at their weapons, though inwardly dreading how many times they would be needed.

* * *

Ensil looked at his work, with a sense of pride. He'd been the weapons master in Silvaren for an extraordinarily long time. In all those years, he had matched countless warriors to their weapons. Each time, it filled him with a sense of satisfaction. "Now to teach you how to use your new weapons."

"I believe Eliséo and Shadow will be able to assist you in that, Master Ensil."

At the sound of Lady Eléna's voice, Ensil looked up and smiled bitterly. It still gave him a nasty turn to remember that she was no longer his Queen.

"A most wise observation, my lady Eléna," he agreed. Her suggestion had only been a thought away from his own lips. How well she knew him! "Shadow, Eliséo, if you will."

Together, the three of them instructed the four newly armed Outworlders in the basic use of their weapons. The lesson lasted for the better part of the morning, until the students were exhausted from the physical exertion. In addition to the swordsmanship lesson for Rilla, Ensil carefully taught her to shed some of her own blood before sheathing her swords. It was not something she could afford to forget. One mistake could curse her blades so that they would never take blood again.

* * *

After the lesson, the Paradisians went to place their new weapons in their rooms before rejoining Eliséo at the lake beneath Silva to relax the afternoon away.

They sat by the side of the lake, lazily moving their feet moving through the water. Tika lifted his head suddenly.

"Eliséo, can you teach us to swim?"

"You don't know how?" Eliséo asked in amazement. It was a skill all elves and coast dwellers learnt as soon as they could walk.

"There weren't any lakes in the Paradise," answered Plyke.

"That's true," returned Rilla, "but there was a stream that ran the whole way through. I doubt anyone other than myself dared swim in it." Eliséo hid a smile as the boys looked at Rilla in astonishment.

"You know we weren't allowed to swim there," Arishen reprimanded her.

"Like that ever stopped me before." She rolled her eyes. "Rhanya taught me to swim when no one was watching."

"Well then, Rilla, you can help me teach the boys," Eliséo suggested before the conversation became heated.

They spent the remainder of the day swimming and lying on the bank of the lake in turns. Other elves came to spend time with them, or give them pointers on how to float or swim beneath the water.

Eliséo watched them all intently. He had been surrounded by humans most of his life, but they never ceased to amaze him with the burdens they placed on themselves and the simple joys they missed out on. He wondered if he would ever understand them completely.

Chapter Twenty-Nine – The prophecy

Eléna sat in her room early the next morning thinking about Rilla. There were few people who had ever been manipulated as much as she already had and further would be. The poor child had no idea that most of her early life had been planned before she was conceived. Even the decision to return to the Outworld had been prophesised.

The only major event that had not been planned or prophesised had still been out of Rilla's control. In a single moment, Eliséo's tree had changed her life forever. To the elves and Elessa, the immediate changes were stunningly obvious, but to the girl herself, they were things she would have to come to terms with gradually.

Eléna regretted revealing the girl's identity in such a dismissive way. Had she known Rilla herself had set up the deception, she would have eased into it during their time in Silvaren. As it was, she'd disrupted the fragile relationship between Rilla and her companions, save for Tika.

Silva, where is the child? Eléna had been bound to Silva at birth. She had helped to shape the most magnificent tree in all of Silvaren. Liessa, too, had begun to lend her dreams to the tree, but Silva did not appear to be taking her suggestions.

She lies awake, by the lake. She is troubled, Eléna, as are they all. Has Shadow yet mentioned to them that they will be departing together? Do any of them have an idea of where their journey will lead them? You must talk to them. They are frightened and can only do harm to the child of prophecy.

I'm trying, Silva, Eléna sighed. She had learnt from a young age how to shield herself from her family's tree. Anything that Silva knew could be easily passed on to another elf bound to her. Eléna's secrets had always been too important to allow that to happen. Her father had been in a somewhat similar situation himself and had taught his daughter to shield her mind from their tree.

As a result, Silva had no idea that Rilla had been bound to an elf's tree a few days before. Nor had she witnessed the many secret conversations between Eléna and her ambassador. It had become a usual occurrence in their lives. Initially, Silva had inquired about the gaps in her knowledge, however, after many years, she had come to understand the need for such secrecy when more than one elf was bound to a single tree.

Liessa had never been taught this skill. Eléna could access her every thought if the need ever arose. As she walked quickly and silently down the many levels of Silva, she reminded herself that one day the need might arise when she was not in a position to teach her.

She found Rilla where Silva said she would, by the lake below, lying by the same mossy stone she'd previously favoured. The lake was deserted but for the two of them. Eléna wondered what the child was doing out of her room at such an early hour.

"Rilla, is everything alright?" she asked, gently, as she approached the girl.

"That's an odd question to ask, Lady Eléna." Rilla opened her eyes and stared straight at Eléna. "I don't think *everything* has ever been alright in my life. It just happens that, since I left the Paradise, less things are alright than before. For example, the very people I left to protect have stopped talking to me.

"I've discovered that both my father and I are lintep, which means he was murdering people for having the tiniest amount of power when he could do so much more than them. He never taught me to use my powers – in fact, he never even hinted to me that I wasn't human.

"And, to top it all off, an elf's tree decided to bind herself to me without even asking, or telling me what was involved, until it was too late. Oh, did I forget to mention that the only person who can protect us in the Outworld is so angry with me that I feel lucky she hasn't murdered me herself?"

"Rilla, I understand how you must feel ..." Eléna had barely begun to sympathise with her before Rilla cut in again.

"You *understand* how I feel? Exactly *how* do you suppose you can understand that?" Rilla's voice grew louder alongside her anger. "Has your life suddenly swept out of your control? Or did you recently realise that nothing in your life was ever as it seemed? Perhaps you mean to tell me that your best friend in the entire world was murdered just so that you could leave a prison, only to be thrown headlong into another?"

Eléna muttered a few words under her breath as the girl ranted. Her angry words were gradually silenced. Rilla put a hand to her mouth where Eléna had created a small pocket of thickened air.

"Now that I have your attention, little one, perhaps I can explain." Eléna seated herself on the mossy stone. "I have lived through more things that you can possibly imagine. To you, it seems as though nothing could be worse for you than it already is. But you are mistaken. There are so many more hardships that you will have to endure. I do not say this to dishearten you, but to make you understand that I honestly do know what you are going through.

"Long ago, when I was barely more than a child in the eyes of the elves, my future was abruptly changed. I lived in relative happiness with my mother and father. But that situation did not last long." Eléna closed her eyes against the nostalgia that swelled inside her. She opened them once more and focused on Rilla.

"I was still young when my parents were poisoned by a traitor. My position as princess and only heir to the throne was elevated quickly to Queen of the Elves. I begged my parents' advisors to turn back time, to bring back my parents and release me from my duties. They couldn't do that of course, but I didn't want to understand. I became a frightened and confused ruler.

"We never found the traitor, so I was constantly in fear for my life. The situation became so bad that I refused to trust my own advisors for, in my mind, no one was in a better position to kill my parents than those who were closest to them."

Rilla had finally stopped trying to speak and listened intently to the former queen.

"Silva was my saviour. As much as I couldn't trust anyone else, I found myself confiding in a tree I barely knew. It's different for the royal family and their tree. We don't bond quite so easily as other elves do with their trees. When your tree is not yours alone, there are things you learn to keep from it.

"I had spent the better part of my life with Silva learning how to block her out of my mind. When my parents died, she was my only companion, but it took me years to realise she was there for me."

Eléna had removed her air block from Rilla while she was speaking so that when the girl tried to answer, she finally could.

"I'm ... so sorry, Lady Eléna. I had no idea." Her voice caught in her throat.

"Of course you didn't, Rilla. But I needed you to understand what I'm trying to tell you. No one is ever in control of their own lives. You can only make the best decisions to change your circumstances, but there will always be situations that you cannot escape.

"Elessa has irrevocably changed your life. For better or worse we cannot yet know, but what we *do* know is that she will always be there for you. If you learn to trust her, confide in her, she will be able to help you with the most difficult decisions you will ever have to make."

"What about Eliséo? He now has to share his tree for the rest of my life."

She does not understand how Elessa has lengthened her lifespan, Eléna thought to herself. To Rilla, she only nodded.

"Eliséo already knows how to block Elessa out, if need be. He may forget to do so on occasion, but I doubt it will take long for him to learn that lesson. Come now, I did not find you to speak of this. There are other things we need to discuss."

"Yes," replied Rilla in excitement, "you just used your magic on me to stop me from speaking. How did you do that? Can you teach me?"

Eléna shook her head in frustration. "Rilla, that is the least important matter at the moment. I need to help you understand the prophecy."

"I understand it perfectly," Rilla answered abruptly.

"Little one, you have only recently learned of the prophecy naming you. There is no imaginable way that you can possibly understand it. You may think you know what it says, but that does not mean you are any closer to knowing what it means."

"And I suppose *you* will be the one to explain it all to me. After all, you seem to know me better than I know myself."

Eléna bit her tongue. She hadn't had to deal with such petulance in many a year.

"When a crystal heart beats in the body of another,
Their song will destroy that which was created.
Every being will bow down to the child of Paradise,
All will hail Rilla."

"I told you, I *know* the prophecy," Rilla repeated herself, almost angrily.

"Then tell me what it means." Eléna raised an eyebrow, curious to see what Rilla herself had made of her future.

"I will destroy something and everyone will bow down and praise me."

"Is that the extent of your imagination, little one?"

"Stop calling me 'little one'!" the lintep shouted.

Eléna ignored the outburst. "I think you may want to think some more on the words. Do you know of any creature with a crystal heart?"

"I assumed it meant a cold-hearted person. That's the way the boys and Shuut see me, so it seems appropriate."

"We do not have long before the earliest risers of the elves come to refresh themselves in this lake. It would be wise of you to put some thought behind your words."

Rilla looked up defiantly at the elf, but re-answered her question. "If the crystal dragons really do exist, then I suppose it could be talking about them."

"Better," Eléna replied, instantly following up on Rilla's renewed interest. "The crystal dragons do indeed exist. Your mother and father were asked to conceive you in their mountains. As you do not have any memory of visiting Silvaren before you entered your Paradise, I do not presume to think that you could possibly know that you lived in the Drakos Mountains for the better part of two years before leaving the crystal dragons."

"*I* lived with the crystal dragons?" Rilla asked, incredulously.

"You will come to understand that most of your life has been meticulously planned to fit the prophecy. It is assumed that, in essence, a crystal heart beats in your body because you were surrounded by those dragons in your earliest years.

"The song has long been thought to mean the lintep's song. Once you reach Illaria, you will be taught all you need to know about that."

"I'm going to Illaria?" Rilla interrupted her. "How will I find the way if not even Shuut knows it."

"Arishen, Tika and Plyke are under the impression that you see and hear more than anyone else does. I'm beginning to doubt them. You have not been directly told who knows the way to Illaria, but I thought you would have deduced that by now."

Rilla flushed crimson. "I suppose an ambassador might know the way, but I don't see how that helps me."

"That's simply because you don't follow your thoughts through to conclusions."

"Eliséo can't possibly come with us," Rilla protested. "*If* Shuut agrees to take us back into the Outworld with her, there is no chance that she will take on another companion."

"Shadow will understand the fact that she does not have a choice in the matter." Eléna ended the debate. "Shall we continue?"

Rilla crossed her arms. "Fine. Exactly what is it I'm meant to be destroying?"

"Do you know what happened to the races, other than humans, when the lintep warrior princess died?"

Rilla shook her head.

"Then I shall tell you." Lady Eléna patted the stone beside her, and the lintep sat down. She paused before speaking, tired, and gathered her thoughts. She'd barely slept since the arrival of the Outworlders. Strictly speaking, Elves did not need as much sleep as other beings, but Eléna had not slept well even before this latest disruption.

"Before the war, each magic-infused race had their own stronghold. The lintep had Illaria, the karliki had Goraburg and we elves had Silvaren. Illaria was already difficult to find, unless you knew the way there. After the war, the lintep increased their security by creating a magical barrier around the edges of their stronghold. Now it is impossible for any to pass through the barrier unless they are accompanied by a lintep or have special permission."

"And Eliséo has permission?" Rilla asked.

"Of course he does. It is of the utmost importance that the elves be able to contact the lintep if the need arises. As ambassador, he is given most of the privileges of every other race." Eléna brushed aside the question.

"The karliki used to live both above ground and in their mountain dwelling, Goraburg. After the war, they retreated completely into the Lesa mountains, which has its own natural defences. It is an underground city. The only way to get there is through a maze of subterranean tunnels. Without a karlik to guide you, you would wander around those tunnels directionless until you died.

"We elves were not so fortunate as either the lintep or the karliki. The only place we have ever lived is Silvaren. The only one of us who has significant magic ability is the Queen or King, but even their magic is not great enough to put a barrier around our forest. I'm sure you and your companions could feel the magic of the trees as soon as you entered our home. Most humans don't like that feeling, so they will not venture to the inner regions of Silvaren.

"However, many of the elves used to have their trees on the outskirts, near the sand crossing. Those poor elves were attacked many times by humans, their trees dying with them. That is why there are no longer any trees right up against the sandy banks on the northern edge of Silvaren. My elves are afraid."

"Why would people do that?" Rilla asked in shock.

"Humans are afraid of what they do not understand," answered Eléna in resignation. "Humans don't understand magic and so, to cover their fear, they attack anyone with the ability. After the war, some humans wanted a safe place to retreat to – a place where magic doesn't exist. Do you know the story?"

"Shuut told us that Paradises were created by some lintep for whichever humans wanted to live free from magic," Rilla replied, looking quite pleased with herself.

"Now follow that thought through with the prophecy." Eléna watched closely. If the child could figure this part out on her own, she might be more inclined to accept it. The child of prophecy said the words aloud to herself. Eléna found herself holding her breath in anticipation.

"The lintep song, which I should learn in Illaria, will destroy that which was created." Rilla's eyes opened wide. "You mean to tell me that I'm meant to destroy the Paradises?"

"You, of all people, should understand why they must be destroyed, Rilla."

"You can't be serious," the girl whispered in a frightened voice. "How can that even be possible? It took more than just a single lintep to create the Paradises. How am *I* meant to undo all of that?"

"You will find a way, little one," Eléna assured her. "Everyone who knows of the prophecy believes that *you* and you alone can right past wrongs. Paradises should never have been created in the first place. It simply gave humans an easy way to hide from magic."

Rilla stared at her incredulously. "How can you ask me to do this? I've only just learnt of the prophecy. What if the prophecy isn't even talking about me? There could be another Rilla out there somewhere – another lintep girl."

Eléna stared out over the lake, biding her time, trying to form an answer that the girl would accept.

"My young friend, I do not expect you to accept, or even truly understand, any of this today. I realise it will take time for you to come to terms with everything you have been told. I believe this is one of the reasons that Elessa bound herself to you. The trees are often wiser than the elves. You have many questions now. They will only increase as your journey continues. Elessa will be there for you when you are ready to hear the answers. She will help you come to terms with what has happened in your life and what people will be expecting from you."

"I see." Rilla's voice had turned cold once more. "You had the throne of the elves thrust upon you when you were so young you didn't know what to do with it and now that you don't feel like being their Queen anymore, you abdicate.

You're running away from your destiny but you want me to face up to mine. The only thing you're offering me in return is the companionship of an elf's tree."

"I will not be chastised for my abdication by a child." Lady Eléna rose to her feet once more, towering over the seated lintep. "There are reasons for my choice which you cannot possibly begin to understand. Do not dare to question my decision."

Eléna did not look back as she walked into the pre-dawn light.

Chapter Thirty – Burdens

Plyke walked down the quiet hall to Rilla's room. He had no idea what he would say to her, but he knew he would have to talk to her sooner or later, if for no other reason than to appease his Partner. It almost felt as though Tika knew that Rilla was keeping a secret for him – but that couldn't be possible. His guilt was playing tricks on him.

As Plyke approached Rilla's room, he saw Gioshué was worriedly peering through the glittering vines. When he saw Plyke, his face became an impassive mask.

"What's the matter?" he asked the young elf.

"It is not my place to interfere with Queen Liessa's guests," Gioshué answered evasively.

"Is it your place to keep me out of Rilla's room if I wish to enter it?"

The elf's eyes flickered back and forth between Plyke and the hanging vines. He answered slowly, "I believe it would not be in Rilla's best interest for me to refuse you entry."

As Plyke entered her antechamber, Rilla's choked sobs reached his ears. He looked back to find Gioshué watching him with pleading eyes. Plyke turned back towards the inner room and walked hesitantly towards the lintep. To see her crying unsettled him – she always seemed to be the strongest of the four of them.

"Rilla?" he called out softly, as he peered into her room. She lay curled up in a ball on her bed, her back towards him.

"Rilla?" he repeated a little louder. Her sobs stopped instantly, the shaking body now frozen in place. "What's wrong?" Rilla curled up, even tighter, into herself.

Back in their Paradise, Plyke had never really spoken to the girls. In fact, he had barely spoken to anyone other than Tika and Kora. When children cried in their dormitory, he exerted all his energy to block out their pain. Where other children would turn to watch the commotion, he had always kept his eyes firmly closed, humming to himself to muffle their sobs.

Blocking the Paradise from his mind, he took a steadying breath and walked over to the now silent girl. He sat on the far side of the bed from her. Neither of them spoke. Neither of them moved. As he sat there, Plyke leaned his head back against Silva's trunk.

Comfort her. A voice sounded inside his head. He sat up straight and looked around the room, eyes scanning for any movement. There was none. Hesitantly, he leaned his head back until it touched the smooth wood. *If nothing else, put your hand on her back.*

Not knowing whether to trust the voice or not, Plyke rested his hand lightly on Rilla's back. Her body trembled beneath his touch. She was still crying, just not out loud.

Plyke closed his eyes to the overwhelming fear he felt rushing in from Rilla. It felt as though it was crushing him, closing his throat so he couldn't breathe.

Trying to provide some comfort, he stroked the crying girl's long fiery curls, the way Kora had done with Tika when his mother had died. He couldn't understand it, but the fear began to recede. There was still the feeling of overwhelming pressure, but the edge had disappeared from the fear.

"Rilla, I want to apologise to you." He felt pathetic, apologising to someone in their weakest moment. "I should never have been so angry with you in the throne room. I had no right to presume you would tell me you were a lintep."

"It doesn't matter now. *Everyone* knows that," her soft voice trembled out a reply.

"But not everyone knows about *me*. That's the point. I was angry with you because you kept your secret, but you're still keeping mine. You have no reason to do that anymore."

Rilla turned her head just enough to look at him. "I never had a reason to keep your secret, Plyke. I just didn't say anything because you clearly didn't want anyone to know about it."

"That doesn't make sense," he pointed out.

"What happened in the throne room – that would happen to *you* if I say anything. Why would I want anyone to do that to you? Do you have any idea how horrible it is to have your secrets stripped away from you so suddenly?"

"I can only imagine." He looked away from her watery green eyes. "Is that why you're crying?"

"No." She barely got the word out before tears overflowed again. Plyke moved closer, leaning over and hugging her. The frightened girl didn't pull away. She simply lay there, crying.

Not knowing what else to do, Plyke held her until she stopped crying. He had no idea how long he'd been in her room by that point, but the sun was visible through Silva's branches.

"Do you want to know why I asked Shuut about my name?" Rilla sniffed out a reply, as she finally sat up on the bed.

"I suppose so," he replied uncertainly. "She was fairly angry when Lady Eléna told her what it is. How does she know who you are, anyway?"

"She said my mother and Erton passed by here on their way to the Paradise."

"Erton's not from our Paradise? What happened to your mother?"

Rilla shook her head in frustration. "None of that really matters."

"Sorry. So, what's the big secret about your name?"

"Just forget it." She waved him off. "You're obviously more interested in other things."

"I'm interested in why you're crying. If that has to do with your name, then I want to hear about it." For the first time he pulled aside his messy hair to look at her properly with both his brown eye and his green one. She wasn't surprised. Why wasn't she surprised? Did she really know everything about him?

"Did you know there is a prophecy that names me?"

Plyke shook his head.

"*When a crystal heart beats in the body of another,*
Their song will destroy that which was created.
Every being will bow down to the child of Paradise,
All will hail Rilla."

He looked at her with a blank face. It made little sense to him. She wiped at her wet cheeks with her shirt sleeve.

"What does it mean?" he asked her.

"According to most people, it means that I will destroy all the Paradises."

Plyke blinked, shook his head and looked at her in confusion. "Exactly how are you meant to do this?"

"That's the thing – no one knows. It's something to do with a lintep song that Lady Eléna thinks I'll learn in Illaria. Shuut told me about the prophecy when I asked her about my name, only I didn't tell her what my name was after that because I didn't want her confusing me with the person named in it."

"But it turns out you really *are* the person it names?" Plyke asked cautiously.

"That's what everyone seems to think. Apparently no other lintep was allowed to call their child Rilla until I was born and they all have it fixed in their head that this Rilla has to be a lintep."

"So, let me get this straight. You are supposed to learn some song to destroy all the Paradises?" Rilla nodded her head. "How can one person possibly do that by themselves? Weren't they created by *lots* of lintep?" Again, she nodded. "It's too big for you! How can anyone possibly ask that of you?"

Rilla smiled sadly. "That's what I wanted to know. Lady Eléna assures me that I will find a way – that I *have to* find a way, or everyone with even the slightest touch of magic in any Paradise will be killed."

"I'm sure that's not the case," Plyke's answered automatically. "They couldn't do that."

"Isn't that what made you and Arishen leave?"

His shoulders slumped at the memory. Tika had made the choice easier for him but, Rilla was right – he would have had to leave sooner or later. It would have been too difficult to hide his skills from Erton forever.

"We'll find a way, Rilla. I promise you." He drew her close to him and let her head rest on his shoulder. She wasn't crying anymore, but he could still feel the weight pressing in on her.

Kora had told him that was one of his powers. On a weekly basis, she had made time to talk to him, to let him tell her anything that he had noticed during the preceding days. More often than not, he would tell her how he imagined he could feel what other people were feeling, if he was close enough to them.

He clearly remembered the day when she had told him that she was his mother and that they were lintep. She had explained to him that he must never allow anyone to know about it. He must keep his knowledge about others to himself. If he didn't, Erton would find a way to make sure he stayed silent. He had only been four or five years old at the time, but even at such a young age he had understood what she meant.

Plyke looked down at Rilla, pity welling up inside of him. Not only had she never been told what she was, but she'd had no one to train her in any way. At least he'd had stolen moments with Kora.

He tried to imagine only finding out what he was once he'd left the Paradise, but could not. That, alone, would have been enough to deal with. But now Rilla had the added pressure of the prophecy.

"I'll help you any way I can."

"Thank you," Rilla mumbled into his shoulder. Plyke smiled as he felt the crushing weight on her mind ease slightly.

* * *

"What do you mean, you don't know where he is?" Arishen questioned Tika indignantly. "He's *your* Partner, isn't he? You should know where he is."

Tika looked up into the taller boy's clear blue eyes and took a deep, calming breath. "I don't know what your Partnership with Parthak was like, Arishen, but Plyke and I don't feel the need to tell each other where we'll be every moment of every day."

It was true – Tika didn't *know* where Plyke was. But he had his suspicions. Something had happened when Ensil had given Plyke the double axe. They hadn't spoken about it, but Tika had felt it. The immediate, swift, sideways glance towards Rilla had meant something. She probably hadn't noticed it. Plyke may not have done it consciously, but Tika had been watching him closely. He had seen the guilt and sorrow in that look. No matter how many arguments they'd had over Rilla, it didn't change the fact that Tika could read his Partner like an open book.

At the rebuke, Arishen was instantly silenced. It had been a low blow, and Tika knew it. The seer's brisk walk to an empty chair by the food-laden table exposed his anger. It would take a long time for that wound to heal, if it ever did. Tika almost felt sorry for having brought up Parthak, but then reminded himself that Arishen had questioned his Partnership with Plyke. He'd had no right to do that.

Moments later, Shuut entered the room. Tika saw her glance between the two of them, eyes narrowing slightly. Tika was thankful she said nothing of the tension in the air. He knew that if anyone pressed the matter, Arishen would be angry for the better part of the day. It seemed to him that their stay in Silvaren was not doing any of them the good they had been hoping for.

Shuut sat down wordlessly across from the seer and began to eat. Tika sat beside the banwep and followed her lead, ignoring Arishen to the best of his ability. He could feel the seer's gaze burning into him, but refused to look him in the eye.

It wasn't long before Rilla and Plyke walked in, side by side. Tika, his mouth full of food, carefully watched Arishen's reaction. The seer was seething with anger. No matter how badly he had treated Rilla, he still craved her attention. It was obvious, the way that Rilla and Plyke walked so closely together, that her attention now lay elsewhere.

Tika waved a hand in greeting, catching Plyke's eye. There was sadness in his Partner's face. Through their Partnership, Tika had been aware of every emotion Plyke felt. This was the deepest sadness he had ever seen. It was coupled with despair and hopelessness. What had the two of them spoken about? If he insisted on finding out, Tika was certain this was one of the times they would not see eye to eye.

Plyke had been pulling further and further away from him recently. There was nothing Tika could do about it. If he tried to cling to their Partnership, it would only drive a further wedge between them. His only hope was to let his Partner be, and simply hope that Plyke would confide in him in his own time.

When they were both seated, Plyke next to Tika and Rilla across from him, Shuut stopped eating long enough to tell them this was her last day in Silvaren.

"Where are we going this time?" Tika asked, secretly glad to be leaving the elves he had so longed to see.

"*We* are not going anywhere. I will be leaving Silvaren to return to the crystal dragons. You are free to go wherever you wish from here."

"We're not *free* to do anything, Shuut, and you know it." All eyes turned to Rilla. "In the Outworld, we will die without your help and you know the elves won't let us stay here forever."

"This is all *your* fault, Rilla," Arishen suddenly lashed out. "If you hadn't forced us to leave with you in the first place, we wouldn't be in this position."

"I never forced you to leave the Paradise," Rilla replied calmly, turning to face Arishen. "And I believe it was your dream that facilitated our departure from Turon."

"Twist the facts any way you like." Arishen raised his voice, threateningly. "We would never have had all these troubles in the Outworld if it weren't for you."

"I'm surprised you feel that way, young Arishen." They all turned to see Lady Eléna standing in the entrance to the room. "From what I understand, you owe your life to Rilla of the lintep." The four Paradisians stood up immediately, a reflex reaction learnt from Erton's idea of respect.

"Lady Eléna," Tika addressed her hesitantly, "will you force us to leave when Shuut does?"

"My dear boy, I would never force you to do something against your will." Tika saw the elf catch Shuut's eye with a deft shake of her head. "However, things in Silvaren do not move as quickly as in the Outworld. I am certain that you would eventually decide to leave of your own accord, to live the life you were meant to."

"Does that mean we can stay on tomorrow when Shuut leaves?" Plyke asked with as much trepidation as Tika.

"Not this time, young Plyke. Shadow will be taking you with her. She cannot abandon you *here* any more than she could in Turon."

"Lady Eléna, I think you will find ..." Shuut's reply was cut short, her mouth moving without the sound of words to accompany it. Tika saw Rilla's half hidden smile and wondered what had happened.

"Shadow, you must deal with the consequences of your actions. You cannot take four Paradisians into the Outworld and expect to leave them in the first town you come by. You will find a place where the four of them either can live safely until they learn the ways of the Outworld."

"Does such a place exist?" Arishen mumbled as he slumped back down into his chair.

"I realise things have not gone according to your liking, young seer, but that is not the way of life." The former Queen glared down at him. "Shadow will find it in her best interest to take you with her when she leaves. Perhaps you will learn to make the best of the situation rather than vent your frustrations on your companions."

Without another word, she turned to leave the room. Only after she was out of sight could Shuut make herself heard again.

"I don't know what the two of you have been planning, but don't think for one moment that I will let you travel with me once we are out of sight of this cursed place." Her cold grey eyes stared at Rilla.

"That is exactly what I told Lady Eléna, Shuut," Rilla replied with a sigh. "She seems to think that you will change your mind."

"We'll see about that." Shuut pushed her half empty plate away before standing from the table and leaving the room. Tika watched Rilla take a deep breath and hold it. She raised her eyes to meet Plyke's before exhaling.

"Congratulations, Rilla. You've done it again." Arishen didn't lose a moment before striking out. "We have to leave yet another place because of you. Not to mention, Shuut is as angry with you as she could possibly be."

"Why don't you just shut up and leave her alone?" Tika bit his lip at his Partner's reply. He wished he knew what had happened between them to make Plyke completely change his mind about the lintep.

"Oh, and I suppose you'll try to make me if I don't." Arishen stood up, hands spread out on the table, staring down at Plyke. Tika could see Plyke's clenched fists beneath the table and held his breath. Out of the corner of his eye, he saw Rilla shake her head ever so slightly.

"Rilla can fight her own battles, Arishen. I just thought you might want to finally grow up."

Arishen looked at the three of them, trembling with rage, and slammed his fists down on the table. They jumped involuntarily at the sound, and kept their eyes averted as he walked away.

"Nicely handled, Plyke," Tika said sarcastically.

"*Someone* had to tell him." His Partner shrugged the comment aside.

"And that *someone* just had to be you, didn't it?" Usually Tika would wait until they were alone for such a conversation, but there was no way to leave Rilla out of this one.

"You could have simply said nothing." Rilla's agreement stunned Tika. "He wouldn't have done anything."

"Do I really need to remind you that the last time he *did nothing*, you ended up with a chisel in your ribs?"

"It hasn't even left a scar. I wouldn't care if he did it again." Rilla brushed away his concern.

"Next time you might not be so lucky. What if he aims for your heart? Or slits your throat while you're sleeping?" Plyke's face was flushed. "Not even being a full blooded lintep makes you invincible, Rilla."

"Then at least he would free me from a future I can't avoid any other way." Rilla's voice was barely more than a whisper, but Tika heard it as clearly as though she had shouted at the top of her lungs.

Tika waited for his Partner to tell Rilla that her future wouldn't be so bad, but the assurance never came. That's what they must have spoken about earlier that morning.

"Do you really think Shuut will let us travel with her to the crystal dragons?" Tika asked, attempting to ease the tension a little.

"I don't know Tika," Rilla sighed. "Lady Eléna seems quite convinced that she won't have a choice once we leave. I think I know what she's planning, but I have a feeling Shuut won't like it."

They finished eating their morning meal in silence, all three of them deep in thought. When they were done, Rilla excused herself from their company. Tika watched his Partner as she left the room. He was aching to find out what had happened between the two of them. The only thing he knew for certain was that Arishen had misinterpreted it. Rilla's attention *was* focused on Plyke, but not in the way that the seer's was on the lintep.

Chapter Thirty-One – Ensil

Rilla found Gioshué waiting for her outside the dining hall. The young elf, leaning against Silva's trunk with two other guide elves, immediately stood to attention as he saw her.

"Isn't there something else you'd rather be doing than waiting on me?" Rilla asked with a raised eyebrow. The young elf smiled mischievously at her. She smiled back at him. "Well, go on then."

Gioshué ran off, yelling back over his shoulder. "Be back by sun down. There will be a surprise waiting for you in your chamber."

Rilla watched the young elf run towards something more enjoyable and envied him his happiness. She walked, head down, past countless elves doing their daily chores. Some of them tried to get her attention, but she avoided talking to them all, with a quick smile and a curt nod.

She stopped by her room to collect her swords. Once on the forest floor, Rilla walked as far from Silva as she dared without fear of getting lost. She found a quiet clearing, more than large enough to extend both sword arms without getting close to any tree trunks.

Closing her eyes, she composed herself and laid her hands on her swords. Breathing slowly, she unsheathed both blades and slowly fought against an imaginary opponent. Over and over again, she practiced the motions taught to her the day before. She blocked out the chirp of birds, the rustle of leaves in the wind, the ocean waves crashing against the rocky shore. Nothing else existed save for her new weapons. She marvelled at the way they began to feel like extensions of her arms, just when she wasn't concentrating too hard.

"Would you care to bout with me?" The sudden gruff voice behind her made Rilla jump. Turning quickly, she saw Ensil, armed with a long sword.

"I ... really don't think I'm good enough for that, just yet." Rilla stumbled over her words. There was a strange iciness in the elf's eyes that she hadn't seen the day before. The very way he stood felt threatening to her. Her heartbeat quickened as her breathing became shallower and more rapid.

"Come girl, you won't get any better fighting against the air. On your guard!" He settled into the attack, sword pointing at her heart. Rilla instinctively took a step back and raised both her swords just enough to deflect his blade.

"Ensil, I really don't think this is a good idea." Her voice trembled. The elf's only reply was to attack again, his blade darting towards her left shoulder. Rilla twirled on her right foot, swinging out of the way. She looked at him in shock. That was a killing stroke. He had not held back at all.

"Ensil, what are you doing?" she cried out in fear, catching his blade between her two from another attack.

Attack him! The order came from inside her mind. Immediately reacting to it, Rilla circled the weapons master, eyes wide with terror. She lunged with the long sword in her right hand, while deflecting Ensil's attack with the shorter sword in her left.

Time and again, they circled each other, one striking and the other defending. Not used to the physical exertion, Rilla soon began to tire. She knew she couldn't simply give in. He would not stop just because she was tired. In a last effort to stop him, Rilla lunged forth with both swords, simultaneously.

"Ensil, NO!" The shouted words came from behind her attacker. Ensil turned to face Eliséo, deflecting only Rilla's longer sword as he did so. Her shorter one struck the muscle just under his right shoulder. Crying out in pain, he fell to the ground. Rilla dropped both her weapons and crouched by his side, Eliséo joining her.

"What have you done?" he murmured. She looked between the elves, not understanding what had happened. Ensil lay bleeding before her, gasping in pain.

"Rilla, stay with him." Eliséo ran off towards Silva without another word.

"I'm done for, child," Ensil whispered between snatches of breath. Rilla stared down at him, eyes glazed over with tears. What had she done? He was going to bleed out before Eliséo could come back with help. She had seen wounds as bad as this in their Paradise. Only Rhanya had been skilled enough to heal them, and even then, only if he'd reached them in time.

Without a word, she placed her left hand over the wound and closed her eyes. She cried out, instantly feeling his pain. It was so much more intense than the fringa's injury.

Stop the bleeding. It was the voice in her head again. Without thinking twice, she obeyed it. She found each vein where blood was pouring out and willed them one by one to bind together. For every vein she healed in his body, her skin tore open in the same place.

That's enough. She took her hand away from the elf's wound and opened her eyes. He was staring up at her in silence. Paying no attention to his cold eyes, she ripped off the sleeves of her shirt. She scrunched up one of them and placed it over his wound, covering it with his left hand. He pressed the cloth into his wound, understanding her effort to slow his bleeding, as she did likewise with her own.

Exhausted from both the swordplay and the healing, Rilla sat on the bloodied grass, leaning back against the trunk of a nearby tree. She payed close attention to Ensil's breath, listening for any change.

What have you done? Those had been his words to her. What did he mean by them? Surely *she* hadn't done anything wrong. *He* was the one trying to kill her. Wasn't he? Confused and tired, Rilla kept both eyes on the wounded elf. As much as she simply wanted to close her eyes and make the world disappear, she didn't trust the weapons master to stay away from her.

She couldn't tell how long it was before Eliséo returned. He wasn't alone. Lady Eléna and another elf she didn't recognise were with him. Without looking at her, all three of them knelt by Ensil's side, taking the bloodied sleeve from his wound. Rilla heard a muffled argument, but didn't bother paying enough attention to wonder what they were saying. She finally felt secure enough to close her eyes and succumb to darkness.

"Rilla." She was being shaken awake by the owner of an unfamiliar voice. "Child, open your eyes."

It was more effort than she could be bothered with to keep her eyes open. In front of her was an elf she hadn't met before. She closed her eyes for what seemed like hours before opening them again. Eliséo's face was next to the unknown elf, concern in his eyes. Rilla tried to move, but her arms were too heavy.

"Don't try to move," Eliséo told her, as though reading her mind. "Kari will put some ointment on your wound, to stop it from bleeding."

Kari removed the bloodied sleeve from beneath Rilla's right shoulder. Blood flowed slowly from the wound. Rilla felt the cool yellow ointment being massaged into her skin, instantly easing the pain. She watched a reflection of herself in Eliséo's eyes. Her face was deathly pale, the blood drained even from her lips. Looking further down, her ripped shirt was soaked with blood. Her naked arms lay beside the two swords – the longer one clean and pristine, the shorter one bloodied at the tip.

Slow minutes passed. Rilla looked from one concerned face to the other, eventually having enough strength to look further afield. Lady Eléna knelt by Ensil's side. The lintep strained to hear his breathing. The other elves were masking the sound.

"Ensil?" she asked, having no strength to form an entire question.

"He's alive," Kari answered with a sideways glance towards Eliséo. "It appears he owes both his wound and his life to you."

"Why?"

"Eliséo insists that you weren't wounded when he left and that Ensil should have died before we reached him." Kari had misunderstood the question. All Rilla wanted to know was why he'd attacked her in the first place. "We know that lintep have the power to heal others at their own risk. How you learnt to do this without a trainer is beyond our understanding. Suffice to say that Ensil would not be alive now if you hadn't tried to heal him."

Rilla closed her eyes once more and remembered Ratchin. She had watched on in fascinated horror as the lintep had healed Cheyenne's son, Muyr. It was the only time she'd seen a lintep use their power to heal someone. She wondered if any of the humans Ratchin had helped over the years had ever understood the price that she paid for them, or if they'd given their little offerings of thanks none the wiser.

"What *I* want to know is how you came to pass by at just the right time," Kari asked Eliséo in a low voice, in an obvious attempt to not be heard by either Ensil or Lady Eléna.

"Lady Eléna has charged me with the lintep's protection," he answered without a moment's pause. "In fact, I would have been here sooner, had Shadow not asked me to continue training the Partners. When I realised the girl was not nearby, I left to find her."

Rilla listened intently to his answer, eyes closed lightly, feigning sleep. She had been wondering the same thing herself. She could believe the claim to being charged with her protection – Lady Eléna had implied that he would be travelling with them when they left. She even believed that Shuut had asked him to further Tika and Plyke's training. What she didn't believe, not for a second, was that he came looking for her simply because she wasn't near the Partners.

There had to have been something to alert him to her dangerous situation. Silvaren was not so small a place that he could find her so quickly without knowing where to look. Then there was the matter of the voice in her mind. Had she been imagining it or had someone really been telling her what to do?

The only answer that made any sense was Elessa. The tree could have seen through Rilla's eyes and alerted Eliséo of her situation. As soon as the thought entered her mind, she dismissed it as stupidity. How could a tree possibly see through her eyes? How could it tell an elf where to find her and warn him that she was in danger?

Why do you doubt the truth? It was the same voice again, echoing through her mind. Rilla snapped open her eyes to see Eliséo looking at her, carefully. Kari was no longer by his side. A quick shake of his head warned her to remain silent.

"We will talk soon," he whispered close to her ear. The tall elf stood up and turned to the others. "Lady Eléna," he addressed the former queen. "By your leave, I will take Rilla of the lintep with me." Rilla didn't miss the look in the older elf's eyes as she nodded her assent. Kari barely paid them any attention, focused as she was on the unconscious patient before her.

Eliséo bent to pick up Rilla's swords, drawing a small drop of blood with the clean one then wiping them both on his shirt before returning them to their sheaths. She didn't protest when the elf placed one arm under her knees, the other supporting her back, and lifted her gently from the grass. Rilla found it oddly reassuring to be held close by someone who cared about her – even if it was just because she was the prophecy child. She leaned her head against his shoulder and closed her eyes, welcoming the oblivion of sleep.

Chapter Thirty-Two – Ensil's test

She doesn't understand. Eliséo blocked his conversation with Elessa from the girl in his arms.

She understands. She refuses to accept. Elessa corrected him.

Eliséo carried the girl to his tree, thanking his lucky stars that Elessa was on the outskirts of Silvaren. The fewer questions they encountered, the better. Rilla was the most important person to have passed through their forest in a long time. Her actions and encounters there would be remembered for hundreds of years to come.

It was purely by chance that he'd met the prophecy child. He had been in the throne room, listening in on the Queen's affairs. As ambassador, it was expected of him to understand the political and social situation of his people. He needed to be able to make immediate decisions when it came to other races.

Queen Eléna had summoned him back to Silvaren but, as he was close to Illaria at the time, it had taken him until the day before the coronation to arrive. He wondered how different the girl's life would have been if he'd missed her entirely.

This path leads nowhere, Eliséo. Elessa spoke gently to him. *What would have happened if you'd never met the child is now irrelevant. The fact is that you did meet her and I bound her to myself. No other possibilities now exist, so why dwell on them?*

He smiled to himself. Any other tree would never have thought to chide their elf. But Elessa had already been old and set in her ways by the time they were bound together. He was used to her pointing out when he was in the wrong, or when he was pursuing matters that should be of no concern to him.

As he approached Elessa, Eliséo looked up at her full height. She rustled her leaves, vainly. The only time she saw herself was through his eyes. Every inch of her was ingrained in his memory — every inch except for her newest additions. His gaze rested on the reddish black branch. The swirl of fiery flowers and bright green leaves, which had adorned it earlier, were now mingled with others on the forest floor. Elessa had done her best to avert any attention she may have aroused.

Eliséo ascended the curved walkway up past the common room to his bedroom. Rilla had fallen asleep in his arms, so he placed her as gently as he could on his bed. He turned to the washbasin in the middle of the room and looked down at his shirt. Ensil's blood covered the bottom half where he'd wiped Rilla's swords clean. He took off the shirt and soaked it in the washbasin until the blood had reddened the water. A few words muttered under his breath returned the water to its original state. He wrung the soaking shirt out of the hole in Elessa's trunk that served as a window, leaving it hanging over the ledge to dry. He changed into a clean green shirt and began to pack for the next day. There wasn't much he would need to take with him, but he knew those few items could be invaluable.

It was early in the afternoon when Rilla finally awoke. Eliséo heard her movements in the room above him. He had been sitting silently for hours, his unseeing eyes staring blankly at the book in his hands, thinking of all that he would be leaving behind him this time. It was obvious, at least to him, that many of the elves were not happy with Lady Eléna's decision. The only other monarch who had abdicated in favour of a child had done so because he didn't want the elves to revolt against his chosen heir when the time came for him to take the throne. There had been good reason to fear that happening and people had at least understood the decision, even if they had not supported it.

This was different. Eliséo well understood Lady Eléna's reasons, but he doubted that many others were in such a privileged situation. He feared there would be times over the next months, or even years, when he might be needed here in Silvaren.

He idly wondered how long he would be expected to stay in the Outworld with the lintep. It was another one of his pointless mental paths. There was no way to tell how long it would take them to reach Illaria. It would depend on so many different factors that he couldn't begin to calculate the time.

He looked up before Rilla entered the common room. She came down the curved walkway uncertainly, clutching at the silver tree pendant around her neck with her left hand. Her eyes widened briefly as they came to rest on him.

"Are we where I think we are?"

Her attempt to avoid Elessa's name amused him. Tactfully, he kept the smile from his face and simply nodded in reply, closing his book gently and placing it on the floor beside him.

"How did you know where to find me?"

Eliséo raised an eyebrow at the girl. Elessa was correct in her assumption that Rilla simply did not want to accept the truth.

"I have been told you are well aware of the answer to that question." He calmly watched as she paled slightly and leant back against the inner trunk of the tree. She immediately jumped forward and turned around. Elessa had taken part of her again – a fiery red swirl marked where her body had been.

Elessa, stop scaring the poor child! Eliséo reprimanded his tree. *She's frightened enough as it is without you playing with her.*

"Please take no notice of Elessa." He motioned Rilla to a cushioned chair by his side. "She isn't used to visitors."

"You don't often have visitors?" the girl asked, seemingly in an attempt to avoid complete silence.

"I'm not often in Silvaren. My position as ambassador keeps me away more often than not." He pushed his hands against his knees as he stood up. "Let me see how you're healing."

He untied the sling from around her arm and wiped away the yellow ointment to see the wound. If need be, he could always find Kari again to reapply some. He shook his head in wonder.

"What is it?" Rilla looked down to see the wound had almost completely closed. An angry red scar was forming in its place.

"Move your arm around, in a slow wide circle." She did as he asked her. "Is the shoulder stiff to move?"

Why do you ask her when I'm letting you feel what she feels? Elessa asked impudently.

She wasn't raised with this bond, Elessa. Eliséo patiently explained to his tree while talking with Rilla. *I will gradually tell her exactly what she will live with the rest of her life, but she has enough to deal with today. Please don't argue with me.*

"It's a little stiff, but nothing that feels like it won't go away soon. I still don't understand what happened with Ensil." Rilla avoided his eyes. "Why did he attack me and then ask what I had done when I stabbed him?"

There were many things that he could tell the girl about the weapons master, but none of them would answer her question. It was not his duty to do so. She would have to talk to Ensil herself. He knew she would be angry with him when she discovered his reasoning. After all, every other elf in Silvaren had been. Ensil had had to deal with more anger in his long life than most of the other elves combined.

"I suggest you ask Ensil about that yourself." He walked over to the table on the far side of his common room, choosing a few fruits and breads to place on the glass plate. Returning to his seat, he offered Rilla first choice of the food. Tentatively, she picked out a nectarine and nibbled on it, her eyes darting everywhere.

"Your tree is different to the ones we were invited into the other day."

Eliséo shrugged. "Each tree in Silvaren in unique."

Rilla shook her head even as he answered. "That's not what I meant. Everyone else has ornaments or weapons. I assume they want to be surrounded by their chosen trade. Your tree ... isn't like that."

"You refer to my lack of possessions." He watched her nod, almost timidly. This was not the proud and confident person he had seen in the throne room. Too many things had happened to her since then. "I find it best not to invite people into my life. Unlike the other elves in Silvaren, I spend most of my time in the Outworld. My most important possessions are kept close to me at all times." He saw her search all over, only seeing his weapons and his rucksack nearby. Even a trained eye would not have discovered his most prized possession.

"You're going to need more than a single nectarine to build your strength up for tomorrow." He offered her a piece of flat bread before motioning to the descending pathway. "I'll take you to see Ensil while you finish eating."

* * *

Ensil lay weakly on his bed, Kari by his side. She hadn't asked him what had happened. The only times Ensil *ever* needed her assistance was when another elf got the better of him. He never told her who the elves were, but most of the time, she could guess without too much trouble.

"She's not an elf, you know." Kari held out a glass cup of tepid tea. The weapons master sat up against the trunk of his gnarled tree and took the proffered cup gratefully.

"Would you not have been curious yourself?" His words came slowly, through short laboured breaths. Though Rilla and Kari had done their best to heal him, he was still in a considerable amount of pain.

"I would have let the child be."

"And I suppose if she were to walk into my room, with her wound practically healed, you wouldn't want to examine her?"

The healer's head whipped around to look out the window following Ensil's steady gaze. He regarded the healer thoughtfully. Kari was quite young, by elf standards. When the battle between humans and lintep had been fought, she was only just beginning to learn the mysteries of healing. That had been many years ago. After that time, the lintep had withdrawn into Illaria, with only a few venturing into the Outworld. Rilla was the first seriously injured lintep she had seen.

Ensil frowned slightly. Eliséo was by Rilla's side. Lady Eléna had chosen well. Of all the elves in Silvaren to entrust to Rilla's protection, the ambassador would have been his choice too. He may have been born in the Outworld, but few elves would dare openly challenge his right to live in Silvaren.

Together, they waited expectantly for the two outsiders to arrive. Occasionally, Kari noticed herself holding her breath and let it out softly. Ensil patted her arm with his free hand. He'd had his chance to examine the prophecy child. If there was anyone who understood how the healer felt at the moment, it was him. They listened to the footsteps approaching, one hesitant, the other confident.

"Ensil, are you fit to welcome us?" Eliséo's clear voice carried up from the common room.

"Come up, Eliséo," Kari answered. "Bring the girl with you."

Ensil's hand tightened momentarily on the healer's arm in an effort to calm her, though it didn't work. She could barely conceal her excitement.

As the guests entered, Ensil handed Kari his unfinished cup of tea and gave her a little nudge towards the other side of his room. Annoyed with him for trying to distract her, she turned her back on the prophecy child to place the cup on the only table in the room.

From the moment he saw her, Ensil didn't take his eyes from Rilla. He knew she was fully aware of his attention, though her eyes followed Kari's movement across the room and back again. When she finally did meet his gaze, it was with proud eyes.

"I'm not apologising for defending myself, but I *am* sorry that I hurt you."

"Good for you, girl!" He smiled at her, with as much enthusiasm as his drained body could muster. "I haven't had been this badly wounded since my run-in with Eliséo."

Both Kari and Rilla looked immediately towards Eliséo.

"I should have known." The healer shook her head, angrily. Turning back to Ensil, she tried to reason with him. "I suppose you won't listen if I ask you to stop doing this."

"You suppose correctly." Ensil smiled a little sheepishly. "An elf needs to have his fun *some* way."

"Fun?" Rilla asked, incredulously. "You attacked me for *fun*?"

"We have different interpretations of that word, young Rilla. You see fun as an enjoyable pastime, no doubt, whereas I have a deeper view of it." He took a pillow and placed it behind his head to get more comfortable. "I have been training elves to use their weapons for longer than most in Silvaren care to remember. In all that time, the greatest satisfaction I've ever had was to see how well my students learnt their lessons.

"Most do passably well, with a select few surpassingly so. Eliséo, though a foundling, was one of those few. But since his training…"

"None have come so close to *killing* you." Kari finished his sentence and threw it back in his face. "What if she hadn't been able to start the healing process before I got to you?"

"Then he would have died knowing that I had a fighting chance of surviving in the Outworld. If I hadn't thought my life was in danger, he wouldn't have seen how I would react under pressure." Rilla's answer took Ensil by surprise. Every elf he'd ever attacked had been furious with him over his tactics. They had all been his students much longer than Rilla, so their trust in him had been overwhelmingly strong. For each and every one of them, it had felt like a betrayal when he attacked them. As the weapons master, he understood and expected that.

Rilla though, she wasn't angry with him. She *understood* him. He'd never met anyone who understood him. Queen ... Lady Eléna came the closest out of anyone he'd ever met, but even she had once begged him to stop testing their elves.

"I like this one." He smiled mischievously up at Kari, who simply rolled her eyes at him. Looking back to Rilla, he saw the uncertain smile on her face. She must have been expecting a vastly different conversation with him.

"Child, I'm extraordinarily proud of you. Even Eliséo had been my student for longer than yourself before I tested him. Without exception, the two of you are the only ones to ever come close to killing me on the spot." He watched as she clutched at the pendant around her neck and ground her teeth. "I'm not upset with you for striking at me, girl. I'm glad you did. In truth, I'm indebted to you twofold now. Not only have you given me such a gift of happiness with your skills, you also saved my life. If there is ever anything you need of me, do not hesitate to ask."

"That's very kind of you Master Ensil," Rilla answered politely. "But I doubt there is anything *you* can do to help *me*."

Ensil raised an eyebrow at her but said nothing.

Kari broke the silence. "Come here child, let me look at your wound."

"There's really no need." Rilla tried to brush the healer away.

"Nonsense, Rilla. I must be certain not to let you leave Silvaren with an infected wound, knowing that I could have helped you, had I simply examined you well enough."

Ensil smiled encouragingly towards the lintep, trying to convince her to trust the healer. Calmly, Rilla sighed and walked over to the healer. She stood patiently as Kari took off the sling and undid the bandage around her wound.

Ensil watched closely. The healer's fingers trembled slightly as she got closer to seeing the lintep's skin. Kari dropped the bandage and sling on the floor and took a sudden step back from Rilla, glancing over towards Ensil, then bent in closer to examine the girl.

"Incredible!" Kari exclaimed, as she stepped back to admire her patient. "I almost wish I hadn't tried to heal you myself. Then we really would have been able to see how rapidly your body works to mend itself."

Rilla shook her head and closed her eyes. Abruptly, she opened her eyes and almost fell back.

"Are you quite alright, child?" Ensil asked gruffly. Rilla looked at him with haunted eyes.

"She will be fine, Master Ensil," Eliséo answered. "She simply hasn't eaten enough for the amount of energy her body is using to heal. I apologise, but I think she should rest. Lady Eléna will not forgive me if I allow any more harm to come to her."

Ensil narrowed his eyes at them, but said nothing. Kari opened her mouth to protest but, catching the look in Ensil's eyes, seemed to think better of the idea. They bid Eliséo and Rilla farewell and watched from the window as the pair departed.

"You know something." Kari didn't turn to face him, but her accusation was well aimed.

"I *suspect* something, my dear. It's not the same thing."

"Curse you, Ensil." She turned to face him, anger overwhelming her. "You know *exactly* what I mean. What have you discovered?"

"I have a feeling that Eliséo's protection of Rilla will continue long after the girl has left Silvaren." He lay back down on his soft blanketed bed, placing the pillow beneath his head. "I think I need to rest now."

It was an unsubtle dismissal. Kari would not argue the point with him. As he heard her footsteps descending the curved pathway to the forest floor, he thought on what he'd learned that day.

Eliséo had been the only other elf to injure him so badly. He'd been trained by the weapons master for much longer than Rilla. The girl should not have been able to best him, even considering the distraction of Eliséo's sudden appearance. Some of the moves she used were too advanced. She hadn't performed them exceedingly well, but that wasn't the point. She shouldn't have known how to perform them at all. They were things that only advanced students learnt.

His mind toyed with a dangerous thought. He tried to dismiss it, but could not. Surely if such a thing had occurred, Lady Eléna would know about it. He would talk to her before the prophecy child left. The former queen would not have a choice. He would threaten to expose her most closely guarded secret if she refused to sate his curiosity.

Chapter Thirty-Three – Arishen's story

Telon waited outside the dining hall with the other guides. Arishen stormed out, slamming the doors closed behind him. Telon jumped back in surprise at this violent display. He stepped forward hurriedly to assist his charge.

"Get away from me, elf!" the seer shouted at him. "I want nothing more to do with this place."

Telon jumped away, hands held up, non-threateningly. He waited until the seer had stormed out of earshot before casting a glance at Gioshué. "It's fine if you leave the prophecy child – *she* can look after herself – but what am I meant to do with this one? He goes from bad to worse within minutes and hasn't the training to trust his skills to save him."

"Find Shadow and tell her," Gioshué suggested with a shrug.

"I doubt you'll get any help from the banwep." It was Tameo, Tika's guide, who spoke up. "By the sounds of it, Shadow is hoping to abandon the new Outworlders here when she leaves."

"Wonderful," Telon sighed. "I suppose I'll follow him from a distance. Just the three of you make sure not to let the others near him today. Give him a chance to calm down."

The seer was walking out of his room when Telon caught up with him. The two long daggers in dark brown leather sheaths immediately caught Telon's attention because he hadn't seen the boy wear them before.

Telon took all the shortcuts he knew to reach Silva's root system before Arishen. He knew Arishen would be no match for any elf in a fair fight, but few elves in Silvaren were constantly armed. Only the likes of Master Ensil and Ambassador Eliséo were prepared in that way.

It wasn't long before Arishen appeared from the only exit he'd been shown, and Telon waited for him in the shadows, watching him. Arishen veered away from the weapon master's tree, no doubt in an effort to avoid anyone he'd become acquainted with in Silvaren.

The seer walked at a brisk pace for over an hour. There were only younger trees in this part of the stronghold, none belonging to any elves. Telon wondered if the seer knew this. He stood behind the nearest tree, blending in with the forest as well as he could, awaiting Arishen's next move.

Daggers were drawn from their sheaths. Telon held his breath, not understanding what the seer had in mind. Arishen stood as though ready to face an attacker, feinting the moves Ensil had taught him the previous day. His frustration proved too great for the unresisting air. Walking towards one of the older trees, Arishen struck out as hard as he could, slashing away the outer layers of bark from the glossy black trunk.

"Arishen, no!" Telon yelled at the seer, coming out from hiding. The tall boy turned to him, wild eyed. "What are you doing?"

"I'm practicing the skills Ensil taught me, what does it look like?" Arishen shouted. "What are *you* doing? I told you to leave me alone!"

"I'm glad I *did* follow you. You can't do that to the trees!" Telon gestured angrily at the torn bark.

"What difference does it make to you? It's not as if I'm hurting anyone. These trees don't even belong to anyone – Eliséo told us that the other day."

"It doesn't matter if they don't belong to anyone. They can still feel pain."

Uncertainty flashed in Arishen's eyes. "I don't believe you."

Telon shook his head in anger. "Put down your daggers and place your hand on the tree you just cut."

He saw Arishen bite back a retort and reluctantly sheath his daggers. He walked to the tree and hesitantly placed his left hand over one of the cuts he'd made. Telon didn't have to watch his expression to know what he was feeling. Every elf had felt what Arishen was feeling now. It was a lesson they learnt at a young age. Whichever tree they hurt first, either accidentally or purposefully, they were made to place their skin on that tree to feel its pain. Once was always more than enough. Especially once an elf was bound to their own tree. The thought of hurting *any* tree was more than they could bear.

"I had no idea." Unshed tears glistened in the seer's pale blue eyes. "I'm sorry." He sat down by the tree and rested his head against it. Telon knew he would still be able to feel the pain, even though the hair on his head would not allow him direct contact with the tree. He sat down beside the human, careful not to allow any part of his skin to touch the injured tree. It was not his actions that had caused the pain. He had no need to share in it.

They sat in silence for a while, Arishen drinking in the tree's pain, Telon wondering what had happened to anger him in the first place.

"Thank you." Telon looked up, puzzled at the unexpected apology. "For coming after me when I told you not to. Who knows how much more damage I would have done if you hadn't stopped me?"

"You looked furious when you came out of the dining hall. I was scared of what would happen if I *didn't* follow you."

"She tends to have that effect on me." Arishen turned red, not from embarrassment, but from anger.

"Rilla of the lintep?" Telon asked in surprise. "Gioshué tells us she is ... quite nice." He wanted to say, the nicest, most troubled person he had ever met, but did not think it wise to share what might not be common knowledge.

"She is quite nice," Arishen answered quietly. "She notices everything and keeps secrets for everyone without them ever knowing. Without thinking twice, she automatically does what she thinks is the right thing to do, usually saving lives as she does so."

"And this makes you angry?" Telon couldn't understand the seer.

"It's a long story." Arishen tried to brush the question away.

"We have a long time before we need to be back for the feast tonight. You may find that a willing ear is what you've needed all this time."

Telon caught the seer's gaze, holding it until he finally gave in. He listened attentively to Arishen's tale, occasionally nodding or asking a question, but remaining silent most of the time.

The sun passed its zenith while Arishen related his story, but the seer didn't seem to notice. He was completely absorbed by his own frustration and finished with an enormous sigh.

"Have you ever thought that perhaps she doesn't realise you have any affection for her?" It was Telon's first thought – one that had occurred to him earlier on.

"I wouldn't call it affection." Arishen blushed, cutting him off.

"What I mean to say is that she may not have seen that you just want to be noticed, to spend time with her, to get to know her. Even though you say she notices everything – she seems to only see things that have nothing to do with herself.

"It's possible that she thinks you dislike her. She can't possibly know that you feel bad because she has saved your life twice and you haven't had a chance to return the favour."

"How can she not realise that?"

"You do give her mixed signals, Arishen," Telon explained patiently, not understanding how blind this human could be. "You argue with her constantly, even to the point of stabbing her. Most of your conversations with her seem to end badly."

"But that's just because she makes me so furious."

"Learn to keep your temper. Stop and think before you yell at her. Try to imagine how she feels. You've told me your story, but have you even considered *her* story?"

"Her story is the same as mine." Arishen shrugged.

"I barely know Rilla of the lintep, but even *I* can tell that isn't so. From what you've told me, she had only one friend in the Paradise – an old man who was murdered."

Arishen nodded.

"She never found a Partner, as it seems most other children in your Paradise did. She has kept everyone's secrets, including yours, never once giving them away until absolutely necessary. Yet, when her own secret is revealed, you and Plyke reacted worse than Shadow. She saved your life on a number of occasions and you never thanked her. She discovered she was a lintep, probably with more power than she could have ever imagined, and now she has no one to show her how to use it. Do you still think her story is the same as yours?"

Arishen was staring wide-eyed at him and shook his head, lost for words.

"I don't know how you could understand so much about her from what I told you."

Telon smiled briefly. "Imagine what I could tell you about her if I knew what all four of you know about her. Even the small amount of time that Shadow has spent with her would tell me something."

"Fine, but even knowing what I know and understanding what you've told me, that doesn't mean I'm going to be able to control my temper any better when I'm around her."

"No, it doesn't," Telon agreed quietly. "All I can suggest is that you stop and take two deep breaths before talking to her. It seems as though being a seer has made you blind to what's staring you in the face. You see so much in your dreams that you simply close your eyes to everything when you're awake.

"Try to actually see what's happening around you. Watch her reaction, not just to you, but to your other companions. You may find that she pays just as much attention to you as she does to everyone else, but you simply don't notice it."

"It's a bit difficult to do that here. She seems to be the centre of attention, with little left over for us Paradisians."

"That's to be expected. It's not every day the prophecy child comes to Silvaren." Telon smiled broadly. He was glad he was alive to see her. Whatever else happened in her life, she would change things in the Outworld. It would certainly be an interesting time in which to live.

"What do you mean she's the prophecy child?" Arishen asked in confusion.

Telon was jolted out of his musings. Was it possible that the seer was the only one who hadn't understood just how important Rilla of the lintep was?

"Perhaps you should ask her about it at some point. Why did you think every elf in Silvaren wanted to meet her?"

"I ... I don't know. I hadn't thought about it."

"Arishen, you need to open your eyes. Try something this evening. Just sit back and watch. Don't try to speak to anyone – see how many people come up to you and the other two boys, and how many go up to Rilla."

"I can try," Arishen smiled half-heartedly. Telon could see that it was going to take more than forced smiles to repair this relationship.

"Let's get back then. I assume you won't want to stay here by yourself the rest of the afternoon." Together, they ambled back to Silva.

Chapter Thirty-Four – Forbidden knowledge

"I assume we're not going to talk about this." Tika sat back in his chair, pushing his now empty plate towards the middle of the table.

"Talk about what?" Plyke responded absently, still looking towards the door which Rilla had quietly closed behind her.

"Your overnight reform. I've been asking you since we got here to give Rilla a chance, to try to understand what it must be like for her to have her most important secret revealed. All three of you treated her worse than she deserved and thought you were quite justified in doing so.

"And now, suddenly, she walks through that door with you so close by her side that Arishen practically had smoke pouring out of his ears."

Plyke turned to stare at Tika with an almost panicked look in his only visible eye, the brown one. "It's not what you think."

Tika shook his head, wondering why they were having so much trouble communicating since reaching Silvaren. "I *know* that nothing is further from your mind. I was simply saying that Arishen misinterpreted it, but I'd rather like to know what *did* happen to make him think that."

"I don't think that's something I can tell you," Plyke started, but then hastened to justify his words. "It's not that I don't trust you, but ..."

"It isn't your secret to share," Tika finished his sentence, knowingly.

"How did you know I was going to say that?" Plyke's confusion was irritating.

"Because she's been keeping everyone's secrets her whole life. It only makes sense that when you finally realised that, you would want to return the favour." Tika watched his Partner's face fall. "Plyke, at least you *did* realise it. It may have taken you a while, but you understood in the end."

"How did it happen that you, the most willing to participate in Paradise life, can so easily accept the Outworld and every surprise it holds in store for us? Why weren't *you* blind with rage over Rilla's secret?"

Tika fought the urge to walk out of the room without answering, to leave his Partner wondering what he'd said wrong. He knew if he did that, there would be no chance for them to ever repair their Partnership.

"Haven't you known me long enough to know that I love the very idea of magic? Wasn't I the one who always wanted to meet the elves?" Plyke nodded. "Then why does it surprise you that I'm not upset that Rilla is a lintep? Why do you think I was happy enough to leave the Paradise? There was never any chance that I would meet an elf there, or see any magic."

"I suppose I never quite saw you in that light." Plyke pulled his hair away from his face, revealing his green eye. "I always thought you were ..."

"One of Erton's mindless sheep?" Tika's icy question drew only a silent response from his partner. "Tell me one thing Plyke, why did you ever agree to be my Partner if that's what you thought of me?" Before his Partner could reply, Tika continued. "Oh wait, that's right. You needed to blend in, to disappear. You couldn't afford to let Erton or his minions notice you. Don't think *I* don't know your secret. Just because I've never mentioned it, doesn't mean I don't know exactly as much as Rilla has guessed about you."

Plyke's eyes were wide with terror. "You won't tell will you?"

Tika's chest hurt. "How can you ask me that? You're more worried *I* will give your precious secret away than you are of a girl you've only just befriended."

Plyke was silent for a long while. "How long have you known?"

Tika tried so hard not to cry in frustration. "That you were different? Always. That you are a lintep? I started to suspect it with your completely impassive reaction to Shuut. I saw you watch Arishen's anger, the argument you had within yourself whether to add your voice to his argument or to defend someone who was just like you.

"Rilla's secret being revealed removed all doubt from my mind that I was right. She suspected your secret and you feared that her being revealed as a lintep would cause *your* revelation."

"You saw all that?" Plyke asked in complete bemusement. "Why didn't you ever say anything to me? Why did you ever pick me as your Partner?"

"You just don't understand, do you?" Tika shouted at him. "My Partnership with you is the closest I will ever get to magic. What all three of you seem to be reluctant to have anything to do with is what I've craved all my life! It seems so unfair that it's wasted on people who just don't appreciate it as the gift it is."

"Gift?" Plyke replied, his voice dangerously low. "How is something that could cause any of our deaths a gift?"

"Why do you always see the bad in everything? Just being a Paradisian in the Outworld could kill us. That means *I* could die just as easily as any of you. But at least three of you have magnificent healing abilities and one can dream the future. What protection do I have other than your friendship?"

Tika waited for a response. Realising his Partner's silence would not end any time soon, he left the dining hall, closing the door softly behind him.

Tameo looked up as he came out. With a shake of his head and a wave of his hand, Tika brushed him aside. Much as he had longed to meet the elves, he did not want their company right now. From what he had seen so far, they didn't understand humans too well. He couldn't possibly explain his current situation without revealing the entire story. He would never betray his Partner. Sadly, his Partner did not appear to believe that.

* * *

Raeslin watched silently as, one by one, all but her charge left the dining hall. Most had left in anger or frustration. She knew there was some special bond between Tika and Plyke, so it concerned her when Tika left the room with an air of resigned frustration. She wondered whether it had anything to do with the prophecy child who, it seemed, had an effect on people wherever she went, whether she wanted to or not.

She stood for a long while waiting for Plyke to come out before venturing into the dining hall of her own accord. She found the boy staring blankly ahead of him, his hair swept back off his face. It was the first time that she'd seen him like that, but she soon realised why. There were few people with different coloured eyes. Who knew what the implications of blatantly showing that in the Outworld would be?

"Master Plyke?" she called out to him tentatively, not entirely sure if she should be disturbing him. Panic flashed in his eyes as his face whipped around to meet her. In a practiced sweep, he dislodged his hair from behind an ear to cover the green eye once more.

"What do you want, Raeslin?" He sounded as resigned as Tika had looked.

"You've been in here by yourself most of the morning. Do you not want to see any other part of Silvaren on your final day here?"

"I want nothing more to do with this place," he answered her shortly. "Why would I want to see more of a place that I'm going to have to leave in the morning?"

"For exactly *that* reason," Raeslin answered. "You are leaving in the morning. Today is your last chance to see anything you like in Silvaren. Why would you waste that opportunity?" Raeslin bit her tongue, afraid she'd said too much.

"I don't think you and I see things the same way." Plyke shook his head bitterly. "I didn't want to come here in the first place. I didn't want to leave Turon. I just want to find a place where we can live without fear and danger."

"What makes you think you're in any more danger than anyone else in the Outworld?" Raeslin pressed him further. "Rilla of the lintep probably has more power than many other lintep. Shadow has been well trained as a banwep and has her part lintep heritage to strengthen her skills. Arishen can dream of any harm which may befall you so that every one of you can prepare for, or even evade, an attack. Exactly *how* does that place you in great danger?"

"Well when you put it that way, maybe it doesn't, but what do I care about seeing more of Silvaren? I don't want to look around and discover that I love the place I will need to leave very shortly. That will just cause more pain than I already have to deal with."

"That's a fairly narrow-minded outlook on life," Raeslin replied. "Is it that attitude which is causing you problems with Tika?"

"How dare you question my Partnership with Tika?" Plyke snapped.

"Partnership?" Raeslin narrowed her eyes. "Is that what you call it when one person practically ignores the other except to fight with them?"

"I don't ignore him." Plyke took the bait.

"You could have fooled me." Raeslin raised her eyebrows.

"And we *don't* fight. We might have the odd disagreement, but that's not the same thing."

Raeslin almost laughed, but stopped herself before she insulted her charge even further. "I think Tika might see things differently. *You* didn't see the look on his face when he walked out of here earlier this morning."

"How dare you presume to know more about my Partner than I do?" Plyke replied indignantly.

"I think it's a wonder you still call him your Partner when it's obvious to everyone but yourself that you constantly dismiss him. If you truly value even just his friendship, I would concentrate on drawing him closer rather than driving him away."

Raeslin knew she had crossed the line already, but it might be the only way of opening the boy's eyes to the mistake he was making. Rather than waiting for an answer, she left the dining hall, leaving Plyke by himself.

* * *

Plyke watched the young elf walk away from him, his anger dying away with her footsteps. *Is she right? Does Tika feel that I'm dismissing our Partnership too?* Perhaps that was for the best. If he was honest with himself, he knew that Tika was right – he'd only accepted being Tika's Partner to avoid detection under Erton's deathly grip.

He didn't even know if Partnerships between humans and lintep worked. Had anyone other than a human tried to use the Partnership bond after one Partner died? Perhaps he should talk to Tika about it. Maybe if they spoke about it calmly, Tika would be more willing to simply stop being his Partner.

The decision made, he got to his feet and finally left the dining hall. Tika's room was a few levels down from the dining hall. He wondered if his Partner would still be there.

Raeslin was not waiting for him outside the dining hall. It was the first time he was completely unaccompanied. At least he would be alone when he found Tika. At his Partner's room, he held out his hand to draw the dark silver vines aside.

"I think, perhaps, you might like to change your mind." Plyke heard the regal voice behind him. Turning, he found Lady Eléna walking up the path to Tika's room.

"My Lady Eléna." Plyke bowed slightly. "Change my mind about what?"

"Don't play coy with me, boy," the former queen answered, shortly. "I know more about you than you would care to imagine."

Plyke was instantly on his guard. "If you know so much about me, my lady, then you would understand why I have to do this."

"I understand why you *think* you have to do this, but you are mistaken." Eléna closed the distance between them with a few swift steps. "Tika is not in his room. If you refuse to change your mind on this matter, you will not find him until this evening's festivities."

"I beg your pardon, Lady Eléna, but this matter does not concern you," Plyke told her in a quiet, steady voice. He had always been good at controlling his temper. It was yet another survival technique he'd learnt in their Paradise. Anyone with a bad temper stood out like a sore thumb.

"I do not think this is a conversation for all ears," the tall, elegant elf told him before she closed her eyes and said a few words under her breath. Plyke watched as a swirl of mist gathered around them, thickening into an almost solid wall. Eléna opened her eyes with a small smile of satisfaction. "That should work nicely."

"What did you do?" Plyke asked, tentatively touching the mist surrounding them.

"Making sure that our conversation doesn't reach the wrong ears," she replied evenly. "Plyke, did your mother ever tell you where you come from?"

Plyke drew in a sharp breath. "In our Paradise, children do not know who their parents are. That's one of the most well known rules, my lady."

"We're not going to get very far if you keep blocking me, boy," Eléna told him. "I know you are at least half lintep. Before you ask *how* I know this, understand that I knew your great-grandmother. You have much of her in you – the same expressions." She sighed sadly. "How I have missed her. It was a tragedy when I lost her. She was a good friend to me all those years ago."

"Even if you *did* know my great-grandmother," Plyke answered when his heart started beating once more, "that doesn't mean that you can guess at what blood runs through my veins."

"I kept a very close eye on her family. I know where her children, grandchildren and great-grandchildren are to be found."

Plyke took a step back but was blocked by the mist wall. Eléna reached out a hand to steady him.

"Don't touch me!" Plyke yelled out in a panic.

"Plyke, please try to understand." Eléna withdrew her hand, but kept a steady eye on him. "I'm not about to tell everyone who you are. I keep this information closely guarded. Not even my closest advisors know that I've kept an eye on your family."

"You told everyone who Rilla was," he retorted immediately. "How can you expect me to believe that you won't tell anyone who *I* am?"

"Rilla is the prophecy child, Plyke. She was meant to have been raised with that knowledge. She was meant to have been taught at least the basic use of her powers. I know it comes as little consolation to her, but if I hadn't said anything, every other elf in Silvaren would have realised by now and she wouldn't be able to hide from it anymore."

"Do you have any idea what you've done to her?" Plyke retaliated without a moment's pause. "Do you understand what she's going through now?"

"Better than you can imagine, boy," Eléna replied, tears glazing her eyes. "Which brings me back to Tika."

"Leave Tika out of this. It has nothing to do with him." Plyke's voice was dangerously low.

"For seeing so much around you, you have a narrow outlook when it comes to your own situation." The elf shook her head. "Tika is the only reason you are still alive today." Plyke stared at her blankly. "What do you think would have happened to you if you didn't have a Partner in your Paradise? You would have stuck out as much as Rilla. The only reason she wasn't harmed was because she was the Paradise leader's daughter. *You* would not have had the same immunity.

"If Tika had not decided to leave the Paradise, you would probably have stayed behind. What do you think would have happened once your power started to mature? It would have been too difficult for you to keep your identity secret, even with Kora's help. In fact, you may have placed both your lives in danger."

At the mention of his mother's name, Plyke lost all feeling in his legs and sank to the floor. "You really do know. But, how?"

"Little one, Kora used to live in Illaria. I only ever met her once, but you look just like her, except for your green eye. It stands to reason that Kora is your mother. You have so much of her in you that it would be difficult to mistake you for anyone else's child."

"I don't understand what Kora has to do with Tika," Plyke mumbled.

"Plyke, listen to me. Tika has pulled you through many parts of your life. The fact that you don't realise that is a shame, but it doesn't change the truth. It would be senseless for you to break your Partnership with him just because you're not human. He's known that your entire life. Why do you think that would make him break away from you?"

"The bond won't work," Plyke answered automatically.

"You don't know that for certain," Eléna replied softly. "Besides, it is too late in Tika's life for him to find another Partner. He has known all along that your Partnership may not work, but he chose you anyway. Why rip this one chance away from him?"

Plyke stared at the tall elf. Her black hair, streaked with silver lines, was the only sign of age. He looked into her silver eyes, losing himself in their depth. They held so much wisdom, so much pain.

"I see your skills lie in empathy. That will be good for Rilla. She will need that." Eléna drew him out of his thoughts. "But *I* will not be good for you in that area. I fear my life's worth of pain will only bring you more despair."

Plyke shook his head to clear his thoughts. He felt as though he'd just woken from a sad dream.

"I think it safest for you to stay with Raeslin today." Eléna dispersed the mist wall, her eyes shining brightly. "Go to your room. She will find you there. Tika will see you tonight. If tomorrow you are still intent on destroying your Partnership, I will do nothing to stop you, but in Silvaren, it will not happen."

In a daze, Plyke watched the elegant elf walk away before turning to his own room. He waited there patiently for Raeslin, barely talking when she arrived.

Chapter Thirty-Five – Gifts

As sunset approached, Rilla walked back to Silva alone. At the base of the massive tree, Gioshué was waiting for her, bouncing with excitement. His unabashed happiness made Rilla smile despite herself.

"What has you so excited?"

"I just wanted to walk you to your chamber."

She raised an eyebrow at him. "I know the way to my chamber, Gioshué. Why did you really want to meet me?"

"I want to see if you like your surprise." He motioned her to the curved walkway leading to her chamber. "Then I've been asked to escort you to the common chamber."

Obliging the young elf, Rilla walked quickly and quietly up to her chamber, not entirely certain that she was going to like the surprise he knew was in store for her. As she entered her chamber alone, she was delighted to find gifts on her sleeping pallet. There were green and brown travel clothes and brown ankle boots. Most of her shirts had been torn apart to be used as bandages and had been too big by far. These new clothes looked as though they would fit her perfectly. Sitting next to her rucksack was a rolled up sleeping mat. She smiled at the thought of taking that on her travels. No longer would she have to sleep on her cloak.

Beside the travel clothes was a vibrant green dress, the colour matching her eyes. As she slipped it over her head, there was the same rustling noise that she had become accustomed to from the leaves in her rucksack. The black slippers that had been beside her bed resembled the smooth glossy trunks all throughout Silvaren. She shook her head. Both Lady Eléna and Eliséo had warned her severely not to mention her bond with Elessa to anyone, but her evening clothes practically screamed it out to anyone who might have any suspicion. Perhaps she was reading too much into the gifts.

Gioshué's eyes lit up when Rilla reappeared. "Even if you weren't the prophecy child, all eyes would still be on you tonight." Rilla's heart sank at his words, though she was careful not to let her feelings show. She loved Silvaren, the forest, the familiarity, the peacefulness – but she couldn't wait to get away from people who knew who she was, who expected too much from her. *It's only one more night*, she thought to herself as she followed Gioshué to the awaiting elves.

∗ ∗ ∗

Tika had spent the morning shooting arrows at a target. His arms ached from the effort, but it was a good ache. He was practising a skill that could well keep both himself, and his companions, safe in the Outworld. It was nice to think that he might not need to rely on their skills alone – that he would be able to contribute something to their company. Living in the Paradise, he had grown accustomed to the fact that everyone should have a purpose. It felt to Tika that his bow and arrow had finally given him one.

Resting in the lake below Silva had helped ease the pain in his arms. Tameo called him out of the water as sunset approached. Tika's fingers were wrinkled. He looked at them in curiosity. In their Paradise, he'd never stayed so long in a pool of water for that to happen.

In our Paradise ... It was a dangerous thought. Plyke had really *needed* him there. It had been a way for Plyke to escape Erton's detection. Now what use was he? Even though they were Partners, Tika doubted it meant much to Plyke now. He closed his eyes against those thoughts. Nothing but sadness waited for him there.

He followed Tameo up to his chamber. Alongside his new travel clothes and sleeping mat was a set of more elegant clothes in shades of deep purple, reminding him of the small fringa whose protector he had helped to save the life of. His black slippers had the same glossy sheen as the bird's beak. As he changed into his new clothes, he softly whistled the tune the fringa had taught him in case he ever needed to call on their help.

* * *

Arishen walked back to Silva with Telon. His guide had not left his side since he'd attacked the tree. Arishen was certain it wasn't through fear that he would attack yet another tree, but because of their long talk about Rilla. He wondered why it was transparently obvious to everyone *other* than Rilla what his feelings towards her were.

He would try Telon's advice. He would sit back and watch tonight. If Rilla made his temper flare, he would take two deep breaths before answering her. He hadn't apologised to her for his behaviour since arriving in Silvaren. Perhaps when they finally left the elves, he might be able to find a quiet time and have a calm word with her.

They reached his chamber just after sunset. Inside, Arishen found a set of travelling clothes, a sleeping mat, and another set of clothes for that evening. The trousers were a midnight blue, threaded with silver to match his shirt. He smiled to himself and shook his head at the implications of his gift. In his eyes, they were an overly obvious reference to the fact that his powers only came to him in sleep. He slipped his feet into the dark slippers and walked with Tameo towards the festivities.

* * *

Plyke had spent the day in relative silence. After being reprimanded by Lady Eléna, he had been in no mood to talk to anyone. Raeslin had taken him to her favourite parts of Silvaren, explaining as much as she could about elves. He listened to her distractedly and barely noticed when she became as silent as he was.

They did not encounter Tika the entire day. Plyke doubted it was a coincidence. Lady Eléna had probably instructed Raeslin to keep them apart.

As sunset approached, Plyke followed Raeslin back to Silva and to his chamber. He looked on his pallet in surprise to see travelling clothes, a sleeping mat and a close fitting black outfit trimmed in grey. It was precisely the colour he would have chosen for himself, making it easier to blend into the shadows. He didn't have to wonder who had been the one to choose their gifts. He was certain that everyone else's was ordered to suit their personality as well, though perhaps each person understood something about their outfit that no one else would.

Plyke dressed in his evening clothes, trying to look more jovial than he felt. This was their last night in Silvaren. In the morning, they would finally be leaving the

170

elves. He knew he would have to tell Arishen and Shuut about his lintep heritage sooner or later, but he pushed that thought to the back of his mind. Together, he and Raeslin walked in silence to the common room to greet the others.

* * *

Shuut waited impatiently for the Paradisians to arrive. She might be forced to take the four of them with her from Silvaren, but she was confident there was nothing Lady Eléna could do to push her luck any further than that. As soon as she was out of sight of the elven stronghold, she would simply slip away in the middle of the night. After all, that's what her father had trained her to do best.

As her companions reached the room where she was waiting for them, Farrow arrived and requested they follow him. The five of them were announced as guests of honour as they entered the common chamber.

Queen Liessa rose from her seat. "My elves, we have some very special guests in our company for one last evening. Will you help me send them off with fair memories of their time with us?"

A loud cheer went up and music started anew. The Paradisians dispersed through the crowd. Shuut made herself a small plate of food and retreated to a quiet corner, enjoying the new magic emitted by the music. She inclined her head to greet the elegant former queen who came to sit by her side.

"Tell me, Shadow, will you be going to the Drakos Mountains when you leave us? Have the crystal dragons been fair in their dealings with you recently?" Shuut drew in a sharp breath. "I mean no disrespect in asking, my friend, but you know how I loathe their manipulations."

Outraged by the comment, Shuut threw up her hand to slap the elf's face. Some force prevented her from doing so. She realised, from the sudden shine in the silver eyes, that the former queen still possessed power of her own without the aid of the crown.

"How dare you talk to me like that!" she said in a steady, low, voice. "I am *not* one of your elves."

The elf's power placed Shadow's hand back in her lap. "We were both told how our lives must be, little one, but I found my own way of living it." She paused momentarily. "I see you still have trouble doing likewise. How long will you let them rule your life, child? How long must you serve them before you are satisfied? You know they will release you from their hold if you only ask it of them."

Shuut looked at her, suddenly feeling like the lost and frightened child she once had been.

"My mother is dead, Eléna. How can I be strong without her? I have no one else to live for." Her voice faded to a resigned whisper. "I died with her. My life belongs to the crystal dragons now. They are the last ones who will take me."

"Do you truly believe that? Is there nothing you can think of? No person who needs you as much as you need them? No dreams or hopes to live for?"

"Unlike yourself, my lady, *I* must live in the Outworld where hopes and dreams have no place," Shuut answered dejectedly.

Eléna nodded as she rose slowly to her feet. "There is still one other who needs your help, if you have courage enough to give it." Shuut followed the elf's gaze as it came to rest on Rilla. Astounded, she opened her mouth to object only to find that Eléna had disappeared.

171

Between tunes, Eléna caught Rilla's eye. The lintep girl managed to excuse herself from the dance with some difficulty.

"I've been rude, Lady Eléna, for not thanking you for my clothes." Rilla smiled at her and smoothed down the material of her emerald dress.

"It was not my gift," Eléna demurred. "Those gifts were from Queen Liessa." She saw the confusion on Rilla's face.

"I do not mean to offend our hostess, but she does not seem to have as much insight to the boys and myself as you do," Rilla replied cautiously. "It seems as though our clothing for this evening was specifically designed. They either suit the person's personality, or serve to remind them of a significant part of their life. Without knowing us as well as *you* seem to, it would be impossible for anyone to choose such perfect garments for us all."

Eléna smiled slightly. "I see you've regained your observation skills. Queen Liessa wanted to make a gift of clothing to her guests, but left the details up to me. However," she added with narrowed eyes, "I doubt your companions have noticed that any other than their own garments are personally significant to the wearer."

Is this another way in which I am different from the others? Rilla thought to herself, sadly. *Will I never be able to become invisible again, to hide away?*

Little one, a voice echoed in her mind, *I did not mean to upset you. You were born different. It is a good thing that you are beginning to prove yourself worthy of the prophecy.*

Standing side by side, Eléna had but to touch the lintep to speak directly to her mind. Rilla pulled back instinctively and walked away without a word. Eléna watched her swift departure, exasperated. The child would need to learn and accept so much before she could fulfil the prophecy. If she kept fighting it, there would be no hope for the Outworld, and no respite for the elves.

"You scare her." A strong voice made her turn around. Eliséo was standing behind her, his eyes stony.

"She will forget her fear soon enough. She's a strong girl," Eléna assured him.

"She *is* strong," he agreed with her. "But she is frightened. There have been too many changes in her life too quickly. She had barely discovered that she was lintep before you named her as the prophecy child in front of everyone. It doesn't matter to her that the elves would have soon discovered it for themselves. Her companions and Shadow would still have been in the dark if you hadn't spoken."

Eléna looked at him wide-eyed, a slow smile spreading to her face. "You are drawn to her power. I hadn't noticed it before, but now I wonder how I could have missed it."

"I am not drawn to her at all, whether her power or her self," the ambassador answered icily.

Eléna answered him in a quiet voice. "You do realise her power is as great, perhaps even greater than your own. You cannot deny that this draws you to her."

At these words, the young elf turned to face her, responding just as quietly. "I have no great power, your grace. You know this." Eléna looked at him in disappointment. "You *do* know this," he repeated, forcefully. "When I was a child and we used to pretend that I was casting spells, you always used the magic in your crown to make me believe I was using my own." She shook her head at him. "But you told me so!"

The tall elven lady looked sadly at him. "Have you chosen what you will do on the morrow?"

"No!" Eliséo snarled softly. "You will *not* do this to me. We finish this tonight. Do you hear me?" His voice trembled with rage and fear.

"Tonight then." Eléna nodded. "Tonight, in my chambers, when the last note has been played."

As Eliséo strode angrily away from her, Eléna felt Ensil's attention dwell on her. She closed her eyes and prayed to the stars that he had not understood what was happening. When she opened them again, the weapons master was standing in front of her, his unwavering gaze locked onto her face.

"You and I need to have a chat, my old friend." His gruff voice brooked no argument. Eléna knew this was one time she would not be able to evade him.

"Master Ensil, what a lovely surprise to see you've healed well enough for this evening's festival."

"Funny you should mention my health," he answered her with a strained smile. "That's just what I wanted to talk to you about. Shall we?" Eléna smiled through clenched teeth and slipped a hand over the arm he offered her.

Chapter Thirty-Six – Eliséo, Ambassador of the Elves

"Why don't you go ahead and protect us with that mist of yours?" Ensil suggested casually once they'd entered Eléna's chambers.

"You know I can't do that without the crown, Ensil." Eléna declined his request with a steady voice. If she wavered now, she knew he would win.

"Eléna, we've known each other for too many years for you to fool me. I *know* you still have power and I'm certain you don't want eavesdroppers to worry us now."

Eléna weighed her options. She had known Ensil her entire life. He had already been the weapons master when she was training. There were few elves whom she would have said held any power over her – Ensil was one of those few. With a sigh, she muttered a few words under her breath and together they watched in silence as the shrouding mist formed around them. Only when the spell was complete did Eléna speak.

"Exactly what part of your health is such a delicate topic that we have need of this mist?"

"I don't begrudge the girl her killing stroke, but she would never have had such an opening if the ambassador hadn't distracted me."

"You brought me all the way up here, in such secrecy, to complain that the ambassador distracted you?" Eléna feigned surprise.

"No. I brought you all the way up here to ask you how in the Outworld that boy knew where to find us," Ensil barely paused for breath. "I knew where she was because I'd followed her all the way from Silva. No elf followed me. Of *that* I am certain. I didn't live to be this ripe old age by letting people creep up on me unawares."

"What are you suggesting, Ensil?" Eléna barely trusted herself to speak.

"I'm suggesting that the boy had just enough time to run, full pelt, from Silva to where the prophecy child and I were once I attacked her. How could he know where she was if someone hadn't told him?"

"Are you suggesting I had the trees spying on Rilla so that I could tell Eliséo where to find her?" she groped for any answer that might fool him.

"I'm not in the mood for your games," the weapons master growled at her. "You know very well that I'm asking you whether Eliséo's tree has bound the girl to herself."

Eléna regarded the weapons master in silence. She had warned them both to be careful no other elf discovered what had happened. Clearly, that warning had fallen on deaf ears.

"Ensil, please don't make me answer that question," Eléna felt like a child once more, begging her advisors to undo everything, to bring her parents back to life so she wouldn't have to be their queen.

"We've lived thousands of years together, you and I," Ensil sighed. "Don't you think it might be time for you to actually begin to *trust* me? You're not the queen anymore, Eléna. You don't have to protect yourself as much as you did before."

"How can you think I don't trust you?" She sank into one of two chairs in her chamber. "You know all of my most closely guarded secrets."

At that, Ensil laughed softly. "No, my dear friend, I know only those secrets which you deign to tell me. No more, no less. Even Silva doesn't know your most closely guarded secrets."

"How could you possibly know that?" Eléna whispered in fear.

"Who do you think taught your father to close his mind from his tree?" Eléna felt him watch her closely. "His own parents would have disapproved of that, had they known he had *found* a way to do it."

"Who are you, really?" Her words were barely audible.

"I'm your friend, Eléna." He knelt by her side and took her hands in his, looking up into her eyes. "I was once more than that, if you'll remember?"

Eléna closed her eyes to bring the images back to her mind. That had been hundreds of years ago. "I remember, Ensil."

"Then you should remember that I never told anyone. I kept your secret as well as I did mine. All I ask is that you open yourself to me once in a while. Did Elessa bind Rilla to herself?"

Tears fell as Eléna nodded her head. She collapsed into his welcoming arms crying into his chest. All the weight on her shoulders disappeared as he held her tightly, kissing her hair. They both knew they could go no further than that. The last time they had let their guard down, Eléna had had to make the most important and dangerous decision of her life. So instead, they held each other closely for what seemed like hours, Ensil kissing the tears from Eléna's cheeks, only to have them replaced almost instantly.

Through their skin contact, Eléna could sense everything. The more she needed him, the stronger his yearning for her. Ensil was so close to breaking. If he couldn't have her, then he didn't want to be this close to her.

The weapons master disentangled himself from Eléna. He stood on shaking legs and held a hand out to her. She took it, only to help herself up. The instant they were both standing, she dropped his and their skin contact was broken. Eléna wiped the tears from her eyes and rinsed her face with the cool water from the washbasin. She could feel Ensil's gaze burning into her, but could not turn to face him. In an effort to dispel the tension in the air, she softly spoke a few words under her breath and the mist fell away from them.

"Lady Eléna, Master Ensil, good evening." Eliséo's voice was stiff with formality. He stood to one side of the chamber. In their distraction, neither had heard him enter the room.

Eléna froze at the sound of his voice. "How long have you been standing there?"

"Only long enough to wonder where you were and then watch you appear out of thin air." She turned to face him and silenced him with a single look. She incanted the same words he'd heard her use a hundred times over with the crown. A mist swirled up around them.

"You told me, and everyone has believed for thousands of years, that this much power only comes to those who call it when they wear the crown."

"Do you not believe your own eyes, boy?" Ensil asked him. "Your mother has more power than she would have us believe."

"My mother?" Eliséo asked icily. "I am a foundling. No one knows who my parents are."

"You never told him?" Ensil asked incredulously.

"I never told him that *you* knew." Eléna looked away from them.

"You really do hold your secrets close to your heart, don't you?" Ensil's words cut her deeply. These were the elves she most trusted and yet they both knew she kept secrets from them. Words failed her as she looked from one to the other.

"Boy, this power runs through your family. The only ones who need the assistance of the crown are those who don't share the natural gift." Ensil explained.

"I don't understand why you know so much about this." Eliséo replied coldly.

"I have lived longer than every other elf in Silvaren. I am the only one who remembers what it was like in the time of King Daelan." The weapons master sighed tiredly. "I alone remember the real reason he abdicated the throne. I started the story that only the wearer of the crown has power, to stop the bitter rivalry between siblings."

"*You* started that story?" Eliséo repeated in disbelief. "Why would you do that?"

"What do you think would happen if there were two heirs to the throne – the eldest with very little power and the youngest with more than enough to not need the assistance of the crown?"

Eliséo did not need to answer. They all knew the answer to that question. Both elves would have an equal right to the throne. The only chance to avoid any sort of rivalry would lie in the hands of the younger, more powerful sibling.

"Have no fear," the ambassador told them. "I don't want to be tied down with a crown. Being ambassador gives me more freedom than most elves."

Eléna exchanged glances with Ensil. "My dear child, you may not be given the choice. If anyone were to find out, they would see only two options – you must be the king or you must die."

"That's a bit dramatic, don't you think, Lady Eléna. I could simply choose not to fight for the crown." He shook his head in anger. "Besides, *I* know how to keep this secret. It will never go further than this room that you are my mother."

* * *

Rilla tossed restlessly on her blanketed bed. She knew it was her last night in the elven stronghold and she was glad about it. But the leaves, which had escaped from her rucksack and were floating over her head, troubled her. They seemed to reflect her emotions.

She stepped softly from her room, hoping to find some peace as she walked the hauntingly silent pathways through Silva. The leaves swirled around her as she clutched her silver tree pendant. She wandered absentmindedly throughout the enormous tree, following where the leaves slowly pulled her.

Finding herself at the entrance of a lit chamber and craving companionship, she looked in to see Lady Eléna, Ambassador Eliséo and the weapons master, Ensil, in deep conversation with one another. A strange mist surrounded them.

"I'm sorry," she said as she turned to leave.

At her words, all three elves stared incomprehensibly at one another. Ensil spoke first.

"I know how strong your spells are. How are they not affecting her?" Rilla stopped in her tracks as she heard his words. "Can she hear us as well?"

A single word from Eléna ended her spell. Rilla turned to find the three elves watching her closely.

"What have I done?" Leaves swirled rapidly around her. "Was the mist shrouding you so that I should not see or hear?" She looked, searchingly, from one face to the other.

"Rilla, do not be afraid." The queen's mother spoke before Rilla had time to panic and flee. "Come, sit with us. There is much the four of us need to discuss." Hesitatingly, Rilla followed Lady Eléna to a place where they could all sit. The elven lady spoke commandingly.

"Eliséo, would you do us the honours? There are no others in the stronghold with power enough to see or hear through it."

The elf shook his head, but a look from Eléna quickly persuaded him to do as he was told. His eyes changed from a dull slate colour to a brilliant silver as he softly spoke the words. The disbelief in his eyes matched hers.

"Rilla, what did you overhear just now?" Ensil asked her as soon as the incantation was complete.

"I ... wasn't really listening," Rilla told him nervously, the leaves around her starting to settle down to the floor around her.

"Nonsense, child," he snapped. "Even if you weren't paying attention, it doesn't mean you didn't actually hear something."

She heard what you said, Eliséo. Rilla stared instantly at Eliséo. He returned her look impassively. Ensil watched the silent exchange between them.

"Out with it boy. What did she hear?"

"What makes you think I would know what she heard?" Eliséo replied calmly.

"I know your tree bound herself to this girl, so don't go pretending you don't know everything she does."

Eliséo showed no reaction. "Master Ensil, I think you will find you are mistaken," the young elf's voice was low and dangerous.

Rilla's leaves fluttered around her.

"Eliséo, please understand." Eléna looked at him with tears in her eyes. Eliséo stared at her silently for a moment.

"I think I've heard all I want to for one night." Hands on his knees, Eliséo was ready to stand.

"You haven't heard nearly enough yet, boy." Ensil placed a firm hand on the elf's arm. Rilla felt Elessa's distress at the situation.

"Ensil, this is difficult enough without you making matters worse." Eléna tried to ease the tension. "Eliséo, there's something I need to tell you. It's true, I brought you into Silvaren as a foundling. I made everyone believe that the lintep found you by chance and that, when they asked me to take you in, I'd never seen you before."

"I *know* that, Lady Eléna," he replied stiffly.

"Yes. However, you don't know that Ensil and Kari helped me in that endeavour. Kari was a gifted young healer who was still quite impressionable and Ensil ... well, he is your father."

"I don't think I should be here." Rilla voiced her doubts quietly. Completely ignoring her, Eliséo stared between his mother and father in disbelief.

"Exactly *who* in Silvaren have you not told your secrets to, Eléna?"

"I needed a healer, Eliséo." Eléna tried to explain. "I knew I could trust her more than the older healers. Ensil came to watch over us, to protect his family, even if we could never tell anyone about it."

"So why are you telling me now?" He flicked his head towards Rilla. "Why are you telling *her* now?"

"Even if I hadn't asked you to keep the prophecy child safe until she gets to

Illaria, I am not unaware to the fact that you would have followed her anyway." Eliséo made no comment.

"You are drawn to each other's power and now you are bound through Elessa. Your lives are forever connected, whether you want it or not. For that reason alone, Rilla needs to know all that you know. It's too dangerous for you to travel the Outworld with her if she doesn't understand exactly how important it is for your bond to remain secret.

"As a powerful heir to the throne of Silvaren, you are in danger. If anyone finds this out, it could be the death of you. None of us are certain what Elessa's bond with Rilla has done, but you may be certain that your death would cause at least some damage to her."

"Are we not now in *more* danger because you've told her everything?" Eliséo shook his head at his mother. "Could you not have left her in ignorant bliss?"

"She heard your words in passing, my son. What do you think would happen if she had forgotten about the knowledge she holds and the crystal dragons manipulate it out of her? Did you even stop to consider that possibility?"

"Then we'll just be certain to stay away from those creatures, won't we?"

"You may not have a choice." Eléna cut him off. "You will not be leading their party – Shadow will. You know she belongs to those beasts. She will insist on visiting the Drakos Mountains even before going to Illaria, to tell them she has found their prophecy child."

Rilla began to understand the danger surrounding her. Suddenly, Ensil started laughing, wincing in pain whenever his arm moved too much.

"What a mess!" His rough voice found its way through his laughter. "And all because you touched his tree."

Rilla wanted to scream out, to tell him it wasn't her fault. She hadn't known it was Eliséo's tree and she hadn't known what it would do to her – to *them*. But she remained silent. She didn't want the weapons master knowing any more about it than he needed to.

Thank you. The words fell gently in her mind. It wasn't Elessa's voice. She looked up to find a smile of gratitude on Eliséo's face, but only for a moment, and then it was gone.

"Well, it seems as though we'll have quite a busy day ahead of us. I don't know about Eliséo, but *I* will need my rest for that." Rilla excused herself as politely as she could and got to her feet. Eliséo said a single soft word and the protective mist fell away from them. Rilla left Eléna's chamber for her own as quickly as she dared, her leaves trailing in her wake.

Chapter Thirty-Seven – Leaving Silvaren

Morning came burdened with mixed feelings. Rilla was glad they were resuming their journey. She had enjoyed her time with the elves enough for it to be a bittersweet departure. Dressing in her travelling clothes was only a reminder of what she was leaving behind. She did not know the Outworld well enough to be able to find this elven stronghold again without Shuut's assistance.

The fact that they had only spent a few days in Silvaren did not detract from the attachment Rilla felt to the forest. Aside from their Paradise, it was the longest she had stayed in any one place. This was as close to *home* as she knew she would feel in a long time.

After she packed her belongings and attached her new sleeping mat on the outside of her rucksack, Rilla strapped her new swords to her sides and joined her companions to walk to the throne room.

As they entered through the glittering vines, Rilla immediately noticed Eliséo standing a little apart from the other elves, dressed in his own travelling clothes with a rucksack by his feet.

"Eliséo, what do you think you're doing?" Shuut asked gruffly.

"I should think it quite obvious," he answered with a smile. "I'm coming with you."

Shuut shook her head in protest. "I won't allow it." A gasp heaved through the gathered elves.

"As you wish," Eliséo replied with a shrug. "I'm going to be travelling in the same direction as you though, so you might as well enjoy my company." His smile was so mischievous that everyone else began to laugh and smile themselves. Shuut scowled darkly. She had no choice but to accept the change in plans.

Farewells were made all around. Kari made a final check of Rilla's rate of healing before hugging her. Ensil patted her on the shoulder, whispering encouragement. Rilla curtseyed to Lady Eléna and Queen Liessa, making certain that at no point was there any skin contact between them. She did not want any more of Eléna's secret words in her mind.

When they passed by Elessa, Eliséo lingered back to caress her trunk lovingly. *I must go away, my friend. May our bond remain as strong as ever while I'm gone.* In her mind, Rilla saw the explosion of tiny silver flowers on her branches. She watched enviously, noticing that the buds and leaves she had created were now nothing more than a memory. She knew she couldn't touch Elessa herself. The risk of anyone seeing her branches redden and the twisted curls of fiery flowers she would create was too great. Rilla walked ahead with the Paradisians and Shuut, leaving Eliséo to his farewell.

As they neared the sandy strip to the rest of the Outworld, the elf caught up with them. Rilla met his gaze for only a moment, but that was all it took for her to feel his pain at having to leave his tree behind so soon.

* * *

They had been walking for hours, not even stopping for a midday break. Eliséo could see the boys were starting to struggle. Shadow set a fast pace, her anger fuelling her. To their credit, the boys were not complaining, but it must have been obvious, even to the banwep, that they could not keep this pace up all day.

"Where are we going, Shadow?" he called out to Shuut, forcing her to slow down in order to respond. "It seems as though we are heading towards the Drakos Mountains."

"We are." Her answer was firm.

"I do not like that region of the Outworld. Why are we going?"

Shuut turned and walked up to him. "You know very well why we're going there," she told him vehemently. "I've found their precious prophecy child and if I have to travel with her, then I'm going to lead her straight to them."

"That is a waste of our time," Eliséo told her, without hesitation. "We should be going to Illaria."

Shuut glared him into silence. "You will *not* tell me what we should and should not be doing. As long as you wish to travel with us you will follow where I lead and not question my decisions."

Eliséo cocked his head to one side, looking at her sharply, then shrugged and continued walking in the direction of the Drakos Mountains. Their argument had at least given the boys a brief chance to rest.

He was concerned about visiting the crystal dragons. He wanted to keep Rilla away from them, but his mother had requested a favour of him, should they happen to pass through the region. Either way, he was bound to follow Shadow as long as Rilla and the boys did.

* * *

Arishen was bent over, hands on knees, trying to catch his breath during the short break Eliséo had managed to give them. He heard Shuut call Rilla the prophecy child, just as Telon had. What did they mean? He had never heard Shuut talk about any prophecy.

His mind was a swirl of questions that he had no way of answering. He couldn't possibly ask Rilla himself. Shuut was angrier than he'd had ever seen her. He was still annoyed with Plyke, and there was no way to get Tika away from his Partner to ask *him*. That left Eliséo.

He was still uncertain why the elf had joined them. There was no reason for him to travel with them. He didn't even want to go where Shuut was going, but insisted on staying with them all the same. It all came back to that one question. What was the prophecy? Much as he wanted to, Arishen couldn't bring himself to ask the elf. He'd barely spoken to him in Silvaren. They didn't know each other even nearly well enough for him to ask what might be a very delicate question.

* * *

When night fell, Tika dug a deep pit and lit a fire in the centre of the circle made by their new sleeping mats. He did not want to spark another lecture from Shuut, not in the mood she was in. Together, he and Plyke distributed the food they'd brought with them from Silvaren. It would be the best food they would eat in a long time to come.

180

Sitting beside his Partner, Tika found himself across the fire from Arishen. He couldn't help but look at the seer every once in a while. Those pale blue eyes kept darting towards Rilla and then away again. Tika inwardly sighed at the seer's obsession with the girl.

"Why does everyone call Rilla the 'prophecy child'?" Arishen's sudden question shocked him. Tika had only heard Shuut call Rilla that earlier in the day. What did Arishen mean by "everyone"? He looked over at Plyke to find his Partner avoiding his gaze. *This* must have been what their secret conversation had been about in Silvaren.

Silence fell. Anyone who knew about it was reluctant to say anything. Rilla's eyes were intent on the fire in front of her. Tika watched her with interest. She was clearly not happy about the prophecy.

"When a crystal heart beats in the body of another,
Their song will destroy that which was created.
Every being will bow down to the child of Paradise,
All will hail Rilla."

It was Shuut who finally spoke. As the words sank into Tika's mind, so much about Rilla finally made sense. If Erton had known about the prophecy when Rilla was born, it was no wonder he kept people from calling her by name. He must have been trying to hide her from someone.

"Why didn't you tell us?" Arishen looked towards Rilla.

"Why didn't you tell anyone about your dreams?" Rilla countered, continuing to stare into the fire.

"That's different." The seer crossed his arms.

"I don't see how," Rilla replied, finally looking up at him. "In the Paradise, your secret would have seen you murdered. In the Outworld, my secret was likely to have the same effect."

"But you didn't know that, did you?"

"Not exactly," Rilla answered unflinchingly. "But if Shuut is correct, then only a *lintep* named Rilla could possibly be the one in the prophecy. That alone could have seen me murdered."

"How do they know you're the Rilla mentioned in the prophecy?" Tika timidly asked. "Couldn't it be anyone named Rilla? It doesn't say anything about lintep. Why would it have to be you just because you're a lintep and your name is Rilla?"

"It also says that she will come from a Paradise," Shuut told him, almost smugly.

"Well, it also says she'll have a crystal heart," Tika retorted almost instantly, "and I don't think you could say any part of Rilla is made of crystal. She may not be human, but she still bleeds and functions the same way."

"You shouldn't argue about things you have no knowledge of." Shuut narrowed her eyes. "It doesn't *literally* mean she will have a crystal heart. It just means she was first raised with the crystal dragons and then taken to a Paradise."

"That is merely one of the interpretations of the prophecy, Shadow." Eliséo's ethereal voice carried softly over the fire. "The crystal dragons are renowned for manipulating events to suit the prophecies they wish to control."

"I don't recall anyone asking for your opinion." Shuut lashed out at him. Eliséo regarded her in silence, looked at Rilla's downcast eyes and shook his head in what Tika could only assume was frustration.

The ambassador fascinated him more than any of the other elves had. He seemed to know so much, but even if something happened that would make anyone else angry, he simply took it in his stride. He must have been the strangest elf in Silvaren, especially since his position as ambassador would keep him away from the elven stronghold more often than not.

Trying to ease the tension, Tika asked Eliséo if he could play his wooden flute for them, so that they could once more enjoy the strangely enchanting elvish music. Far from refusing, the elf immediately took the flute from his rucksack and began to play. As the music flowed from his instrument, Tika stood up, took an unresisting Rilla by the hand and drew her outside their circle of firelight to dance. Soon enough, Plyke joined them, with Arishen not far behind.

* * *

When the music stopped, Shuut moodily told them all to get some rest. Eliséo was given the first shift of the night. Rilla lay close by his side. Even though she was exhausted, she could not fall asleep. Her thoughts wandered everywhere until it occurred to her that the music Eliséo had played that night was different to the previous times she'd heard it.

When she was certain the others had fallen asleep, she sat up and whispered to him. "Why did the music you played tonight feel different from when we were in Silvaren?"

The elf immediately turned to her. "What do you mean *feel* different?"

Rilla shrugged. "I don't know exactly. It just didn't feel the same. I recognised some of the tunes you played, so it wasn't that they were simply unfamiliar. They just didn't draw me in as much as the first time I heard you play."

"Rilla, you must not repeat that to anyone. Do you understand?" He looked into the shadows to make certain no creatures were there, then looked over to the sleeping figures to assure himself that they were indeed asleep. His actions confused and frightened her.

"When my mother was there, I pretended to use magic – magic that I didn't know I truly possessed until last night. All elves can play magic through their music, but it only goes so far as to make the listener feel empathetic to it. I played magic through my music just for you that first night, to make you notice me. I didn't know it had worked and I can't always do it. People would start to realise eventually and I would put us both in danger. Do you understand?"

Nodding in annoyance, she lay back down. It didn't seem to matter how much she wished that magic was not a part of her life, it always followed her around. She wondered if that was the reason that the elvish music felt so right to her – the reason that it flowed through her, making her a part of it. She drifted off into a troubled sleep with different tunes playing in her mind, trying to pull her in all directions at the same time.

Chapter Thirty-Eight – Forgiveness

Plyke sat on a log, on higher ground than the camp. His attention was completely focused on his five companions. He didn't notice the bandits behind him. They crawled down the hill on their bellies, keeping as low to the ground as they could to avoid detection. There was too much wind swirling through the trees for Plyke to hear them coming. If he turned around now, he would still have time to defend himself, or even run back to camp to get help from the rest of them. Only if he turned around right NOW.

Arishen woke with a start and looked around him. Plyke was gone. Everyone else was still asleep. The wind was blowing fiercely around them, making it difficult to see through the dirt and leaves swirling in front of him. He stood and looked up the bushy hill where Plyke had been sitting on a log in his dream. He couldn't see him anywhere.

Unsheathing his two long daggers, Arishen ran up the hill, calling out Plyke's name, certain that he wouldn't like what he found. Hearing the commotion, the others woke and instantly armed themselves, searching for the disturbance.

By that time, Arishen was already halfway to the log where he knew Plyke had been. Before he could go any further, he saw four humans creeping towards their camp. He knew there were too many for him to attack by himself, but he had no choice. His heart pounded in his ears as they saw him and got to their feet, brandishing daggers of their own.

Arishen yelled as he ran up to them, swinging his long blades wildly. Everything Ensil had taught him was forgotten. The attackers stayed out of range, encircling him, making him constantly turn around to watch his back. He focused on the man in front of him, seeing only two blades as his arms. As they came forward to pierce his skin, he moved aside and slashed out at his attacker, cutting a deep wound in the man's belly. He heard two cries of pain and realised one was his. Evading one blow had placed him closer to another of the attackers. The blade had gone straight through Arishen's left arm. Dizzy with pain, he dropped his left dagger and swung wildly with his remaining one, trying to keep his attackers at a distance.

In confusion, Arishen watched as one after the other, his attackers fell motionless to the ground. Behind each of the fallen bodies stood one of his companions, with only Plyke missing. Looking blindly past their questioning faces, Arishen turned to continue up the hill to the log where he knew Plyke should have been. Tika and Eliséo followed him closely.

He'd woken up before the dream told him what the men had done to Plyke. Arishen didn't know if the boy was dead. A groan escaped Plyke's lips as Tika shook his shoulders, trying to wake him. All three of them breathed a sigh of relief at the sound. He was alive.

"Tika, tell Rilla to come here." Eliséo bent down to speak to the small boy. "Don't let Shadow give you no for an answer."

Tika nodded and reluctantly left his Partner's side and ran to find the only healer among them. Arishen watched it all happen as though through someone else's eyes. He didn't notice that Eliséo had spoken to him until the elf repeated himself.

"How did you know to find Plyke here?"

Arishen looked at the elf as though seeing him for the first time. "I dreamt he was here, sitting on that log." He pointed to the log beside which Plyke was lying, motionless.

* * *

Rilla ran up the hill with Tika. When she saw Plyke lying motionless on the ground, she knelt immediately by his side and searched his body. Probing carefully, she found a small, bloodied lump at the back of his head, near his neck. Rilla placed her hand over the wound and cringed with sudden pain. Taking care not to harm herself more than necessary, she took some of his pain, spreading it all over her body as she had done when healing the fringa. As soon as she noticed Plyke's eyes flickering, she took her hand away from his head, remembering Ratchin's warning not to overexert herself when others couldn't help her.

Unsettled, she sat down on the log. Eliséo came to sit by her side. He spoke to her softly, so the boys wouldn't hear.

"Do you think you can stand any more?"

Rilla looked up at him questioningly. The elf pointed to the motionless seer. His face was pale from more than just shock. Rilla ran her eyes over the tall boy. His left arm was dripping blood over the grass. She closed her eyes, took a deep breath and nodded. Eliséo's hand on her arm stopped Rilla before she could stand.

"Who taught you to heal like that?"

"I saw a lintep healing a human in Turon. I just copied what she did." She shrugged.

"That's not what I meant." The elf shook his head. "When you healed Ensil, his wound opened up in your shoulder. You just healed Plyke in a different way. What did you do and who taught you to do it like that?"

"Oh, I see. I spread his pain out through my whole body, so I wouldn't be injured as badly as him. I guess with Ensil, I just panicked so I forgot to do that. Ratchin didn't teach me that, I just ... I don't know, figured it out myself I suppose."

"Do you think you could try something a little different with Arishen?" He asked slowly. "If you cover his wound with one hand and cover my arm with the other, could you spread the wound over both you and I?"

"I ... don't know," Rilla replied uncertainly. "I suppose it might work, but I couldn't say for certain."

"Well, you're going to have to try. His wound is more than you can handle by yourself and we need to get away from this area as soon as possible. That band of humans may not have been working alone and if their friends find half of our number too wounded to defend ourselves, it may not go well for us."

Without waiting for her reply, Eliséo stood to bring Arishen to the log. He had lost so much blood that he could barely stand. Tika stood behind Arishen to make sure he didn't fall over.

Hesitantly, Rilla placed her right hand over Arishen's wound and her left one on Eliséo's arm. She closed her eyes to focus on the stab wound, instantly gasping in pain. An identical wound began to open in her own left arm.

Rilla, focus. The words fell into her mind, jolting her into action. She slowed down how quickly she was healing Arishen, then began to spread the pain around her own body. She saw that the blade had gone all the way through his arm. The

184

best way she could think of healing him was to close at least one side of the wound. As she began to mentally stitch his skin back together, the pain in her own body increased. When it was almost too much to handle, she managed to push the pain through her skin bond with Eliséo. She only stopped when the elf suddenly took her hand off Arishen's wound.

Rilla looked over Arishen's shoulder to see one side of his wound was completely healed. There was less blood flowing out of his arm, but enough that it would still hurt him if something more wasn't done.

"Tika, could you get my rucksack? Rhanya's healing pouch is inside it." Only when he was gone did Rilla turn to Eliséo. He was holding his hand over a fresh wound in his left arm. Angry tears stung her eyes.

"Why didn't you tell me you wouldn't be able to do the same thing?" She yelled at him. "I could have just healed him a little less, or taken a little more for myself. Now I have to try to heal both of you with what little herbs and ointments I managed to take from our Paradise."

"You were already weak from healing Plyke," Eliséo answered her calmly. "There was no way you could have helped Arishen enough on your own. As it is, I'm not certain we've helped him enough, but it's all I could allow you to do."

Tika returned to see Rilla's smouldering look. Timidly, he held out her rucksack. She took it silently and pulled out Rhanya's healing pouch, examining each clay pot within until she found the one she was looking for. Ripping one of her oversized spare shirts, she applied the ointment over both Arishen and Eliséo's wounds before bandaging them with the strips of material.

Without a word, she left her rucksack and ripped shirt, taking only Rhanya's healing pouch to where Plyke lay. He was still motionless and disorientated on the ground, his eyes looking about him almost in a panic. Rilla called Tika over as she applied a different ointment to the back of Plyke's head, that she hoped would reduce the swelling. Plyke visibly calmed at the sight of his Partner.

Rilla took her rucksack and left the four boys on the hillside, heading back down to Shuut and their slain attackers. The banwep was searching through their clothes and examining their blades.

"Can I help?" Rilla asked, willing to do anything to take her mind off her pain and anger.

"Check their bodies for anything we might find useful. There's no point leaving them with things they can no longer use. Boots are a good hiding place for coins. You'll have to check everywhere you can think of to hide anything of value."

Rilla scrunched up her nose, regretting her offer of assistance. She pulled off first one boot and then the other of the man in front of her. The stench made her gag. Leaning as far away as possible, she searched within both for any hidden pouches. To her surprise, there was a pouch in the left boot containing three silver coins. In the other was a tiny sheath with a matching blade. She placed her findings on the grass next to her rucksack and continued to search anywhere she could think of in the man's clothes. There was nothing else of interest.

Taking what she'd found, she went over to where Shuut was looking through her own loot and placed the coins and dagger with the rest of it.

"I don't understand it." She looked up at Rilla in confusion. "These men had more than enough silver to last them for the next few months. What were they thinking to attack a camp of six people, including an elf and a banwep, when they would surely have come across easier targets before their coin ran out?”

Rilla had no answer for her. The Outworld still didn’t make much sense. She could not even hazard a guess as to what might have been going on in their minds when they attacked.

“Are we going to burn their bodies?” That’s what they had always done in her Paradise.

“No,” Shuut answer firmly. “A fire would only attract attention. That’s something we should avoid if possible. The vultures will take care of whatever the larger beasts don’t get to first.”

Shuut gathered what they had salvaged from the attackers and stowed the spoils in her rucksack. When she was ready, Rilla led her up to where the others were waiting. By the time they reached the boys, Plyke was sitting up against the log where Eliséo and Arishen sat. All four boys got to their feet as they approached.

Arishen was still pale, but seemed to have regained some of his strength. Plyke stood a little unsteadily, but Tika was instantly by his side to hold him up. Shuut took one look at the damage the attack had caused and shook her head.

“Eliséo will be scouting ahead of us today. We don’t know if these men were working alone. No one is to be left behind. If any of you struggle with the pace I set, tell me. We can’t afford for any of you to weaken to the point where you will be of no use in a fight.”

Her words caught Rilla off guard. Even with the explanation, she was still surprised with Shuut’s leniency. Eliséo headed in the direction of the Drakos Mountains, quickly disappearing from view. The five remaining companions followed slowly behind him. Shuut asked Rilla take up the rear. She grimaced as she realised Shuut had no idea that she felt just as weak as the injured boys.

* * *

Shuut had allowed the Paradisians a midday rest, knowing they couldn’t possibly maintain her pace all day long. It was nearing dusk and she knew she still needed to speak with the seer before nightfall. Half turning to face the Paradisians, she called out behind her.

“Arishen, by my side.” She did not wait to see if he had heard her, but continued walking ahead. When he caught up to her, she spared him a sidelong glance. “Explain to me what happened this morning.”

“I had a dream,” he told her plainly.

“That much is obvious, boy. I need to know every detail.” She did not snap at him. Sometimes a gentler tone reaped more answers. Arishen tried to please her, leaving out no detail no matter how insignificant. When he had finished recounting the morning’s events, Shuut looked at him thoughtfully.

“I think it’s time you start up your night shifts again.” It was less a request than an order.

“Are you sure?” he questioned her hesitantly. “Shouldn’t you ask the others if they agree?”

“It’s possible we owe our lives to you Arishen. I don’t think the others will have a problem with my orders.” She hid a smile at the pride in his face. She hadn’t seen that look in a long time.

Soon after their conversation, Shuut called a halt for the day. Without being told, the Paradisians immediately started to make camp. Plyke and Rilla dug a pit and lit a fire. Arishen and Tika set out all their sleeping mats in a circle around the fire. She hated to admit it, but Shuut was impressed that the Paradisians had learnt so much and had matured to the point where making and breaking camp had become second nature to them. They never complained or argued about whose turn it was to do what. They simply fell into their roles as though they had been doing it all their lives.

"How will Eliséo know where to find us?" Tika asked between mouthfuls of an apple.

"He is an elf, Tika. I can assure you he's had his eye on both us and our surroundings all day. You may not have noticed him, but he will certainly know where we have made our camp." Shuut had travelled with Eliséo once before. It had been Queen Eléna's idea for the ambassador to practise those particular skills. Shuut had not minded so much. It had relieved her boredom in the quiet evenings. During that time, she had noticed some similarities between them. Neither of them really fit in anywhere. He was a foundling elf who spent most of his time away from Silvaren. She was a banwep. At the time, it had almost suited her to travel with him. This time, it was different.

Eliséo was not the reason Shuut had been forced to take the Paradisians with her from Silvaren, but he *was* the reason she would not be able to abandon them at the first opportunity. Strangely enough, she was less irritated by that fact than she had been the day before. This troubled her. It was dangerous for a banwep to create any personal ties, and especially with Paradisians. They would only bring her more trouble than she already found by herself. At least one good thing would come of it – she would bring the prophecy child to the crystal dragons, fulfilling a task they had set for her years ago.

* * *

"Good evening," Eliséo said as stepped into the firelight. Under his arm, he held a live chicken. "Tika, would you help Shadow with this chicken? I trust it will be sufficient to fill your bellies tonight."

"What do we do?" Tika stepped forward excitedly.

"You could have at least finished the job." Shuut looked up, irritably. "We didn't particularly need to sleep with the stench of blood tonight."

"I will not be partaking of your meal this evening, Shadow," Eliséo replied, unfazed. "Perhaps you would prefer if I simply allow the bird to go free."

"No!" Tika cried out. "Please Shuut. We can just take it further away from the camp where it won't matter what kind of mess we make."

Without a word of thanks, Shuut took the chicken from under Eliséo's arm. She walked off in the direction from which he had come, Tika following close on her heels. He liked the small human's enthusiasm for anything new.

"Do you irritate Shuut on purpose?" Arishen looked to Eliséo for an answer. "It seems as though everything you do annoys her."

"No, Arishen," Eliséo sat on his sleeping mat. "Shuut and I, we are both fiercely independent people. The difference is that I embrace company where I can and she shies away from it."

Plyke joined in with the questioning. "Why did you come with us, Eliséo? From what we heard, you had only just returned to Silvaren. Didn't you want to stay there a while before leaving again?"

* * *

Rilla turned her eyes towards the fire. This was not a conversation she wanted to be part of. She just wanted to fade away. Pretending that it was possible, she closed her eyes and wondered what it would be like to simply disappear.

Stop that! A voice in her mind forced her to open her eyes in surprise. Eliséo was not looking at her, he was still talking with Arishen and Plyke.

Elessa? she asked hesitantly.

Of course. The voice sounded angry. *Who else would have noticed what you were doing before you got yourself into trouble again?*

What was I doing that was so dangerous? Rilla asked in confusion. All she had done was close her eyes.

Your companions may know what you are, but they are keeping silent on the matter, which is more than I can say for you. Rilla started in surprise. *You are still an untrained lintep travelling through the Outworld. It would not do for you to flaunt your powers so openly.*

How can you reprimand me now for something I didn't realise I was doing but not chastise me when Eliséo asked me to heal Plyke and Arishen this morning? Rilla was becoming increasingly annoyed by all the conditions and expectations people were placing on her.

"Rilla?" The voice came from far away. She wouldn't even have noticed it but for the light touch of a hand on her shoulder. She looked beside her to where Plyke had sat down. "You looked like you were in a completely different world for a moment."

"I was just ... thinking." Rilla found that she wasn't a good liar. She had never needed to lie in their Paradise. She had never cared that Erton would punish her for what she had done and there was no authority higher than her father. Most people hadn't cared enough to even talk to her, let alone ask delicate questions.

"Your eyes were unfocused and ..." he hesitated, "well, it almost looked like they were glowing."

"Glowing?" Rilla asked, with what she hoped didn't sound like a nervous laugh. "Are you sure it wasn't just a reflection from the fire?"

"Maybe." Plyke's eye narrowed momentarily. Rilla felt a pang of guilt, but made certain to mask it. She knew Plyke's powers lay in empathy.

Rilla was saved from more questions by Tika and Shuut. They walked into the firelight, Tika proudly parading the plucked chicken they had skewered on a long straight branch. Shuut hurriedly placed four other sticks, two on each side of the fire, deep in the ground and motioned Tika to place the long branch on the small brackets she had made for it.

"How long will it take to cook?" Arishen asked, his eyes wide with happy anticipation.

"Long enough for you to work up an appetite by sparring against each other. And don't even think to get out of it with an injured arm. You can just use your other arm." Shuut cut off the question before it was out of the seer's mouth. "Tika,

188

no arrows for you. It's too dark. Get out your dagger."

Rilla was glad for the distraction. It would allow her to practice and keep her mind off everything that had happened to them since they'd met Shuut. She stood to one side of the firelight, both swords at the ready, watching the others arm themselves.

"Eliséo, would you do us the honours. I don't want any more injuries today." It wasn't really a question, but Rilla could all tell that the elf didn't mind. He walked over to each of the Paradisians, eyes glowing slightly, and mumbled a few words. They could not see what he had done and all four of them looked at him, puzzled.

"You won't be able to draw blood from each other, but don't let that stop you from defending yourselves. Bruised bodies can often hurt just as much as bleeding ones," Eliséo explained.

Rilla placed the flat side of her shorter sword on her right forearm, tilting it towards the sharp edge only to find it dull. On closer inspection, she realised the blade wasn't touching her skin at all but had a thick layer of air as a barrier.

Tika and Plyke were matched against each other, with the smaller boy protesting the unfair advantage his Partner had over him with a double axe.

"You don't get to choose what weapons your attackers will have, Tika," Shuut reminded him shortly. "Learn to be quick and creative."

They sparred until the chicken was completely roasted. Shuut took it off the skewer and dealt out portions to all but Eliséo. No one questioned him about it.

Rilla sat silently, as far away from the others as she could without drawing attention. Plyke had said her eyes were glowing. She knew it wasn't a reflection from the fire, but the alternative scared her. Elf eyes glowed when they used their magic, but she had never taken notice whether Eliséo's eyes glowed when he spoke to Elessa or not. It was a disturbing idea.

The elves and the tree had tried to explain to her exactly how much her life had changed in that single moment when Elessa had bound them together, but it was too much to take in. If her eyes were glowing, did that mean she would be able to use the same kind of magic as the elves? She knew she would not age as quickly. After all, Elves lived for hundreds, even thousands of years, even more than the lintep. What would she do with all that time on her hands? She had never really thought past the next day in their Paradise – not until Shuut had appeared. Even then, her only thought was to safely get the boys away from Erton and keep them alive in the Outworld. Those thoughts had consumed her so completely that no thoughts of the distant future had entered her mind. What would happen when they found the lintep? Would she and Plyke be trained in their skills? What about Arishen and Tika? Would the boy be allowed to stay with his Partner in Illaria? Would the seer ever find a safe place to live, where people wouldn't try to kill him just because of his dreams?

Rilla was jolted out of her thoughts, once again, by someone saying her name. She looked up to see everyone staring at Shuut.

"Sorry, I wasn't listening. What did you say?"

"I said Arishen will take the first shift tonight, followed by Plyke, Tika, you, Eliséo then myself."

Rilla looked at the expressions on the boys' faces. All of them looked uncomfortable. That morning had obviously scared them all, but she knew it wasn't her place to question Shuut.

"Shadow, it may be prudent to double our watches for a while." Eliséo's voice was quiet, but commanding. "It will only be a little less sleep for each person, but that sleep will be sounder with the knowledge that there are two pairs of eyes watching over the camp, rather than one."

Shuut glowered at the suggestion. "Do as you will," she replied icily. "Wake me for the last watch. I do not wish to be caught unawares in the early hours of the morning." Without another word, she lay down on her sleeping mat and turned her back towards the fire.

"Rilla and I will take the first watch." Eliséo stole their attention away from the banwep. "Tika and Arishen, you'll take the middle watch. Plyke, you will share the last watch with Shadow. Be careful tonight. This morning's attack was not provoked by desperation. They may not have been working alone and their companions may come looking for us tonight."

Rilla saw the Partners exchanging worried glances. They had been frightened enough without his *encouraging* words. Had he meant to scare them even further? Quickly and quietly, she stood up from her sleeping mat and walked out of the firelight, starting her ever widening circular path around their camp. She did not wait to see if the boys had lain down to sleep, or if Eliséo had followed her. If she couldn't disappear, then she just wanted to be by herself.

Chapter Thirty-Nine – Attack

Eliséo had been watching Rilla all evening. Whether through his own eyes or Elessa's, he had been watching her – and he knew something was wrong. In the short time he had known her, she had changed from a strong-willed, carefree young woman, to a terrified, insecure child.

She can't just keep running away from everything. He had been blocking his thoughts from Rilla since he'd discovered she was bound to Elessa. It made talking to his tree more of an effort, but she was worth it.

Did you see what she tried to do this evening? Elessa explained about Rilla's attempt to disappear. *She grows stronger and bolder with her powers every day. You think she is trying to run away, but in doing so, she only discovers more things she can do. We need to get her to Illaria, my friend. I do not know how long she will last without the lintep masters.*

Eliséo didn't need to voice his concerns on the matter. They knew Shadow planned to visit the Drakos Mountains first. Admittedly, the banwep had no idea that she was leading her companions away from Illaria, but at this point he doubted whether it would make a difference to her if she knew. The crystal dragons had a strange hold over her. She felt indebted to them – he knew this – but if she could only see them for what they truly were, she might not be so eager to do their bidding.

You need to train her with what little you have learned from the lintep these past years. You've seen the way they school their young. Try to explain it the same way the masters do. It may be our only chance to help her keep her powers until we reach Illaria. Elessa's advice was sound. He knew it was. But he was afraid of Rilla losing more than just her powers. From what he had seen so far, her power was already so great that it would almost certainly take her life in leaving her.

When their shift was over, Eliséo watched from his sleeping mat as Arishen and Tika began their circular paths around the campsite. He decided to talk to Rilla the next evening. Even if Elessa hadn't told him, he would still have been able to see with his own eyes that the young lintep wanted to be left alone. She had gone to the extreme of trying to disappear. There was no chance that he could talk with her that night, but the next night was a possibility. If he pulled her aside before her weapons training, she would be able to use her power with her swords. He had watched weapons masters in Illaria training many young lintep. If he remembered their explanations, it might be enough to help the prophecy child on her way.

Although he eventually lay his head down on his sleeping mat, Eliséo did not close his eyes even for a few minutes that night. He thanked his lucky stars once more that elves had less need of sleep than other beings.

The attack from the previous morning had left a sour taste in his mouth. Either the men had been paid, or someone had played with their minds. Neither explanation appeased him. Unless someone knew the prophecy child travelled with them, there was nothing of value in their travelling party. Perhaps Rilla had been wise to disguise her true identity in the Outworld. Eléna had removed that layer of protection from her. He fervently hoped it wouldn't lead to her death.

Morning did nothing to raise Eliséo's spirits. It was an overcast day. If it rained, any attack would be hidden until the very last moment. The night had passed uneventfully, but that did not convince him that they were safe. If someone powerful or rich enough was determined to find them, they would not stop at hiring one group of mercenaries. He was certain there would be more.

As he had done the day before, he scouted ahead and to the side of his companions. He was lighter and quicker of foot than the rest of them. When they stopped for a midday meal, he did not join them. Instead, he walked a wide circle around their small party.

Increasingly throughout the afternoon he felt that something was amiss. The lack of an attack was a contributing factor to that feeling. Even if only those four men had been hired, surely their employer would check to see if the job had been done. It didn't feel right to have such loose ends.

* * *

They were setting up camp when the next attack came. Eliséo was still on his way back to them. Shuut had gone to find them something to eat for the night. Preoccupied as she was, Rilla neglected to keep an eye on her surroundings.

She heard some leaves rustling behind her as booted feet walked quietly over the forest floor. Expecting to only see either Shuut or Eliséo entering their campsite, it took her a moment to alert the boys.

"To arms!" she yelled as she drew her swords. Once again there were four attackers. Once again, they were all massive men. She tried to calm her mind, to remember everything Ensil had taught her. Behind her, she could hear the boys hastily drawing their own weapons. The leader of the pack came straight for her, blood lust in his eyes. His iron-studded mace gripped tightly in his hands.

Rilla took an involuntary step back. He gave her a toothy grin as he advanced. Once in range, he swung at her. Rilla crossed her two blades in front of her to block the attack. The blow was so heavy that it jarred both her arms. She managed not to drop her swords, but her arms fell momentarily to her sides. Wincing in pain, she lifted them again in time for his next blow. Again, and again, she dodged his attacks but he kept coming.

Attack him! Elessa's voice insisted. *Don't just be defensive. Strike him.*

It took a moment for Rilla to realise the instruction was meant for her. She turned to avoid the mace, and instead of stepping further away, she continued to turn until she was behind her attacker and then buried both swords in his unprotected back. He roared in pain and fell to his knees, half turning to face her, mace still gripped tightly in his hands. Rilla pulled her swords out of his back as he moved, and swung the longer one at his arms. To her horror, the blade sliced through both his arms, leaving uneven stumps behind. She stood, frozen, staring at the mutilated man in front of her, unable to tear her eyes away.

A high-pitched cry of pain made Rilla tear her eyes away from the bloodied man at her feet to see a serrated sword go straight through Tika's left leg. Without hesitating further, Rilla ran up behind the man and slashed first with one sword and then with the next, cutting deep wounds in his back and then his front as he turned, unarmed, to face her. Roaring wordlessly, he put both hands around her neck and started to choke her. Terrified, throat burning, Rilla dropped her swords and desperately clawed at his massive hands. Her vision closed in until she could not see.

The hands went slack around her throat. Rilla fell to the ground, limp and gasping for air. Slowly, her vision returned but she lay motionless on the cold, damp grass, breathing in as deeply as she could, eyes shut tightly to the mayhem around her. It wasn't until Eliséo came to check she was still alive that Rilla opened her eyes again. She saw herself lying on the grass, blood sprayed over her clothes and body. Confused, she blinked and saw Eliséo's concerned face staring at her intently.

"Is everyone alive?" she asked hoarsely.

"Everyone is alive." His voice was cold and distant. "Tika is badly injured."

Will you be able to heal him?

Tired and weak, Rilla sat up and looked around her. Plyke was by his Partner's side, helplessly holding his hand. Arishen was watching the two of them from a distance, a glimmer of envy in his eyes. He had escaped with only a few cuts and two astoundingly dark bruises. Shuut was already searching the fallen bodies for anything they could use.

Eliséo held out his hand to her. Rilla took it, knowing she had no choice but to heal again. It was now certain that the first attack was not a random event. There would be more to follow. They could not afford to stay in one place for any great length of time. Tika's injury would slow them down considerably, no matter how much Rilla was able to heal him, but she had to do something or he would more than likely die.

As she approached Tika, Plyke looked up with angry tears in his eyes. Rilla barely notice. She was completely preoccupied with the problem that faced her. Without making eye contact with Tika, she sat by his side and looked at the serrated blade still lodged in his leg. She didn't know what to do. If she pulled it out, the blade would do even more damage and there would be twice as much for her to heal. She had little choice, though – the blade could not stay there.

"Arishen, I need my rucksack." Rilla waited for him in silence. When the seer returned with her rucksack, she searched through it for Rhanya's pouch. Inside, she found what she was looking for – a small vial of red liquid. Putting it to one side, she pulled out a scrap of leather Kora had given to her before they left the Paradise. Eliséo handed her a short, fat twig. He knew what she intended to do. Rilla's hands trembled as she wrapped the scrap of leather around the twig.

"Open your mouth," she instructed Tika. Hesitantly, he did as he was told. Rilla carefully poured a single red drop from the vial onto his tongue. "This will help to numb the pain. I doubt it will be enough. Bite down on this." She placed the leather-bound twig in his mouth, and watched his teeth clench down on it. She handed Tika's Partner one of her discarded shirts. "Plyke, take this cloth and be ready to hold it firmly over his leg. As soon as the sword is out, well ... I don't know how much blood there will be, but I will need your help."

For a moment, Rilla had nothing left to do. She stared at the hilt of the sword, wondering how difficult it would be to draw out. It had gone into his leg easily enough. She gingerly placed her hand around the hilt.

"Wait." A firm hand on her shoulder made her turn around. Eliséo looked down at Tika. "If we can seal the wound, you might not need to use as much power to heal him."

"We can do that?" she asked, barely trusting her voice.

"Arishen, put as much wood as you've gathered on the fire." Without a moment of hesitation, the seer turned to his task. Eliséo walked over to another one of the motionless bodies, and took up a flat-edged sword.

"As soon as the fire is strong enough, we hold the blade there until it turns white." He left the rest unsaid. Rilla cringed and turned to a wide-eyed Tika.

Arishen picked up as much firewood as he could and carried it over to the small pit he and Rilla had dug. He placed as much as he could in the pit, being careful not to smother the small flame. Eliséo stood, ready and waiting with the sword. His eyes glowed as he said a few words under his breath. Suddenly, the fire cracked into full force. Arishen took a few steps back from the blazing blue flame. Rilla watched in fascination as the elf held the tip of the sword in the fire, waiting for it to turn white.

"Plyke, Arishen, hold him down." Both boys rushed to do his bidding. "Rilla get ready to pull out the blade." He waited for them to all be in place before nodding to Rilla. She gripped the blade, pulling with all her might. It came out more easily than she had expected, her extra force sending her tumbling backwards.

Eliséo paid her no attention as he pulled the sword out of the fire and walked straight over to the terrified boy. Tika's sobs became a howl when the white-hot blade seared the skin on both sides of his leg. He fought against Plyke and Arishen's grip to get away from the pain. They held him firmly.

It seemed like hours had passed since Rilla had first walked over to Tika, but it was only been a few minutes before the most painful part of the process was over. Tika was sobbing into Plyke's shoulder as Arishen stared mutely as the elf stabbed the heated blade into the grass. Rilla watched from where she had fallen with the bloodied sword. She saw Shuut finally stand up and walk over to them.

"What was the point of that?" she asked the elf, irritably. "There will be so much damage that it won't heal properly without a healer. You should have just taken the leg off."

"Rilla is a healer," he replied as he motioned Rilla to her feet. "She will do what she can now."

"That little pouch she carries around with her does *not* make her a healer, Eliséo." She pointed to Rhanya's pouch and rolled her eyes at the elf's stupidity.

Ignoring her, Rilla joined Tika. She placed one hand over the newly seared skin, breathing in sharply with the pain, then placed her other hand over the same part of his other leg. She searched out the difference between the two legs – blood flowing where it shouldn't, muscles torn jaggedly apart.

Carefully, she willed the veins to mend themselves so that the blood flowed properly through them. Her pain increased with each repair. She began to stitch the muscles back together. She didn't stop until Eliséo gently pulled her hands away.

Tika had stopped crying. Rilla found him staring at her in wonder. He had watched her work on both Plyke and Arishen the previous morning, but clearly had not understood what she had done.

"What did you just do?" Shuut asked suspiciously.

"I healed him as much as I could," Rilla replied evenly. "He won't lose his leg now."

"Who taught you to do that?" Shuut pressed her. "There was no one in Silvaren who could have taught you that."

Rilla hesitated for a moment. Would Ratchin want Shuut to know? "No one really *taught* me."

"Don't play word games with me, girl! Where did you learn to do that?"

"I watched Ratchin heal a boy in Turon. I just ... copied what I thought she had done."

"Ratchin knew you were a lintep and didn't tell me?" There was fire in the banwep's eyes. "Did she know you copy her in this?"

"Not exactly." Rilla shrank back into herself, trying to hide away from Shuut anger. "She knew that I had copied her before, but that was just taking some heat out of water. It wasn't healing anyone."

"But she took you with her to heal someone in Turon, knowing that you wouldn't be able to help but try the same thing yourself."

It wasn't really a question. Shuut knew the truth as well as Rilla did. Ratchin had known full well that Rilla, once she'd realised her potential, would not be able to resist trying out everything she'd seen. Her final warning replayed in Rilla's memory. *Do not overstep your boundaries ... the thing that may seem small and insignificant to you, could end up costing you your life.*

Rilla didn't really miss Ratchin, she had barely known the lintep lady, but she missed what she could learn from her. Ratchin hadn't actively tried to teach her anything, but Rilla had learnt so much from simply watching and talking to her.

Shuut growled. "Double watches. Same pairs as last night. We'll break camp before dawn tomorrow." Her words did little to comfort anyone.

Chapter Forty – Training

Rilla looked at the aftermath of the attack with unseeing eyes. It just didn't seem possible that someone could want anyone in their party dead enough to pay at least eight silver coins to get the job done. Shaking her head, she walked over to her fallen swords. Ensil and Shuut had repeatedly told all of them that their weapons were to be cleaned after use. A weapon left bloodied would eventually turn to rust but, even before that, the blade would become weak and possibly fail during an encounter.

She bent to pick up her two swords, keeping her eyes firmly averted from her handiwork. Staring at those uneven severed arms was more than she could bear. With great care, she thrust each of her blades into the soil up to the hilt and pulled them back out. With her already bloodied shirt, she gently wiped the wet soil from each blade, leaving them as clean as they had been before the attack. Standing, she replaced her swords in their sheaths.

Not quite certain if she was ready to face the night, Rilla took a deep breath before going to find Eliséo. As hungry as they had all been when they'd made camp, the thought of food was enough to make any of them sick now. Following Shuut's example, the boys were already preparing themselves for sleep.

"Follow me," Rilla looked up at the sound of Eliséo's voice. It was gentle, but commanding. "You and I need to have a little talk." She raised her eyebrows at him, but said nothing.

* * *

Eliséo walked until they were well out of hearing of the camp. He did not turn to face Rilla immediately. He did not know how to begin.

Why are you treating her so delicately? Elessa asked in annoyance. *Just tell her she will die unless she does exactly what you tell her and be done with it.*

It's times like this I almost agree with Lady Eléna that it was foolish to bond with such an old tree. His reprimand was enough to silence her. They both knew he would never want to trade his bond with her for another tree, even if that were possible, but it was all he could ever say to put her in her place.

"Rilla, have you been told what can happen with lintep if they don't receive the training they require?" He turned and looked straight into the girl's piercing green eyes.

"Ye-es," Rilla drew out her reply. "Ratchin mentioned that if they haven't learned to control it, it will leave their bodies."

"Did she mention that if their power is too great, it will kill them when it leaves?" Rilla bit her lip and nodded wordlessly.

"I would hope you had figured it out yourself by now." He barely knew how to get the words out. "You are one of those lintep, Rilla. If we do not get you to Illaria before your power begins to peak, you *will* die."

Eliséo watched as tears welled up in her eyes but did not spill.

"What will happen to you and Elessa if I die?" Her answer took him by surprise.

Physically, we will be fine child. Elessa answered for him. *Though we would rather prefer it didn't happen, if you don't mind.*

"How much time do we have left?" Rilla asked.

"It is difficult to tell. Often the most powerful reach their peak swiftly. If they are not already near Illaria at the time, then there is little hope for them." Eliséo watched the lintep closely, trying to gauge her reaction.

"Is there a reason you've decided to bring this up now? Or are you just trying to warn me that I could die, possibly quite soon?" There was no bitterness in her voice, just a cold steadiness.

"There may be a way to slow the process, if you'll allow me to try." Rilla's only response was a questioning look. "I've spent a lot of time in Illaria. I've seen things that only lintep would normally see. If I remember well enough, I can try to train you in some small ways."

"How will that help me?"

"It is in learning to control their power that a lintep can hold onto it. I was allowed to observe many lessons while in Illaria. If I show you the exercises they taught young lintep, perhaps it will be enough until we reach the stronghold ourselves."

Rilla listened attentively. Her eyes started to glow, but Eliséo heard none of the conversation. He was irrationally irritated that Rilla could speak privately with Elessa.

"What's going on in there?" He took her by the shoulders and turned her to look him in the eye.

"I'm not the only one who needs your help." Rilla lowered her green eyes.

"I know that, but Plyke has his power under control for the moment. At least *he* knows when he is using it."

Rilla looked at him wide eyed. "How do you know about Plyke? Did Elessa tell you?"

"I don't need Elessa to tell me something like that. I sensed his power the first day we met." He looked up at the moon suddenly. "We're wasting valuable time. You need to start training."

"We need to be keeping watch," Rilla admonished him. "I won't live long enough for my power to kill me if we aren't careful."

"I can assure you we will be quite safe the rest of tonight. It would be extremely unlikely for another group of men to sneak up on us. My ears are sharper than you can imagine. If we have any more unexpected visitors on our watch, I will not be caught off guard."

"Well then, teach me."

Rilla stood looking at him, a blank expression on her face. The girl confused him. She should feel strongly about this – happiness, apprehension – it was life or death for her. But there was nothing. Eliséo cleared his mind and searched through his memories for the ones in Illaria. He had spent many years there in his position as ambassador. It was only because of Queen Eléna's relationship with the lintep that he had been privileged enough to be present at training sessions. Most of those had been advanced lessons. He had never seen a lintep have their very first lesson.

"What have you been shown, or learnt yourself, so far?"

"I know how to heal people," she answered immediately, then stopped to think. "I can take heat out of something. Though I haven't tried it, I know it works the same way in reverse. Oh, why didn't I think of that at the time?" She closed her eyes and shook her head.

"Think of what?" Eliséo was in the dark. Elessa was keeping Rilla's mind separate from his, so he could not see what she was thinking or go through her memories.

"When I took heat out of the water, I only took as much as I could until I overheated and started to sweat." She opened her eyes to reveal anger behind the lids. "If I had thought about it, even for a moment, I would have realised that I could get rid of that heat somewhere else and not just keep it within me."

"Was anyone there when you tried this the first time?"

"Ratchin was there, but she was busy healing someone. I had seen her warm bath water with her own heat and simply assumed that it would work the other way around if I wanted it to."

"You mean no one showed you how to do that with your power?" He raised a questioning eyebrow.

"Ratchin is the only lintep I've ever seen using their magic. I watched her and tried a few things I'd seen her do. But she never *actually* taught me anything."

"Is that everything you saw Ratchin do and so try for yourself?"

"Not exactly." Guiltily, she turned away from him.

"What else did you do?" It was like talking to a child.

"I, sort of, projected my mind to follow a fringa around Dell's Inn." After her initial hesitation, words tumbled from her lips. "Ratchin explained that she could make her mind follow a person as they were leaving a room, or that she could project her mind into a room that she'd been to before. So, the fringa and I decided to try it when the others were out. He wandered around the inn, eventually finding Ratchin, and I followed him. Ratchin was furious with me when she realised what I'd done. She said it was foolish."

"She was right," Eliséo agreed unsympathetically. "It was extremely foolish to try that. Imagine what could have happened if anything went wrong. You were simply lucky that everything went according to plan."

"How was I supposed to know that?" Rilla snapped back at him. "No one ever took the time to tell me, so exactly *what* made you think that I knew it was dangerous?"

"Common sense should have prevailed there. But let's move on." He waved his hand dismissively. "Is there anything else you've tried?"

Rilla took a long, deep breath before answering. "I can fade into the background, if I want to. I don't think it's exactly disappearing, because some people can still tell that I'm there or that something isn't quite right and one person has even managed to see me. It's a lot easier to do it when people are used to ignoring you or don't really pay much attention to you anyway."

"Show me." He folded his arms and stood back a little way from her.

"I ... don't know if I can do it while you watch."

"Your life may depend on it at some point. You need to learn to do it with people watching you," Eliséo told her bluntly.

She closed her eyes and took two deep breaths before beginning. Eliséo watched her blur into the background. Rilla opened her eyes once more.

"Not bad for your first attempt," he conceded. "It was more difficult for me to keep you in focus, but you did not fade away. If I had turned my eyes away for a moment, we may be having a different conversation right now. However, you cannot count on your enemies to look away from you when you want them to."

Rilla's cheeks flushed then Eliséo lost sight of her.

"Are you trying to do that?"

"Trying to do what?" she asked wearily.

"You just disappeared. Completely." He watched as she reappeared before his eyes.

"I wasn't thinking about it. But isn't that what you wanted me to do?"

"Rilla, you need to concentrate," Eliséo did not raise his voice but he heard the irritation creeping through. "You need to be able to disappear when you want to and not have it happen accidentally without you even thinking about it."

"Shall I try it again?"

"Yes."

Eliséo watched as she disappeared again, purposely and completely.

"Good." A small smile escaped him. "But it needs to be a lot faster than that. Again."

He kept her practicing for the rest of their watch. By the time they made their way back to the camp, the girl was exhausted but delighted. She could now disappear in a moment's notice and stay that way for as long as she needed to without Eliséo being able to find her.

Chapter Forty-One – Lesser trees

Dawn was breaking when Eliséo woke Rilla. Tika and Arishen were sleeping peacefully. Shuut and Plyke were still out on their watch. He knew he should have done this last night, but if she had been angry with him, they would never have started her training. The lintep followed him away from the two sleeping Paradisians, waiting until they were out of earshot before questioning him.

"Are we doing some more training?" Rilla rubbed the sleep from her eyes and tried to stifle a yawn.

This isn't lintep training. He spoke to her through their link with Elessa. *This is elf magic.*

Rilla was instantly alert.

Place your hand on this branch and shape it like this. He placed his hand on another branch and shaped it so that one end curved like a crescent moon. *Elessa will help you.*

The lintep placed her hand on the branch he'd pointed out to her. She smiled as the end curved just as Eliséo's one had. Once that was done, Elessa showed her how to detach the branch from the tree. Her smile instantly disappeared. Eliséo blocked himself from her pain.

"How could you make me do that?" she asked him in a wounded voice. "You knew how it would feel for me to force that tree to give part of itself to me."

"It was necessary," he replied bluntly. "We cannot afford to wait for Tika's leg to heal any further before leaving this place. The alternative of allowing him to lean on the rest of us would weaken us all. If we are attacked again, we will need as much strength as possible."

"Why did you make *me* do it?" she repeated. "Why couldn't you have done it by yourself?"

He paused for a moment, considering how best to answer her. *I needed to teach you more about your powers. Since Elessa bound you to her, you will have power over any lesser tree. If you ever need to do something similar again, now you know how.*

"I will *never* do that again," she told him in a quiet voice as she walked away from him.

Arishen and Tika were awake when Rilla returned. She nodded a silent greeting to them before kneeling over her sleeping mat. Eliséo followed her, carrying the branches they had created. Shuut and Plyke were only a few steps behind him. Eliséo held out the branches to Tika.

"Try these. They may help you walk until your leg is better healed." He placed the curved end under each of Tika's arms and showed him how to walk with them.

Grinning happily, the small human thanked him. Eliséo nodded in acknowledgement, then quickly walked away to roll up his sleeping pallet. He did not bother trying to catch Rilla's eye. She would be angry with him for some time over those branches. There was no point trying to talk to her about it now with everyone surrounding them.

It did not take long for everyone to break camp. They were all as eager as each other to make a move. No one knew if there would be another attack in the same place, but they did not intend to find out. A single look towards Shadow confirmed Eliséo's idea that it would be best for him to stay close to them rather than scout ahead.

The six of them set out in a sombre mood as they passed the bodies of the dead men. Shuut had dragged them outside the circle of firelight, but she could not make them disappear.

Tika visibly paled at the sight of them. Plyke, seeing his Partner's reaction, gently turned Tika away from the man who had injured him. Arishen walked past without a second glance. Rilla stopped and stared at the four men. Her handiwork was visible even from a distance. She had hacked both arms off one man. His stiff blue body lay there, reminding her of the horrible act she had performed. Eliséo walked up and gently placed a hand on her shoulder in an attempt to console the girl. She turned around with fire in her eyes.

"Don't touch me." Her voice was low and threatening. Eliséo dropped his hand immediately, unprepared for such a reaction. He simply stared after the lintep as she walked away from him.

"What did you do to her?" Shuut asked with some amusement. "She doesn't even speak to Arishen like that – and he stabbed her in the chest and punched her in the nose."

"Nothing that should not have been done," Eliséo answered evasively. "She'll deal with it eventually."

"So, you did do something to her." The humour went out of the banwep. "You had better make sure she deals with it sooner rather than later. If she struggles to be amiable today, it will not go well with the boys. Much as I hate to admit it, she is the soul of those Paradisians. If you have wounded her somehow, the others will suffer just as much as she does."

Eliséo kept his eyes firmly fixed on Rilla and away from Shadow. He knew what she said to be true, but he could think of only one way to right the situation and *that* would have to wait until nightfall.

You should never have placed the child in this position, Elessa reprimanded the elf. *You made her harm another tree for the first time without warning her what she would feel. That is inexcusable.*

There was no time to explain it to her, Elessa. We are in danger in this Outworld. She may now understand the urgency to reach Illaria, but she refuses to accept what we may have to do in order to get there in time. Eliséo felt a pang of guilt. *If she hadn't done this, we would not be able to travel even half the distance we need to today. Even one day could make a difference, especially if that fool of a Shadow insists on visiting her damned crystal dragons first!*

Elessa backed down as she felt his fear and frustration. She embraced him, as only an elf's tree could, and comforted him. *I will talk to her, little one,* she promised him.

* * *

Rilla walked by herself for most of the day. She was so furious with Eliséo for making her manipulate a lesser tree that when Elessa tried to talk to her, she forcibly attempted to keep the tree out of her mind.

Stop that this instant, you petulant little child! Rilla was shocked into inaction. *If you would but listen to what I say, you may eventually find it within you to forgive Eliséo his actions this morning.*

Reluctantly, Rilla listened silently as Elessa explained to her what would happen each time she manipulated a lesser tree, even though she insisted she would never do it again. She was instructed how to protect herself from the pain she would cause those trees.

Then Elessa did something Rilla was not expecting. She showed her Eliséo's memory from the first time *he* had been asked to manipulate a lesser tree. Rilla recoiled from it. She felt so naïve. She had thought Eliséo did not understand what he had done to her, what he had asked her to do. She saw that what he had felt his first time was a thousand times worse. He had been raised to love and respect trees as living creatures. To make matters worse, the first time he'd had to manipulate a tree had been during training – not out of necessity. There were no reasons he could offer to the lesser tree, for it to be manipulated and broken for the elf.

Rilla felt the hot tears trickle down her face. Immediately, she practised her new skill of fading out of focus. There was no way she would be able to explain away a sudden burst of tears if any of the others saw

* * *

Throughout the day, Shuut watched Rilla from behind and noticed her fade in and out of focus. A few times, she lost sight of the girl completely and almost panicked before she reappeared moments later.

"Rilla, by my side." The lintep looked around and waited until Shuut caught up with her.

"What are you doing?"

"I ... don't know," Rilla replied evasively. "What *am* I doing?"

"Don't play games with me, girl. You've been fading in and out all day. You've even disappeared completely from sight a few times."

The lintep beamed. "It works!"

"What works?"

"That's exactly what I was trying to do – disappear."

"Would you kindly *stop* doing that?" Shuut tried to keep her temper, but it was flaring all the same. "If you hadn't noticed, we're being hunted. Whoever is after us will become all the more intent on killing us all if they discover you are a lintep."

"No."

"I beg your pardon?" Shuut stared at the girl.

"No. I won't stop practicing my magic." Rilla stared at her defiantly. "We aren't heading towards Illaria. You've decided it's more important to visit the crystal dragons instead. Which means the only way I'll get to keep my powers, and quite possibly my life, is if I practice as much magic on my own as possible."

"How did you get that notion into your head all of a sudden?" She followed Rilla's gaze as it came to rest on Eliséo. "I should have known you were behind this."

"You almost sound surprised, Shadow." The elf walked up to them.

"You should know better," Shuut chided him. "If the person trying to track us isn't human, it will be all the easier for them with Rilla using her powers."

"So, what you're trying to tell me is that I need to choose between dying when my power reaches its peak because I haven't learnt control, or dying because I'm practicing my magic but allowing someone to track us down." Rilla stared unflinchingly at Shuut. "It's not much of a choice, Shuut. Don't you think it would be better for everyone if we simply headed for Illaria now so that I don't *need* to practice magic in the Outworld anymore?"

"I'm telling you to stop using your powers until we reach Illaria." Shuut remained firm in her resolve. "We're going to the Drakos Mountains first. We'll get to Illaria in plenty of time."

"How can you possibly know that?" Rilla asked angrily. "You don't even know where Illaria is. For all you know, we're heading in completely the opposite direction and it will take us too long to reach the lintep."

"She makes a strong argument, Shadow. You *don't* actually know where Illaria is." Eliséo smiled mischievously at her. "But I do."

"I don't care!" Shuut yelled at the two of them. "We're going to the Drakos Mountains first and that's *final!*"

* * *

The boys stopped in their tracks at Shadow's outburst. Rilla took a step back, dumbfounded. Eliséo only hesitated a moment before taking command of the situation.

"Nightfall is near enough. Make camp over by those trees, then begin your sparring practice. Rilla with Plyke, Arishen with Tika." The four Paradisians headed immediately towards the trees Eliséo had pointed out. When they were far enough away, the elf turned on the half-caste.

"What is wrong with you?"

"Nothing." Her reply was almost sullen.

"Don't 'nothing' me," he said more calmly than he felt. "You're acting almost as young as your companions. What is the matter with you?"

"The two of you were pressing me too far," Shadow replied defiantly. "This is *my* journey and I will go where I like. If you and Rilla don't like it, you can just leave."

"You know very well that isn't going to happen. At this point, none of the Paradisians want to part ways with you. I can't take Rilla away from them. She simply won't agree to that. You know that."

"Who are you to lecture me, Eliséo? You're barely more than a child yourself."

With that, Eliséo knew something was terribly wrong. Shadow had spent enough time with the elves to know that they did not age the same as humans, or even lintep. She knew Eliséo was much older than she was.

Keeping his eyes on the banwep, Eliséo called out to Rilla. The lintep raised her head at the sound of her name. He motioned her over. Thankfully, she walked briskly over to them without argument. Eliséo went to meet her half way and whispered in her ear.

"Do you feel any magic?"

Rilla looked at him worriedly for a moment, then closed her eyes. "Yes," she whispered, just as softly, back to him. "But it doesn't feel the same as ..."

"Careful what you say." He cut her off. He knew she had almost voiced aloud an admission of her bond with Elessa. "Can you tell me anything about it?"

"I don't know where it's coming from, but it feels ... discordant somehow."

Eliséo took a deep breath. He knew exactly what was going on. "We need to disrupt that magic, right now." He eyed Rilla, wondering whether she had the strength and control for what he was about to ask her. Would she even trust him enough to do as he said?

"I'm going to use the incantation that was said in Eléna's room the night before we left Silvaren. I'll need your help to make it strong enough. Do you think you can do that?"

"I think so," she answered warily.

Together, they led Shuut to their camp site. Rilla looked uncertainly over at Eliséo.

"What happens if I'm not strong enough to help?"

"You will be fine," he reassured her, knowing that his own power would have been strong enough. He simply could not allow anyone else to know understand that. It was all just a ruse to convince them he had very little power of his own. Turning to the others, he told them, "Someone outside our camp is using magic against us. I'm not sure if it's directed at everyone, or only at Shadow. I will try to counter it. Rilla will lend me her power to strengthen the spell. I need everyone to stay close together. Don't move too much."

The boys looked worriedly at one another and then at Rilla, who smiled reassuringly back at them. Eliséo was glad they at least trusted Rilla. He nodded to the lintep. She reluctantly took his hand and listened as he recited the same words he had practiced countless times with his mother. His eyes glowed a soft silver as the magic began to work. Rilla squeezed his hand tightly as he began to draw on her strength. The air around their camp thickened until it was practically solid. Eliséo saw everyone, other than Shadow, looking in wonder at the mist.

"Thank you, Rilla." The elf released her hand and turned to the banwep. She was shaking her head, eyes closed, as though trying to clear her thoughts. Eventually, she opened her eyes and saw the mist around them.

"What's happening?" she asked in confusion. "I feel like I've been dreaming."

"Someone was using their power on you," Eliséo told her bluntly. "I've created a shroud of invisibility around us all, with Rilla's assistance. It stops people seeing and hearing us. It also prevents any magic entering it."

Shuut looked over to the lintep girl now standing as far away from Eliséo as possible.

"You're helping to create this?" she asked, motioning to the mist around them. Rilla nodded slowly. "Thank you, Rilla."

"Does anyone else feel like they have just woken from a dream?" Eliséo asked the boys. They shook their heads, confirming his thoughts. "Then Shadow was the only one affected."

"Why would it only affect her?" Arishen questioned him.

"It is more than likely that the magic was directed specifically at her." Eliséo thought it best not to dissemble at this point. "I would assume the one responsible for this is same person hiring the bands of men that attacked."

"But why would this person only direct their magic towards Shuut?" Tika asked.

"We do not have time to think on that at present. We need to get as far away from here as possible." He held his breath for a short moment. "Goraburg is closer than the Drakos Mountains."

Shuut's face reddened slightly. They needed to find a safe place. Though the crystal dragons might provide better protection, they were further away. Until they knew who their attacker was and what they wanted, she would have no choice but to agree with Eliséo. Everyone was watching her closely. She merely inclined her head towards him. Eliséo smiled his thanks to her.

"Rilla, I need to ask for your further assistance. This mist needs constant power if we are to move. I cannot do it on my own." He looked carefully at the young lintep, trying to gauge her response to lending her strength to his spell. She had held up better than he had expected. Hopefully, by the end of the evening, she would not be much the worse for wear.

To Eliséo's annoyance, Shuut watched closely as Rilla seemed to internally debate helping him, before she reluctantly held out her hand to him.

Being careful not to release the lintep's hand, Eliséo modified the incantation and took a few steps forward to test the magic. The mist moved with him. He smiled, satisfied with the result, and nodded to Shuut who immediately divided his and Rilla's load between herself, Arishen and Plyke.

They turned towards Goraburg and travelled at a good pace for half the night. Tika was using the manipulated branches as best he could to keep up. Plyke eventually took his Partner's pack, not allowing him the chance to protest, and added it to his already heavy load.

Eliséo kept a close eye on Rilla. He wasn't certain how she would cope with maintaining a spell over such a long period of time. She barely showed any signs of fatigue. He knew it was a simple spell, but was still astonished that she was able to give him so much strength without any distress.

You think I have nothing to do with that? Elessa's voice was in his mind.

I'm sorry, my friend, he replied absently, *I did not realise you had been watching us.*

I always watch my little ones, Eliséo. You should know this by now.

Does she know? He glanced sideways at Rilla. Her eyes were firmly fixed on the moonlit woods in front of them.

There was no way to help without her feeling it, she replied, unperturbed. *I believe she is grateful to me for it.*

Of course I am. Rilla joined in the conversation. *We should stop soon though. I don't think Tika can go much further tonight.*

Eliséo looked across at the small human. Even with Plyke taking his pack, Tika was still struggling to walk with his branches.

"Shadow, do you agree we have travelled far enough tonight?" Shuut followed Eliséo's gaze to Tika and nodded her head almost imperceptibly.

"Yes, I agree." She turned to Arishen and Plyke. "Make camp."

Tika immediately slumped down to the grass, his back against a tree, and carefully placed his branches within arm's reach. As Shuut and the other boys made camp, Eliséo carefully restored Rilla's strength to her before releasing his grip on her hand. The young lintep did not look at him as she walked as far away as the protective mist would allow. Eliséo had modified the incantation so that they could stay in one place.

"Rilla." Shuut called out hesitantly. "I want to thank you for, well, I guess for all your help tonight. I realise without you, our mystery stalker would probably have found us."

The lintep did not say a word. Even Eliséo was surprised by the banwep's admission that she needed help. Shuut abruptly turned away.

"I suggest you all get as much sleep as you can while we're here. Eliséo will keep watch over us all." Shuut addressed the Paradisians, her back turned towards Rilla.

"Why do you need to keep watch?" Arishen asked in confusion. "Won't the mist keep anyone from finding us?"

"It will, Arishen. But I must remain awake for the mist to work," Eliséo replied.

"Won't you get tired?" the seer's voice betrayed his own fatigue.

"We elves are a sturdy race, Arishen. We can survive without sleep for much longer than any human or lintep."

The boys needed no further encouragement. They hastily followed Shuut's example, lay down on their sleeping mats and closed their eyes. Rilla alone remained seated and staring at him.

Eliséo waited until he heard the deep breathing of their companions before speaking. "Your eyes are awhirl with thoughts, Rilla."

"And what do they tell you?" The lintep replied, not giving anything away.

"I do not presume to know." He lowered his eyes. "I can only guess they are angry thoughts."

"Not anymore, Eliséo." She smiled sadly. "I want to apologise for my behaviour this morning."

"What do you mean?" Eliséo looked up at her. "I was furious with the person who made me do that for the first time."

"I know," Rilla replied quietly, "I saw your memory. Elessa showed me the necessity of what we did. At least I have that small comfort. You had nothing your first time. I'm sorry you had to go through that. I have been selfish to let you think I was angry with you all day. I just didn't know how to tell you."

"Thank you, Rilla." The words were almost inaudible as Eliséo pulled a book out of his pack and opened it. Rilla looked at him a moment longer then lay down on her sleeping mat and quickly fell into a deep sleep.

Chapter Forty-Two – Sparring

Eliséo woke his companions as the sun began to rise. He wanted to maintain a good distance between them and their pursuer. The Paradisians still needed to practise the skills Ensil had taught them and they would need more space than the mist could provide. With a single look, Shuut understood his intentions. She gave the order to break camp.

As the others were packing up, Rilla checked on Tika's leg. It hadn't healed visibly from the night before, but at least it looked no worse. With his permission, she placed her left hand over the wound and her right hand over his other leg. Tika smiled broadly at her as he tested the pain while walking with his curved branches. Rilla shyly returned the smile. Eliséo sighed at her continued lack of confidence.

"I know it is much to ask of you, but would you lend me your strength again today so that I can maintain this mist while we travel?" he asked Rilla. She nodded wearily and held out her hand.

"When are we going to stop?" It was mid-afternoon by the time Plyke dared to ask. "We haven't had a break all day and we travelled half the night."

Eliséo exchanged glances with Shuut. They both would have preferred to keep travelling, but there was no point exhausting the Paradisians before their sparring practice.

"Very well." Shuut stopped dead in her tracks. "Make camp then get out your weapons." She smiled as the faces of her companions fell. Eliséo released Rilla's hand and the mist dissipated. He noticed Shadow and the boys heave unconscious sighs of relief. They had been enshrouded by his mist since the previous day. While they had been able to see the forest around them slowly give way to open fields, the mist had blurred their view of it. He hoped they were far enough from their pursuer that the open fields wouldn't give their position away.

Each of the Paradisians brought their weapons to him. Once again, he thickened the air around them so that no one would be gravely injured during the sparring session.

Shuut marked out a line with her rucksack, then walked fifty paces away from it with Tika's branches. She dug two holes in the ground and placed one branch in each hole, so that the curves of them formed a half circle. Approaching the apprehensive boy, she motioned for him to get his bow ready.

"From this rucksack, you must aim for your arrows to go through the half circle your branches make." She instructed him.

"That's impossible!" Tika complained. "No one can do that. It's too small a target and too far away."

Without hesitation, Shuut took the bow, nocked an arrow and drew the string back to her cheek. Effortlessly, she aimed and fired. The arrow flew straight through the centre of her target, landing in the grass behind it.

"Nothing is impossible," she said as she handed him the bow and walked towards the other Paradisians. Tika stared after her, thunderstruck. He looked down at the bow in his hand. Gripping it tightly, he turned to face his target, drew an arrow, nocked it, aimed and fired. The arrow flew wide of the target. He cursed and tried again.

Eleven arrows later, he had barely improved and his quiver was empty. Angrily, he limped the fifty paces to his branches and kicked them over before gathering his misfired arrows. Eliséo joined the boy as he carefully replaced the arrows in their quiver.

"Shadow is older than you." Tika startled at Eliséo's voice above him. "A banwep is bound to have had a fair deal more practice than a Paradisian. You cannot expect to hit the target on your first attempt."

"I'll *need* to hit a target on my first attempt if anyone attacks us again." Tika thrust the last arrow into the quiver before looking up with fire in his eyes.

"The angrier you become, the further your arrows will stray from their target," Eliséo replied calmly. "When you have been fighting for your life as long as Shadow, *then* I would expect you to hit every target on your first attempt. For now, be patient and practice."

Tika grudgingly nodded his head, and they returned to the campsite where Eliséo watched the human shoot another two quivers of arrows before turning his attention elsewhere.

Eliséo was amazed at Rilla. She had used so much of her energy to heal her companions in the past few days, not to mention helping him maintain the protective mist. If it had been any other person, lintep or otherwise, she would certainly have been exhausted by now. Yet to look at her, one would think she had been through no more than her companions.

Rilla was sparring with Plyke. Two swords against a double axe was an odd match, but you never knew who would attack you in the Outworld, nor what weapons they would carry. Not that he had expected any less from Ensil, but it had been a wise decision for the weapons master to match each person with their perfect weapon, rather than give all the Paradisians the same type of weapon.

* * *

Plyke had only sparred with his Partner and the seer since receiving his axe. It had felt, as soon as Ensil handed him the weapon, like an extension of his body. He assumed that was a normal feeling, until he noticed how awkward Arishen and Tika were with theirs. Perhaps it was a lintep trait to be one with his weapon. Rilla seemed to be as comfortable with her swords as he was with his axe. The thought caused him to hold back any time he had sparred with Tika and Arishen.

Rilla was more skilful than the boys. She would push him further than they did. Holding his axe in both hands, he took a defensive stance. Rilla attacked with her long sword. He blocked the attack, swinging his axe sideways. The short sword made its way around his parry before he had a chance to attack.

It was a defensive bout for Plyke. He immediately realised he would not get very far with her if he held back. Making a rash decision, he let his inhibitions go. He became one with his axe just as Rilla was one with her two swords. The battle became a pyrrhic dance. Their fluid movements fed off each other. Plyke was no longer solely on the defensive. He occasionally had the advantage and was exhilarated by the intensity of the fight.

"Enough." Shuut's commanding voice stopped the two of them in mid attack and defence. Plyke blinked, as though waking from a dream and saw Rilla do likewise. He looked around to see everyone staring at them. There was little chance he would be able to explain away his skill with his double axe.

Cursing his stupidity in possibly revealing himself, Plyke walked briskly away from his companions. He went only so far as he thought Shuut would allow before sending someone after him. He needed to be by himself – to consider what he had done by showing the others that he had been concealing his ability with the weapon until now. Had they all noticed or were they too absorbed in their own practice? He and Rilla had not noticed the others. She had been just as surprised as he was to hear Shuut commanding a halt.

Plyke held his head and shut his eyes in pain. Letting himself go had released the senses that he normally held in check. He could feel his companions back at the camp, the small creatures that lived in the fields. It was an overload of information. He could not shut it out. In amongst it all, he could feel Eliséo approaching him.

"I can help if you will allow it." Plyke did not acknowledge the elf. He didn't want to talk to anyone. "It will only get worse if you don't protect yourself."

Plyke opened his eyes in confusion. "What are you talking about?"

"I know what you are, Plyke." Plyke recoiled in fear. "I will not let anyone know. I simply want to help you."

"How do you know what I am?" he asked wildly. "Who told you?"

"Your companions do not know what you are. If you want to keep it that way, you need to let me help you."

Plyke hesitated. He barely knew anything about the elf. He closed his eyes to try to collect his thoughts but that only made things worse. Shutting off one of his senses simply made his lintep sense intensify. He almost cried out in pain before Eliséo clapped his hands in front of his face. Plyke instantly opened his eyes and stared at the elf in shock.

"Look into my eyes. Concentrate on them." Plyke felt he wouldn't be able to look away even if he wanted to. "Notice the patterns within them. Let them become your whole world."

As Plyke stared into those silver eyes, he felt himself relaxing slightly. His lintep sense became slightly muted. The more he concentrated on Eliséo's eyes, the more attention it required. It seemed as though those intricate patterns had some meaning. There was some puzzle within them he needed to solve. He concentrated ever more.

As time passed, it almost seemed to Plyke that the elf's eyes began to glimmer slightly. Plyke thought about nothing except those eyes. He could still sense everything around him, but the information was no longer overwhelming. The pain had been dissipating, but Plyke had not noticed until it was almost completely gone. He blinked in surprise and shook his head to clear his thoughts.

"How did you find out what I am and how to help me?" Plyke finally asked him again.

"Plyke, I am the Ambassador of the Elves." Eliséo smiled faintly. "I have probably spent more time with the lintep than with my own people."

Plyke's heart raced.

"Do not worry yourself. I will not reveal that which you choose to keep hidden from the others."

"It's not a choice," Plyke replied instantly. "If they knew what I was ..."

"They may have turned against you in the Paradise." Eliséo finished the sentence for him. "What was the point in leaving that place if you still allow it to rule your life?"

Plyke didn't answer. He knew Eliséo was right. It was ridiculous for him to let the Paradise rule his life when he no longer lived there. In truth, it probably wouldn't be so bad to let Shuut and Arishen know the truth about him. After all, one was a seer and the other a half-lintep. Why then did he still hesitate?

Eliséo stood up to return to the campsite. "You may find that the others will not take the news as badly as you fear."

Plyke watched as the elf walked away from him. He had no idea what to do. Should he pretend nothing had happened and refuse to answer their questions? Or should he finally tell them who he was? He had been hiding his true self for so long that he had no idea who he would be without his disguise.

Plyke walked back to the camp with his head held high. Just because he had momentarily lost control of his power did not mean everyone had noticed. Arishen probably hadn't seen anything. Shuut may have observed something but her ability was more in reading minds and Plyke had been careful to always shield his mind against her.

"What was that?" Shuut barely waited for Plyke to be within hearing distance before questioning him. Maintaining his steady pace towards the camp, Plyke inspected the barriers to his mind, making certain there were no cracks through which Shuut could pry.

"What was what?" He kept his voice even.

"Don't play coy with me, boy." Her grey eyes narrowed. "I've been watching all of you quite carefully since Ensil gave you your weapons. Against Arishen and Tika, you spar as if you're no more than their equal. Had that been the case, Rilla would have left bruises all over you. Yet we all saw you defending yourself a little too well against her attacks, even managing to turn the tables on her a few times."

"You're saying you *don't* want me to defend myself well against Rilla?" Plyke had no idea how far he could push the lie, but he intended to find out.

Shuut took a deep breath and turned to Rilla. "You didn't seem surprised that Plyke could challenge you."

Rilla avoided Plyke's gaze. His heart beat faster. *Does she know how to shield her mind?*

"I obviously haven't watched him as closely as you. While he has been sparring with the others, I have likewise been occupied. Why should I be surprised that he can challenge me when I've never sparred with him before?" Rilla's answer gave Plyke hope. Perhaps he would be able to keep up the charade a little longer.

"You weren't surprised because you already knew about him." Tika's soft voice shattered Plyke's hopes. Shuut turned to face him.

"She already knew *what*?"

Plyke stared at Tika in anguish, silently pleading with him to stay quiet.

"That he is at least part lintep." Tika's jaw trembled slightly.

Shuut cocked her head to one side in astonishment. "I beg your pardon?"

"That's not true," Plyke replied immediately.

"Don't you think it's about time you stop pretending?" Tika looked straight at him, stony faced. "Rilla and Eliséo know now too. So really that just leaves a seer and another lintep. Exactly who do you think you need to hide from?"

"What are you doing?" Tika's betrayal overwhelmed Plyke.

"You obviously don't have the courage to stop hiding, so it looks like I'll have to force you."

"So, you save me in the Paradise only to risk my life in the Outworld?"

"You're being ridiculous!" Tika yelled at him, long-held back fury bubbling over. "I kept you safe from Erton without ever asking anything in return and you accuse me of risking your life. Did it not occur to you that *you* are the one putting all of our lives at risk? Don't think for a minute that I don't blame you for my leg. If you had fought against those brutes the way you just sparred with Rilla, then perhaps I wouldn't have been injured at all!"

Plyke stared at him, confused and scared.

"Exactly when did you two become Partners?" Shuut asked curiously.

"We were in our sixth year," Plyke answered softly. "But I didn't know Tika knew until we were in Silvaren."

"I knew something was different about him before that. By our sixth year, Kora must have already started teaching him to hide his abilities. It wasn't until we met you that I started to suspect exactly what he was."

Shuut drew in a sharp breath. "Why didn't you tell him you knew before Silvaren?"

"What would have been the point of that?" Tika looked at her angrily. "Plyke might have panicked and if anyone had observed his reaction, I would have put him in greater danger."

"So, you couldn't tell me because *I* might have panicked, but you expected me to tell you then and everyone else now. What if *you* had reacted badly?" Plyke knew was clutching at straws, but couldn't seem to help himself.

"Don't be daft, Plyke," Arishen spoke up for the first time. "Tika has always been the person most interested in magic in our entire Paradise. Everyone knows that. It's a wonder Erton didn't do something about it while we were still there. He would never have reacted badly to *this*."

"And you can tell me this from experience, can you? Your Partner ..." He didn't get a chance to finish.

"Parthak gave me a chance. It was more than she thought I deserved, but she gave it to me anyway. She was Erton's prize little sheep." Arishen choked back his tears. "If even *she* was willing to hide me from Erton's attention for a short amount of time, I can guarantee you that Tika would have hidden you from Erton his entire life."

"Well now we'll never know, will we?" Plyke retorted. "He didn't hide me from you and Shuut, did he?" He ignored Tika as his Partner picked up his quiver to retrieve his arrows from the field.

"You don't deserve a Partner like him," Arishen told Plyke angrily.

Plyke looked away as Arishen stormed off. His gaze went straight to Rilla who barely had time to open her mouth before he berated her. "And don't you start. You can't possibly tell me what I should or shouldn't have done. You never even had a Partner."

"How dare you!" Her eyes brimmed with tears. "I never had a Partner because no one our age would even *talk* to me. The only person who dared defy Erton to become my friend paid for it with his life. Don't you *dare* tell me that I don't know what it's like to have my life in someone else's hands or hold their life in my hands. Rhanya gave his life for me and Shuut, or did you not realise that's why Erton had him killed?"

Plyke had the decency to stay silent after her outburst. Rilla, tears streaming down her face went to help Arishen with the fire. Shuut and Eliséo quickly busied themselves, and Plyke could tell they would not be drawn into the argument.

Chapter Forty-Three – Healer's gift

Shuut set the night watches with a little more care than usual. She had thought living the life of a banwep would save her from social politics but even in a group so small she now had to make certain not to put the wrong people together for a shift otherwise she could endanger all their lives. Rilla would share the first shift with her, next Eliséo and Plyke and, lastly, Tika and Arishen.

The boys fell asleep quickly and quietly, even the elf. Shuut barely gave them a second glance as she and Rilla began walking their rounds. They walked in opposite directions around the campsite, circling wider and wider until they were certain no attackers were nearby. Eventually they returned to the camp and sat with their backs against each other, staring into the distance, maintaining their watch.

* * *

"How long have you known about Plyke?"

"Can we please not talk about this?" Rilla hadn't stopped thinking about Rhanya since earlier that evening. It had taken all her strength to stop crying.

"I just wonder if there are any other secrets you hold." Shuut pressed. "You've appointed yourself holder of secrets without even noticing. How much longer can you go on like that? Eventually you'll break and just blurt out everything you know."

"If that's what you think," Rilla replied instantly, "then your nightly rummaging through our minds has told you nothing about me."

"I stopped doing that weeks ago!" Shuut protested a little too quickly.

"No, that's what you told us, but not what you actually did." Rilla felt Shuut's back stiffen against hers. "You've stopped doing it while we're still awake, but I've woken every time you've tried it on me in my sleep."

"Old habits die hard," sighed Shuut, shrugging. "Is that why you keep everyone's secrets?"

"I've never really thought about it," Rilla answered after a moment's pause. "I suppose I noticed things no one else did because I had no distractions. There was no point in telling anyone what I saw because it would have only caused pain and suffering. Erton was adept enough at that without my help. So, I continued to observe and, in my own way, help them to stay hidden."

"I just don't understand." Shuut shook her head. "If you had nothing to gain by keeping their secrets, why do it? They never even knew to thank you."

"Rhanya knew," Rilla whispered barely loud enough for Shuut to hear.

"Then why didn't *he* say anything?"

"He was a *healer*, Shuut." Angry tears coursed down her face again. "If he mentioned any of what we knew to Erton, he would have been harming people. He would have undone all of his work as a healer if he did that."

"Is that why you did it too? Because you were going to become a healer?" Rilla didn't answer. She was overwrought by the memory of her loss. Seemingly unwilling to let the matter go, Shuut pressed on. "Do you ever wonder if the boys know why you left the Paradise?"

Rilla drew a deep breath and held it for what felt like an impossibly long time.

"Please don't tell them." She realised that Shuut must already have guessed the truth. She had been careful to hide Rhanya's letter away from everyone since she'd finally had the courage to open it.

"Why don't *you* tell them?" Shuut asked, oblivious. "It might make them respect you a little more and not lash out at you like that idiot boy of a lintep just did."

"You must be joking." Rilla turned her head in astonishment. "Do you honestly believe that?"

"Do any of them appreciate the fact that I wouldn't have even taken them as far as Turon if it hadn't been for you? They would have survived there very long, but they would have died before then if it hadn't been for you."

"You can't tell them. *Please.*"

"Why does it mean so much to you to keep them in the dark?" Shuut pounded her fist into the grass, obviously frustrated.

"Apart from Rhanya, they're the closest thing to friends that I've ever had. If you tell them, that will end in an instant."

"Friends?" Shuut started in surprise. "Tika, I can see is a possible friend, but the other two? One breaks your nose, stabs you with a chisel and argues with you almost every time he talks to you. The other barely speaks to you at all except to call you a hypocrite. These are the *friends* that you are now sworn to protect."

Rilla didn't answer. There was no point. How could Shuut possibly understand what it had been like to live in almost total isolation in a place as small and crowded as their Paradise? How could she expect the banwep to understand that one civil conversation with any of the boys was more than they'd ever shared in the past fifteen years? They were dearer to her now than she ever believed possible. It surprised her to realise that, now, so was Shuut.

The following morning, Tika and Arishen woke the others. Little was said as they ate a cold breakfast and broke camp. There was no need for words. Everyone went about the tasks they knew needed to be accomplished before they started walking. Rilla, once more, cursed herself for not tending to Tika's leg the night before. It was healing quite well with her help. She felt some small amount of satisfaction, if not happiness, that within a day or two he would be able to walk without the assistance of the makeshift crutches.

At the thought of the mutilated branches, she inwardly cringed. There were so many things she had done to cause pain to others. Healing people was really the only way she could think to make up for that pain. She silently wondered if that was the way Rhanya had felt too and had to blink back the tears that threatened to engulf her again.

Why was she thinking of him so much now when she had managed to push the rest of her life from the Paradise to the back of her mind? She knew better than to think it meant something. She was no seer. Perhaps it was because she'd had to heal so many people in recent days. She couldn't help but think of Rhanya when she was healing. How long had it been now? Weeks? A season? She couldn't even remember how long they had been in the Outworld. The days and weeks blended together. All she could remember was Turon, Silvaren and now the attacks and healing.

Mind your surroundings.

The voice in her head brought an abrupt halt to her musings. She blinked away her thoughts and looked around to see if anyone had noticed how preoccupied she'd been. As usual, no one had. They were walking on oblivious to her. The others never noticed anything about her, but why should she be surprised? They'd never noticed her in the Paradise, why would a change of scenery make a difference?

Rilla, mind your surroundings!

The tone of Elessa's voice brought Rilla up short. She immediately looked around her to see what was the matter. Tika and Arishen were walking at the head of their party with Shuut. Plyke was a few paces behind, watching them with an angry set to his shoulders. Eliséo brought up the rear behind Rilla herself. There was nothing out of the ordinary.

That is not anger.

Trusting the tree's perception, Rilla looked once more at Plyke. She sped up her pace until she drew alongside, and then looked across at him. What she had mistaken for anger was, in fact, intense concentration. His brow was tightly creased. Something was confusing or scaring him. She tapped her teeth together for a moment, then sighed.

"Plyke?" She hesitated. What could she possibly say to him?

"Go away." He didn't sound angry, just irritated.

"What's the matter?"

"Leave me alone."

"No. What are you concentrating on?" she persisted.

Plyke turned to face her in astonishment. "Who says I was concentrating on anything?"

"Plyke, please, just believe me when I say I *know* something is bothering you and tell me what it is." He looked at her for a few moments, uncertainty written across his face. Eventually, it seemed that common sense won.

"I can feel something bad is happening, but I don't know what."

Rilla looked warily around them. They were travelling through open plains and she couldn't see anyone but the six of them.

* * *

Eliséo caught Rilla's eye and immediately understood something was wrong. He quickened his step to reach them and asked Plyke directly, "What do you feel?"

"I don't know. Something bad." Plyke shook his head in annoyance.

"Where is it coming from?"

"What do you mean?"

"Is it ahead of us or behind us?

"I don't know!" Plyke raised his voice in frustration. Shuut immediately turned to see what the commotion was about. The other boys followed her as she walked back to them.

"What's going on here?"

"Nothing!" Plyke responded angrily.

"Plyke can feel something bad, but he hasn't been trained well enough to understand what is happening." Eliséo ignored the look Plyke gave him. He'd had to deal with much worse than petulant teenagers before.

"Can you help him?" the banwep asked.

"I can only try." He looked at the now frightened boy and told Plyke to close his eyes while motioning Rilla and Shuut to keep a close watch on their surroundings. Plyke looked nervously at him. "Plyke, close your eyes."

The young boy violently shook his head. "It will only get worse if I do."

"Plyke, look into my eyes." Before he could think twice about it, the lintep looked straight into Eliséo's glowing silver eyes. "Feel your companions around you. Feel their fear that you will refuse to help them."

Plyke instantly cringed and hugged himself.

"Close your eyes," Eliséo's voice was laced with command. Plyke was now spellbound by his eyes and voice. The boy struggled to keep his eyes open, but his will was no match for Eliséo's.

"Let your senses go. Feel your surroundings." Eliséo waited until he saw Plyke flinch. "Feel the disharmony in the air. Focus on it."

There was an intense look of concentration on Plyke's face. Eliséo had managed to both calm him down and cast his senses further afield.

"There is someone ahead of us."

"Are they alone?"

Plyke shrugged. "I can't feel anyone else but it's too loud for me to really tell."

"What is too loud?"

"There's a roaring sound."

"A roaring sound like water flowing rapidly in a river?" The elf was trying to guide the boy as much as possible, but it was so much more difficult with a Paradisian lintep than a lintep in training in Illaria.

"I've only ever seen a stream – in our Paradise. It didn't sound anything like this."

Eliséo cursed under his breath. "Can you *see* anything, Plyke? Anything at all?"

"No," he shook his head. "I can't see anything. Please let me open my eyes."

"I am not keeping you from opening them," Eliséo replied calmly, regretting the lie he had to tell. Plyke instantly opened his eyes and stared suspiciously at him, but Eliséo turned to Shadow.

"The only roaring sound he could have heard is the Bramble River. If there is something happening there, whoever is targeting us is likely damaging the ferry so we can't cross. We need to change our direction."

"No!" Shuut answered forcefully. "We're going to the crystal dragons and that's final."

"Shadow, are you hearing me?" Eliséo asked her carefully. "If we continue along this path, we will be walking directly into a trap."

"I don't care! I'm in charge here and you will all do as I say!"

Eliséo and Rilla exchanged worried glances. Something was wrong with Shuut. A banwep would never knowingly walk into a trap if they could avoid it.

"Bad magic!" Plyke cried out, seconds before Shuut fell limply to the ground.

"Everyone to me!" Eliséo commanded the Paradisians. Without a moment's hesitation, they were instantly by his side. He wasted no time in conjuring up the thickest layer of mist he had ever woven. Without asking her permission, Eliséo took Rilla's hand to strengthen it even more. The lintep was too stunned to react, sagging slightly from the sudden drain on her energy.

"Is she still alive?" asked Tika.

"I'm not sure," Eliséo replied.

"She is, but barely," Plyke answered in a pained voice.

"Tika, we need you to walk without your sticks. Can you do that?" Eliséo waited for Tika to nod before continuing. "Get Shadow's sleeping mat and place it between the sticks. Use any rope you have and tie it together. You boys will need to carry her."

"Plyke, can you still feel something?"

The frightened boy closed his eyes and concentrated. Eventually, Eliséo put his hand on the boy's shoulder. Plyke opened his eyes.

"I can't feel anything apart from the six of us."

Eliséo thanked the boy before turning due west and walking on, clutching Rilla's hand firmly, no longer heading towards the ferry crossing. Plyke and Arishen carried Shuut on her converted sleeping mat, while Tika had shouldered the banwep's rucksack.

"Where are we going now?" Arishen spoke up first.

"We are heading for the Bramble River," Eliséo replied shortly.

"Isn't that where you told Shuut we *shouldn't* be going?"

"No, I told her we should not go to the ferry crossing."

"Wait, what's the point of going to the river if we aren't going to the ferry crossing? How are we meant to get across?"

Eliséo stopped in his tracks, unintentionally jerking back on Rilla's hand as he did so. "The closest safe haven for us now is with the crystal dragons. The fastest way to get there is through Goraburg. We need to reach the other side of the Bramble River for that to become a possibility. The only way to safely cross the river is to go straight through it. We will need this spell to protect us as we walk across the riverbed." He gestured at the mist around them with his free hand.

"What if it doesn't hold?" Plyke asked in near panic. "I can't swim!"

"That will be the least of your concerns if that happens," Eliséo muttered under his breath.

"What does that mean?" Rilla glared at him, the only one within hearing distance.

Eliséo took a deep breath. "It means that should the mist fail anywhere within the river, the sudden pressure of the water caving in on our bodies will crush us to death." He watched as their expressions turn to horror.

"Do you have enough power to make sure that doesn't happen?" Plyke asked ever so quietly. "I mean, you wouldn't take us through unless you knew we'd be safe, right?"

"Wrong." He attempted to continue walking but was held back by Rilla's firm grip.

"Exactly what does *that* mean?" Her voice was now threatening. "You don't have enough power, or you'd take us through the river without knowing we'd be safe?"

They were wasting precious time. He knew they wouldn't want to go through the river if they knew how dangerous it really was, but Rilla was so stubborn that she would refuse to move one step closer to the river without knowing what she was leading her friends into.

"I don't have enough power, but I'm hoping you do." Fear rippled across the boys' faces but Rilla flushed angrily. "We don't have much of a choice. Illaria is too far away to make for with someone intent on attacking us. The ferry crossing has certainly been turned into a place of ambush. I don't know why we are being targeted, but whoever it is isn't taking chances. We need to do something unexpected. This person can't possibly expect us to walk straight *through* the river so, in every imaginable way, that is our safest path."

The river was the safest place for them to be, if Rilla had the power to keep them safe. The lintep turned to look silently at each of the boys.

"Let's go then," she said and walked on without looking at him.

Chapter Forty-Four – River crossing

They heard the Bramble River long before they saw it, but the sun was already nearing the horizon by the time they reached the brambles which gave the river its name. Eliséo cursed under his breath, thankful that no one heard him. The rapidly flowing river was at least two miles wide. He was certain they would not reach the other side before the sun had set. Crossing the river was going to be dangerous enough the way he planned to do it. Crossing in darkness would be completely reckless.

"We can't cross now." Everyone started at his announcement as he released Rilla's hand. He understood their confusion. They had walked at an unforgiving pace all day to reach the river and now he was telling them it was all for nothing.

"Why not?" asked Tika, doubled over to catch his breath. Walking without the branches had clearly been a challenge for him, but he wouldn't complain while Shuut lay unconscious and the other four were either shouldering her or keeping them safe inside a misty dome.

"It will be too dangerous to cross in darkness."

"Why can't we just light a fire and take it with us?" Arishen and Plyke placed Shuut carefully on the ground as the seer asked his question.

"Does anyone have oil?"

Everyone shook their heads. They hadn't needed oil for their other fires. They simply gathered enough firewood for the night whenever they were safe enough to light a fire.

Rilla has her leaves.

Eliséo knew Rilla heard Elessa as well. The lintep instantly looked at him but Eliséo did not immediately return her gaze. A few moments passed before he turned to her slowly, as though a thought had occurred to him.

"Rilla, do you still have the leaves that Lady Eléna gave you?"

She nodded.

"They may help us if you don't mind losing a few along the way."

* * *

Rilla flinched. She'd had the leaves for as long as she could remember. It was true that she'd forgotten where they had come from or that they were special in any way, but they were among her most precious possessions. The thought of losing them momentarily stopped her heart.

"How can they possibly help?" she asked, hoping Eliséo wouldn't find a good enough reason.

"Eléna gave you the leaves from her very own tree, Silva. That tree is the heart of Silvaren. More than any other tree in our forest, Silva has a life and strength all its own. Those leaves will each burn for longer than an entire branch of a tree from the Outworld."

Rilla's shoulders slumped. It felt like he'd dealt her a physical blow.

"Let's start crossing now," she said, hoping to delay the inevitable. "The more ground we cover before night falls, the fewer leaves we'll need to use."

"We can't do that," Eliséo told her. "We need you to start burning the first one now. You will not be able to deal with that distraction later."

Rilla held her breath and tapped her teeth together. She knew there was no real choice. If she didn't agree, their pursuer could find them before they had a chance to cross. She took off her rucksack and rummaged through it until her hand touched the leaves. Not knowing how many they would need, she took a small handful and pulled them out. Leaving one in her hand, she carefully placed the rest in her pocket, within easy reach.

"Now what?" she asked the elf.

"Hold it out in front of you and light it." The ease with which he answered her made Rilla's blood boil. She was absolutely furious with him. These leaves belonged to *her*. They were a *gift*. He was so easily asking her to destroy them.

She held out the leaf before her, trembling with anger. Before she realised what she was doing, her anger gathered into a ball of heat at her fingertips. The leaf burst into flames.

Rilla yelped in surprise and pain and she let go of the burning leaf. To her amazement, it didn't fall. It floated in front of her. Her eyes momentarily met Tika's through the image of the flame and she saw her astonishment mirrored in his.

Eliséo took her hand again and motioned the others to pick Shuut up. Barely waiting for them to do so, he began walking straight for the river. Rilla made no attempt to stop him. She was too surprised and confused. Wherever she moved, the leaf kept its distance in front of her. If she moved sideways, it likewise moved to the side. She was experimenting with it while they were walking and only took in the rest of her companions when Eliséo roughly tugged at her hand to get her to keep moving with the rest of them.

As they neared the river, Rilla's focus turned from the burning leaf to the rapid waters now filling her entire view. Sudden panic gripped her. The thought of keeping so much water out of their bubble of mist was terrifying. If she failed, they would all die. *All* of them. She stopped dead in her tracks.

"I can't do this," she said it mostly to herself, but the others heard her.

"You have no choice," Eliséo replied as the boys gathered closer. "If you don't do this, then we'll all die."

"Are you looking at the same river as me?" She pointed to the Bramble River incredulously. "How can I possibly keep *that* out?"

"'I'll help." Rilla turned in surprise to Plyke. He shifted his stance uncomfortably as she stared at him. "If you can lend your strength to Eliséo, I can lend mine to you."

"Would that even work?" Rilla asked with a glimmer of hope.

"I don't know." Plyke shrugged. "We may as well try. Your power seems very different to mine. You can heal people just by touching them. Maybe it will work the other way around if you just sort of take some strength from me."

Rilla looked uncertainly from Plyke to Eliséo.

"It could work," the elf conceded. "You would both have to be very careful. Rilla, do not take too much too quickly. Plyke, you *must* tell Rilla when you have no strength left to give. We can't possibly manage if we have two bodies to carry. Do you both understand?"

They both nodded. Rilla stood hesitantly as Plyke held out his hand towards her. Tika, without being asked, walked over to take Plyke's place by Shuut. Rilla wondered if he could carry Shuut the whole way across the river with his injured leg, but there was no choice left for any of them. If this plan failed, they were all dead.

Everyone watched as Rilla took Plyke's hand. Nothing happened.

"It's not working." Rilla lowered her eyes.

Child, you must draw strength from him. It can't simply happen by holding his hand. Elessa was instantly in her mind.

"Try harder," Plyke urged her.

Remember how it felt to take heat away from something. It will be the same as taking his strength. Just squeeze his hand and pull the strength into yourself.

Rilla took a deep breath and squeezed Plyke's hand. She could feel the strength in his grip as it tightened around her hand. Reaching out for that strength, she imagined tying a knot between her strength and his. Then she pulled.

Plyke fell to his knees, dragging Rilla's arm down with him. Eliséo was shouted something at her but she couldn't hear it through the surge of energy within her. She focussed her eyes to see what was happening and found Plyke pale and breathless on the grass. She released her hold on his strength and the colour came back to his cheeks.

"Now I understand what you were trying to warn us about." Plyke smiled as he shakily got to his feet.

"I'm sorry." Rilla's hands shook. She hadn't realised what she was doing until it was almost too late. She could have killed Plyke if she'd pulled any harder.

"We're all learning here without a teacher." He squeezed her hand gently. "No harm done."

Rilla took little comfort at his words. She wondered if *he* realised how close she had come to killing him. She turned to the river and walked right up to the bank, past the thorny brambles. The river was calmest on the bank where it met the resistance of hardened soil. She squeezed Eliséo and Plyke's hands, closed her eyes and stepped into the water.

She stepped on stones, but her boots remained dry. Rilla opened her eyes in confusion and looked down. The mist in front of her feet had become more solid. She smiled and looked over at Eliséo.

"It's working!"

He didn't return her smile. "Don't get too excited. This is the easiest part. It will become more difficult as we get further in."

Rilla frowned at his lack of enthusiasm for their success. Behind her, Arishen and Tika picked up Shuut, readying themselves for the crossing. She waited until they were ready before continuing into the river.

Walking unsteadily over slippery rocks, Rilla concentrated on the mist. It became thicker the further into the river they walked. Once they were away from the bank, the flow was much stronger. It took more effort to keep that amount of pressure out of the mist. Before long, the mist was completely submerged in water. Though it meant that the river wasn't pushing them too hard from the sides, they now had added pressure of the weight of the water on top of them.

Rilla strengthened the mist as much as she could without draining too much energy from Plyke. It was a two-mile journey across the Bramble River. Walking at a normal pace, it wouldn't have taken them more than an hour or two to cross. Unfortunately, they were walking slowly. With three of them attempting to keep the river out and the other two carrying Shuut, there was no way they could set that sort of pace. Rilla hoped that she would have the strength to get them all safely to the other side.

Time passed. The water became darker around them as the sun began to set. The burning leaf in front of Rilla allowed them to see everything within the mist, but very little outside it. The only way Rilla knew they were still heading in the right direction was because of the extra pressure on her right side. The river had been flowing from right to left, as long as that pressure stayed on her right, they should be heading straight towards the other bank.

She tried to keep her thoughts focussed on three things – making sure the extra pressure was on her right, watching Plyke's face to make sure he was still capable of giving her strength and keeping an eye on the burning leaf in front of her to make sure they weren't plunged into darkness. The last two were worrying her. The leaf had almost disappeared and Plyke looked like he would collapse if she held on to his strength much longer.

Rilla stopped walking suddenly, jerking on Plyke and Eliséo's arms. The Paradisians looked at her in confusion. Eliséo had immediately guessed what was concerning her from one glance at the leaf and Plyke.

"Plyke, can you reach into my pocket and pull out another leaf? This one is fading," Rilla asked him. As Plyke held the second leaf to the first, his fingers trembled with the effort. He dropped his hand as the second leaf burst into flames.

"I gave you one order, Plyke," Eliséo said roughly. "You were to tell Rilla when you couldn't give any more strength."

"I can hold on a little longer," Plyke insisted, his voice faint.

"No, you can't." Eliséo's reply was brusque. "Rilla, let him go."

Rilla tried to let go as gently as possible. First, she stopped pulling his strength into her. Draining as that was, she knew she had to go on. She mentally untied the knot between them and let go of his hand.

* * *

Eliséo caught Rilla as she fell from the lack of strength. He refused to feel guilty about the ruse. He could have kept the mist solid all on his own, but his eyes would have shined so brightly that none of the boys would ever forget it. If they ever mentioned it to someone who knew anything about elves, his secret would be revealed.

He allowed Plyke to assist Rilla, the boy put his arm under her shoulders to hold her up. Slowly, they continued across the riverbed. Plyke took on the responsibility of watching the burning leaf. Eliséo kept the mist going and ensured they walked in the right direction.

By the time the second leaf had burnt itself out, Rilla could barely walk. Plyke had recovered enough of his strength to pick up the lintep and carry her. There was no resistance. Her eyes were closed and her head slumped against his shoulder but she wasn't sleeping. Eliséo knew it was by sheer will that she managed to keep herself alert enough to help him maintain the mist.

* * *

Tika was struggling. His leg had been throbbing for at least an hour. Much as he tried to push the pain away, to make it just part of the background, it was still there.

221

* * *

Arishen was too distracted by jealousy to notice anything other than Rilla and Plyke. Why couldn't he have been the one to help Rilla? This would have been a perfect chance to get close to her. If only he had thought to swap positions with Plyke once it was clear he was recovered and Rilla was faltering.

* * *

"We are almost at the far bank." Eliséo couldn't help but listen in on their thoughts. They were shouting them so loudly within themselves. "The riverbed has started to slope up again. We all just need to hold on a little while longer."

There was relief from all but Rilla. He didn't know if she could even hear him. *How is she?* he asked Elessa.

Fading quickly, little one. Her reply did nothing to ease his concern. *I am passing her much of my own strength, but there is little more I can do for her. If you think the others won't notice your eyes, then I suggest you take a little more of the burden for yourself. Otherwise, I doubt she will make it out of this river alive.*

Eliséo could no longer justify the pretence that could kill them to keep his secret safe. He squeezed Rilla's hand and passed as much strength as he dared back to her. She stirred, but said nothing.

That should be enough. Elessa comforted him as only an elf's tree could. Eliséo was careful to keep his eyes slitted. Even so, he kept them averted from the others. They must have been shining so brightly that the grey would be a glittering silver.

It wasn't much longer before he felt the pressure on the mist changing. There was less pressure on top and more on the sides. They were coming up out of the water. He quickened his pace, not wanting to burden Rilla any longer than necessary and not wanting to give the boys too much of a chance to see how brightly his eyes were shining.

As soon as they were completely out of the water, he muttered a single word to dissolve the mist protecting them. Rilla immediately began to breathe easier, but she did not awaken. Arishen and Tika gently placed Shuut on the ground a little way from the riverbank. Plyke did likewise with Rilla, then covered her with the cloak from her rucksack.

A single look at the three boys told Eliséo all he needed to know. They were all too exhausted to carry Rilla and Shuut any further from the river. Their pursuer had been at the ferry crossing when the attack had come. Even if the one tracking them had guessed what they had done, there was no chance the six of them could have been pursued across the river. They should be safe enough for the night.

"Set up camp," he told the boys tiredly. "No fire tonight."

Silently, the boys set about putting everyone's sleeping mats on the ground as close to each other as possible. Without a fire, they would need each other's body heat to keep warm.

"There are no shifts tonight. I will watch over you all until dawn."

There was no complaint. Tika was the only one who looked like he was about to protest, but instead he gratefully sank down under his blanket. Within minutes, all of them were asleep.

222

What are you going to do now? Elessa gave him little time to relax.

The only thing we can do. Go to the karliki and hope that they lead us through their tunnels to the Drakos Mountains.

Are you sure you want to go to either of them? she asked in concern.

We have little choice. Whatever was done to Shadow, her best chance is with the crystal dragons. We are too far from Illaria for the lintep to help us.

At that, his tree left him in peace. She knew he was right, but that didn't mean she had to like his decision.

223

Chapter Forty-Five – Thistlehall

It was an uneventful night. Eliséo kept his senses attuned to their surroundings. No elf could ever be caught unawares if they were alert. He did not have to take his eyes off the Paradisians and the banwep to know if they were being watched or approached.

He needed a plan. He knew the thoughts he'd shared with Elessa weren't enough. With Shuut unconscious it would take too long to even get to the karliki. If they passed through Thistlehall, they might be able to find a horse and wagon. It was a small town, but if enough gold changed hands, anything was possible.

Eliséo's thoughts turned to his companions. In the morning, Rilla would need to heal Tika's leg further. There was every possibility that the boy had set back the healing process by days, by straining as much as he had that evening. That meant he would not be able to ask Rilla to do anything else. He wondered if even sleeping the rest of the night would allow her to recover. That left Plyke.

Eliséo was going to have to do something extremely dangerous. A fully-trained lintep would shy away from the task, but this boy, who shied away from his power was their only hope. Eliséo needed to see what had happened to Shadow. It was obvious she had been attacked by a magical force, but no elf could have cast their power over such a great distance with such devastating effect. It had to have been another lintep. Knowing what was wrong with her would give him an indication of how soon they needed to reach the crystal dragons.

He waited patiently for the sun to rise before even contemplating waking them. As soon as there was enough light to see comfortably, he woke Plyke. Even though the others now knew he was at least part lintep, he doubted the young boy would want them to witness such a difficult task. As he sat up, Plyke looked around at the other sleeping Paradisians in confusion then over to Eliséo questioningly.

"I need your help with Shadow. We need to find out what is wrong with her and how long she can possibly last like this."

"And exactly how do you think *I* can help you there?" Plyke asked, rubbing the sleep from his eyes.

"We don't have time for you to dissemble." Eliséo tried to hide his irritation. "I need you to see what happened to her."

Without another word, Plyke quietly went and sat by Shuut's side. Eliséo followed him, but remained at a respectful distance. He didn't want to interfere more than necessary.

The young boy closed his eyes and took a few steadying breaths before looking closely at the half-caste. He hesitantly placed one hand on her forehead and drew back with a start.

"What's wrong?" Eliséo rushed over and knelt beside Plyke.

"She's trapped," he said, averting his eyes from the banwep. "There's something around her mind. She scared me when I went in there. I don't even know if she realised I was there, but her mind is jumping all over the place, trying to free itself."

"You have to go back in there." Eliséo made it clear that the boy had no choice in the matter. "If what you're saying is true, she will only weaken herself faster by fighting against it. We need as much time as she can give us or she won't survive. You need to tell her that."

"I ... I've never done that before." Plyke lowered his eyes, almost in shame. "I was only taught to listen, not to speak."

Eliséo looked at him in surprise. That was not what most lintep were taught, however, most lintep who left Illaria did so because they disagreed with their teaching principles. Considering that, it wasn't so strange that whoever mentored Plyke withheld that sort of knowledge from him, especially when it could only do him harm in a Paradise.

"From what I saw during my time in Illaria, all you need to do is think about something without letting anything else distract you and the rest should take care of itself. All you can do is try, Plyke."

* * *

Plyke shivered in the morning chill, rubbing his arms with his hands distractedly. He didn't want to do this. He'd been furious with Shuut for doing the same to him. How could he now do it to her? His only comfort was that he had no choice. She might very well die otherwise.

Bracing himself for the chaos within Shuut's mind, Plyke once more placed a hand on Shuut's forehead. He flinched at the intensity of her fear and frustration, but didn't pull back this time. In his mind he called her name over and over, eventually seeing that it was having a calming effect on the trapped banwep. He hoped that meant she could actually hear his thoughts.

You need to stop fighting. He couldn't hear any reply, but his strength lay more in empathy. She was confused and frightened. He knew it was difficult for her to trust anyone, even the innocent Paradisians she had rescued.

We're going to find help for you, but you need to stop fighting or you won't last long enough. There was less confusion but her fear was still there, being held back by sheer force of will.

Plyke took his hand away from her forehead and sighed with relief. "I think she won't fight anymore."

"Did she say anything?" Eliséo asked anxiously. Plyke shook his head. "Well done, Plyke. That was a brave thing you just did. Hopefully you have given us enough time to save her. Now, wake the boys."

* * *

Eliséo didn't tell Plyke how worried he was that Shuut could not speak. It was not a good sign. He already knew the magic was powerful, but this made matters worse. Only lintep masters and mistresses could do things like this.

Trying to dismiss that problem from his mind, Eliséo crossed to Rilla and knelt by her side. He touched her arm lightly, not wanting to startle her awake. She barely stirred. His brow furrowed as he gently shook her. Her eyes still did not open.

Elessa, can you get through to her?

She is resting, Elessa replied shortly.

Wake her. We need to go. They needed to reach Thistlehall that day to have any hope of getting help for Shadow.

I told you she is resting. Elessa's tone brooked no argument. Eliséo knew better than to try to persuade her. Instead, he stood and turned to the boys.

225

"Rilla is still tired from last night. I will carry her today." He could see the boys were worried. Thankfully, they said nothing. "Plyke, Arishen, you two take Shuut on her sleeping pallet. Tika needs to rest his leg as much as possible today."

Tika almost protested, but obviously thought better of it and simply picked up his own and Rilla's rucksacks.

Eliséo walked silence, Rilla in his arms. It was a long and slow journey. He stopped often to allow them all the chance to rest. All four of them were carrying more than their fair share and the effort was beginning to tell on the Paradisians.

It was late evening when they neared the tiny town of Thistlehall. Eliséo would have preferred they had arrived earlier in the day. It was going to be difficult enough as it was to convince the innkeeper to give them a room, but they were bound to be less inclined to take such odd travellers at night. He'd always found humans to be more mistrustful in the darker hours of the day.

As they walked down the main street, the villagers stared at them in open curiosity. Most of the men scowled at them, while the women looked pityingly at Rilla and with open hostility towards Shuut. No banwep was ever welcome in small towns throughout the Outworld.

Eliséo quickened his pace until he had reached the inn, the boys keeping pace behind him. He had barely opened the door before the innkeeper came bustling forward.

"No room, no room." The thin man waved his hands in front of him as he attempted to bar their way.

"Good innkeeper," Eliséo appealed to him in his distinctly elvish voice, "all we ask is a room for the six of us for a single night."

"Even if I had such a large room, how would you pay for it?"

Eliséo had met many men like this before. They had exactly what he most needed and would to only give it to him at an exorbitant price. He had not left Silvaren unprepared. A silver coin should have easily covered their room for a week but Eliséo was in no mood to bargain. Shifting Rilla in his arms, he drew forth a gold coin. He dropped it into the innkeeper's bony hand and waited for his mood to improve.

"Follow me." The sinewy man barely spared their company a glance as he turned down a passageway. He was more preoccupied with the gold coin than anything else, biting it to test its worth as he led them to their room.

"Your room is here," he said as he handed them a key. "The baths are down the end of the hall on your left."

Eliséo thanked him before ushering in his companions and locking the door behind them. The trouble with using gold coins to get what you wanted in the Outworld was that people became greedy. He had learnt early on in his travels that the Outworld was a dangerous place for those who exhibited their riches.

He looked around the room and shook his head. A gold coin wasted on such a shabby room. It didn't have proper beds, just pallets barely thicker than their sleeping mats. Tika immediately set about laying their own sleeping mats over them. Arishen and Plyke carefully laid Shuut down on hers before flopping onto their own. Eliséo laid Rilla gently onto the mat furthest from the door. She still hadn't opened her eyes and he was beginning to worry.

She will be fine, Elessa reassured him. *She simply needs to rest.*

You keep saying that, but she hasn't stirred all day. Eliséo was unusually short with his tree. She could easily have roused Rilla if she'd wanted to, but had instead decided to push her further into a deep sleep. They didn't have time for this. He didn't know how long they had before their pursuer found them again. Eliséo looked up from Rilla to find the boys watching him for answers. "She'll be fine." He tried to reassure them, but knew he lacked conviction.

"She hasn't stirred for an entire day and night. How can you possibly know she'll be fine when she isn't waking?" Arishen voiced their concern.

Not knowing what to tell them, Eliséo changed the topic. "Get some rest. I'll keep watch again tonight."

"No." Tika spoke up. "I know elves can go without more sleep than humans, but surely you need to rest even if only for an hour or two. I will take the first shift and wake you when it's your turn."

Eliséo's eyebrows shot up. Tika had always seemed the most timid of the boys. He did not argue with the small boy. In truth, he was grateful. Without a word, he lay himself on the mat closest to the door. Any danger would surely come from there and he was the only one in a position to protect them in any way.

A firm hand on his shoulder woke Eliséo from his deep slumber. He looked up to find Tika staring at him with a serious face. Something was wrong.

"I think my leg is worse. It hurts more than it did before. I don't know if I'll be able to walk tomorrow without Rilla's help. When do you think she'll wake up?"

Eliséo looked over at the sleeping lintep. "I don't know, Tika. It took a lot for her to get us through that river. She just needs to rest."

"You keep saying that, but what if she doesn't wake up at all?"

"Trust me, Tika. She *will* wake up." He sent the boy to bed before he could dispute the matter further. Not bothering to wait for the deep breathing signalling sleep, Eliséo spoke to Elessa.

Wake her.

Well, good evening to you too. Elessa greeted him irritably. *I'll wake her when I'm good and ready.*

Wake her or we're all as good as dead.

These humans have got to you. His tree replied without sympathy. *They may die if I don't wake Rilla, but you certainly won't and neither will she.*

You don't know that, Elessa. Eliséo tried to reason with her. *All we know about our attacker is that they could hurt Shadow from miles away, and that they have employed many men to track her over long distances and kill. How can you possibly know for certain that I won't die trying to protect my charges?*

There was silence.

You would die to protect them?

Eliséo didn't answer.

I see.

Rilla began to stir. Eliséo immediately went to her side.

"Did it work?" A whisper escaped her dry lips.

"It worked." Eliséo breathed a sigh of relief. "You brought us through the river quite safely."

He watched as her eyes fluttered open. She had been asleep for so long, her eyelids were stuck together with gummy muck. Lazily, she rubbed her eyes until she could see properly. She glanced around the room, taking account of everything and everyone there.

"I didn't do it alone."

"No, Plyke lent you more strength than he should have."

Rilla shook her head. "No. I mean, I remember that, but *after* that, towards the end when Plyke carried me, *you* stopped drawing as much strength from me." She looked at him accusingly. "Why didn't you just do that the whole way?"

"You know why, Rilla." He spoke calmly and quietly to her. They should really be having this conversation through Elessa, but he was purposely blocking the tree from both their minds. He did not need her chiding him or scaring Rilla.

"Then why did you do it at all?" she rubbed her eyes again, trying to wake herself further. "Did they not notice anything?"

"No." He shook his head. "They were all too, shall we say, preoccupied, to notice."

"But your eyes." Eliséo cut her off before she could continue.

"As I said, they were preoccupied and my eyes were barely open."

Rilla didn't press him any further on the subject. "Where are we?"

"Thistlehall. I hired a room in an inn. We shall be leaving in the morning."

"But it's the middle of the night. Why did you wake me now?"

"Tika needs your help." Rilla's shoulders slumped. "He helped carry Shuut the entire way through the river and still had to walk unassisted until we reached this inn. If you heal him in the morning, you won't have the strength to walk."

Silently, Rilla walked over to Tika's sleeping mat. He barely twitched as she lay her hand on his leg. She drew back with a cry. Eliséo leapt to her side to catch her before she fell and woke the boys.

"What happened?"

Rilla shook her head angrily. "I'm tired. I wasn't paying attention. I drew his pain into me without thinking."

"Concentrate, Rilla," Eliséo told her patiently, "You don't need to take any of his pain, just mend the muscles a little."

"If it's so easy, then *you* do it!" she snapped at him. "They're all asleep now and no one will see your eyes."

"It doesn't work like that, Rilla. I'm not a healer." He spread his hands out helplessly. "I can't do what you can."

Tapping her teeth together, Rilla turned away from him. Eliséo watched as she walked to the only table in the room. Taking the mug with the most water in it, she walked back over to Tika. She placed her right index finger in the water and her left hand on Tika's leg once more. Soon the water began to boil.

She removed her finger from the water and placed her right hand over Tika's other leg and stayed there motionlessly for a few minutes. Eliséo was at the point of pulling her away when Rilla took her hands off Tika and sat back on her heels.

Rilla went to her pack and pulled out Rhanya's healing pouch. She rummaged through it until she found the dried chamomile flowers. Taking a few of them, she placed them in the mug with the boiled water, held the mug in her hands and let out a huge sigh.

Eliséo watched her in amazement. He had lived with the lintep for many years, watching as they passed their knowledge down to each new generation. None of them had managed to simply pick up the skills that Rilla had so quickly, especially not without assistance from another lintep. She was truly unique.

They sat in silence, Rilla drinking her tea, Eliséo desperately trying to find any faster way to the Drakos Mountains than through Goraburg. Rilla was barely halfway through her tea before she fell asleep. Eliséo deftly caught the mug before it fell to the floor. He placed it on the table and picked her up, laying her down on her sleeping pallet. She was too weak. Eliséo doubted she would be able to walk for even a few hours the next day.

In this tiny village, he would be forced to pay outrageous amounts to buy even the worst horse and wagon available. It would have to wait until the morning. He could sense almost the entire inn was asleep. Almost. There was someone coming their way. Eliséo opened the door with his sword held low, but ready.

"Have you lost your way?" His calm voice stopped the blacksmith in his tracks. His wheezing breath stank of ale as he looked guiltily up into Eliséo's eyes.

"I took a wrong turn is all," he slurred and turned to leave. Eliséo shook his head in dismay. This man had only come to rob them of their coins, not their lives and in that he was unusual. At least their travelling group was large enough to discourage *those* sorts of thieves.

Chapter Forty-Six – Dreams of Paradise

As dawn broke, Eliséo woke the boys and Rilla. With a silver coin, he had convinced the innkeeper to send food and water to their room. The Paradisians sat down and ate ravenously while Eliséo managed to pour some water down Shuut's throat without choking her. He could sense the boys' relief that Rilla was awake, but they were too hungry to talk about it.

"I need to go out for a while," he told them once he was done with Shuut. "Lock the door after me and do not open it until I return. Is that clear?"

The Paradisians nodded. Tika stood to lock the door behind him. Eliséo did not waste time looking for a horse at the inn. No traveller with a horse would part with it for *any* amount of gold.

Thistlehall was not a large village. It took him less than a few minutes to walk the length and breadth of it. During this time, he managed to spy a sturdy horse and a passable wagon. It was easier to haggle with the wagon owner than the horse owner, but eventually he managed to purchase both and hitch them together. Thistlehall had drained him of more coin in a single visit than most of his complete journeys through the Outworld.

Heading back to the inn, Eliséo heard a great ruckus. Even from outside, he could hear banging on a door and raised voices. Trusting no one would be able to get very far with the horse and wagon before he returned, Eliséo dropped the reins and ran towards their room.

He had barely made it half way down the hall before the innkeeper and a few others he had gathered to his cause had managed to break down the door Tika had locked in his absence. He saw the four Paradisians at the ready with their weapons, being sure to keep themselves between the villagers and Shuut.

"What is the meaning of this?" he shouted. The villagers didn't slow their pace. The Paradisians at least spared him a glance before moving to defend themselves.

"Stop!" Eliséo's voice was laced with command. His eyes would be glowing faintly. He hated using his powers on humans, especially those who were already mistrustful, but he didn't want any harm to come to his companions. The villagers were momentarily frozen in place before he released them. They tumbled to the floor, their legs tangled together.

"Explain yourself." He directed his order to the innkeeper who looked up at him guiltily from the floor.

"You hired the room for a single night. When you left without the rest of them I assumed you weren't coming back. They refused to open the door to pay for another night and so we were just trying to get them to leave."

"I see." Eliséo's voice was calm and even. "Well, clearly I am back to collect my companions. If you will kindly leave the room, we will gather our belongings and be out of your way." As the villagers got up to leave, Eliséo turned to them. "It would be in your best interest to make sure my new horse and wagon are waiting for us at the front of the inn when we come out. I would hate to lose my temper with the villagers of Thistlehall."

The men mumbled their assurances as they quickly shuffled back down the hall. Eliséo waited until they had disappeared from view before stepping inside the room and closing the door. One look at his tired and injured companions made him understand the boldness of the villagers' attack. They were a sorry group without him. He only hoped they weren't attacked again before they reached the karliki. None of them were in a state to fight. The three boys had all been injured too recently and Rilla was still exhausted from the river crossing and the healing she'd had to do since her encounter with Ensil.

"We're leaving. Pack your things and meet me at the front of the inn. Rilla, get Shadow's sleeping mat and come with me." He knelt down to pick up the banwep before heading out of their room, Rilla close on his heels. There was no point in staying any longer. Thistlehall could offer them no protection from their unknown attacker and if they stayed any longer, the villagers themselves might grow even bolder.

He carried Shadow down the hall. As they walked through the inn, he noticed all eyes glance up and then quickly turn away. If he had been human, they would probably all be dead by now, including the banwep. The horse and wagon were waiting where he had left them. Rilla arranged the sleeping mat in the wagon before Eliséo gently placed Shadow on it.

The boys did not leave them waiting long. They had not bothered packing their things properly, but carried everything bundled in their arms. They placed it all in the wagon around Shadow and walked alongside it as Eliséo drove the horse forward, eyes darting everywhere on the alert for another attack.

* * *

Less than an hour later, Thistlehall was hidden from view. This side of the Bramble River was densely forested with gum trees. Eliséo had told them that humans did not like travelling too close to the Lesa Mountains. It was a well-known fact that the karliki dwelled here.

With that knowledge, Plyke at least did not need to be alert for another attack. Instead, he walked by Tika's side, carefully watching for any sign that his Partner would fall.

"Tika." Plyke and his Partner looked up at the sound of the elf's voice. "Come and take over from me. Your leg should rest as much as we can afford it. Besides, I hear you were to work with horses if you had not left the Paradise."

Tika smiled instantly. They all knew his leg could use the rest and it had been such a very long time since he'd had anything to do with horses. The last time they had even seen one was a few days before the Choosing. Tika quickly climbed up into the wagon and took the reins from Eliséo.

Plyke took the opportunity to walk closer to Rilla, leaving Arishen to bring up the rear with Eliséo. They walked along in silence for a long while, Plyke occasionally glancing sideways at her. Eventually, he spoke.

"Next time, *I* decide when to stop lending strength to you."

Rilla missed a step and briefly closed her eyes. "You couldn't have lasted any longer. I didn't have a choice."

"You could have at least told me what would happen to you," he persisted, trying to hide the hurt from his voice.

"I ... I didn't know what was going to happen, Plyke." He knew it was the closest she could come to apologising. "I've never done anything like that before."

Plyke was silent for a moment then placed his hand on her shoulder. "You were asleep for more than a day. We thought we were going to lose you. Don't ever scare us like that again." Rilla smiled shyly at him.

* * *

Arishen watched as Plyke put a hand on Rilla's shoulder. He couldn't hear what they were saying, their voices masked by the horse's footfall. Remembering what Telon had told him, he counted to ten and slowly let out the breath he had unconsciously been holding.

He was angry that Plyke felt he had a right to touch her, but what irritated him the most was that she didn't shy away from his touch. She would never have let *him* get close enough for that to happen.

"Did you dream last night?" Eliséo's voice dissolved his anger.

"Yes," he answered warily. No one had ever really taken an interest in his dreams before, not in a good way.

"Do you dream every night?"

"Most." Arishen didn't know much about Eliséo. He still wasn't entirely sure why the elf had joined their group, but if Rilla and Shuut trusted him then there wasn't any reason for him not to, and yet he found himself resisting.

"Better to tell me than no one at all, isn't it?"

"I write them down, that's enough for me." Eliséo raised an eyebrow at his response. "Fine," sighed Arishen, "I dreamt of the people we left behind in the Paradise."

Eliséo hesitated a moment. "You didn't dream of the innkeeper trying to evict you?" Arishen, looking straight ahead, shook his head. "What *did* you dream about?"

"Kalid made locks for her door and windows. She's afraid they're coming for her next. She sleeps uneasily. At meals, she always sits in a different seat so they can't poison her. She doesn't let anyone use her tools and she locks them in her room at the end of each day."

"Is this the first time you've dreamt of this person, Kalid?" Arishen shook his head. "Then it may be nothing more than just a dream."

"I never know for certain if a dream is more than just that." He shrugged uncomfortably. "But I don't think this is just a dream. It's like I've been watching her since we left. Kalid's the one who helped me take some of the carpenters' tools to protect ourselves out here. She warned me not to trust Shuut just because she agreed to take us with her."

"She sounds wise," Eliséo ventured carefully. "I'm sure she can look after herself."

"You don't know what our Paradise was like," Arishen told him flatly. "It doesn't matter how careful, clever or strong you are. If Erton wants you dead, one way or another, he'll succeed."

"Is Kalid the only one from your Paradise that you've dreamt of since leaving?"

Arishen bit back tears. He shook his head. "I've watched two others die and someone flee after an attempt on their life."

"Who fled?" Eliséo asked.

"Kora," replied Arishen. "She was a tailor."

"Kora?" Eliséo exclaimed incredulously.

232

At the sound of her name, Plyke turned around and Tika stopped the carriage. Rilla watched on in fascination. Kora was the only person who had ever noticed her in the Paradise when she didn't want to be found. Ratchin had told her that meant she was a lintep.

"Kora will be fine," she reassured Plyke. "I think she's a lintep. I'm sure she can look after herself." Plyke looked at her with haunted eyes.

"Oh," Rilla whispered half to herself, "she's your mother, isn't she?"

"Kora is your mother?" Eliséo asked in shock.

"Yes," replied Plyke in confusion. "Do you know her?"

"Everyone in Illaria and Silvaren knows her." They all stared at Eliséo. "She's one of Princess Rilla's grandchildren."

"*One* of her grandchildren?" Rilla asked, drawing away from Plyke. "How many grandchildren does she have?"

"There were five of them, actually, but only two remain. Kora is one of them."

"Who's the other one?" Tika asked the question that Plyke was too shocked to voice.

Eliséo averted his eyes from Rilla. "Nyssa."

Rilla felt the blood drain from her face as Eliséo said her mother's name.

"Nyssa is alive?" She barely whispered, but they all heard her. All but Eliséo looked at her in confusion. She looked at the elf accusingly. "You *knew* the whole time?"

"I promise you, I had no idea who Plyke's mother was." He was evasive.

"But you knew who *my* mother was, which means you knew *exactly* who I was and never told me. Were you ever going to tell me that she's alive?"

Eliséo held her gaze unwaveringly. "I am the Ambassador of the Elves, Rilla. I know more about the elves, lintep and karliki than anyone else. I am *always* going to know more about those three races than you."

"Answer the question, Eliséo." She snarled the words out. "Were you ever going to tell me that she's alive?"

"There is very little chance you will ever meet her, Rilla. I didn't want you to get your hopes up needlessly."

"We're cousins?" Plyke's voice broke through Rilla's anger. She looked at him in confusion. She hadn't been thinking about that. All she knew was that her mother was alive. Nyssa hadn't died after abandoning her in the Paradise with Erton.

Plyke moved forward, arms outstretched to embrace her, but Rilla turned away from him. She didn't want anyone to touch her. She wanted to be alone, to figure the whole mess out, but it was the last thing she could do. Instead, she unthinkingly started walking in the direction they had been heading all morning.

You can't run away from everyone, Elessa's voice bore into her. Instinctively, Rilla blocked her out with full force.

Eliséo caught up with her and grabbed her arm roughly. "Rilla, stop that. Your eyes are shining."

Elessa, don't bother her now.

Rilla heard the thought and knew she'd be safe from their tree for at least a little while, but it wasn't enough.

"I don't want *anyone* to bother me now." She shrugged free of this grasp and continued walking straight ahead. As Plyke ran to catch up to her, she saw him glare back at the elf. Rilla could hear the others drop back to give her some space. She barely glanced at Plyke, but he said nothing, simply walked beside her in silence.

They broke for their midday meal, none of them talking. No one had said a word since that morning's debacle. Rilla healed Tika's leg a little more and then they set off again. She purposely kept her eyes averted from Eliséo the entire time.

"You know, you can't stay angry at him forever," Plyke ventured, once they'd resumed their journey.

"Why not?" Rilla's anger was unrelenting.

"For one thing, at least he let us know that we're cousins." Plyke smiled shyly at her. It was something none of the other Paradisians would ever be able to claim about someone.

"I don't see why that makes you so happy." Rilla shook her head at him. "It's not like it changes who we are. In fact, it doesn't really change anything at all."

"It changes things for *me*," he said quietly, but refused to say more when she glanced over at him.

* * *

They'd been walking almost the entire day in silence. Tika had been resting while driving the horse and wagon most of that time. By mid-afternoon, he decided it was time to stretch his legs out a bit and see how well he could walk after Rilla's brief healing session at midday.

"Rilla, why don't you take over?" It wasn't really a question. All the Paradisians were still worried about her from the river crossing. Tika was more than capable of walking the rest of the day and insisted she take a break. Grudgingly, the still-furious girl walked over to the horse and let him smell her hand, patting his nose before climbing up into the wagon.

Tika went to walk beside Eliséo. This journey was the best chance he had of becoming friends with an elf. He wasn't going to waste any opportunity to talk to him.

"How often do you visit the karliki, seeing as you're the ambassador and all?"

"I used to visit them every year." Eliséo twisted his lips a bit. "That was a long time ago, though."

"What happened to make you stop going?" Tika asked heedless of the pain he might uncover. He never shied away from asking questions that most others would avoid.

"My best friend challenged me to a duel, only in jest, but he was overheard by other karliki. I could not tactfully decline, so we duelled with the entire population looking on. I could not bring shame to Master Ensil by allowing the karlik to best me, so I eventually overcame him.

"I don't understand why that made you stop visiting them," Tika persisted.

"The karlik in question was the youngest son of the clan leader." Eliséo smiled sadly. "His father did not take it very well that an elf had bested a member of his clan. I was politely asked to leave and have not been invited back since."

Plyke called out from behind, "How long ago was that?"

"Fifty years ago," Eliséo answered without hesitation.

"Fifty years?" Rilla exclaimed. She had been silent the entire time, but all the Paradisians had been listening closely to the conversation. "How can that even be possible? You don't look a day older than Shuut."

"Shadow is younger than the elf children who were your guides in Silvaren and they are hundreds of years my junior."

"Hundreds of years?" Arishen echoed from behind him. "Exactly how old *are* you?"

"I am a foundling, so we will never know my exact age. It's safe to say I'm over six hundred years old."

"How old is Lady Eléna?" Tika asked, awestruck. He knew more than the rest of them about elves, but this was almost more than he could believe himself.

* * *

Eliséo hesitated. This was not how he wanted Rilla to discover how long elves could live. "The Queen Mother is well over two thousand years old," he answered without offering any extra information.

He was careful not to look too long on the lintep girl. Since she'd blocked them both out earlier that morning, neither he nor Elessa had tried to contact her. Had it occurred to her yet that she could quite possibly expect to live the same length of time?

The Paradisians took their time to digest the information. Eventually, Rilla ventured another question. "If Lady Eléna is over two thousand years old and looks around the same age as Erton, how long do most elves live?"

The Paradisians looked at him in curiosity, but the only one he had eyes for was Rilla. "We elves do not generally discuss such things, but I have known an elf or two to be over four thousand years old before choosing to die. Having said that, many elves have died before their time of choosing by some catastrophic event."

"What do you mean 'choosing' to die?" Tika asked ever curious. "And what kind of thing could kill them?"

"Another time, Tika," Eliséo told him. "We should make camp for the night. I'll keep watch by myself tonight." Tika looked about ready to protest when he caught his Partner's eye and saw the warning in them.

Eliséo frowned but said nothing. He led them onwards until he found a suitable clearing for the evening. Plyke set out the sleeping mats in a circle around the small fire pit that Tika and Rilla created. Arishen helped Eliséo carefully carry Shadow from the wagon to her sleeping pallet. Together, they managed to get a small amount of water down her throat without choking her. There was no chance they'd be able to feed her until she was cured. Eliséo hoped they would reach the crystal dragons before it was too late. They were the only creatures within travelling distance that he thought stood a chance to help her.

"I'm going hunting," Rilla announced, once all the chores were done.

"Not by yourself, you're not." Eliséo replied. He was unwilling for any of them to stray too far. It had been easier with Shadow around. One of them stayed with the Paradisians while the other hunted. He didn't quite trust any of the Paradisians to keep themselves alive without him.

"I'll go with her," Arishen volunteered. It was not quite the solution Eliséo was hoping for, but when he saw the smouldering look Rilla cast his way, he had no choice but to accept.

* * *

"Rilla, wait for me," Arishen called after the girl when she got too far ahead of him. She slowed and turned to wait for him. "What are we hunting for? I haven't seen any animals the entire time that we've been in these woods. Have you?"

"No," admitted Rilla. "Just the odd bird here and there."

"Then what are we doing out here?" he asked her bluntly. "Or was this just your excuse to get away from Eliséo?"

Rilla looked at him in surprise. "I ... don't know," she replied uncertainly. "I mean, we *do* need to find something to eat."

"That's true, but we're unlikely to be able to hunt anything. I think we'd be better off trying to find some fruit or berries."

Rilla nodded. "I'm sure we can do that. I used to do it in our Paradise. I saw some while I was riding in the wagon." Arishen raised his eyebrows at her, but Rilla just shrugged. "There wasn't much to look at from the wagon other than the plants."

"Okay then. What are we looking for?"

"Orchids," Rilla smiled. "I saw some White Fingers earlier today. The tubers are quite nice."

"Orchids it is." Arishen couldn't help but smile back. He had lived in the same Paradise as Rilla for over ten years and had never done more than half the things she took for granted.

They searched for the small, beautiful flowers, digging up the plants and being careful not to damage the roots. Arishen hadn't noticed them at all before Rilla pointed them out, but now he saw them scattered all over the forest ground. Not just white ones either, there were also little Pink Fingers scattered here and there.

When they had enough for themselves and their companions, they stopped digging. Rilla sat on her knees, the tubers on the floor in front of her. She stayed, staring at them for a few minutes in complete silence. Arishen brought over the last of his finds, adding it to the pile.

"Let's head back." Arishen looked up as he spoke. "It's starting to get dark."

When Rilla didn't move, he looked closely at her face. "Rilla? It's time to go now." If she heard him, she didn't let on. She just sat staring at the floor. Arishen was getting worried. The last time he'd seen her like this was at Rhanya's funeral pyre. He'd had to carry her back from the flames so that she wouldn't get burnt. He wasn't sure if she had even felt the heat.

Unsure of what to do, he knelt beside her and placed a hand gently on her shoulder. Immediately, her head snapped up, her eyes looking wildly into his. She shook her head and actually seemed to see him.

"Would you have left the Paradise if it weren't for me?"

It was the last thing Arishen was expecting.

"Yes," he told her. "Parthak threatened me a few days before the Choosing. She'd realised there was something different about me because of my dreams. She wanted me out or ..."

"Or dead?" Rilla asked without hesitation. Arishen only nodded.

236

"How would you have done it?"

"What do you mean?"

"I mean, if Rhanya had lived and I'd gone to his room instead of Shuut's, what would you have done?"

Arishen rubbed his cheek. "I don't know Rilla. I would probably have just gone to Kalid's room and asked her to help me get out."

"They would have killed you before she could help you."

"Well then, I would have just walked to the boundary and left." Arishen shrugged uncomfortably. "What difference does it make now?"

"I just want to know if everything was worth it." Rilla looked up at him sadly. "If the three of you would have left the Paradise and survived without Shuut, without me going to her first, was anything that happened afterwards worth it?"

"If that's what you're worried about, then stop." He frowned as he looked at her. "Don't think any of us haven't realised by now that we're only alive because of you. Tika *may* have chosen Shuut without you, which means so might Plyke, but she would never have been persuaded to take us even as far as Turon if it weren't for you."

"But are any of us actually happier out here than we were in our Paradise?" Rilla looked away, refusing to be placated.

"Rilla, we're *alive*." Arishen took her chin in his hand and lifted her face so she was forced to look him in the eyes. "We're alive because of *you*. You would have been miserable staying there after Rhanya was murdered. I would already be dead. Plyke would have had to hide who he was his entire life. Tika would never have found the elves."

"I would have been dead by the time of the next Choosing." Her comment surprised him. "Plyke might have been too, depending on how powerful he turns out to be."

Arishen looked at her for a moment longer, before turning his eyes back to the darkening sky. "Then stop this and help me get these tubers back to camp. We're all alive and we need to get Shuut to the karliki. That's all that matters right now."

* * *

Rilla hesitated briefly before helping Arishen pile the tubers into the makeshift pouch he made by holding out his shirt. Before long, they were back within view of the camp. Eliséo, standing watch at the edge of the clearing, visibly relaxed once he saw them approach. She pointedly ignored him as she showed the boys how to cook the tubers over the fire.

It was a quick and quiet meal. Everyone was worried about Shuut. Plyke spoke to her with his mind again, reassuring her that they were well on their way to the karliki if she could just try to save her strength rather than fight against the spell.

Tika watched the process curiously. "How are you doing that?" he asked when Plyke was done.

"I don't know," Plyke replied evasively. "If I'm touching a person's skin, it's only a step away to their thoughts."

"Can you do it too?" the short boy turned to Rilla.

Rilla immediately shook her head. "I don't want to try it."

"Yes, but *can* you?"

"I think so," she admitted, "It was the day Rhanya died, so I don't even know if it was real. I would never do it on purpose the way Shuut used to do with us."

Tika nodded. "Do you need to be touching them like Plyke, or can you do it the same way as Shuut?"

Rilla took a deep breath, not really wanting to have this conversation. They had only just started to trust her. She didn't want that all to change so soon.

"I think it's the same way as Shuut, but it only happened a few times. I knew Arishen and Shuut were hiding the truth from me so when they spoke, I heard their minds say something different to what they actually said. I think I'd struggle to do it on purpose."

She glanced over towards Arishen, hoping this latest secret hadn't destroyed their fragile relationship. He only looked at her curiously.

"Could you try it on me?" Tika asked with a spark in his eyes.

"What?" Rilla was aghast. "Why?"

"Just to see if you can." When Rilla shook her head, he pleaded with her. "You know all of my secrets already. You can't possible find out anything that I want to hide from the rest of you."

"Tika, I'm tired and I really don't want to do this right now."

"Oh," he mumbled in reply. "I understand."

You're just like Plyke, Tika thought to himself. *You don't think your powers are a gift and you don't want to use them. What a waste!*

"That's not true at all," Rilla replied. "I *do* want to use my powers. I try to use them as much as possible. I just don't want to hurt anyone, including myself, when I do."

Tika looked at her in shock. "You *heard* that?"

"You didn't say that out loud?" Rilla replied, just as shocked. Tika shook his head as the others looked on with interest.

"What did he say?" Plyke asked, curiously. Rilla looked at him uncomfortably. Perhaps Tika didn't exactly have secrets, but his thoughts were his own. She didn't want to damage their turbulent Partnership any further by exposing his thoughts.

"I said your powers are wasted on you. You don't want to use them and you don't think they're a gift." Tika replied unflinchingly. Rilla was glad he hadn't made things worse for her, but she was worried about what he was doing to his Partnership.

"That's a little unfair, Tika," Arishen pointed out. "He's using his powers right now with Shuut."

"Yes, but only because he has to and only because Eliséo asked him to in the first place."

Plyke only hesitated a moment before replying. "You still don't understand. I lived almost my entire life in fear. Kora was very clear about what would happen to me if anyone found out about my powers. All she taught me to do was to keep them well contained inside me. If I release my control, everything comes flooding in whether I want it to or not. So, forgive me if I think a gift that I can't control and physically hurts me is not exactly something I'd like to use."

Tika had the good grace not to argue further and Eliséo quickly stepped in before Rilla was questioned about her powers again. She knew there was a fine line between lintep and elf powers but since she hadn't been using either for long, it wasn't something she would be able to distinguish herself. If she spoke too much about it, she could accidentally expose her secret.

"I'll take watch tonight. The four of you need rest more than I do," Eliséo told them.

Rilla noticed her sleeping mat had been put on the opposite side of the fire from Eliséo. She looked up at Plyke as they got under their respective cloaks and smiled appreciatively. He returned her smile knowingly.

* * *

Eliséo listened as one by one, the Paradisians fell asleep. Plyke alone stayed awake. The boy soon came over to sit by him. Eliséo watched him approach curiously, but said nothing. They sat together in silence for quite a while before the boy spoke his mind.

"You know, she's only so strong and she doesn't trust very many people." Eliséo looked over at Plyke questioningly. "Whether Arishen and Tika realise it, Rilla's the only reason we're all still alive today. If you *ever* do anything else to hurt her, I won't forgive you."

"I have never done anything to intentionally hurt Rilla," Eliséo replied evenly. He couldn't believe that he was being reprimanded by a child.

"Intentions don't matter when it comes to her. You kept the truth about her mother from her. That anger alone will keep burning for a good long while." Plyke brushed the hair back from his differently coloured eyes. "I have no idea why it mattered so much to her, but something you said about the elves living so long scared her half to death today."

"Perhaps she made the connection that all other races, including lintep, live longer than humans." Eliséo tried to brush aside the comment, but Plyke seemed startled by his reply.

"Lintep live longer than humans?"

Eliséo avoided breathing a sigh of relief as he managed to steer the conversation away from a very dangerous topic.

"Did Kora never tell you that? Some have been known to live over two hundred years."

"Two hundred years?" Plyke was taken aback. "What about half castes?"

"Are you a half caste?" Eliséo was surprised that Kora would have mixed her blood with a human.

"I'm not certain. I haven't really paid attention when Rilla hears the lintep whistling to see if I do too."

"Well, that's a bit of a grey area. There are different levels of half castes. But I think it's safe to say if you have any lintep blood in you, the likelihood is that you will outlive all of your human friends."

"Tika will be crushed," Plyke cried out in anguish. Eliséo placed a firm hand on his shoulder and looked squarely at the boy.

"Tika is your Partner. His spirit will live on as long as you do."

"You don't know that," Plyke choked out a reply. "Have you ever known a human to become Partners with a lintep before? The magic might not work."

'That's true," Eliséo conceded. "But have you thought of the possibility that the magic could be stronger precisely because you're a lintep? Get some sleep, Plyke. You're going to need it for tomorrow."

Eliséo watched as a troubled Plyke lay down for the night. He had dodged a very dangerous topic. How were they meant to do this their entire lives? Was it even going to be possible? If nothing else, once Rilla lived past a few hundred years, people would begin to suspect.

You always look too far in the future. Elessa's voice in his head was not a comfort to him.

You don't look far enough into the future, he reprimanded her. *It's your fault we're in this mess to begin with.* He closed his mind to her. Unlike most other elves, sometimes he needed a break from his tree.

Chapter Forty-Seven – Building Walls

Eliséo watched his companions in silence the next morning. By unspoken agreement, Tika had hopped up into the wagon leaving Plyke to walk with Rilla. Arishen walked ahead of the wagon with Eliséo

"It seems as though you're all trying to protect Rilla from me," he commented to the seer.

Arishen looked over without smiling. "It's interesting you think she needs protecting from you."

"That's not what I said," Eliséo corrected him. "I wouldn't have tried talking to her today, even without your intervention."

"Then why don't you leave her alone?" Arishen persisted.

"I haven't spoken a single word to her. I haven't approached her at all. How else am I to leave her alone?" Eliséo didn't add that he had forcibly kept Elessa from her mind which was more than he should have done.

"You can stop looking at her." Eliséo opened his mouth to protest. "You think she doesn't notice it when the rest of us do? It will only make her angrier with you."

Eliséo rolled his eyes at the idiocy of the situation. "I will never understand humans, no matter how much time I spend with them."

* * *

Rilla had been thinking half the morning how to save herself from her current situation. She knew Eliséo was keeping Elessa from her mind, and she was grateful for that, but she knew there was only so long that he could or would do it.

"Kora was your mother, so she taught you everything you know, right?" She turned to the boy beside her.

Plyke shook his head almost imperceptibly. "It's better to think that she taught me how *not* to use my powers and to block my mind from everyone."

"I think that's what I need to learn." Rilla nodded to herself. "Ratchin showed me a few basic things and I've ... amended them to suit other circumstances. But she never intended that I would do that. We knew her for such a short amount of time that she couldn't really teach me very much at all."

"And yet look how far you've come," Plyke smiled at her. "Just imagine what you'll be capable of when the masters and mistresses at Illaria get their hands on you."

Rilla held her breath. "That's only one of the things I'm afraid of." She rubbed her forehead with both hands, trying to clear her mind. "I need you to teach me how to keep people out of my mind."

"What?" Plyke's response was so loud it made Tika turn his head towards them. One glance from his Partner was more than enough to make him direct his gaze away again. "Rilla, I can't teach you."

"Why not?" Rilla asked bluntly. "You know how and I don't. Just tell me how you do it."

"I can't." Plyke shook his head incredulously. "Don't you understand? Kora taught me to do this from before I can even remember. I do it now out of habit. There have only been two times I've broken that. First was when I sparred with you that time. Second was when I had to reach out my mind to see where our attacker was. Both times I only managed to pull myself back together with Eliséo's help."

Rilla refused to give up. "True, but both of those times, you lost control. I'm not in that position. I have complete control of my mind and powers, I just want to hide them from prying eyes."

Plyke grew slightly concerned with the turn of the conversation. "Is there something you're not telling me? Has someone already tried to pry into your mind?"

"Shuut used to try it all the time." Rilla deflected. No matter how close she was becoming to Plyke, there was no way she could tell him the truth. "Eliséo tells us the crystal dragons are manipulative and the lintep are masters in reading thoughts. I'll never feel safe or comfortable with any of them if I can't protect myself as well as you can."

Plyke looked about to protest again. Rilla rested a hand gently on his forearm. "Plyke, I'm only asking you to tell me what you do. I'll try to figure it out from there. I know you can't actually *teach* me anything."

With a deep sigh, he agreed. "Seriously, all I can tell you is that I build a wall."

"What do you mean, you 'build a wall'?"

"Just that," he replied. "I build a wall around my mind, brick by brick by brick. I leave my surface thoughts outside the wall so that people will see something and just think I'm a little dim witted or dull. It seems to have worked for the most part."

Rilla threw up her hands. "I'll try it. I'll build a wall around my mind."

"Just like that?" Plyke's eyebrows shot up. "You can't just do it in a matter of minutes."

"Not on the first try, no," Rilla conceded. "But I hope to have a decent wall up by the end of the day." Plyke began to smile until she continued. "Then you can try to break through."

"No! Not a chance. I'm not doing that." Plyke couldn't believe what she was asking of him. "It's the very reason why Kora had taught me in the first place. So no one could ever read my mind. She taught me it was a violation for anyone to try to read someone else's mind!"

"I need you to do it, Plyke," Rilla pleaded. "You're the only one who can test it for me before we meet people I don't know if we can trust."

Plyke shook his head. "You just try to build up a wall, we'll see if you can convince me to breach it later."

"Will you ... watch out for me today?" she asked him shyly.

"For my cousin, anything," he replied with a smile. Rilla smiled back hesitantly, still not at all understanding why being related made such a difference to Plyke. Nonetheless, she appreciated being able to work on such a difficult and important task with someone watching out for her.

She immediately began. The first thing she did was examine her own thoughts and how they were arranged. There were thoughts that she often kept hidden even from herself. They were buried deep in her mind. She knew that the knowledge of her bond with an elf's tree was trying to join those thoughts even though it touched her life every day. Eliséo blocking them both from her mind would make it a little easier for her to start building.

There were thoughts such as seeing the trees and the barely noticeable path that they were travelling along that were right on the surface, just like Plyke had described. She couldn't see a clear separation between them, but she could certainly try to build a wall so that most of the surface thoughts were on the outside with everything else on the inside.

It wasn't difficult, but it took a long time. She didn't notice anything going on around her as she built her wall. She pretended she had an endless supply of bricks at her disposal and began to place them around her inner thoughts. It wasn't a circle wall, but as close to it as she could manage. Not knowing whether the shape would make a difference, she just assumed it would be easier to not have crevices all over the place. She thought it would weaken the entire structure.

* * *

Eliséo had been watching Rilla curiously, though not openly. She had a determined and faraway look in her eyes. He had no idea what was causing it, but he had no mind to ask her. He knew that would only irritate her further and he was already far enough in her bad graces for his liking.

"Do you think we're travelling quickly enough, Eliséo?" Plyke distracted him.

"We're travelling better than I had hoped, mainly due to the wagon. I think it would help if Rilla healed Tika's leg a little more ..."

"I'm fine," Tika immediately assured him. "I'm resting it quite a bit in the wagon. It will keep healing by itself until tonight."

"What will we do when we reach the karliki?" Plyke asked before Eliséo could insist on Rilla's assistance. "I mean if they still remember why you haven't been back in fifty years. What options do we have?"

Eliséo knew they were purposely keeping him from talking to Rilla, but he held his tongue, only answering the questions posed to him.

What is happening? Elessa asked him irritably. *You're keeping me from the girl and you have no idea what she's doing. Just look at her face. She's doing something she doesn't want us to know about.*

That's exactly why I'm blocking you from her! She needs her privacy until she learns to block us out herself when she needs or wants to. Eliséo replied quickly before blocking the tree from his mind. He never completely blocked her out. She could always read his thoughts, but he stopped her from talking to him and distracting him further.

"I can only hope that my friendship with Ilya Mikhailovich is as strong as I had imagined. He's the only one who can reason with his father to grant me entry once more." Eliséo touched his pocket briefly, knowing that what it held would be his best chance of that.

"What if that doesn't work and we are refused entry?" Plyke asked matter of factly. "How will we get Shuut to the crystal dragons soon enough for them to heal her?"

Eliséo looked skyward and bit his lower lip before answering. "I don't know, Plyke. I'm not sure we'll make it to the Drakos Mountains in time to save Shuut if we can't go through the Lesa Mountains."

"Isn't there *anything* else we can do to help her?" he asked in exasperation.

"No Plyke," Eliséo sighed. "Unless you or Rilla have the means to release her mind, then we're stuck. Elves don't have the power to heal like that. Kari *might*, but she's a trained healer. In any case, she's too far away. I have no chance of helping her myself."

"How much longer until we reach the karliki then?" Plyke asked impatiently.

"If we walk double the pace of this morning, we can make it before nightfall." This last comment threw them into action.

Plyke dropped back to the wagon and Tika leaned down as they spoke quietly. With a glance towards Rilla, Tika nodded.

"I need to stretch my legs out," Tika answered Eliséo's unasked question. "She can always heal me a little tonight if I overdo it."

Tika moved to one side of the wagon, while Plyke took the other so that both he and his Partner had control of the reins.

Eliséo held his tongue the entire day about whatever it was that Rilla was doing. He knew Plyke was a part of it and, by default, so was Tika. Arishen didn't appear to have anything to do with it, but all three boys were doing their best to keep him away from her. Walking as quickly as he thought the Paradisians could handle, they were fast approaching the main entrance to the tunnels. Whatever Rilla was doing, she'd need to stop and tell him about before they entered. It would be too difficult to have her in this trance-like state around the karliki. He stopped suddenly. The boys looked around, trying to find the entrance to the caves.

"Are we there?" Tika asked in excitement. "Is there a secret entrance somewhere?"

Eliséo shook his head. "We're about an hour away. We should still make it before nightfall, but we can't arrive with Rilla like that." He gestured to the vacant expression on girl's face.

"I think we should leave her alone," Plyke immediately protested. "She ... doesn't want to be disturbed today."

Eliséo was increasingly worried.

"Plyke, whatever it is she's doing, we need her to stop right now. If you don't want me to disturb her, you're going to have to do it yourself."

Plyke looked up at Rilla and then turned back to the elf, barely catching his eye before lowering his eyes. "I'm not sure if I can."

Eliséo's slow temper was starting to rise. "Why not?" Plyke didn't answer. "Plyke, tell me what she's doing." Plyke shook his head, almost imperceptibly. "Tell me what she's doing." Eliséo laced his voice with power. It was the second time in a matter of days he'd had to do it.

"She's building a wall around her mind."

Eliséo panicked. "She's doing *what*?"

Plyke looked over at the other Paradisians who simply stared back at him questioningly. He took a deep breath before relating his entire conversation with Rilla that morning.

"Get her to stop this instant!" Eliséo yelled at the boy. At the same time, he unblocked Elessa from his thoughts. She instantly knew they were going to assault her at the same time as Plyke. They knew her well enough to know that if she was even close to finishing her wall, there was no way she would ever let them back in and that could be extremely dangerous for all three of them. They only waited for Plyke to place his hand on her arm before shouting as forcefully as they could.

Rilla, come back to us. Plyke pleaded with her.

Girl, stop this nonsense instantly! Elessa chided.

Rilla, don't finish the wall! Eliséo called out barely concealing the panic running through him.

* * *

The force of three different minds calling out to her broke through Rilla's concentration. She was *so* close to finishing the wall.

Just a few more minutes, she thought to herself. *I only need a few more minutes.*

Rilla, please stop. It was Eliséo. The elf was more worried than she'd ever felt.

I can always finish it later, she told herself as she cleared her head and looked at her companions. She was surprised to find Plyke tightly holding her arm, his eyes mirroring the concern in Eliséo's. Her brow creased as she shrugged herself free of his grasp.

"I guess it didn't really work so well then," she said softly.

Plyke cocked his head to one side looking at her curiously.

"It worked better than you think," he told her, not offering up any extra information.

"What do you mean?" she pressed him, while the others watched on in silence. An uncomfortable silence. "You broke through to me quite easily. It can't have worked very well."

He shook his head, refusing to answer. Plyke was angry with her, but she couldn't understand why. The others weren't angry with her. She felt nothing from them.

Was it panic I felt in Eliséo?

Arishen and Tika were standing a little way back, watching the exchange in interested silence, but that was all. Rilla was about to press Plyke further but Eliséo jumped in before she had the chance.

"I understand you've been building a wall around your mind today, but you need to stop that now." Before she could argue, the elf continued. "We are fast approaching the karliki and I need everyone to be on their guard. I can't have you in a trance as we plunge ourselves into possibly the most dangerous place I will ever take you.

"*If* we are admitted into the Goraburg, we need to be trusted the entire time we are there. Even having visited more than any other human, elf or lintep, I would still be lost without a guide in those tunnels. If, for any reason, we are suspected of being a danger to the karliki, they will not hesitate to lead us away from the entrance so that we would never find our way out. Do I make myself clear?"

Rilla suspected his comments were aimed towards her. Eliséo turned and continued his brisk pace towards their destination. Before he'd gone more than ten paces, he stopped and faced them again.

"No one is to mention Rilla is the child of prophecy. If you agree, we may in fact use your assumed name of Karinya until we are well clear of both the karliki and the crystal dragons." Rilla nodded mutely. "Arishen, it would be best to keep your dreams to yourself in Goraburg unless you fear we are in grave danger. Plyke, Tika, no one will mind humans or lintep, so the two of you should be fine." He turned his attention to all of them once more. "Offer as little information about yourselves as possible. We do not need them knowing that we have been attacked numerous times since leaving Silvaren or they may suspect that we have led our enemy straight to them."

Rilla quickly hopped down from the wagon and helped Tika up. She hadn't really noticed that they had allowed her to ride most of the day. Guilt trickled through her, but she pushed it aside. Her mind was more difficult to protect than Tika's leg. She could always heal his leg more once they stopped again.

With little communication between them, Tika settled into the wagon while Plyke gave Shuut a quick drink. Through trial and error, they had found that soaking a small rag and swishing it around in her mouth until she started sucking was the most effective way to get water into her safely. At least they were managing to keep her hydrated. Once he was finished, he went to walk beside the horse, following Eliséo's fast fading figure through the trees.

Arishen and Rilla took up the rear. They walked in silence for a long time. Rilla often felt his eyes on her but every time she turned to look at him, he quickly looked forward again. She put up with it for a while before it became annoying.

"What is it?" she asked him sharply.

"What?" Arishen turned to her, eyebrows shooting up.

"Why do you keep looking at me and saying nothing?"

"I ... I didn't mean to," his stammered apology was quite unexpected. The Arishen Rilla had come to know was brusque, unyielding and completely unapologetic. When he saw the look on her face, he continued. "You just don't realise what you do to the people around you. That's all."

"What's *that* supposed to mean?" Rilla asked, more confused than ever. By his silence, she assumed the seer wasn't going to answer her. Almost angrily, she started to shake her head at him.

"Rhanya loved and helped you, even though he knew it might cost his life. Shuut took four Paradisians into the Outworld with her because of you. Eliséo left Silvaren after he'd only just arrived, seemingly to protect you. Plyke now automatically does anything he can to help you, with Tika close on his heels." He sighed and shook his head. "The worst part is that you must notice what they do, but you're blind to the fact that all of the people around you would die to protect you in a heartbeat."

If Rilla was stunned by his uncertainty before, she was completely shocked by this. Gathering her wits, she mumbled a half-hearted reply. "That's because they all think I'm the prophecy child."

* * *

It was her way to escape his praise and he let her have it. She had to see that what he said was the truth and it had nothing whatsoever to do with some stupid prophecy.

Remembering what Telon had told him, he took ten deep breaths as they walked on. She had always been different to the rest of them. He didn't know why she shied away from the knowledge that they all held her in such high regard, but it was obvious the thought made her uncomfortable. It seemed no matter what he did, what he said to her, the outcome would always be the same – Rilla's discomfort.

They continued the rest of the way to the tunnel entrance in silence. Rilla stepped as lightly as she could, making as little noise as possible. Arishen noticed what she was doing and tried to follow her lead with less success. By the time Eliséo called a halt, he was thoroughly frustrated with both his attempt to talk to Rilla and his lack of success in treading silently over the leaf covered forest floor.

Chapter Forty-Eight – Goraburg

Eliséo spied an old, twisted snow gum, it's brown and red stripes oddly out of place amongst the pure white of the ghost gums in the Lesa Forest. Elessa, of course, was his favourite tree in the world, but this unique gem held a special place in his heart. It was a lone tree in the middle of a forest as much as he had ever been alone among the elves. Aside from that, it was the key to Goraburg and to his best friend.

It had been fifty years since he had seen Ilya. He had no doubt the karlik still remembered and would immediately welcome him. What he doubted was his friend's father's ability to do the same. Mikhail Alekseevich was a proud karlik, and more stubborn than most people Eliséo had ever met. Hoping that he was doing the right thing, he bent down to the tangled roots of the snow gum, his fingers expertly searching for a hidden latch. He felt the cool touch of metal, grasped it firmly and turned it.

Acting quickly, he moved his companions close to twenty paces away from the roots. They barely had time to question him before the ground in front of them slid open. The karliki were well known for their skills in metalwork. The Paradisians were still gaping, when a stout karlik appeared at the top of a long set of stairs.

Eliséo immediately stepped forward to introduce himself. "Dobrey den Messenger of the Karliki, I am Eliséo, Ambassador of the Elves."

"Dobrey den, Ambassador. I remember you." The karlik tugged at his coarse, blonde beard. "You will not be readily welcomed by Lord Mikhail Alekseevich. Why have you come?"

Eliséo did not recognise him, but he may easily have been one of the many karliki who had gathered to watch him spar with Ilya. He had spent enough time with this race that he could tell this particular karlik was not ill disposed towards him.

"My companions and I need safe and quick passage through Goraburg to the Drakos Mountains." He smiled slowly. "I would also dearly love to see my friend, Ilya Mikhailovich."

"Friend?" the karlik snorted. "I saw the position your *friend* put you in the last time you were here. If you are willing to forgive him that, I will see what I can do."

Eliséo's smile broadened at the memory. "It was all in good fun. Perhaps the greatest shame is that Lord Mikhail Alekseevich did not see the humour in the situation and I have been forced to miss my friend these fifty years."

"I will try to persuade my lord to grant you an audience with his youngest son."

"If you would be so kind, please present this gift to Ilya Mikhailovich for me." Eliséo pulled a multicoloured stone carved in the shape of a flower in full bloom and handed it to the karlik. "It is of the utmost importance. He will not believe I am at his door without you placing that in his hand and his hand alone."

The karlik took the stone and held it with great care. He finally looked behind Eliséo and took in his companions, including Shadow lying motionless in the wagon. "Wait here for my return."

He disappeared down the steps and the forest floor slid closed behind him. Eliséo walked over to the wagon and sorted through their belongings. The Paradisians were still staring at the floor uneasily.

"He won't be back soon," Eliséo told them without looking up. "It's a long way down the stairs and he will need to convince Lord Mikhail to grant us an audience before coming all the way back up again. We'll be lucky if he returns before the stars appear."

His companions looked up at the sky. It was late in the afternoon, but the sun had not yet begun to set. Tika walked over to Eliséo and watched him taking his branches out of the wagon.

"Will we need to carry Shuut again?"

Eliséo nodded as he began to put together the branches with her sleeping mat.

* * *

"Rilla, do you think you can heal my leg a bit more before the karlik returns?" Tika asked. "I *may* have walked a little more than I should have on it this morning."

Rilla looked up through red curls as he sat stiffly beside her. She deftly plaited and tucked her hair under her cap. "It's the least I can do for you."

He inched closer as she held out her hand towards him. Rilla placed one hand on his good leg and the other on his injured one. Nothing happened. She couldn't see the muscles in her mind, couldn't feel the pain. She looked up at him, confused. "Are you sure you need my help?"

"Can't you feel it?" His eyebrows creased.

Rilla shook her head and tried once more. Nothing. She couldn't see or feel anything. *What's the matter with me?*

You built a wall. A voice crept in from a distance. It was Eliséo. He sounded sad. *You should have asked me. No, not asked. You should have told me before you tried doing that.*

Why? Rilla tried to keep her panic at bay as she closed her eyes. *What's happened to me? I can't feel Tika's pain or see the muscles in his leg.*

Plyke is not a lintep master. He explained to you what he did and how he survived in the Paradise. What he didn't tell you, probably because he has no idea, is that building a wall does not just keep people out of your mind. It also keeps your powers held safely inside.

Isn't that a good thing? Rilla was so scared she was barely listening.

If you had finished the wall in the way I assume you had intended, you would not be able to access your powers at all and we would not be having this discussion. From what I can see, you've built yourself a kind of tower protecting your mind. You will need to lead your power to the top of that tower so that it can come out and help you. You must not finish building your wall.

Rilla felt his panic once more. In trying to save herself, she had almost irreparably damaged herself. *I'm sorry.* She whispered to him. *Maybe when we're somewhere safer, you can help me build a different, better wall?*

When we're safe, I'll see what I can do. Eliséo agreed. *For now, learn to use your powers again. Tika needs you.*

Rilla opened her eyes and saw both Tika and Plyke watching her in concern. She forced a smile. "Looks like I built a better wall than I thought."

Plyke walked off stormily towards the wagon to help Eliséo and Arishen. Rilla watched him go, still uncertain why he was so angry with her.

"Can you help me?" Tika asked, turning away from his Partner.

Rilla shrugged and replaced her hand on his leg. She closed her eyes and tunnelled down into the tower in her mind, searching for her lintep power. Eventually, she found it and gently pulled it up to the top of the tower. She allowed it to spill slowly over the sides, making sure not to let all of it out at once. Instantly, she saw the muscles in Tika's leg and felt the pain in her own. It was duller than before. She was grateful for that.

It was only after a few moments of trying to knit Tika's muscles together that she realised her healing powers were working slower than usual. It took her a good few minutes to repair the damage of the day and more to heal it further. She knew she probably shouldn't exert herself too much, but she was so close to healing his leg entirely that she just kept going until it was all fixed. She pulled her hand away from his leg and sluggishly opened her eyes.

"Try that."

Tika bent his legs to get up and looked at her in amazement. He jumped up to his feet and ran on the spot. "It's perfect!" He barely waited for Rilla to get to her feet before hugging her. "Thank you."

Tika smiled and ran over to Plyke to show him. Eliséo was watching him closely. His gaze eventually drifted over to Rilla.

How did you find it?

Much more difficult than before. But he's all healed now so I shouldn't have to help anyone until you can help me. She inwardly sighed with relief.

It seems as though your wall is numbing you to your own pain. I can feel a small tear in your left leg. At least your own healing powers shouldn't be affected. You'll probably have healed by the time the karlik returns.

Rilla wasn't certain, but she felt as though the elf was reprimanding her. She lent heavily on her left leg, raising her right foot slightly. She felt a small, dull ache, but nothing significant. If Eliséo hadn't mentioned it, she quite possibly would not have noticed it.

* * *

The moon had risen half way into the sky by the time the forest floor slid open again. They watched and waited as the sturdy, pale karlik emerged once more.

"Lord Mikhail Alekseevich, at the most ardent insistence of his youngest son, has agreed to grant you access to Goraburg." Eliséo smiled with unreserved relief at the news. "I, Grigori Nikolayevich, will take you to your rooms where you will make yourselves presentable for my lord."

"Many thanks, Grigori Nikolayevich." Eliséo bowed slightly towards the karlik. "You must have a silver tongue."

Grigori shook his head. "It was not my silver tongue, but your gift to Ilya Mikhailovich, that changed my lord's mind."

Eliséo smiled to himself. The gift was one that Ilya and himself had been trading back and forth for years. It was the strongest reminder of their friendship he could have sent down into the tunnels.

Grigori waited for Eliséo to send their horse on its way to greener pastures before beginning the long journey down to the heart of Goraburg. Once they were all below ground level, he turned a hidden latch to make the opening slide closed once more. The Paradisians held their breath. It was pitch black and they were on a steep stairway. Grigori instantly lit a torch for them thought Eliséo knew the karlik needed no such help himself.

They walked down the stairs for the better part of an hour, through both narrow and wide passages. Eventually, they began to pass through small caverns with stalactites hanging over stalagmites. In some of the caverns, there were columns where the two had met. Each cavern reflected the light of the torch so that they were never in darkness.

Eventually, Grigori slowed his pace in a somewhat larger cavern than most of the others they had passed through. He carefully selected a staircase leading up. Eliséo made sure no one was left behind as they followed him up into a smaller cavern. He immediately spotted a stone table sparsely covered with food.

"It appears Lord Mikhail Alekseevich has provided refreshments for you," Grigori told them. "I will leave you to your meal and will come to escort you to the main chamber where my lord and his sons will receive you."

Eliséo thanked the karlik. Grigori hesitated and sidled up to him.

"Ambassador Eliséo, might I have a private word with you?"

Eliséo knew better than refuse the karlik who had already done so much for him. He instructed the Paradisians to wash themselves as well as possible with the bowls of water scattered throughout the small cavern before following the karlik back outside.

When they were well out of earshot of the others, Grigori turned and looked at Eliséo gravely. "Your audience with my lord is of the utmost importance."

"I am aware of that." Eliséo replied in all seriousness.

"No, you do not understand." The pale blue eyes turned stony. Grigori took a deep breath before continuing. "I was made a member of Lord Mikhail's council a few years after your last visit. I enjoyed my position there for thirty-four years. It has been ten years since I was relieved of my position. In fact, there are few I sat with then who still enjoy that position today and 'enjoy' may not be the correct term to use anymore."

Eliséo knew it was a grave injustice to have been serving on the council and now be a lowly messenger.

"If Lord Mikhail removed you ..." Eliséo left the sentence hanging. There was no way he would be able to reverse the clan leader's mind over the decision.

"Vladimir Mikhailovich removed me," the blonde karlik corrected him without hesitation.

Eliséo was stunned. "And Misha allowed it?" He lost all sense of etiquette, using the most familiar term of Mikhail's name he was ever privileged enough to use.

"Misha would never have allowed it if he knew what was happening." Grigori smiled bitterly. "Vladimir has been trying to rule in his father's stead. He keeps Misha in the dark about so many things. I am certain he used a similar ruse about me as he used about all the members who went before me – we chose to step down to allow for fresher and younger blood in the council." He shook his head angrily, throwing his hands up in the air. "Who ever heard of such rubbish? The council is meant to have old blood in it to prevent old mistakes from being repeated."

"Does Ilya know of this?" Eliséo asked earnestly. "Surely he would not allow his father to be blinded by Vladimir."

"Ilya is in danger of falling out with his father because of his loud voice against his brother," Grigori explained. "Vladimir has planted so many seeds of doubt and betrayal in Mikhail's mind that it is all Ilya could do to keep in his father's good graces. If he so much as breathes a word of politics, it has been made clear that his father will send him away from Goraburg."

Eliséo stared in utter disbelief. The caring, loving man he had known fifty years ago would never threaten his son with exile. He now understood Grigori's insistence of how important his audience with Lord Mikhail would be. He was wrong to have stayed away for so long. He had abandoned his best friend in his time of need without even realising it.

Cursing himself for his stupidity, Eliséo's thoughts ran to Vladimir. The dark-haired brother had never been the most agreeable of karliki, but Eliséo had badly misjudged him if he had stooped to trying to usurp his father's position, which would have come to him in the fullness of time anyway.

* * *

"There's been a change of plans." Eliséo informed his companions sharply as he rejoined them in their cavern. "Arishen, if you have any dreams at all while we're in Goraburg, no matter how insignificant you think they might be, you tell me instantly. Do you understand?" The seer looked up at him in confusion, but nodded.

"Rilla, the karliki never had an interest in the prophecy about you before. We'll have to play it by ear to see whether we tell them of you or not. Your presence could tip us one way or the other so we'll still need to be careful. In the current circumstances, we cannot hide your true name. If it is later revealed that we lied, things could get worse for us than I had imagined."

"How are you going to keep my identity hidden from them without changing my name?"

"I'll try not to introduce you all individually. The likelihood is that they won't particularly care who you are anyway."

She looked at him with fear. "I'm going to pull down the wall around my mind."

Eliséo said nothing.

"I don't know if that's such a good idea Rilla," Plyke said hesitantly. "I know you've had a different experience with your power, but if I ever let my powers loose suddenly, they try to escape. Eliséo was the only reason I didn't lose them last time it happened."

Rilla looked up at him expectantly.

"We don't have time for this," Eliséo told her simply. "If the same thing happens with you, I don't know if I can help you the same way. As Plyke said, your powers are vastly different. If something goes wrong, we may have two people to carry through the tunnels, if they even allow us safe passage."

Please, Eliséo. She pleaded with him through their link. *I'm scared of being powerless to help my friends.*

Remember that feeling next time you decide to do something so drastic without talking to me first, he chided her.

Rilla instantly pulled away from him, hurt and confused. Eliséo saw her reaction and closed his eyes to hide the torment in them. When he opened them once more, he was calm and composed.

"We don't have much time before Grigori returns. What sort of wall did you build?"

"It's a tower. A really tall tower. But I didn't finish it, so the top is open." She looked at him expectantly. Eliséo rubbed his chin thoughtfully, nodding his head slowly.

251

"Until Grigori comes back, you are to start lowering your tower." She smiled at him gratefully. He looked at her sternly, not returning her smile. "This is important, Rilla. Do *not* pull down the entire thing. I want you to do it as slowly as you built it, brick by brick. Even if you only pull down a few rows, it will still make it easier and faster for you to pull your power out. Do you understand?"

She nodded her head gravely.

"Before we do that, wash your face and hands. You won't have time later and I won't have you looking like that when we are presented. That goes for the rest of you too. I want you all to wash the travel dirt away from your faces and change into the clothes you received in Silvaren. You can eat after that."

The boys and Rilla rushed over to the basins of water scattered throughout the cavern. Eliséo followed close behind them. They washed their faces and changed, Arishen going to the extra effort of wiping Shadow's face before sitting down to devour the food on the stone table.

* * *

When she was ready, and Eliséo had forced her to eat a few mouthfuls, Rilla sat a little way from the boys and waited for the elf to sit across from her. She took a deep breath and looked into his silver eyes. They looked so dull when he wasn't using magic. He couldn't read her thoughts any longer. She had made certain of that. He could only hear what she purposely said to him in her mind.

"Look at my eyes at all times. Do not dare to look away. Pull down one brick at a time, *slowly*. When I tell you to stop, you do so immediately. Do I make myself clear?"

Rilla nodded, making certain not to take her eyes off him. It was more difficult to work on her wall while focussing her eyes on something, but she knew it would be dangerous to try it any other way.

The tower she'd built must have been over a hundred rows high. She felt an overwhelming sense of failure for her current task, before she'd even started it. Trying not to think about it, she started with the top row. She took away a brick but didn't know how to dissolve it from her mind. Not knowing what to do with it, she placed it at the bottom of her tower, beside one of the other bricks. She would change her wall from a tall single brick tower to a short double brick tower. If nothing else, it would give her an ample supply to build it up again if she needed to.

Slowly, but surely, she continued one brick at a time and placing it down the bottom before going back up to remove another one. She hadn't removed more than six rows before she heard Eliséo's voice calling out to her.

"Stop now." His eyes glowed a soft silver as he said those words. Rilla realised he was taking no chances that she wouldn't listen to him. He was using his powers on her. She stopped and looked around her.

"Why? Grigori's not back yet and I've barely taken away enough to make a difference." She bit back any further protests, hearing how petty her complaint sounded. Eliséo didn't bother to reply. Instead, he drew his sword and opened a small cut on his left forearm.

"Heal me." His instruction was dispassionate. Rilla stared at him, speechless. "Now, Rilla."

His words moved her into action. She placed one hand over the cut. The pain wasn't instantaneous, but it didn't take quite so long to feel as with Tika earlier that evening. She wasted little time in first dispersing his pain through her entire body and then knitting his skin together again. It wasn't a deep cut. Nothing that should have been too strenuous for her, but she found it difficult anyway. In a matter of minutes, she had finished and Eliséo's arm was back to normal.

"Well?" He waited expectantly for a reply.

"It wasn't as difficult as with Tika. It still took longer than it should have, but I suppose the more I do it the faster I'll become."

"Go invisible." Eliséo barely waited for her to finish speaking before testing her again. This time, Rilla didn't bother talking. She tried to fade into the background, as she had so many times before. Eliséo was still looking straight at her. The more she tried, the less she felt she was succeeding.

"Well?" she asked him.

"As you said, it took longer than it should have and you were only half transparent. You might be able to get through a crowded room unnoticed, or even down a quiet tunnel if you weren't expected, but if anyone had their eyes on you, all you'd do is make it difficult for them to focus on you. That's all we have time for, I can hear Grigori approaching." He turned to the boys. "Get your things together. Plyke, Tika, get Shadow. We're not leaving anything or anyone behind."

Chapter Forty-Nine – The Audience

Grigori led them to the audience cavern. Eliséo found he was nervous about the audience. It was an unusual feeling for him – in the past he had always been welcome both as the ambassador and Ilya's best friend. Between dealing with the mess Rilla had created for herself and making sure they all looked as presentable as possible, Eliséo hadn't even had a chance to think about how he was going to approach the problem of Mikhail's blindness to Vladimir's scheming. He knew he'd be helping more karliki than just Grigori if he could open Mikhail's eyes.

He slowed his breathing as he walked behind Grigori. He would have preferred to hold up the rear, but the karliki always made a point of entering a room by order of importance. He would not allow himself to seem unimportant in their eyes.

The most important part of their audience would be to secure safe passage through Goraburg. Everything else could fall into place after that. He was still uncertain about revealing Rilla to them. It should not make a difference to them either way, however, if he did not reveal her identity, Vladimir could find some way to turn it against him.

The audience cavern was large, with tiers of seats carved out of the stone in intricate patterns. Unusually, for any cavern in Goraburg, all the stalagmites had been removed.

Eliséo took in everything in a glance. His audiences with Lord Mikhail Alekseevich had previously seen the chamber less than half full. Today, every carved seat was occupied. Some karliki were even seated on the stone stairs or standing behind the last row of seats.

Eliséo fought the urge to shake his head. Mikhail had made this too serious. The only options now would be his eternal exile or complete forgiveness. However much he hoped for the latter, everything pointed to exile.

The council members were seated closest to the front. Less than half of the faces were familiar to Eliséo. Vladimir had been hard at work getting rid of the influential karliki and replacing them with his own loyal followers.

"Dobrey den Lord Mikhail Alekseevich." His voice was calm and even. It echoed eerily off the stone walls.

"Dobrey den Ambassador Eliséo," Mikhail returned his greeting coldly. "Let it be known that you were only granted an audience at the insistence of Ilya Mikhailovich. If it had been solely my decision, you would never enter Goraburg again."

"Father!" Ilya cried out aghast. "You do Ambassador Eliséo a grave injustice. I've told you time and again that we challenged each other only in jest."

"That *jest* ended with a sword at your throat. Never again will an elf be in a position to threaten my son."

Eliséo could already see the situation rushing out of his control, but he could not speak again until he was addressed again.

"Eliséo is both the ambassador and my best friend. You can't exile him for *your* mistake," Ilya reasoned with Mikhail.

"How dare you challenge our father?" Vladimir called out angrily.

Ilya glared at his brother, ignoring his comment.

"Lord Mikhail Alekseevich," Ilya addressed his father formally, "we have not yet heard the reason for Ambassador Eliséo requesting an audience. The least we can do is ask for an explanation."

The return to formality, and his son's reasonable argument, swayed his father. Mikhail turned towards the outsiders and gestured for Eliséo to speak.

"Lord Mikhail Alekseevich, I humbly ask your permission to travel through Goraburg to the Drakos Mountains." Eliséo could see the karlik was about to protest. He hurriedly continued, motioning towards Shadow. "One of my companions has been struck down by some foul magic and our only hope to save her rests with the crystal dragons."

"I can see your injured companion is a banwep. What concern is she of mine?"

Under normal circumstances, Mikhail would not have challenged his request. It irked Eliséo that Vladimir had managed to change his father so much.

"Shadow is a person of great importance to my other companions, two of whom are lintep in the blossoming stage of their power. They refuse to travel anywhere without her by their side."

"Once again, I ask you how this concerns me." Mikhail was still cold and distant. Eliséo's hand was being forced. He could not think of any way around the situation. He would have to reveal Rilla. He motioned her forward.

"May I present to you, Rilla of the lintep. She comes from a Paradise with her three friends. If she does not reach Illaria before her power reaches its peak, she will die."

"Are you implying it would be my father's fault if this unfortunate event occurs?" Vladimir was immediately on the defensive, not allowing his father to respond. "In any case, how can we trust that she is who you say? She could be any lintep, if a lintep she is indeed."

He was right, of course, and everyone in the audience chamber knew it. Unless they had met Princess Rilla, they would not notice the similarities. Unless they had met Rilla before she entered the Paradise, they would not know who her parents were and that she had been raised with the crystal dragons for the first years of her life.

"You can trust me because I would never lie in my position as Ambassador of the Elves. You can trust me because I have no reason to deceive you. You can trust me," he paused, "you can trust me because my best friend is Ilya Mikhailovich and I would *never* jeopardise that friendship."

Ilya smiled at him warmly. Eliséo found himself easily returning that smile, despite his difficult situation.

"Permission to speak, Lord Mikhail Alekseevich." The voice came from behind him. Eliséo turned slightly to see a grey haired karlik stand in the front row of seats. He recognised him instantly. It was Kazimir Sergeyevich, Mikhail's oldest friend and most trusted advisor. Vladimir would never be able to make him stand down from his position in the council.

"Kazik, permission is always granted to you." Mikhail's face melted into a smile and his voice lost its harsh edge. If there was anyone who could turn the tide, Eliséo knew it would be Kazimir. The karlik carefully avoided his gaze as he spoke.

"It would seem as though we have two choices. The first is as Vladimir apparently wishes, take these people back to the entrance they came from. Doing that, we can be assured that at least three of them will die reasonably quickly and whether we care or not, we *will* be responsible for their deaths." Mikhail nodded.

"The second option is to admit we may have slightly overreacted to a friendly jest fifty years ago, put all of that behind us and lead them to the Drakos Mountains." Before Vladimir had a chance to speak, Kazimir continued.

"Ambassador Eliséo has served in his position for hundreds of years. He has been Ilya Mikhailovich's dearest friend for as long as your son has known him. It is doubtful he would cast aside all of that willingly.

"If he believes this child to be Rilla of the lintep, that should be enough for us. Would you really want to take the risk that perhaps she isn't and let her die only to discover later that she is and you are responsible for her death? You'd have the elves, lintep and crystal dragons thirsty for your blood."

"And if she isn't the child of prophecy?" Mikhail asked after a long pause.

"Then you lose nothing. You will still have saved the lives of three people. All six of them will be forever in your debt. It can't hurt." He finished with a shrug.

Eliséo had been carefully watching Vladimir during this exchange. His expression had darkened considerably.

"Father, you can't change your mind so easily. Kazimir Sergeyevich is too attached to the elf to see things objectively. They could be spies sent in by the humans to learn our weaknesses," Vladimir pleaded with his father.

"Rubbish," Ilya replied immediately. "All they want is to be taken to the Drakos Mountains to heal their companion. Where else could they possibly heal her?"

There was a rustling towards the back of the audience chamber as a karlik with thick blonde hair and green eyes stood up. She was younger than half of the council members – much younger than Mikhail and Kazimir, but Eliséo recognised her instantly.

It was Anya Nikolaevna, the stonemason. She was the karlik who had carved the flower that he and Ilya passed back and forth to one another on each visit. Many years ago, they had entered her workshop, daring each other to take something without her noticing. The multicoloured flower had immediately caught their attention and they managed to steal it away before Anya noticed. She had never found out who had taken it and they planned to keep it that way. Eliséo blushed at the memory, hoping that she wouldn't piece it together just by looking at his face.

"Anya Nikolaevna, why do you stand?"

Eliséo reflected that at least Mikhail was as confused as he was.

"I would urge you to take Kazimir Sergeyevich's advice and quickly. We need to discuss what your father, Aleksandr Ivanovich, left behind for the three of us to guard."

Eliséo had no clue to what she was referring. He was certain that Mikhail would dismiss her request instantly.

"Let it be known that I grant safe passage to Ambassador Eliséo and his companions as far as the Drakos Mountains. Anyone who hinders or harms them will answer to me." Mikhail's voice was loud and clear as it echoed around the chamber.

The decision signalled the end of the public audience and Eliséo's apparent forgiveness. Eliséo looked over to Ilya but only saw confusion in his eyes.

They waited impatiently for the gathered karliki to vacate the audience chamber. Eventually, the only ones who remained were Eliséo and his companions, Mikhail and his two sons, Kazimir and Anya.

"Has the situation changed?" Mikhail asked Anya as soon as the sound of footsteps had receded.

"It has, but I will not speak of it with Vladimir Mikhailovich here. It has nothing to do with him."

Vladimir face reddened. "Father, she means to turn you against me. I demand to remain. There can be no reason why Ilya can stay and I can't."

"Vladimir, go now." Mikhail sounded weary. If Vladimir was like this every day, Eliséo could well understand his weariness.

"Father!" he cried out in protest.

"Vladimir, you will listen to me." Mikhail's voice turned stony again. "I am still the leader of the karliki and you will obey my command. Go now, before I decide to punish you for your insolence."

Furious, Vladimir turned on his heels and stormed out of the chamber, his footsteps echoing loudly. Mikhail was about to speak again, but Eliséo put out a hand to stop him. He muttered under his breath. The Paradisians moved quickly to ensure Shadow was close to them. A thick mist began to surround them.

Mikhail watched in silence until the dome was complete. He tugged at his red beard when it was done.

"Does this do what I think it does?" he gestured to the mist.

"It does, Lord Mikhail," Eliséo confirmed his suspicions. "We are safe from prying eyes and ears."

"Enough with this Lord business. Let us put all of that behind us. You were foolish to challenge my son and I was foolish to hold you to it."

"You took your time to come to that realisation Misha." Eliséo smiled warmly, placing a hand on the karlik's shoulder. The smile was returned with a huff.

"Now, Anushka, what's this all about? I thought we agreed to complete secrecy between the three of us."

Mikhail's familiar use of her name led Eliséo to understand that they were old friends. It made no sense to him given Anya's lack of position on the council and her comparative youth.

"We did, Misha, but things have changed. What Aleksandr entrusted to the three of us could help this banwep."

"But you told us, in quite a state as I recall, that it was stolen." It was Kazimir who spoke.

"It was stolen," she replied steadily. "However, I found out fairly soon afterwards who had stolen it."

"Why didn't you tell us?" Misha cried out in a mixture of relief and anger. "Who stole it?"

Eliséo and Ilya froze as the stonemason gestured to the two of them. Kazimir laughed uncontrollably at their expression. The two best friends were at a loss to explain his reaction. They knew they should be punished for their actions and yet.

"It was safer this way. I've been keeping a close account of it. It has been passed back and forth between them each time Eliséo visits. For the past fifty years, it has been travelling the Outworld, but even there it was safer than here."

Ilya regained his composure first. "Why would grandfather Aleksandr entrust a stone flower to the three of you?"

Mikhail stared at them in disbelief and then joined Kazimir in his laughter. Eliséo and Ilya shared a confused look.

"Now you understand why it was safe with them." Anya smiled.

"Are you going to let us in on the joke?" Ilya had a more even temper than his brother, but it had reached its limit. Anya turned to explain to them.

"The two of you stole what you *thought* was a stone flower. What you never realised was that it was so much more than that. Aleksandr Ivanovich entrusted the heart of a crystal dragon to the three of us. He told us how to use its powers and made us swear to keep it secret.

"To do that, we agreed that I should carve it into a flower so no one would ever suspect its true nature. It was at that point the two of you stole it. I was frantic when I realised it was gone until I discovered it was the two of you."

"What I don't understand," Mikhail interrupted her explanation, "is why you thought it was safer being swapped and carried all over the Outworld than it was in our care."

Anya and Kazimir shared an awkward look, neither wanting to meet Mikhail's eye. Eventually, Kazimir yielded.

"Misha, how long have we known each other?"

"It must be over three hundred years," Mikhail answered easily

"And in all that time, have you ever known me to lie to or betray you?"

"Come, Kazik, what is this all about?"

"Answer the question," Kazimir insisted. Eliséo held his breath.

"No, never. Not even when I wish you would have lied to me."

"This will be one of those times," Kazimir told him gravely. "You have been blind to many of Vladimir's actions. He is not satisfied to wait for your position to fall to him naturally."

"You are walking in treacherous tunnels, my friend," Mikhail warned him.

"Exactly why do you think almost half of your council members have been replaced with *his* friends in the past thirty years?"

"He told me they were standing down to make way for younger voices on the council," Mikhail answered with little hesitation.

"And does that not strike you as odd?" his friend questioned him. "Is not the council meant to be comprised of the older generation to prevent mistakes being repeated because of a lack of experience or memory of past events?"

"That is the general idea, yes." Mikhail thought on it for a few moments. "But what other reason could there possibly be for them stepping down?"

"Stepping down, indeed!" Kazimir retorted angrily. "Every single one of them was forced out of the council by Vladimir. He threatens them in such a way that they would not dare confront you about it."

"If his plan was to remove my most trusted advisors, then why do you still remain?" Mikhail was not prepared to yield.

"I have no family for him to threaten. There is no one he can harm to keep me silent."

"What you are suggesting is a monstrous crime."

"And your son has committed it. Now do you understand why Anushka thought it was safer to let the heart pass between the two boys?"

Mikhail nodded, not trusting himself to speak. Eliséo knew the betrayal of his eldest son would weigh heavily on him. He could not leave him unpunished, and yet, to punish him was almost unthinkable. The punishment for a crime of this magnitude was either death or permanent exile. How could he impose either on his son?

"I don't understand why the heart had to be kept safe. It's just a piece of crystal in the end. What difference would it have made if Vladimir knew it was here?" Ilya broke the silence with the question Eliséo was dying to know the answer to.

It was Anya who replied. "The crystal heart was given to the leader of the karliki when the first crystal dragon died. No, perhaps I must go further back than that. Thousands of years ago, the karliki had powers too. They slowly expended them in various ways by working them into the tunnels of Goraburg. They created farming caverns where the stone emits a light similar to that of the sun, but nowhere near as powerful. Some wove their powers into their stoneworks.

"Two karliki carved a crystal dragon each and breathed life into them with their power. Their names were Sascha Vladimirovich and Nadya Grigorevna. In the end, the power they gave was not enough and through this process they also gave their lives. It was a gift the crystal dragons never forgot. We do not know how it happened, but they have changed vastly in size and shape since the first pair were created.

"In return, when the first crystal dragon died, it's heart was given to our clan leader. Since that time, this knowledge and the power it brings along with it has been passed down. Very few know of it. In fact, only the three of us knew of it until recently."

"What power does it hold?" Eliséo asked curiously. He knew the karliki had once had power of their own, but he'd never heard this story before.

"As the karliki were left powerless, the crystal heart was the perfect gift. It would heal any magical ailment without requiring us to travel to the crystal dragons themselves. We three are the only ones who know the words to unlock this power. What I am suggesting is that one of us tries it on your companion. She doesn't look like she will last the journey to the Drakos Mountains otherwise."

Ilya pulled the crystal heart from his pocket and held it out to Anya. The stonemason glanced at Mikhail and Kazimir, but neither of them made a move to take the heart. Seeing her step towards Shadow, the Paradisians made way for the karlik, though Eliséo noted that they still stood protectively around her.

Anya knelt and held the crystal heart over Shadow's forehead. She murmured a few words. Even Eliséo, with his enhanced hearing, could not hear what she said. When nothing happened, Anya looked up questioningly at the two older karliki.

"Perhaps it needs three karliki," Kazimir suggested with a shrug. "Why else would Aleksandr have involved all of us?"

The three karliki knelt around Shadow's head. The Paradisians stood back further. Eliséo watched intently while the three karliki mumbled together.

Shadow's eyes flew wide open. She sat up and instantly fell back down. Eliséo moved quickly and caught her head before it smashed on the stone floor. He had known she would be weak, but this was worse than he had expected. She would never be able to walk through the tunnels. Not unless they stayed and rested for a few days first.

"Rest, Shadow." He stroked her forehead gently. "We're in Goraburg now. It won't be long before we can travel to the Drakos Mountains." There was gratitude in her eyes. Eliséo looked up at Ilya. "She needs food and water. She's been like this for too many days."

"Of course." Ilya looked over to his father. "Let me and Misha out of your mist. We'll walk to my cavern where there will be plenty of food for your companions. If the rest of you follow with that mist, we won't be disturbed."

Mikhail readily agreed to the plan. Eliséo muttered one word under his breath to create a break in the mist. Father and son stepped carefully out of it before the rift closed behind them. Once they were ready to start moving, Eliséo held his hand out to Rilla. She stared at it a moment before comprehending. She walked over and took his hand with both Anya and Kazimir looking on curiously.

"This will probably be the best way to show you that I really am a lintep." Rilla smiled at them as she started to walk forward. The mist moved with her, Eliséo at her side. Tika and Plyke quickly picked up Shadow. It worried Eliséo that she did not protest at all.

* * *

Arishen felt useless as his companions took to their tasks. He took Shuut's pack as well as his own and followed the others, with Anya and Kazimir close on his heels. The two karliki watched everything with great interest, but didn't speak to anyone. Arishen took the opportunity to observe the tunnels. Within a few minutes, he was completely confused. All the tunnels looked the same, only sloping in different directions. They didn't pass through very many caverns, but there were a lot of cross tunnels. His favourite section was when they emerged from a tunnel into a water cavern. A shaft of light came down from the top of the cavern to illuminate the bright blue water beneath the thin pathway.

Three karliki jumped out of the water, pulling Eliséo, Tika and Arishen's feet, making them lose their balance. Knives glinted in the dim light from the water.

Arishen closed his eyes against the image and fell over backwards, right into Anya and Kazimir. The karliki caught him awkwardly, calling out to his companions. Eliséo turned around, pulling Rilla with him. The mist stopped suddenly and jerked back with them.

"What did you see?" Eliséo asked immediately. Arishen shook his head, standing up again slowly.

"Nothing," he lied.

"Arishen, we're in enough trouble as it is. Don't make things worse by hiding things from me."

"It was just an image, really," he dissembled. "Not a whole dream."

"I don't care if it was a glimpse of your Paradise. Tell me now!" Eliséo commanded him.

"Three karliki jumped out of the water and tried to pull you, me and Tika down. They had knives." The words were out before he could stop them. "That's all, I swear."

"Did you see their faces?" It was Anya, not Eliséo, who asked him. Arishen shook his head.

"No, I never see faces. Besides it all happened so quickly. The cavern shifted a bit, so I don't think it was this same one, but almost everything looks the same to me down here."

"This mist is protecting us now and Lord Mikhail and Ilya are waiting for us," Rilla reminded them. "We can talk about it when we reach them."

They walked the rest of the way in silence. Arishen noticed Anya and Kazimir glance his way. He didn't know whether they had seers here, as sometimes happened with humans but, from their reaction, he didn't think so.

Once they reached Ilya's cavern, Eliséo let go of Rilla's hand and the mist dissolved. Kazimir quickly related the events to them, explaining their delay.

Arishen was asked more questions, but the conversation soon drifted away from him. He moved away from as quickly as he could to help Tika and Plyke with Shuut.

* * *

Once she'd had a few sips of water, a whisper escaped Shuut's lips.
"Plyke?"
Instantly, he moved close to her, tucking his hair behind his ears so he could look at her properly.
"Thank you." She gripped his wrist. Plyke smiled broadly.
"Ah well, you've saved my life who knows how many times. It's about time I returned the favour." His reply was loud enough for everyone in the cavern to hear it, even though he meant it for her alone. Kazimir looked over to them in confusion.
"What is the banwep thanking you for? Did you do something before she was attacked?"
Deftly dislodging the hair from behind his ear, he turned to Kazimir. With his face slightly downcast, he replied quietly, "I'm at least part lintep. I convinced Shuut to stop fighting against the mind snare. She was weakening herself too quickly and wouldn't have survived the first two days if I hadn't said something. I told her we were coming here in the hope that you could get us to the Drakos Mountains faster."
"Why do you not hold your head up high when you tell us of such wonderful deeds?" He walked over to Plyke and reached up to raise his chin. "You should be proud of your powers, not ashamed or afraid. We karliki were unwise to part with our powers. How many wonderful things would we have been able to do with them? That gift is now lost to our entire race. I would never wish that loss on anyone."
Plyke looked up and smiled. Perhaps Tika was right – his power was a gift that he should fight to keep it at any cost. Tika grinned, ran over and gave him a fierce hug.
"That's what *I've* been trying to tell him. Obviously, I wasn't qualified enough."

* * *

Rilla watched Arishen during this exchange. He hid it fairly well, but he was hurt that no one ever reacted to his gift in the same way. Either it wasn't trusted as being true, or he couldn't give enough detail.
It was quite unfair that she and Plyke got all the attention when he had saved their lives before too. Arishen had taken a small stone plate of food and was sitting unobtrusively in a corner of the cavern. Rilla went to sit next to him and gingerly took a sweetly spiced bread from his plate, smiling as she took a bite from it. She smiled even further when she saw the stunned look on his face.
"What happens now?" he asked her. She shrugged and looked towards Eliséo and Ilya.
"We still have to get to Illaria," she answered. "I suppose it will depend on Shuut now. Either we go to the Drakos Mountains first, or we go straight to the lintep."

261

Chapter Fifty – Through the tunnels

"Ilyusha. I've missed you my old friend." Eliséo smiled warmly and embraced the karlik when they finally had a moment together.

"I dare say not as much as I've missed you." Ilya returned the embrace fiercely. "Vladimir would never have been able to change so many things if you and I weren't in Misha's bad graces."

Mikhail turned at the sound of his name and joined them.

"Ilyusha, Eliséo, forgive a stubborn, old karlik," he said as he took each of their hands. "My pride was wounded and I could not bear to look at either of you. It was a constant reminder. Unfortunately, I wounded myself even more by exiling one of you and ignoring the other."

Eliséo was overjoyed by the apology. He and Ilya hugged Mikhail until he pushed them away.

"Enough of this," he said in a mock gruff voice. "What are we to do now? Will you still travel to the Drakos Mountains? Your companion is healed, so there is no rush."

"Rilla and Plyke still need to get to Illaria as soon as possible," Eliséo said, shaking his head.

"Surely you don't think they are so powerful they will die?" Mikhail asked in annoyance. Eliséo glanced at the two lintep.

"I have seen Rilla's power for myself. It is amazing what she can do without ever having been trained. I can only imagine how powerful she will become when her power peaks. She will most certainly die without the help of the lintep masters."

"What about the boy?" Ilya asked, curiosity getting the better of him as he turned to glance at the Plyke.

"It's hard to tell with him," Eliséo answered guardedly. "He was raised in a Paradise where his mother taught him to hide his power. She did a magnificent job of teaching him to do this.

"I know his powers are still reasonably strong with the walls in his mind built up to hide them. What I don't know, and can't discover myself, is how strong his power would be without those walls. We can't even tell if he is a full lintep."

Eliséo thought back to the one day that Plyke had relaxed his hold on his power just a little when sparring with Rilla. That one glimpse of his power chilled him to the bone. It wasn't necessarily stronger than Rilla's power, but was so much more intense because it had been held in check for such a long time. If Plyke lost control again, Eliséo wasn't certain he'd be able to help the boy contain it as he did that one time.

"I don't want to take a chance with either of them." He shook his head once more, finalising his decision. "We'll stay only until the Paradisians have rested. It must be the middle of the night above ground. They'll be too exhausted to make the journey now."

Ilya nodded. "They will rest here, in my chambers." His father looked as though he was about to protest. "Father, if the seer's vision is anything to go by, they won't be safe anywhere else."

Anya and Kazimir had joined them, seeing that the conversation had turned serious. The stonemason spoke up instantly.

"Do you trust his visions?"

It was a difficult question to answer. Eliséo had only witnessed one of Arishen's dreams himself and it had saved their lives. He knew of others that had not come to pass because circumstances had changed and others that they wouldn't ever know had come to pass because they were of his Paradise.

"He has saved his companions' lives with his dreams."

"That doesn't answer my question," Anya replied.

"I have no reason *not* to trust them," he tried to evade the question. It was unfair to ask him to judge the boy's skills. He knew Arishen truly was a seer, but he hadn't been trained to hone that skill or to distinguish between dreams and visions.

"Does it disturb you that he doesn't see faces? Or that he didn't have a vision of the audience when it was so important to you?" Anya asked.

"I have trouble understanding how he can tell who the people in his dreams are without seeing their faces," he continued before Anya could press her point. "However, the one dream I was there for, he picked exactly who was being attacked and where. He knew exactly number of attackers and how they were using the wind to cover their footsteps. It didn't matter that he couldn't see the faces."

"I understand you want to defend your companion, but it would benefit everyone in this room if he could identify who the karliki in his vision were. Without that, we're left blind. It's almost impossible to take you to the Drakos Mountains without passing through a cavern with water. The only other way to change his dream is to make sure the karliki concerned are otherwise occupied."

Eliséo looked over to Arishen. He was happily sitting with Rilla beside him. Neither of them speaking, but it was really all the seer wanted. Eliséo did not want to disturb this rare moment for him but he had no choice. They must know more about his dream.

"Arishen, come here please." Arishen looked up, exchanged a worried glance with Rilla then joined Eliséo and the karliki.

"I've already told you everything I saw." He clenched his fists defensively. Eliséo made to speak to him, but Anya jumped in first.

"I understand you don't see faces." Arishen crossed his arms tightly.

"All I want to know is if you saw any distinguishing feature. Hair colour, clothing, anything?"

"I already told you everything I saw," Arishen said, reddening in frustration. "There were three karliki who jumped out of the water to pull us down by our feet. They had knives. That's all I saw."

Rilla came over when she saw how defensive Arishen was becoming. Eliséo noticed how he tensed up at her approach. He almost wished he'd thought to tell her to stay back.

"Was I walking with you?" she asked. Arishen's eyes clouded over as he went through the vision again.

"Yes, but you were in front of the three of us."

"Who was carrying Shuut?" she followed up immediately. "Was it Plyke and I or was it you and Tika?"

Plyke and Tika, upon hearing their names, instantly looked up at the seer.

"No one was carrying Shuut." He shook his head in confusion. "She was walking right there next to you."

Anya smiled broadly. "Which karlik was leading you through the tunnels?"

"The messenger from the entrance to Goraburg – Grigori Nikolayevich." Arishen answered confused by her smile.

"We have our answer then. If Shuut walks out and Grigori leads you all, then the seer's vision may come to pass. It could be that Vladimir knows of the existence of the heart and may piece it together when he sees the banwep is healed. She must be carried out, so that no one other than the ten of us know what transpired. Perhaps Ilya and I can lead you out together so that we need not chance it with Grigori."

"I suppose that means we should leave now," Rilla piped up. "If no one is to know that Shuut has already been healed, it will seem suspicious for us to linger."

Kazimir patted Rilla on the back. "I like this one, whether she is the prophecy child or not. She has a clever head on her shoulders." He looked at Ilya's laden table. "Pack as much food in your rucksacks as is left and that will have to do you."

Eliséo watched Mikhail's face grow longer by the second. Kazimir and Anya exchanged a worried glance. Finally, Mikhail shook his head and cleared the glazed look from his eyes.

"Kazik, my old friend, I will need your help more than ever in the coming weeks. Vladimir must be punished and his followers must stand down from the council." Kazimir nodded, knowingly. "Ilyusha, go with Anya but hurry back. You will not like it and I doubt you ever wanted it, but you will need to fill Vladimir's shoes now."

Ilya took a step back, shaking his head and hands. "Father, that is the last thing I want."

"Nevertheless, it now falls to you. I cannot possibly keep Vladimir around when he was not content to wait for something that would have rightfully been his. He is too dangerous. I didn't even see what he was doing." Mikhail walked over to his son and took his rough hands in his own. "I know I ask a lot of you, but you will see that there is no other way. We'll talk more when you return – just make sure this boy's vision doesn't change suddenly to have *you* with a knife at your throat."

Eliséo was stunned. Not only had he just named Ilya as his heir, but hinted that changing the circumstances around Arishen's vision might only affect who was threatened at knifepoint. The thought that Anya's plan might backfire hadn't occurred to him until Mikhail pointed it out. Distractedly, he motioned the Paradisians to fill their rucksacks with food.

"Father, you can't be serious," Ilya pleaded. "Vladimir will not stand down without a fight."

"The laws on this matter are clear," Mikhail responded, unflinchingly. "Traitors must be exiled or put to death. I can't say I want him dead even after what he's done to me, so exile it will be."

"He won't go," Ilya argued. "And if you somehow manage to force him out, you would have to exile all of his followers. Then what? You have a band of rebel karliki outside the tunnels, plotting some way to take their revenge on you and get rid of me?"

Eliséo listened to the exchange in silence. He completely agreed with Ilya, but his solution was not one he cared to voice aloud. Kazimir turned to face him once his son had finished speaking.

"You are an ambassador. Surely you have a solution to the problem Ilya foresees." Kazimir's words cut him. The old karlik *had* to know what he was thinking. Why would he put him in this position? Mikhail, Ilya and Anya all looked expectantly at him.

"This is a family matter. I have no place putting forward my opinions."

"Come," replied Mikhail, "you are Ilyusha's best friend which almost makes you part of our family. What say you?"

Eliséo felt his palms begin to sweat as he ran every scenario he could think of through his mind. He wiped his hands on his pants as he looked Mikhail squarely in the eyes.

"I do not say this lightly and I do not expect you to act on my words. Ilya speaks truth when he says Vladimir will resist. If you do exile him and his friends, they will be able to openly plot against you. They may even be able to convince humans to join them with promises of wealth." He took a deep breath and rushed through the next sentence. "I would put to death all of the traitors for if you only put Vladimir to death, it would fan the flames in his followers and they would try to overthrow your entire family."

Ilya's jaw dropped. "You want my father to kill my brother?"

"No!" Eliséo was quick to reply. "I don't *want* him to at all. I could not imagine him doing it. But I was asked my opinion as an ambassador, not a friend of the family. As an ambassador, I see the political intrigue Mikhail is mired in and the only way out is to well and truly rid himself of the traitors in his midst."

"I agree with the elf," Kazimir said, lifting his chin in defiance. "Vladimir has poisoned so many karlik minds. He cannot be trusted either within the tunnels or without. The only problem is that we don't know who all of his followers are."

"We can at least get rid of the ones we know of," Mikhail answered, scratching his beard. "Those who he used to replace my council members, all of whom I shall replace immediately."

"But father, you won't really get rid of Vladimir, will you?" Ilya protested. "Would you so lightly get rid of me too?"

"Ilyusha, I'm not doing any of this lightly." His father placed a heavy hand on his shoulder. "*You* would never give me a reason to get rid of you and for that I am eternally grateful. I do not think I could bear to lose you too. But think of what Eliséo and Kazik have said. What good could really come of exiling Vladimir? It seems as though we would waste more lives in the future if we let him live to raise a rebel army against us. Can you not see it?"

Ilya dropped his eyes in defeat. Eliséo knew the brothers had no great love for each other, but it must be difficult to agree to this plan.

"We're ready," Rilla interrupted. "Plyke has convinced Shuut that we will carry her to the Drakos Mountains."

Eliséo bent low to embrace Mikhail. "Do svidanya, Misha. I hope we meet under better circumstances next time."

"Do svidanya, Eliséo," Mikhail replied with tears in his eyes. "I am so sorry to have exiled you for such a long time. Vladimir would never have had a chance ..." Words failed him. Kazimir pulled him away gently and shook Eliséo's hand.

"Take care through the tunnels. We cannot afford to lose two heirs in one day. Do svidanya."

The Paradisians had been standing awkwardly, waiting for him. Finally, Eliséo turned to face them. Tika and Plyke had already taken their posts with Shadow. Rilla and Arishen had finished dividing the heavier packs between the two of them.

They exited Ilya's cave single file, Anya first, followed by Rilla, then Arishen with Tika and Plyke following him as they supported Shadow. Eliséo brought up the rear with Ilya. If it was to be such a short visit, they were determined to spend as much time together as possible.

Chapter Fifty-One – Escape from Goraburg

Once they had left Ilya's cavern behind and the light from within it grew dim, Anya lit two torches. She handed one to Rilla and asked the other to be passed back to Eliséo. Rilla understood it was more dangerous for their party to be so well lit, but only karlik eyes were well enough accustomed to the dark for them to be able to see unaided in the tunnels. If Vladimir had indeed realised what was happening, then they would need all the help from they could get.

"How long will it take us to reach the Drakos Mountains?" Rilla asked the karlik walking in front of her.

"We cannot take the most direct route as there are too many karliki we would need to pass. Going another way, it will take at least a day. Less if we don't rest too often."

"They are seasoned travellers by now, Anushka," Ilya called out from behind. "If they've been travelling with Eliséo all the way from Silvaren, I doubt there would have been much time for resting. I should know from the time I ever travelled the Outworld with him."

"Between Eliséo and Shuut, we must be among the best travellers in the Outworld," Tika piped up. "Had it not been for our adventures along the way, we may have had more chance to rest."

"What of your adventures?" Anya turned her head to momentarily look at the small human. Tika glanced at Eliséo before relating everything that had befallen them since leaving Silvaren. It took a few hours, with both Anya and Ilya asking questions, for Tika to finish his story.

"But what I'd really like to know is why you all decided to leave your Paradise and how Rilla came to use her powers in the first place." Ilya had been completely engrossed by all the turn of events.

Arishen, Tika and Plyke easily answered why they had left. Their reasons weren't secret anymore. Rilla, however, still hesitated.

What's wrong? Eliséo asked through their bond with Elessa.

I don't want everyone I meet to know everything about me. She pushed the thought as hard as she could towards him. *I don't even know half the answers to those questions myself.*

You can trust these karliki, Eliséo tried to reassure her.

That's not the point, Rilla told him. *I haven't even told the boys and Shuut why I really left the Paradise. Elessa only knows because she went prying through my mind the first time I touched her. I suppose that means you know as well.*

Then just tell them whatever you want to, Eliséo told her.

Rilla saw Anya glance back at her questioningly. Her eyes widened.

"Your eyes are ... quite bright," the blonde karlik gasped. Rilla understood immediately what had happened. She immediately cut her contact with Elessa and moved the torch further to the side.

"The torch must be playing tricks with light." She attempted to shrug it off. "As for me, I left the Paradise because it just wasn't for me and I started using my powers when we met a lintep in Turon. It was then that I realised what I might be capable of and tried my hand at a few things I saw Ratchin do."

"I've never seen Ratchin do even half the things you've done," Shadow pointed out, quite unhelpfully. Rilla cringed inwardly.

"She gave me ideas of what to do and I took it from there. If you boys would stop injuring yourselves, I wouldn't have to use my powers so often."

"Why haven't *you* tried to do what Rilla does, Plyke?" Ilya asked with greater curiosity.

"It's complicated," Plyke replied. "The simplest answer is that my power works differently to Rilla's. My power seems to be more to do with the mind than the body."

Rilla thought back to that first day she purposely tried to use her power with the fringa's help. She had followed him with her mind, so she must have some mind power as well. She hadn't tried it since then because of the blasting she'd received from Ratchin over it. She might be able to try it again more safely once they reached Illaria.

"How long will it take us to get to Illaria after we leave the crystal dragons?" There was no answer to her question. She turned around. "Eliséo?"

Ilya and Eliséo had stopped walking. There was a knife at Ilya's throat and another in the small of Eliséo's back.

"Any of you move and they're both dead."

"Stanislav, what are you doing?" Anya asked incredulously.

"Vladimir has spies everywhere. I was sent to follow Ilya when he left the audience chamber. My surprise at the rest of you appearing out of nowhere was nothing to the knowledge that Mikhail intends to murder his own son."

Rilla was only half listening to the karlik. She was thinking of a way to save them. Eliséo should be quick enough to save himself, but she knew he wouldn't sacrifice his best friend's life for his own.

Closing her eyes, she dived down into the tower in her mind, hauling her power up to the top and letting it flow down over the sides. The effort of containing it in her body was almost more than she could bear. She slowly pushed it out of herself in a thin tendril, reaching slowly to where Eliséo stood.

It was just like in Turon – she knew where he was standing and led her power there with her mind. Once it had reached him, she saw where the knife was digging into his back and concentrated her power on that one point. As carefully as she could, she drew heat from the torch into her body and down through her tendril of magic all the way over to the knife. She was wary of letting the heat of the torch linger in her so once she had made the connection, she pushed it as hard and as fast as she could into the knife.

In the distance, she heard a scream of pain and a clatter before she smelled the metallic scent of blood. Quickly and quietly, she withdrew the tendril of power from Eliséo back into herself and locked it safely away in her tower before opening her eyes. Stanislav was lying dead on the cave floor, blood covering his body.

Almost everyone was looking at the dead karlik. Almost. Plyke was looking straight at Rilla, disbelief in his eyes.

"Rilla? What ... how did you do that?" At the sound of his voice, all eyes turned on Rilla. It was the last thing she was expecting. She shook her head, dropped the now unlit torch and covered her face.

"I don't know. I panicked."

"*That* was anything but a panicked action," Anya said from behind her. "No matter how you made Stanislav drop the knife, it was the cleverest thing you could have made happen. The elf is the only one quick enough to have responded and you knew that. What did you do?"

Rilla listened with her eyes closed and her head in her hands. She didn't want any of this attention. She had just wanted to save Eliséo's life, but she knew she'd have to give him a chance to save Ilya for him to justify his actions. She hadn't even known if it would work or if the tendril of magic was just her imagination.

"I don't know," she mumbled as she opened her eyes and held her head up. "I just want to get out of here. Please can we keep walking?"

"She's right." Eliséo immediately came to her rescue. "It's too dangerous for us here. We'll talk about this when we're out of the tunnels."

They walked the rest of the way in silence, through ever narrowing passageways. Rilla barely noticed any of it. She was still reeling from the fact that it hadn't been her imagination and she had actually done that. Anya was right. It had been a calculated move. She knew that and so did everyone else.

The one thing she couldn't understand was the look in Plyke's eyes. He was hurt and angry and stunned. She didn't know why he would be hurt and angry but it wasn't the first time he reacted that way to her and the way she used her power. Perhaps he thought that she shouldn't be trying to use her power without a trained lintep around. Maybe he didn't approve of what she did with her power. After all, he had been taught to hide his power and not use it unless absolutely necessary.

* * *

It was nightfall when they eventually exited the tunnels. The Paradisians were exhausted. Eliséo could see it in the way they carried themselves. They hadn't slept in two days and they'd been walking almost the entire time. The four of them tried to hide it, but as soon as they were out, they sank down to the grass and fell asleep where they lay. In a way, he was glad. It would give him a chance to speak with Ilya and Anya alone.

The two karliki slowly helped him dig a fire pit and light a fire. He knew that they didn't want their meeting to be so short, but it could not be helped. Eliséo had to escort Shadow to the crystal dragons, then Rilla and Plyke to Illaria as quickly as he could. Ilya and Anya had to return to tell Mikhail of the attempted assassination of his new heir. Ilya looked down, hands in his pockets, and shuffled his feet.

"We could stay until they wake up, if you like."

"No, we can't," Anya told him firmly. "Your father needs you."

"I know." He nodded, choking back tears. "I just ..."

"... don't want to say goodbye," Eliséo finished his sentence as he bent down to embrace his friend. "Ilyusha, I will come back as soon as I can, I promise. Send me word of anything important. I doubt we will stay long with the crystal dragons, but they will be able to get a message to me if needed. They know the way to Illaria."

He went to pass the crystal heart to Ilya, but Anya stayed his hand. "I don't think that will be safe in Goraburg just yet. Better keep it with you."

"May I ask you a question?" he turned to the blonde karlik as he placed the carved flower in his pocket. "Why did Aleksandr Ivanovich include you as one of the three karliki he told about this?"

"One of you were bound to ask me that. I'm much younger than Misha and Kazik." She smiled and nodded. "My brother, Grigori, and I share a family secret that most but Aleksandr have forgotten. We are descendants of Sascha

Vladimirovich and Nadya Grigorevna. Aleksandr thought it fitting to choose one of us as the third karlik."

Eliséo turned at approaching footsteps. Grigori suddenly burst from the tunnel, straight into them, bowling them over.

"Anushka, I found you!" he panted as he helped his sister to her feet.

"What is it, Grisha?" Anya asked him.

"Vladimir has escaped," he told them while catching his breath. "He had spies everywhere."

"We know," Ilya told him bitterly. "One of them tried to kill us on way here."

"What do you mean he escaped?" Anya kept to the point at hand. "Has Mikhail already executed the other traitors?"

"He called a meeting, of only his old council, as soon as you left. He told us his plan to immediately put to death all the traitors." Grigori shook his head in despair. "We searched everywhere for Vladimir, but he has disappeared."

"You must go quickly." Eliséo turned to Ilya. "He won't be coming out of this exit, not when he knows we were heading this way. He won't want to take his chances in a duel with me. Do svidanya, Ilyusha."

"Do svidanya, Eliséo." Ilya nodded, shook his hand and led the way back into the tunnels. Grigori followed him closely. Anya stayed only a moment longer to remind him to take care of the crystal heart.

"If Vladimir heard about the executions there's no telling what else he heard." She shook his hand and made to leave before he held her back.

"Take care of Ilyusha for me. I don't know how long it will be before I can return. He'll need all the help he can get in the coming months." She nodded before running down the tunnels after Ilya and Grigori.

Eliséo watched them go sadly. He should never have stayed away from Goraburg for so long, even if Mikhail had all but exiled him. For fifty years he had missed seeing his best friend and now that they had finally met again, he had to leave so soon.

Kicking the stones at his feet, he paced around the clearing anxiously. The Drakos Mountains were so close, and yet he had to wait for his companions to rest before reaching them.

Do not be so eager to meet the crystal dragons, Elessa chided him. *I don't think any of us will enjoy that visit, especially if Lady Eléna's sources are correct.*

That's not the only reason I want to get away from Goraburg, Eliséo interrupted her abruptly. *I know I told them Vladimir would not follow me, but that was only a guess. He's like a trapped animal at the moment, knowing that if he is caught he will be put to death. That makes him more dangerous than ever. For all I know, he could be thinking that I would be the perfect bargaining chip for his life. If he knows about the crystal heart, he might try to steal it from me and force one of the three to reveal the words to unlock its power.*

There is nothing you can do about Vladimir nor the crystal dragons right now, she reminded him. *So, keep watch for your companions and try to rest as much as you can.*

Chapter Fifty-Two – Drakos Mountains

Dawn broke and his companions still hadn't stirred. Eliséo knew they were tired, but he couldn't justify letting them sleep the day away. Not with Vladimir's disappearance and not when the Drakos Mountains were so close.

He woke Rilla first. Her red curls had come loose overnight and were covering most of her face. She looked so peaceful that he didn't want to wake her. She had been through so much already and this day would probably be the worst of all. If Eléna's sources were correct …

"Rilla, wake up." He touched her arm gently. She woke instantly at his touch. Her eyes locked on his, forehead creased.

"What's the matter?"

He shook his head. "It's nothing. Wake the others and get ready to leave."

"Are you angry with me?" The lintep refused to give way. "Is it about what I did in the tunnels?"

The tunnels? Eliséo hurriedly thought to himself. *What had she done in the tunnels?* The memory came rushing back to him. With everything else that had happened since then, he'd completely forgotten.

"I'm not angry with you, Rilla," he reassured her. "That's not to say that I'm not curious how you even thought to do something like that, let alone actually manage it before Stanislav killed me and Ilya."

"I panicked."

"Yes, you said," he replied slowly. "However, Anya was right when she said that the idea and consequent action were not those of a panicked person."

"I know. I just don't know what to tell you." She tapped her teeth together. "I knew you could save yourself but you wouldn't if it meant Ilya died, so I did the only thing I could think of to help you save him. I don't think I even had a plan other than to get my power over to you and do something. Anything."

Eliséo looked at her curiously and not without worry. "The sooner we get you to Illaria, the better. If you can do something like that with a mental tower around your power, I don't know how we're going to keep you alive. Was it difficult?"

Rilla shook her head. "Not really. The worst part was controlling my power immediately after I pulled it out of the tower."

"Wake the others while I scout around." Eliséo shook his head in disbelief as he walked away from her.

* * *

Before they began their journey towards the looming cliff faces that were the Drakos Mountains, Plyke ensured that Shuut ate and drank, convincing her that she needed to stay on her converted sleeping Drag mat until they reached the crystal dragons. Rilla enviously noticed that Shuut had a newfound trust for Plyke – a touch of respect. The banwep disliked Rilla most of the time and had only grudgingly accepted her after the first time Rilla saved her life. She was accepted and nothing more.

Things had only grown worse after they arrived in Silvaren and Shuut discovered who Rilla really was and that she'd purposely concealed all of that from her. It frustrated Rilla that almost every time she forced Shuut's hand, or the banwep discovered a secret about her, it happened in circumstances that were out of her control.

All the good things Rilla had done, the times she had saved their lives with her quick thinking or her powers barely even balanced the score. It wouldn't help that Shuut had already been in the mind snare when Rilla had done her most spectacular magic and would probably not believe what she had done.

She lifted her face to the cool wind, which was whipping her curls around her. Without thinking, she started to plait her hair and hide it under the hat she had taken from their Paradise. It was something she did every morning in the Outworld. Shuut had told her it would be easier to blend in as a boy rather than to stand out with her fiery hair loose to her waist. As she stared up at the sky, she noticed that it looked like rippling water.

"Tika, do you see that?" she asked, as he was walking closest to her. He looked in the direction she pointed and nodded curiously.

"Eliséo," he called out to the elf, still looking up. Eliséo walked over and looked up where Rilla was pointing. A smile spread over his face.

"You found the crystal dragons." He nudged Rilla proudly. "They won't be happy to have been found out."

Rilla shook her head. "I don't see any dragons."

"Neither do I," Tika chimed in. "Just a ripple in the sky. Wait! It's moving down."

The small ripple in the sky soon became a large ripple covering almost their entire field of vision. They watched as it came closer, becoming less a ripple and more like crystal in the sun, sparkling with dazzling colours. Arishen and Plyke had stopped walking and placed Shuut on the ground. The crystal dragon landed between the travelling party and the Drakos Mountains. It was enormous – bigger than Rilla had imagined possible.

"Who are you?" a deep voiced growled.

"Groldor, it cannot be that long since you last saw me to not remember me," Eliséo answered in a calm and level voice.

The dragon sniffed disdainfully. "It's *you*, elf. What do you want?"

Eliséo raised his eyebrows in mock surprise. "This is how you treat the person who has returned your precious Shadow to you?"

"Shuut? Where is she?" The crystal dragon pushed his snout towards the group, finally seeing the banwep lying still on the ground. He turned back to Eliséo, baring his sharp crystal teeth. "What have you done to her?"

"He didn't do anything to her," Tika defended Eliséo angrily. "We risked everything to save her life and bring her to you."

Groldor peered closely at the small boy. "Apologies Master ...?"

"Tika." He furrowed his brow and crossed his arms defensively.

"And can you tell me, Master Tika, how Shuut came to travel with such a large party and be the only injured one?"

Before Tika could answer, Eliséo replied. "Your concern is only that she *was* injured and is now healing. Now surely you do not intend to question us out here in the open, where anyone can listen in. Celtan may not approve of that. Nor will he be impressed that Shadow has returned and you have kept her from him."

Groldor growled deeply, trying to intimidate them all. Rilla thought it may have worked on the Paradisians had they not seen the smug smile on Eliséo's face and started smiling themselves.

"I will take her to him, you follow behind me," the dragon retorted angrily.

"I think not." Eliséo shook his head firmly. "If you take Shadow, you take all of us. Otherwise you can wait for us to walk there with her."

Groldor growled, a deep rumble. Rilla and the boys stepped back as his massive belly began to glow orange. He raised his snout skywards, roared and shot fire into the air. Rilla watched, mesmerised, as the ball of fire in his belly flowed out of the dragon.

Soon, the air above them shimmered. Another dragon was coming to meet them. It was amazing to see the entire sky shimmering like water for the second time.

Once the dragon landed, Rilla realised they were trapped. Groldor was in front of them, blocking the way to the Drakos Mountains. The new dragon had landed behind them, cutting off their retreat. The thought came unbidden. They shouldn't *need* to run away from the dragons. They had come to the dragons because it was what Shuut had wanted.

Why do I feel trapped? she wondered to herself. It surprised her when there wasn't a response from either Elessa or Eliséo. Without meaning to, she found herself looking over at the elf, questioning him with her eyes. He caught her glance sharply, barely shaking his head.

"Loreli," Eliséo greeted the dragon with tight lips. "So glad you've come to bring us to Celtan yourself."

"If I'd known I was being summoned to help *you*, elf, I'd have left Groldor to his own devices." Her voice was clear and sharp, and only fuelled Rilla's uncertainty. For the first time in the Outworld, she felt that she would not be able to keep the boys safe. She knew the crystal dragons had sent Shuut to search for her. She knew they had mapped out her entire life before she was even born. If they realised who she was, would she really be trapped? Could they keep her against her will? Would they use her friends against her? She felt anxious and on the edge of panic.

Suddenly, Arishen was by her side, slipping his hand into hers. The contact brought her back to her senses. She glanced at him and instinctively tried to pull away. He kept his eyes firmly averted and squeezed her hand tightly. Strangely, instead of making her angry, his grip on her hand calmed her. She felt a strange sense of role reversal. In their Paradise, Arishen had always been the one to cause a scene while Rilla had diverted the attention from him. The seer prevented her from drawing attention to herself. She squeezed his hand in return, and gently disentangled her fingers from his before looking back to the dragons.

"The elf is refusing to let Shuut out of his sight, so I'll take him as well as the other girl." Groldor told Loreli. "You can take the boys and that ridiculous contraption."

Rilla looked as he pointed a massive talon towards Shuut's converted sleeping mat. She looked at Eliséo, certain he would be angry with the proposal, but he was looking about nonchalantly.

Rilla walked slowly over towards the elf and the banwep, not wanting to let Groldor touch her in case the crystal dragons had powers like lintep. One touch could be all he needed to break through her carefully built walls. As if he knew exactly what she was thinking, even without using their link with Elessa, Eliséo reached out and placed his bare hand on Groldor's foreleg while positioning himself near Shuut. Reassured by this, Rilla quickly covered the remaining distance and stood beside him.

Once they were ready, Groldor and Loreli picked up each person and settled them carefully between the spikes on their backs. Rilla was glad to be behind Eliséo. As Groldor spread his wings to take flight, she suppressed the urge to squeal and held onto the elf tightly, turning so that the side of her head was flat against his back.

Groldor took flight and Rilla felt her stomach lurch. She held so tightly to Eliséo that her nails bit into his skin and she felt him flinch. Holding onto the spine in front of him with one hand, he loosened her grip on him with the other, squeezing her fingers in reassurance. The air roared past them deafeningly – words would be of no use.

Rilla watched, petrified, as they flew higher than the mountains themselves. The jagged peaks became higher and higher until, quite suddenly, they gave way to a large flat valley. Dotted on the valley floor were dozens of other crystal dragons in every colour she could have imagined, lazing in the sun. From this height, they looked like what Rilla had imagined the originals made by Sascha Vladimirovich and Nadya Grigorevna would have been. With their descent, the image changed, revealing just how large the dragons could be. Groldor and Loreli were large, but they were not the largest in their flight.

Clouds of dust and grass billowed as they descended, wings beating back to smooth their landing. The crystal dragons swiftly placed Shuut on her sleeping mat once more and reached up to allow their passengers to alight from their backs.

A few of the other dragons lazily lifted their heads to see what the commotion was about but all of them seemed to lose interest quickly. Strangely, it made Rilla feel better. The dragons couldn't even tell who Shuut was from a distance, so there was no reason they would catch her out.

Groldor asked Loreli to wait with the travellers while he went to fetch Celtan. The massive clear crystal dragon lay on the ground, curling her body and tail around them. If she had been friendlier, it would have been a touching gesture. As it was, it made Rilla feel more like a prisoner than a guest.

Loreli barely spared a glance for the Paradisians, dividing all of attention between Shuut and Eliséo. Rilla wondered how their apparent hatred of each other had begun. It was clear there was no love lost between the elf and the crystal dragons, and Rilla knew there must be a story behind the strained relationship rather than simple dislike.

Rilla was aching to talk with Eliséo. She had a dozen questions but she knew better than to ask any of them, with or without the aid of Elessa. Instead, the six of them waited in silence. Plyke watched over the sleeping Shuut. Arishen and Tika sat close by the two of them. Rilla had initially started pacing, but soon came to rest by Eliséo's side. Every time she tapped her feet on the ground or drummed her fingers on her arms, he rested a hand on her shoulder.

They were not kept waiting for too long. Groldor soon returned, another dragon following close behind. Rilla studied him as he approached. Whereas Groldor and Loreli were clear crystal and the other dragons in the clearing were mostly pale colours, *this* dragon was a bright sapphire. Ridiculously, it made Rilla inclined to like him more than the others instantly, as if colour could actually make a difference to the beast's personality.

"Celtan." Eliséo inclined his head slightly towards the sapphire dragon. "We're here to return your Shadow."

"So I see." Celtan's voice rolled out smoothly. "Though she is not quite as well as when I last saw her. What happened?"

"We were hoping you might tell us," the elf replied evasively. Rilla knew there was little he could tell the crystal dragon about their adventures that wouldn't reveal something they wished to keep hidden. "We were travelling towards the Drakos Mountains when her mind was attacked. She fell and has only just started to recover."

Celtan eyed Eliséo for a moment. "Groldor, Loreli, resume your watch in the sky. Your duty always comes first."

"Celtan ..." Loreli's temper flared quickly, fire curled in her belly.

"Loreli, I will brook no argument." Celtan bit out a command. "Shuut will still be here when you finish your watch. You can talk to her then, if she's awake."

Groldor growled at Eliséo before taking to the sky. Loreli followed closely behind him and soon they were lost to sight, not even visible as a shimmer.

"Now then, tell me what really happened." Celtan said quietly. "My little Shuut is a clever banwep. How did she find herself burdened with so many companions? How do you know her mind was attacked? And, possibly most importantly, how did she miraculously begin to recover without the aid of the lintep or the dragons?"

Rilla remained silent, as did the boys, too afraid to answer any of those questions. They were all exactly the things they were trying to hide. Eliséo gestured towards them as he spoke to Celtan.

"Your Shadow did indeed find a Paradise, she said you had sent her to do that very thing. However before she could find your prophecy child she was forced to escape with these four. She owed them a life debt, which is why you find her with such a large company."

Rilla realised she was holding her breath.

"I see." The dragon didn't press the point, though Rilla felt certain he must know the truth was being hidden from him. "And how was she attacked?"

"That is the part we are uncertain about." Eliséo glanced at a pale Plyke before continuing. "We had already been attacked twice by groups of four men with plenty of coin on them. It was after that, when we neared the Bramble River, that she began to behave rather strangely. Soon afterwards, she fell to the ground and nothing we did could rouse her. She was unresponsive, and stayed like that for days. We travelled to, and through, Goraburg to bring her to you as swiftly as we could."

"She was healed in Goraburg then?" Celtan asked in what could only be described as a whisper.

"I see you understand how that happened."

"They told me it was lost," Celtan said uneasily.

"They thought it was and it's best that everyone remains under that impression," Eliséo cautioned him. "Vladimir has been exposed as a traitor and fled Goraburg. His followers are to be put to death though I cannot tell if any of them have also escaped."

"Does trouble always follow you, Eliséo?" Celtan asked with a hint of mirth. "It seems we never meet under pleasant circumstances."

"I would have thought you'd be happy that I returned Shadow to you, but if you want me to take her away before she wakes up, that can be arranged." Eliséo smiled for the first time since they'd arrived at the Drakos Mountains. It instantly made Rilla relax.

"You know I would never agree to that. Come now, name your favour, for I know you like your debts paid as soon as they arise." Celtan looked around at Rilla and the other Paradisian. "Each of you may name a favour as you are all responsible for bringing my little Shuut back to me."

Rilla's heart quickened at the thought of a favour from the crystal dragons. She wanted most to ask after her mother but it was too much of a risk. Besides, she had no way of knowing if Nyssa had ever contacted them again after abandoning her in the Paradise.

"My favour is actually carried forward from Lady Eléna," Eliséo spoke confidently.

"Lady?" Celtan asked in surprise. "What happened?"

"*Lady* Eléna has stepped aside for her daughter, Queen Liessa," the elf replied easily. "She is of the understanding that her dear friend Nyssa is residing with you and would like me to pass on a message to her."

Celtan hissed sharply, the boys flinched back as Rilla did. Eliséo tilted his chin defiantly and stood his ground. "You are lucky Shuut is still sleeping."

"No, old dragon, I believe *you* are lucky she is still sleeping. Not that it will make any difference once Nyssa sees her."

"I could refuse to bring her to you," Celtan threatened.

Rilla's head reeled. Her mother was here.

"I could slit Shadow's throat before you even realise I've moved," Eliséo retaliated.

"You wouldn't."

"Try me." The elf raised an eyebrow, hand on the hilt of his sword. Celtan growled, spreading his wings, and took off into the sky. He was already half way across the clearing before the Paradisians let out their breath collectively.

"You wouldn't really have killed her, would you?" Tika asked nervously. "I mean, she's your friend."

"Shadow has no friends, Tika." Eliséo turned towards him. "But that would not have caused me to kill her. These dragons manipulate people. Your Shadow lived with them for many years and is as dear to the dragons as anyone ever was, but she has also been manipulated more than most and is completely in their power. Celtan would never risk her safety for the sake of avoiding an uncomfortable situation. I was simply calling his bluff."

"Why doesn't he want you to talk Nyssa?" Rilla barely trusted her voice as she said her mother's name.

"You will see soon enough, Rilla." Eliséo avoided her eyes. "Now, we do not have much time. Do not answer any questions unless they are directed specifically to you. Plyke, we may need to tell them that you are part lintep to facilitate our departure. Tika, Arishen, if the offer of a favour still stands, ask for a horse for all of us. Time is of the essence now and we need to get to Illaria as soon as possible." Finally, he turned to Rilla. "Do not breath a whisper of your name to them. If anyone asks your name," he paused meaningfully.

"I am Karinya," Rilla finished his sentence woodenly. It felt like she was back in the Paradise again. No one was to call her by name, no one was even to mention it. The only difference was they now had a false name to call her.

She knew that meant she wasn't even able to tell Nyssa who she was. She would have to pretend not to know her – not to ask her the one question that burned inside of her. Rilla barely remembered what she looked like. The last time she'd seen her mother was just after they arrived in the Paradise. Nyssa had barely heard the rules before she kissed Rilla goodbye and walked out of her life, leaving her with Erton.

"I am truly sorry," Eliséo whispered as he leaned in close to her. "It really is for the best that they do not realise you who are. Whatever happens with Nyssa, *please* try not to react more strongly than the others. Do you understand?"

Rilla nodded. The urgency in his voice scared her. Worse, he drew her in for a quick embrace, saying, "I would have told you if I was certain she was alive. I just didn't want to give Shadow another reason to hate you. I'm sorry."

Rilla pulled away from him shakily. "What are you talking about? What's going on?"

"I'm so sorry." He pulled away from her, moving closer to Shuut. Celtan's wingbeats grew louder as he approached. Nyssa must have been nearby for him to return so quickly. Rilla looked over at Eliséo and Shuut. *What does he know that he's too scared to tell me?*

She had no time to guess before the massive sapphire dragon landed beside them, landing so that Shuut was shielded from Nyssa's vision by the rest of them. Nyssa jumped down from Celtan's back without any help and walked calmly over to Eliséo, her wavy brown hair flowing almost to her waist.

"Greetings Ambassador." She bowed her head ever so slightly. "Celtan tells me you have a message from Lady Eléna."

"Greetings Nyssa." Eliséo bowed his head. "Lady Eléna sends her best wishes. We had heard rumours that you were dead."

"Dead? How did that rumour get started?" Nyssa laughed.

"More recently, rumours that you were indeed alive and living with the crystal dragons were reported," Eliséo continued as though he hadn't been interrupted.

"I'll bet that rubbed her up the wrong way, didn't it?" When Eliséo didn't return her banter or even smile, Rilla saw Nyssa's grey eyes lose their sparkle as her expression became serious. "What is your message, Ambassador?"

"Your daughter, Shadow, recently paid us a visit. She has been under the same misunderstanding as we were that you were, in fact, dead."

"Shuut is alive?" Nyssa asked incredulously. "How is that even possible?"

"She is alive and recovering, as you can see." Eliséo stood aside and motioned the Paradisians to do likewise.

"Shuut!" Nyssa screamed her name hysterically as she ran to her daughter's side. "Shuut, wake up! What's wrong with her?" She knelt and grabbed Shuut's shoulder, shaking her almost violently. Plyke placed a hand on Shuut's opposite shoulder, firmly pushing her back to the ground to stop Nyssa from hurting her.

Rilla watched Nyssa in shocked silence. She had almost fallen when Nyssa had run past her. Eliséo was instantly by her side, holding her up. She barely even noticed his touch as she stared at Nyssa and Shuut and then Plyke as he interceded. Her own mother hadn't even spared her a glance. She was nothing compared to her other daughter. Her other *daughter*. That meant the unthinkable – Shuut was her sister. The shock was too much for her, and she sagged against Eliséo's side.

Eyes wild, Nyssa looked up at Plyke before turning on Celtan. "You! You told me she was dead. Sixteen years you've let me believe that. Is that how long she's believed I was dead?"

"Nyssa." Celtan reared up defensively. "You have to understand that it was the only way to fulfil the prophecy."

The mention of the prophecy snapped Rilla back to her senses. They were talking about her now.

"What are you talking about?" Nyssa asked. "What difference could it have made to the prophecy for me to know that Shuut was alive and well?"

Celtan scratched his snout with a long talon, and it seemed to Rilla that he was uncomfortable. "The prophecy child needs to be a full blooded lintep. It didn't take us long to realise that one of Rilla's descendants would be our best chance to create her. So, when you came to us with your daughter asking for shelter, it was beyond our wildest dreams that we might be able to control the prophecy."

"And by that you mean, of course, to lie to everyone around you for the delusional hope that you could manipulate something that is out of your control." Eliséo received a savage growl for his interruption.

"What use is a prophecy child when no one knows who they are? Better to have everything in place so that we can find them at the right time."

"I still don't understand why you told me that my daughter was dead," Nyssa replied stonily.

"You agreed readily enough to the plan, but we needed another lintep." The dragon hesitated. "You are aware of the lintep tradition that any union requires both lintep to take existing children of the other under their wing. It simply wouldn't have worked for you to take Shuut. Erton would never have agreed to any of it with her as a factor. So, we ..."

"Lied to my face and tore my heart to shreds so that I could give you a full-blooded descendant of Rilla."

Celtan didn't immediately answer. Nothing he could say would make what the dragons had done any less horrendous. "We always looked out for her."

"You looked out for her by telling her I was dead and then throwing her back into the Outworld alone? Look at her!" Nyssa screamed at the dragon. "*This* is how you look out for her?"

"*That* was out of our control," Celtan replied defensively. "How could we possibly know that she would be burdened with so many Paradisians and that her mind would be attacked in one journey away from us?"

"To be fair, you *did* intend for her to be burdened with at least one Paradisian. You knew exactly which Paradise Nyssa had left your prophecy child in and you sent Shadow to find it."

Rilla could see that Eliséo was trying to break the dragon's hold over Nyssa and Shadow, if that last was even possible.

"Tell me, did Shadow even know that you'd sent her to find her own sister?"

The dragon was at a loss for words, his plans to control the prophecy crumbling before him. "We did what we thought was best. If Erton does not teach the child to control her powers, then she must make it to Illaria in the next few months."

"My Rilla will be sixteen years in a few weeks, not a few months," Nyssa almost whispered. "How could I be so stupid to leave her with Erton? What if he didn't teach her enough? Unless she's already on her way to Illaria, she might die."

"She might not be as powerful as we imagined she'd be." Celtan spoke gently, as if to calm her. "Perhaps she will only be in danger of losing her powers."

"If you think I'd believe that for moment, you're not as clever as I always thought you were. How could any full-blooded child of mine be anything less than spectacular?" Nyssa was almost in tears.

Rilla was so confused. Her mother was talking about her like she wasn't there. How could she not realise how close she was? Did she regret leaving her for any other reason than the fact that Erton might not have taught her enough? How could she not have known what kind of man Erton was and that he never even told her that she was a lintep?

"Nyssa, you are welcome to join us on our travels." Eliséo looked to her mother. "We can escort you across the Bramble River and then send you on your way to find your daughter."

Nyssa looked at him with a mixture of relief and anger. "Only if we take Shuut with us. I will *never* leave her again."

"You can't take her," Celtan pleaded. "She isn't well."

"She is healing quickly enough," Eliséo replied readily. "And I believe you owe the rest of my companions a favour."

"Horses!" Tika squeaked.

"We'd like a horse for each of us if you have any." Arishen glared at Tika. "A wagon for Shuut as well."

The dragon was stunned into silence. Rilla thought it was because his playthings were being taken away from him, and he was being asked to speed them on their way.

"You will have what you wish for on the morrow." He bent his head sadly as he spread his wings to depart. The Paradisians waited until they thought he was out of earshot before talking openly.

"Is it safe for us to stay so long?" Plyke asked the question that was burning in Rilla's mind. She didn't trust herself to speak. If Nyssa figured out who she was before they left, she might never escape the crystal dragons. Eliséo spared a quick glance towards Rilla before answering.

"We don't have a choice. We have no plausible reason to leave any sooner."

"You have me," Plyke offered cautiously. "You could always tell them we need to get to Illaria as soon as possible for my sake."

"We could," Eliséo conceded, "but that might change Celtan's mind about everything. Instead of horses, he could offer to fly Nyssa wherever she wants and fly us to Illaria. That would certainly be faster, but we'd be in more danger."

Nyssa had stayed by Shuut's side, and Rilla watched as she gently stroked the hair from Shuut's face as her daughter's eyes fluttered open and shut in confusion. The tone of voice of their discussion and the repetition of danger aroused her, and she looked up at them in suspicion.

"Why are any of you in danger from the dragons? And why do you need to reach Illaria?"

Rilla looked to Eliséo for an answer, not trusting herself to speak. The elf did not answer immediately. Rilla knew it was a difficult subject to broach. Nyssa's previous cries had been loud enough for several of the crystal dragons resting in the clearing to raise their head attentively and look in their direction.

To Rilla's surprise, Arishen walked confidently up to Nyssa and spoke just loudly enough for his companions to hear. "I am a human seer. I've had visions of your daughter. I know where she is but she's in danger. We need to get to her quickly, but ..." He bit his lip, feigning uncertainty. "If the dragons realise we have this knowledge, they'll force us to take them to her and then manipulate and control her the same way they have Shuut."

Nyssa's eyes were wide with shock, but she didn't see the small smile on the Paradisians' faces as they realised what Arishen had done.

Rilla watched as Nyssa looked to Eliséo. "How important are the horses and wagon?"

"If we're to travel as swiftly as possible, we need at least one horse. Shadow is in no state to be walking as far and as fast as we must. With one horse, she can ride most of the day and build up her strength."

Rilla sometimes forgot that Eliséo was an ambassador, trained to think quickly in dangerous situations. He hadn't even hesitated before answering. He must have already calculated this when telling the Paradisians to request horses.

"One horse I can get." Nyssa nodded to herself. "They owe me that much and more."

She motioned them away from her and raised her hands high above her head. A moment of concentration later and a stream of fire sprouted from her fingertips, streaming straight up into the air. It only lasted a moment, not even long enough for the sleepy dragons surrounding them to notice.

Rilla stared at her mother in wonder. Such a wonderful display of magic was more than she had ever dared hope to see.

Before she could try to figure out how it was done, Groldor and Loreli appeared in the clearing. One look at Nyssa cradling Shuut's head and the crystal dragons knew what had happened. Groldor shuffled uncomfortably.

"Where's Celtan?"

"I was displeased with him." Nyssa didn't elaborate. "You owe me a favour. You will take the seven of us to the eastern border of the Drakos Mountains. As a parting gift, I request the swiftest horse in your herd. Shuut failed in the mission you sent her on, so I will need to find Rilla myself."

"Has Celtan approved this plan?" Loreli asked cautiously.

Nyssa stared at her with stone grey eyes. "Celtan holds no power over us anymore. He understands that neither Shuut nor I will *ever* do his bidding again. Now find a swift horse and return here instantly."

Loreli growled angrily as she spread her wings and took off.

Groldor's eyes hadn't strayed from Nyssa and Shuut, his gaze shifting between one and the other. "I haven't even had a chance to speak with her. Can you not wait until she wakes?" His voice betrayed a deep sense of loss.

"When she wakes up and sees me, she will know that you lied to her about the most important things in her life. Do you really want to speak to her when she is so angry with you?" Nyssa shook her head, knowingly. "Better for her temper to cool away from the Drakos Mountains so that if she ever meets you again, she won't try to kill you."

"Will you tell her I'm sorry?" Groldor asked quietly. "I never agreed with Celtan on that count. I didn't want to hurt her."

Nyssa's expression softened. "I can tell her you said that, but she won't necessarily believe me. It will be a long time, if ever, before she forgives you and comes back."

"And you?"

"Celtan has lost me forever," Nyssa replied coldly. "He told me one daughter was dead to make me have a second one, knowing he would ask me to leave her behind to come back and tell him where she was hidden. He forced me to give up both of my daughters."

Rilla listened to the conversation in silence. She was discovering what she'd always wondered about without asking any questions. She had been taken to live in a Paradise for no reason other than that it was what the crystal dragons had asked of Nyssa. Her mother had abandoned her in Erton's care for the same reason. The manipulations of dragons were why her life had been so difficult. That her mother had blindly followed what they told her to do only made matters worse.

Had Eliséo known all of this? He had said they only recently heard that Nyssa was alive and didn't know if it was true. Had they truly been fooled just like Shuut?

They can't have thought Nyssa was dead the entire time. Lady Eléna told her that they had passed through Silvaren on their way to the Paradise – that's when she'd given Rilla the tree pendant and leaves.

Instinctively, she reached up to touch the pendant. If Nyssa saw it, she couldn't help but know who she was. She turned away from her mother and bumped into Eliséo. Hurriedly, she hid her pendant under her shirt and buttoned it up higher to keep it hidden. He noticed her panicked eyes and gave her a reassuring nod.

"Did you know all of that?" she whispered to him. They were as far from the others as it was possible to get without arousing suspicion. There was little chance anyone would overhear and she was desperate to know more.

"Not now," he whispered back as her eyes filled with tears. "I promise I'll tell you everything I knew as soon as we're safe." He risked a comforting touch of her cheek. She tilted her head towards his hand as he drew it away. Rilla doubted Nyssa or Groldor would think anything of it if they saw, but better to avoid their notice if possible.

Loreli returned with a chestnut stallion cupped between her claws. Rilla marvelled at how calm the horse was in the clutches of a dragon. He must have lived in the Drakos Mountains from a very young age to be so comfortable with them.

With minimal fuss, the Paradisians, Eliséo and Nyssa were seated between the spikes on Groldor and Loreli's backs. Groldor gently picked up Shuut and her converted sleeping mat, cradling the banwep carefully in his claws while Loreli clutched the now restive stallion. Before any of the other dragons roused themselves from sleep, the two clear crystal dragons were up in the sky, flying east towards the mid-morning sun.

Rilla fared a little better on this flight. If a horse could do it calmly, so could she. They flew over the high peaks and across lower peaks and valleys until they came to foothills. It was the eastern border of the Drakos Mountains. Groldor started the descent with Loreli following close behind him. Together, they landed carefully on the soft grass. Their passengers were barely off their backs before Nyssa dismissed the crystal dragons with a wave of her hand.

Groldor hung his head sadly and took off without a sound. Loreli growled an empty threat before following him. Nyssa watched them disappear into the sky, until there wasn't even a shimmer to betray them. Finally, she turned to Arishen.

"Where is my daughter?"

Chapter Fifty-Three – Sisters

Arishen was taken by surprise. Rilla knew hadn't thought this far ahead. The seer looked over to Eliséo, and Nyssa followed his gaze.

"You said you knew where my daughter is and that she's in trouble," Nyssa pressed him. "If she's in danger, we don't have time for you to check everything with the ambassador. Where is she?"

"She's right there," Arishen pointed to Rilla. Nyssa looked at her uncomprehendingly.

"Rilla?" Nyssa hesitantly took one step forward. "Is that really you?"

Unsure of what to do, Rilla took off her hat to let her fiery red hair down. She unbuttoned her shirt to reveal the tree pendant, just in case Nyssa didn't believe them. All doubt seemed to flee Nyssa's mind. She raced over to Rilla and almost knocked her over with the force of her embrace. Rilla stood still, shocked by the sudden affection from a woman she barely remembered.

"Hello Nyssa," she said quietly.

"Hello *Nyssa*?" her mother asked as she pulled back from the hug. "That's all you have to say to me after so long?"

Rilla tapped her teeth together in annoyance. "Well, what do *you* have to say to *me* after you abandoned me to the care of a murderer?"

"Murderer?" Nyssa looked at her as though she had lost her mind. "What do you mean? I left you in the Paradise with Erton, your father."

"You left me with a man who refused to let anyone utter my name and so forced me into a life of alienation." Rilla looked at Nyssa coldly. "The man who became our leader and ordered so many murders it would make you sick to hear. Is that the father you mean?"

Nyssa looked from Rilla to the others. The boys avoided her gaze. "Rilla, I'm sorry. He wasn't like that when I left you both there."

"Perhaps if had known him better before the crystal dragons asked you to mate with him, you'd have discovered his true nature for yourself."

"Now listen here young lady," Nyssa raised her voice, but suddenly fell silent at the sound of Shuut voice.

"Nyssa?" Shuut mumbled as she struggled up on one elbow. Plyke and Nyssa were instantly by her side. Rilla ached at being so easily forgotten.

"My little girl!" Nyssa cried and hugged Shuut to her. Unlike Rilla, Shuut returned the embrace as though she was holding on for dear life.

"You're alive!" the banwep repeated over and over, tears streaming down her cheeks. "They told me you were dead."

"They told me *you* were dead." Nyssa sobbed as she held ever tighter to Shuut. Rilla watched on enviously as her mother and half-sister clung to each other. She'd already made Nyssa angry. Now it was just a matter of time before Shuut discovered that they'd only been told these lies so that Rilla could be born and manipulated alongside them. Now she understood why Eliséo had kept apologising. He knew Shuut would despise her from that moment onwards. She looked over at the elf, pleading with him to help her.

He nodded and bought her at least a little more time. "Shadow, do you think you can manage to ride if we sit you up on this horse?"

Nyssa disentangled herself from her daughter. Shuut looked from Eliséo to the saddled horse and nodded. "But where are we going?"

"To Illaria. To the lintep." His answer was enough to distract her. Shuut had always wanted to go to Illaria, to meet the lintep.

"But we need to take Rilla to the crystal dragons … don't we?" she mumbled uncertainly, shaking her head. With a sudden moment of clarity, she turned to Nyssa. "Why did the dragons tell me you were dead?" Rilla froze.

"That's not important right now." Eliséo spoke with authority. "We need to get to Illaria before Rilla and Plyke's powers peak. Can you ride?"

It was the mention of Plyke's name that encouraged Shuut. Her eyes brightened as she searched for him and realised her was by her side. He and Nyssa helped her to her feet and together they led her over to the stallion. Tika held the reins and talked softly to the horse to keep him calm and steady as Shuut struggled into the saddle. Even that small effort drained her of energy. She slumped forward onto his chestnut neck and held onto his mane with weak fingers. At a nod from Tika, Eliséo turned and led the party in the direction of Illaria.

They walked in silence for a long while. Eliséo led the way with Rilla a little behind him. Plyke and Nyssa walked either side of Shuut, as Tika steadily led the horse by the reins. Arishen brought up the rear. Away from Nyssa's attention, Rilla retied her hair and shoved it under her hat, avoiding the constant looks she could feel Arishen cast her way. She knew he was worried about her, but she didn't want to talk to him right now. The person she most wanted to talk to was Eliséo and, knowing that, the elf was staying as far away from her as he could.

He had promised to answer any questions she had about her mother, but she couldn't ask them now with Shuut and Nyssa so close. All Rilla really wanted to do was to fade away. Fade into the background, but there weren't any trees to fade into, only grass. Long wavy grass. Swaying back and forth.

"Rilla?" she heard Arishen's voice from a distance but didn't answer him. She just wanted to be left alone. "Rilla!" The voice was now a cry of fear. Rilla shook her head to find everyone staring at her.

"What?" she replied angrily.

"You disappeared," Arishen told her quietly.

Her temper melted instantly into a smile. She hadn't really even been trying and she'd managed it, even with her wall still mostly up. Her smile vanished as she saw Eliséo's look of disapproval. She frowned. Hadn't he said she'd need to practice until things happened more easily with her wall in place?

"Erton taught you to use your powers." Nyssa nodded, pleased with the apparent result.

Rilla turned coldly towards her. "Erton taught me *nothing*. He didn't even tell me I was a lintep."

"Then how?" Nyssa's voice trailed off uncertainly.

Rilla was too angry and bitter to feel anything else towards her mother. "Eliséo, how are we going to get back across the river?" she asked the only question that might divert Nyssa's attention from her. Before he had a chance to reply, Shuut sat up a little straighter in her saddle looking completely bewildered.

"Back across the river? Where are we?"

"Don't you remember what happened?" It was Plyke who replied. Shuut shook her head.

"I barely remember anything. I know you stopped me from dying, but the rest is … a hazy."

Eliséo looked over at the newest member of their travelling party. "Nyssa will probably want to know the story as well. What's the last thing you clearly remember, Shadow?"

Shuut closed her eyes. "I remember telling Rilla to stop using her powers to fade in and out of focus." She turned to try to find Rilla and almost fell out of the saddle. Plyke and Nyssa helped balance her again.

"That was just a few minutes before you fell." Tika took it upon himself to continue the story. "After that, Eliséo got Rilla and Plyke to help with his mist bubble until we got to the river." He explained, in as much detail as possible, everything that had happened until they reached Goraburg, until eventually he hesitated. "Then we travelled through the tunnels to the dragons where we found Nyssa and … here we are," he finished awkwardly.

Shuut was silent for a while longer. Eventually, she ventured a question. "Do we know who attacked me? Or why?"

"No," Eliséo answered firmly. "We don't even know if you were the intended target."

"And since they found us once, when we were a smaller company and all fit and healthy, it is quite likely they will find us again."

No one spoke. Eventually, Shuut slumped back onto her horse's long neck.

Rilla had watched Nyssa carefully during Tika's story. Her mother had often looked back at her enquiringly.

"If Erton didn't teach you to use your powers, who did?" Nyssa half turned to face Rilla, being careful to keep Shuut steady with one hand. When Rilla didn't answer, she called Eliséo over to steady Shuut. The elf reluctantly took her place with a warning glance at Rilla.

She looked back at him utterly confused. Surely Nyssa was one of the only people in the Outworld she should be able to trust. As Nyssa walked towards her, Rilla's mind filled with an image of a younger Nyssa walking towards her in the Paradise, coming to say goodbye. Anger and pain welled up inside of her. Her mother should have been someone who kept her safe, but she had been the one to put her in more danger than anyone else. She had left Rilla in the care of Erton.

Nyssa tried to catch Arishen's eye, but Rilla noticed and immediately reached out a hand and caught his fingers. His face flushed at the unexpected contact, he understood the gesture and kept his eyes firmly averted from Nyssa, staying close by Rilla's side. Nyssa sighed and repeated her question.

"Who taught you to use your powers?"

"Ratchin," Rilla replied without any elaboration.

"And who is Ratchin?" Nyssa asked through gritted teeth.

"A lintep we met in Turon." Rilla almost took pleasure in the difficulty she was causing her mother.

"And she taught you how to heal, disappear and lend your strength to an elf's spell?"

Rilla looked over at Eliséo. Any truthful answer was only going to cause problems. What Rilla did was a dangerous way to experiment with magic, but it was the only way she had. Ratchin had warned her not to overextend herself and Rilla had tried her best to follow those instructions.

"More or less," Rilla answered evasively.

Nyssa huffed and shook her head. "More or less," she repeated, with her hands on her hips. "And did she 'more or less' teach you to be disrespectful to your elders or was that someone else?"

Rilla tightened her grip on Arishen's fingers and glared angrily at her mother, refusing to say another word. Nyssa stormed off towards Eliséo, and Rilla let out a deep breath in relief.

* * *

"I don't know what's wrong with that girl, but if she's anywhere near as powerful as it sounds she is, we won't make it to Illaria before her power peaks. I'm going to have to start her training myself."

Eliséo missed a step as he moved aside for Nyssa to resume her place by Shadow's side.

"You aren't a lintep mistress," Eliséo reminded her. "Only a master or mistress can help her now."

"If some unknown lintep from Turon can teach her to heal and disappear, I'm certain it can't be difficult to teach her the basics."

Eliséo didn't know Nyssa as well as he knew Shadow and was coming to know Rilla, but he understood there was no way he was going to change her mind on this. "If you're going to train one, you may as well train them both. We don't know how powerful Plyke is, but even the loss of his power would be disastrous."

"From the sounds of it, he isn't as powerful as Rilla."

"Actually, we don't know that at all." Eliséo was broaching subjects that he knew were dangerous with Nyssa. She and Kora had very different opinions about lintep magic. That was common knowledge in Illaria. He was certain Kora would not be at all impressed that Nyssa was forced to teach her son, but it was their best chance of helping Plyke retain powers and possibly save his life. "Plyke was taught at a young age to build a wall around his powers. Whatever he does is through that wall. It's possible he's even more powerful than Rilla, but we won't know that until we get to Illaria and they can both safely take down their walls."

"Rilla has a wall too?" Eliséo cursed his slip of the tongue. He hadn't meant to reveal that.

When he didn't reply, she asked him, "Who taught her that?"

"I did," Plyke replied from the other side of Shadow.

"You?" Nyssa, craned her neck to see Plyke over the horse. "But you're just a child yourself. How could you possibly teach her that? And who taught you?"

Plyke shrugged. "A lady in our Paradise."

"Does this lady have a name?" Nyssa asked curiously. "She must have been a very skilful lintep to teach you that by herself."

Eliséo hoped against hope that Plyke wouldn't name his mother. Nyssa seemed to be asking all the right questions in such a way that the boy could not avoid answering. If Plyke told her it was Kora, she would probably ask everything she could about her, even to the point of knowing they had to have been in the very same Paradise for a short period of time. Eliséo held his breath.

"Just someone in our Paradise," Plyke answered casually. "I don't think she was all that powerful, she only taught me to build a wall to protect myself against ..." Plyke bit off the end of his sentence.

"Protect yourself against what?"

"Not 'what', but who." It was Tika who answered, looking back over his shoulder at the lintep. "Protect himself against Erton."

"Why would Plyke need to protect himself against Erton? He's so young, he couldn't possibly be a threat to an adult lintep."

Tika motioned for Eliséo to take over the reins and lead the horse as he went to walk beside to Nyssa. "Erton became the Paradise leader when we fairly young, maybe when we were four or five years. It was only a year or so afterwards that the first death happened. Arishen can probably tell you about most. He used to dream about them."

Nyssa glanced back at the seer who was now walking apart from Rilla. He paled slightly at her attention and crossed his arms defensively.

"Anyhow, we didn't really know what was happening then, but the older Paradisians did and they tried to protect to the younger ones who might be in danger. Anyone who spoke out against Erton or showed that they were different, or had any sort of unnatural gifts were taken care of. It started out as accidents – a horse rearing backwards over a stable hand, a fisherman getting tangled in his nets and drowning. But everyone knew what was happening.

"Our Paradise went from being a sanctuary to a death trap for so many. If Erton had suspected that Plyke was even part lintep, he wouldn't have hesitated in having him murdered."

Nyssa's mouth gaped open. "Did anyone in the Paradise know that Erton himself is a lintep?"

"No," Tika answered darkly. "We thought he hated the lintep and magic of all kinds. He made us all believe that the lintep were dangerous and would kill humans as soon as look at them. The elves weren't much better in his opinion, and he made us believe the crystal dragons and karliki didn't really exist."

Nyssa shook her head angrily. "All of this to hide the prophecy child that he willingly helped to create for the crystal dragons."

Eliséo motioned Tika back to the reins, with a comment back to Nyssa. "I do not think he was trying to prevent the prophecy, if that is any consolation. He did not stop Rilla from leaving the Paradise with Shadow. If he had wanted to make sure the Paradises were never destroyed, he would have had her killed too."

"He couldn't kill me," Rilla called out from behind. "I gave him every reason to. Everyone must have remembered that I was his daughter and I did not conform like all his other sheep. It drove him mad. The only chance he had to get rid of me without anyone suspecting why was when we chose Shuut as our mentor. He tried to convince Shuut not to take us so that he could legitimately execute us all. So, to repay a life debt, she took us into the Outworld with her."

Shuut roused at the repeated mention of her name. "You know, none of this would have happened if you had told me your real name to begin with. I would have taken you straight to the crystal dragons instead of going to Silvaren first."

"That's not fair, Shuut," Rilla responded hotly. "If Lady Eléna hadn't told you, we might still be fine. It was only after you found out who I was that we started being attacked. In any case, if we didn't have Eliséo with us then, we probably all would have died. And you would never have found out that your mother was alive."

"Your mother?" Nyssa picked up on her choice of words. Rilla shook her head angrily.

"You are my mother," Shuut pointed out in confusion.

"Yes but ..." Nyssa bit her lip. "You do know about Rilla, don't you?

"That she's the prophecy child?" Shuut nodded. "Of course I do."

"Well, yes, but that's not quite what I meant." Nyssa tapped her teeth together in that same manner that Rilla had. "You do know that I'm Rilla's mother too, don't you?"

Shuut sat up bolt upright in her saddle. "What?!"

"I thought you knew." Nyssa went pale. "Didn't anyone tell you?"

"Exactly who was supposed to tell me that?" Shuut's voice was dangerously quiet. "The crystal dragons? Is that who? The ones who told me you were dead ..." Shuut looked over at Rilla, her eyes drifting to the other Paradisians before focussing once more on her mother. "Rilla is almost sixteen years old. The dragons told me you were dead when I was nine years old and I'm not yet twenty-six. Exactly how long did you wait to have Rilla after they told you I was dead?"

"I'm sorry Shuut." Nyssa was in tears. They had all stopped walking by now. This wasn't quite the reaction the Paradisians were expecting, Eliséo assumed. None of them had expected Shuut to be angry with Nyssa. "The dragons ..."

"The dragons had you more in their grip than they ever had me!" Shuut was furious. "How could you betray me like that? You replaced me with a prophecy child as soon as you possibly could and with Erton of all people, like my father wasn't bad enough."

Shuut used the last of her energy to kick her horse forward, leaving her mother standing alone and looking lost, while Eliséo quickly turned to get in front of the banwep's horse to lead the way.

* * *

Rilla held her breath as she walked past the still figure of her mother and quickened her pace to overtake the others so she could walk next to Eliséo. The elf looked over at her, his eyes a dull, empty grey, as she fell silently into step with him.

They walked in silence for hours, every now and then allowing Shuut the chance to walk a little to rebuild the strength in her leg muscles. Rilla stayed at the front of the company, unwilling to be separated from Eliséo. As much as she hated not having chosen to be bound to Elessa, Rilla was missing that link now. She had almost completely cut herself off from that connection and didn't know how to find it again. Elessa and Eliséo had managed to break through to her, but she couldn't seem to talk to them unless they had already made the link for her. All morning she'd been searching within her tower for the smallest hint of Elessa and Eliséo.

It had taken her hours, but she'd finally found something. She didn't know if it would work or not, but she tried anyway. It was the memory of her swirling red flowers on Elessa's red tinged branch. She held onto it tightly and shouted as loudly as she could in her mind.

Eliséo! Can you hear me?

The next thing she knew, the elf was on his knees holding his head in his hands, eyes tightly shut. She instantly let go of the memory and bent down to see what was wrong. The others had called out in alarm when he went down. Before panic spread, Eliséo calmly got to his feet.

"Not to worry, it was just my tree playing games with me." He smiled at them reassuringly. "She forgets that distance and time away doesn't make her voice grow any softer. She almost deafens me every time we're separated."

Rilla knew the others had no idea what the bond between an elf and a tree was like. Eliséo could have told them anything and they would have believed him.

Did I do that? She asked him gently, once they were both facing forward again. If the link really was working, her eyes would be glowing a faint green as his would be shining silver.

Yes, little one. You did. It wasn't Eliséo who answered her. Rilla smiled as she felt the tree embrace her mind. *You finally found your way back to us. Next time, do it more gently or you won't just knock him to his feet.*

Funny how I almost feel safer now.

You're far from safe Rilla. Don't forget that, Eliséo reminded her. *Until we reach Illaria, your life is in danger and I'm not just talking about when your power peaks or any attackers we may find along the way.*

How else can I possibly be in danger? Rilla asked.

Nyssa brings danger with her wherever she goes. Eliséo refused to elaborate further.

* * *

It was getting dark and they would need to find a safe place to make camp. Groldor and Loreli had left them in the foothills of the Drakos Mountains but, unlike the Lesa Forest, these foothills weren't covered in trees. They had been walking through tall grass all day long.

Just like the grass Rilla had disappeared into, Eliséo thought to himself.

You almost sound annoyed with her, Elessa remarked.

She doesn't realise what she's doing half the time. Eliséo sighed inwardly. *I can't tell if she's the most powerful lintep I've ever met or if she just learns in a different way because she wasn't raised by them. Plyke could easily be more powerful than her when his wall comes down, but he'll probably have a harder time learning the basic skills because he's purposely been taught not to use his power.*

So, what you're trying to tell me is that you're worried about how the lessons with Nyssa will go. Eliséo didn't answer, but he knew Elessa could feel his chest tighten at the thought. *Just because Nyssa is her mother doesn't mean that Rilla will turn into her. Look how different she is from her father.*

Yes, but Erton didn't want her for long. Eliséo shook his head imperceptibly. *Nyssa has been dreaming about being reunited with Rilla for years. She's bound to try her hardest to reshape her daughter to make up for the loss of so much time.*

Worrying won't stop that from happening, Elessa pointed out. *Together, we can put an end to any silly notions Nyssa tries to plant in her mind.*

Eliséo found a boulder larger than most of the others scattered throughout the long grass and called a halt for the day. The Paradisians set out to make camp with

288

Nyssa and Shuut watching while Eliséo scouted out the surrounding area. Tika led their horse in a large circle, flattening the grass, until there was enough ground for the sleeping mats to be laid out with room to spare.

* * *

Rilla waited impatiently for Eliséo to return from scouting. She itched to be doing something. She walked over to the boys, motioning to her swords. "We should probably start our sparring practices again. Who wants to pair up with me?"

"I want to use my bow and arrows," Tika declined politely.

"You'll just lose your arrows in this grass," Shuut called out sleepily from her mat, eyes still shut. "Don't use that as an excuse not to spar hand to hand with someone."

Sighing, Tika set down his bow and quiver and pulled out his dagger. He and Rilla moved to one side of the clearing, well apart from Arishen and Plyke. Rilla drew her swords, and waited for Tika to face her. She half crouched and waited for him to pounce. Seconds before his dagger bit into her skin, she crossed her swords in front of her to catch the blade and twisted it out of his hand. She waited for him to pick it up before they started again.

It wasn't going to be a fair fight even setting the difference of weapons aside. Rilla hadn't even pulled her power over to cover her swords, but she was still more skilled than Tika. Her mind wandered as they sparred to the point where she was barely concentrating on the bout. If Shuut had been watching, she would have reprimanded Rilla for the tiny errors that caused her to make.

Eliséo ran into the clearing. His sudden appearance startled them. Tika turned to face him, and Rilla stopped mid-attack as she saw his attention shift. Arishen was not as quick as the lintep to halt his attack on Plyke, who turned, leaving himself open to Arishen's daggers. He screamed as one of the daggers sank into his left shoulder.

Rilla dropped her swords and rushed to Plyke's side as Arishen pulled his dagger out. It wasn't a deep wound, but would need healing all the same. Without a second thought, Rilla placed her hand over Plyke's shoulder, grabbing Arishen's shoulder at the same time. The pain didn't hit her instantly, her wall still numbed her senses. By the time she felt it, a small tear had already opened up in her own shoulder. Cursing her stupidity, Rilla spread the pain throughout her body and then through to Arishen. Once that was done, she let go of the seer and placed her free hand over Plyke's right shoulder. Arishen's dagger was sharp and thin, and had left a clean cut. Rilla lightly stitched the muscles back together, trying to replicate the structure of Plyke's other shoulder. She did only as much as she thought they could get away with before pulling away. They were back in the Outworld now, in open grasslands. She couldn't leave herself weak for fear of an attack.

Plyke slowly got to his feet from where he had fallen on his stomach. He worked his arm around in a circle, testing his shoulder. A smile spread over his face as he turned around. Finding Rilla behind him, he engulfed her in a hug. She shrugged him off with a smile.

"Nice work, Rilla, but next time, wait for me to shield your weapons before you start sparring," Eliséo chided them.

289

"That's all?" Nyssa's panicked voice rose above them. "They could have killed each other and that's your warning to them?"

"They're not so unskilled as you may think, Nyssa." Eliséo turned to her. "None of them would actually follow through on a killing strike."

"But Arishen just stabbed Plyke and Rilla wounded herself trying to heal him." She walked over to Rilla. "Next time leave the healing to me. You're just a child. You can't possibly be as skilled as a fully trained lintep. Let me have a look at him."

Rilla's temper flared as Nyssa brushed past her, but she held her tongue. She knew she was a good healer – better than good, in fact. She'd learnt a lot from Rhanya in their Paradise and had watched carefully when Ratchin took her to heal the farmer's boy in Turon. Since then, she'd healed both Tika, Arishen and Plyke, not to mention Ensil, her first and most magnificent effort. How could Nyssa possibly think that she knew anything about healing?

Eliséo came up behind Rilla and placed a hand on her shoulder. The simple touch was enough to calm her.

It's ridiculous that an elf I met barely a few weeks ago knows me better than my own mother.

It's fortunate for you that I do know you so well already. He tightened his grip momentarily before walking towards Nyssa.

The older lintep had finished her examination of Plyke's shoulder. She rubbed a thumb on her forehead just between her eyes.

"I believe you owe Rilla an apology," Eliséo prompted her. "She's a much better healer than you give her credit for. I've seen her heal a number of wounds of varying degrees with amazing results every time."

Nyssa looked over at Rilla, anger and confusion warring on her face. "You are more skilled than I had imagined," she conceded, "but less experienced than you should be to attempt such a task."

"I've healed much worse than that with no one around to help me," Rilla retaliated hotly. "If you're so skilled and experienced yourself, you would have got to Plyke before I even had a chance to touch him."

"I wouldn't have rushed into it as quickly as you and injured myself at the same time," Nyssa retorted. "I would have assessed the situation calmly and then taken the time to heal him completely."

"Well then why don't you just go ahead and finish it off?" Rilla stormed off to the other side of their tiny clearing, snatching up her swords on the way. *No matter where I am, I always feel trapped.*

Rilla sat down, and blooded her swords, before she thought gloomily that she would have even preferred to be back in the isolation hut in their Paradise. She could escape from everyone there. She had faded into the background so many times in Erton's Paradise. Thinking back on it now, she wondered whether it was just her imagination that people ignored her or whether they really couldn't see her all those times.

"Rilla, stop it, you're making me feel sick not being able to focus on you," Tika whispered to her. He had come to sit by her side while Nyssa further healed Plyke.

"Sorry," she mumbled back to him. "I just wanted ..."

"To disappear from your mother?" He half smiled at her, keeping his voice low. "I know how you feel. Sometimes I just want to disappear from Plyke these days. Especially now that he's getting along so well with Shuut. It's like he doesn't need me anymore so there's no reason for me to be here."

Rilla looked at him in shock. "You can't be serious. Of course he needs you –
you're his Partner."

"There's no doubt he needed me in the Paradise. He even needed me to choose
Shuut as a mentor to force him to leave. But now." He shrugged. "He had you from
Silvaren and now he has Shuut. What does he need me for? I can't keep him safe
anymore. We don't even know if the Partner bond will work with us."

Rilla looked at Tika with new eyes. She'd known that Plyke was different
while they were in the Paradise, but she'd also seen that most other people were
distracted from the realisation by Tika. He was always the most talkative person,
drawing attention away from his quiet Partner. Even in that they'd seemed to make
a perfect pair. It hadn't ever occurred to Rilla that Tika knew he might be cast off
when they left their Paradise. He had been prepared to protect Plyke his entire life
in the Paradise, never expecting there to be a real opportunity for them to leave.

"Even if you never protect him again, he should always remember you spent
years saving his life in the Paradise." There was nothing more to say. If Plyke was
too stupid to see that, Rilla thought, he didn't deserve Tika.

Chapter Fifty-Four – Training

The next morning was spent in near silence. With Shuut alternating between riding and walking, Plyke always by her side, Tika was left to tend to the horse. He caught Rilla's eye whenever Plyke ran to Shuut's side to help her. Rilla could understand how he felt Plyke was ignoring him, but the worst part was that Plyke seemed to be doing it without realising the pain he was causing.

"How long until we reach the river?" Arishen asked.

Eliséo called a halt to let Shuut back onto her horse. "Another two days at this pace. We might reach by tomorrow evening, but we're not crossing in darkness. It will give Nyssa some time to train Rilla and Plyke before we're back on the more dangerous side of the river. We'll have to assume that our enemy doesn't know we crossed and is still on that side somewhere."

Rilla's heart sank at the thought of training with Nyssa. She had been looking forward to reaching Illaria and exploring everything she could do with her power. What she had never expected was to have her estranged mother teach her. It was going to be difficult with one teacher between the two of them. Nyssa wouldn't be able to take their particular strengths and weaknesses into account.

With a stab of panic, Rilla wondered if Nyssa would try to teach them to read minds by doing it to them herself.

What if she finds you!

You can always shut her out. Eliséo told her. *Though I doubt she'd make it through your wall before you realise she's there.*

A quick glance towards Nyssa showed she was watching her contemplatively.

You need to stop using our link when you have your eyes open. Nyssa is bound to notice something sooner or later.

Irritated that she couldn't even be free in her mind, Rilla broke her link to Eliséo. She walked over to Tika to give him a break from leading the horse for a while, but her frustration agitated the horse to such an extent that he soon had to take the reins back again.

* * *

By the end of the day, they had entered a sparse woodland and Eliséo called a halt. As soon as their camp was organised, Tika took his bow and arrows off to one side to begin target practice. Shuut had regained enough of her strength to stand by his side and instruct him.

Eliséo thickened the air around Rilla's swords, Arishen's daggers, Plyke's axe and his own sword. He paired the boys together, even though they'd sparred the night before, warning them that they would still sport nasty bruises if they were hit so not to relax their guards.

Feeling how agitated Rilla had grown throughout the day, he led her to a small clearing, within easy sight of their companions, and raised his sword. The two of them had never sparred before. However, he had seen what she was capable of with Ensil and wanted to push her as much as the ancient weapons master had. If exhausting her with swordplay was the only way to diminish her frustration before her lesson with Nyssa, then that was exactly what he would do.

Before Rilla was ready, he lunged forward, anticipating her reactions and caught both of her swords with his, parrying them out to the side and flicking his blade up to hit under her ribs. Rilla winced slightly and lightly stepped out of his reach, raising her swords defensively.

"I think you need to master the use of one sword before using both." Eliséo motioned for her to put her shorter sword away. "In fact, put them both away. I may as well show you how to use them properly. I'm not sure what Ensil taught you before he attacked you.

"These swords are different from most you'll find in the Outworld. Only one side is sharp. The way you tie the scabbard into the belt is with the slightly arched blade facing skyward. This means you have two ways of attacking someone.

"The first is if your opponent is too close to actually draw the blade out, then you just ram the hilt into their face or chest, giving you a chance to back away and fully draw out the blade.

"The second is if your opponent is far enough away for you to completely draw your sword. As you pull it out, the blade is facing your attacker so you can slash at them wherever they are by either angling the blade towards them or coming down in an arch to either slash their face or, more effectively, chop off their arms as you've done before."

He watched as she performed those techniques against thin air, then took a stance in front of her. Over, and over, again she practised each move as Eliséo changed position. By sunset, Rilla was well and truly exhausted. Eliséo could sense that her frustration had faded away. She had been too intent learning her new skills to dwell on anything else.

* * *

Tika had managed to shoot a hare under Shuut's guidance and they were eager to eat a hot meal for the first time in days. Rilla leaned in to start a fire with some heat from her fingers, but stopped herself before she did any more magic without first learning it from a lintep. She didn't want to get in trouble with Nyssa before their lessons even began.

Eliséo, noticing her reluctance, took the flint out of his bag and struck it against a stone to spark the fire into life. It was such a practised motion that it took the Paradisians' focus away from Rilla. Plyke had found a strong thin branch to skewer the hare. He handed it over to Arishen and Tika before going to sit over near Nyssa. Rilla followed his cue and sat next to him, facing her mother.

Nyssa smiled uncomfortably at the two of them. "Right, well, why don't we start by both of you telling me what you already know." She rubbed the top of her left hand absentmindedly. "Plyke, why don't you go first?"

"I don't really know how to do very much." Plyke avoided her eyes. "Why don't you ask Rilla first?"

"You'll both need to tell me before we begin, so just go ahead." Nyssa tried unsuccessfully to put him at his ease.

"I know how to build a wall, a pretty good one I think. It fooled Erton and Shuut anyhow." He shrugged and shook his head. "The only other thing I can do is talk to someone's mind if I'm touching their skin."

"That's all?" Nyssa's eyebrows shot up. "Eliséo said you might be more powerful than Rilla." Plyke shrugged again.

"That's not all," Rilla said. "He's got quite a skill with empathy. All he needs to do is touch someone to feel everything they're feeling. He can also cast his senses out to hear things further away and feel if anyone is using magic."

Plyke looked over at her in surprise.

"That does sound quite impressive," Nyssa conceded. "Have you done this often?"

Plyke shook his head. "I try to avoid touching anyone's skin because I hate prying. And I've only ever once cast my senses out and even then, it was only because we were in so much danger."

"You don't have to defend your actions," Nyssa reassured him kindly. "You're a lintep. Your magic is a part of you and to deny yourself the use of it is to deny who you are."

Rilla and Plyke shared a look. Nyssa's approach was quite different to Kora's, but neither of them wanted to point that out.

"Rilla, what about you?" Nyssa asked. Rilla thought she heard a note of excitement in her mother's voice. She hoped that excitement would win out over anger when Nyssa heard what she had done.

"Well, I only found out I was a lintep a little while before we reached Turon, so I may have been doing things in the Paradise without realising it, mostly trying to fade into the background. But you've already seen me do that. As you know, I can heal as well." She refrained from commenting further on that. Nyssa did not need to know the danger she'd been in a few of those times.

"I can draw heat out of things, but only as much as my body can handle. Same goes for the other way around, I can heat things up using my body heat, but only to a certain extent." Rilla tried to remember what else she'd done.

"There's something I've only tried once, in Turon. I followed a fringa with my mind through an inn until it found Ratchin. But that gave me such a headache I've never done it since. I think that's all." Rilla looked over to find Nyssa staring wide eyed at her. Before her mother could respond to what she'd said, Plyke reminded Rilla of one last thing.

"You also made the karlik in Goraburg drop his weapon so Eliséo could attack him, but I don't know how you did that."

Rilla could have hit him. She didn't want Nyssa knowing about that. It was bad enough that she'd experimented in Turon when she was alone in an inn, but experimenting with something so dangerous in unfamiliar territory with everyone already in so much danger was ridiculously stupid and she knew it. She'd even known it at the time but could not see any other options.

"Oh ... how did you do that?" Nyssa's voice was quite faint. Rilla internally debated saying that she didn't know or that she'd forgotten, but if she was going to start training properly, it would be more important to tell Nyssa the truth than to spare herself from a tongue lashing.

"I sent out a tendril of my power towards Eliséo until I found the point on his back where the dagger pushed in. Then I took the heat from my torch and passed it through that tendril, making sure that it didn't stay inside and burn me, until it reached the blade. I tried to push it through as fast as I could so the whole dagger would be too hot for the karlik to hold. And then he dropped it and I pulled the power back behind my wall."

There was a stunned silence. Even though the others were sitting further away from her than Nyssa, they had all been listening in on her answer. She knew all of them had been itching to know how she'd make the karlik drop his dagger but no one had guessed exactly how dangerous a move it had been.

"What kind of idiot are you?" Nyssa yelled at her. "Didn't Ratchin tell you not to overextend yourself or experiment with anything dangerous?"

"Of course she did," Rilla replied hotly. "But I'm sure she didn't expect me to be put in so many dangerous situations either. What was I supposed to do? Just let the karlik kill him?"

"Eliséo can take care of himself." Nyssa gestured to the elf. "He doesn't need you to act stupidly on his behalf. From now on, don't try anything so dangerous without a fully trained lintep around or at this rate, you'll kill yourself before you reach Illaria."

"You're a fully trained lintep," Rilla pointed out, angry that Eliséo hadn't stepped in to argue that he actually did need her help that time. "So that means I can try anything with you around."

Nyssa's eyes narrowed. "You can try what I tell you to in our lessons and nothing more." Rilla bridled at the restriction, but knew there was nothing she could say to change Nyssa's mind.

* * *

Nyssa looked at her two trainees with some trepidation. She would need to start them on the white stones. *Her* white stones. Every training lintep was given ten white stones in their first lesson. They were used to learn the fundamentals of the use of their power, and then to build on their skills. Nyssa had never lost a single one of her and always kept them nearby. She pulled three stones out of her right pocket, and placed one in front of each of them.

Placing her hands in her lap, Nyssa closed her eyes. She had practised this skill every day in her youth. This was something she could do in her sleep. She lifted the stone in front of herself, moved it in a circle around her head, then placed it gently back where it had started in. Nyssa opened her eyes with a serene smile. Practising the basic skills always made her feel calmer.

"Plyke, you first." Nyssa motioned to the stone in front of him. "Wrap your power around your stone, then lift it and place it back down again."

"How do I do that?" he asked in confusion.

Nyssa creased her brow. "You just wrap your power around the stone and lift it."

"How do I wrap my power around the stone?"

Nyssa looked up at Eliséo helplessly from across their small clearing. He was right. She wasn't a lintep mistress and had no idea how to train novices. In truth, she had never really listened much during her ow lessons. Her power had always been so strong that she had completed all set tasks with ease. She had never had the need to hone her skills the way most other lintep did. Nyssa rarely had cause to regret it, but this was one of the few times she did.

"You just push your power out of you towards the stone, and then wrap around it." It was the best explanation she could give.

Plyke closed his eyes. Sweat beaded on his forehead. Nyssa held her breath.

"Wait." At the sound of the elf's voice, Plyke opened his eyes again. "Nyssa, you should be prepared to help Plyke. If he brings his power out, he may have some trouble controlling it and containing it again."

Nyssa almost protested that she wouldn't need to do that until she saw the fear in Plyke's eyes. Instead she nodded and wrapped her power in a bubble around Plyke and his stone.

"I'm ready, Plyke."

Plyke closed his eyes with a frown. Nyssa staggered under the force of his power as it slammed into hers. It took all of her concentration to keep it safely contained and close to the boy's body. She breathed a sigh of relief when he pulled his power back behind his wall.

"There!" he said proudly. "I did it."

"Well done," Nyssa congratulated him. She'd barely noticed the stone move off the dirt. The force with which his power had had tried to escape could have proved fatal for him if she hadn't been prepared. She looked over at Eliséo, wondering exactly how much the elf had learned of lintep magic during the time he spent in Illaria.

* * *

"My turn?" Rilla asked impatiently. She barely waited for Nyssa to nod before sending her power out towards the stone. Before she knew it, the stone had disappeared. Rilla stared at the ground in front of her and all around, trying to find it.

"What have you done with my stone?" Nyssa asked angrily.

"I ... don't know," Rilla said. "I did exactly what you told me to. I wrapped my power around the stone and lifted it."

"You were meant to put it straight back down again." Nyssa's face flushed as she pulled a fourth stone out of her pocket. "Do it again and this time put it back down. Don't lose another one."

Rilla bit back a reply. Training with her mother was going to be difficult enough without them yelling at each other. This time, she kept her eyes open. She sent her power out towards the new stone and carefully wrapped around it. Then she lifted it. A second later, Eliséo's hand was clenched in front of her face. Rilla almost fell backwards in surprise at his quick elf reflexes.

"What are you doing?" she asked as she balanced herself again.

"Catching Nyssa's stone before you lose another one." He winked at her before turning to Nyssa. "I think this one needs slightly different training. She didn't make the other stone disappear. She simply lifted it so quickly that it shot up into the air. This one would have gone the same way if I hadn't caught it."

Rilla smiled, immediately understanding her mistake. She'd used too much power on such a small stone. As soon as Eliséo placed it back on the ground, she reached out a smaller tendril of power, the smallest she could control, and wrapped the stone in it once more. This time, instead of just trying to lift it up as hard as she could, she lifted it as slowly as she could. Smiling at the result, she made the stone float all around their camp and back again to its original position without moving once.

She looked up at Nyssa to see a strange look on her mother's face. It wasn't pride or even anger. It was shock.

"How did you navigate the stone around the entire camp without looking at it?"

"I don't know," Rilla replied truthfully. "I guess I just remembered the layout?"

"That's probably enough for one night." Eliséo cut the lesson short. "Give Nyssa back her stones, eat and sleep. Rilla and I will take the first watch. Arishen and Nyssa, we'll wake you for the middle watch. Tika and Plyke, you've got the early morning watch."

Nyssa's brow furrowed but she was not bold enough to argue with Eliséo. With their shifts sorted out, everyone gathered round the fire for their share of the hare. It wasn't much once it was shared between the seven of them.

After they finished, the boys walked over to their sleeping mats and immediately lay down. Nyssa went over to Shuut and lay down next to her, heedless of the fact that Shuut was still angry with her.

Rilla watched the gesture in silence. She wondered if she would ever feel close to Nyssa. With a shake of her head, she began walking her rounds in widening circles with Eliséo, making sure the nearby area was still safe before heading back towards the camp. It was a cold night and she wanted to stay as close to the fire as possible. They sat back to back, looking out into the darkness.

* * *

You have to tell her, Elessa finally blurted out. *She needs to learn the difference between lintep power and my power.*

We're not going to be able to keep this a secret forever, Eliséo responded heavily. *It's just not possible. If Nyssa had been looking at her eyes rather than the stone, she would have seen them glowing. Lintep eyes don't glow. It won't be long before everyone realises what's happened and then what?*

Then we make sure to keep you both safe, just like we always do, Elessa reminded him. *Nothing will really change.*

Everything will change. You will need to be kept safe too. Don't think there aren't those out there who wouldn't try to cut or burn you down to stop her fulfilling the prophecy.

Eliséo waited until he was certain beyond the shadow of a doubt that everyone was asleep before talking to Rilla about what had happened with the stones.

"How did you enjoy your first lesson?"

Rilla turned to glare at him. "It wasn't exactly a dream come true. I'd rather be training with Ratchin."

"It may not be much better when we reach Illaria. You will not be given your choice of teachers."

"No, but at least they will have more experience with students than Nyssa does." Rilla hesitated. "How *did* I get the stone to travel all around our camp without bumping into anything? I swear I could see it the whole time, even though I never turned around to watch it."

"If you were any other lintep, I would have said you followed it with your mind, like you followed the bird to Ratchin."

"But?" Rilla prompted him when he stopped.

"But I saw your eyes glow."

"Oh ... well, at least that won't be a problem if you keep away from my lessons."

Eliséo was silent for a while, lost in thought. "I may need to leave you for a while when we reach Illaria."

"Why?" Rilla asked frantically. "Why would you leave me?"

"First, I was never meant to stay with you. My official obligation was to get you and Plyke safely to the lintep and see if I could find Nyssa along the way."

Rilla looked away from him angrily. "Secondly?"

"Secondly," Eliséo continued in a quiet voice, "we cannot keep up this charade. I must speak with Lady Eléna about Elessa. People will soon notice a difference in you, whether it's your eyes, your reflexes or your lifespan. Eléna will tell us what we should do."

"She wouldn't suggest Elessa break the bond, would she?" Rilla asked in a whisper, her head resting gently against his.

"She would never suggest that." Eliséo found her hand and covered it with his own. "We're bound together now for better or worse. But I will have to leave to see how best to navigate these waters."

* * *

Tika and Plyke woke everyone at dawn. They had barely spoken, again. Plyke constantly seemed to be lost in thought these days. Tika's only comfort was that at least he wasn't the only one Plyke was reserved with. Just about the only person he was happy to speak more than two words to was Shuut.

They started out as soon as they had broken camp. There was no food left from the night before. Keeping that in mind, Tika kept his bow close to hand. Whenever they switched over to Shuut walking rather than riding the horse, he handed the reins to Plyke and walked a little away from the company, shooting at any animals he could find.

By noon, he'd taken down four squirrels and two hares, and they stopped to sort out their supplies. While Arishen and Plyke went to search for roots, berries and fruit, Rilla and Tika sat on one side of their clearing, skinning the animals and passing them over to Eliséo and Shuut to salt them. Nyssa sat a little apart from them, not offering to help and seemed to be trying not to turn up her nose at the smell of blood.

"Is this how you travel all the time?" she asked Shuut, motioning to the curing process. Tika kept his eyes focussed on his job, but couldn't help but hear their conversation. He shifted uncomfortably at the tension in the air.

"Since I was made to leave you in the Drakos Mountains and live with my father instead, yes. This is how a banwep survives in the Outworld."

Nyssa sighed. "I didn't mean ..."

"You never seem to mean anything," Shuut cut her off. "You didn't mean to leave me with a banwep, but it happened. You didn't mean to leave Rilla with a murderer, but it happened."

"That isn't fair, Shuut." Nyssa crossed her arms defensively. "How was I to know Erton would become a murderer?"

"Well, you knew my father was a banwep before you let the dragons send me off with him," Shuut replied hotly. "Exactly how many decisions in your life have actually been your own? How many do you take responsibility for?"

* * *

Rilla stopped what she was doing and looked over to her mother and sister. If she had been the one asking these questions, Nyssa would have started yelling at her by now. With Shuut, she was almost apologetic.

"It seems the dragons are more manipulative than I ever gave them credit for," Nyssa replied softly. "I left Illaria with no real idea of what I wanted to do except to find Kora. When she left, I had no one else to keep me there. She disagreed with so much of what we were taught. We argued a lot towards the end ..." Nyssa drifted off for a while. She shook her head. "In any case, I believed in the prophecy and when the dragons offered that I could help it eventuate, I jumped at the chance."

"Did the dragons tell you their plan right from the beginning? To bring me to a Paradise?" Rilla braved asking a question she had been itching to have answered.

"That had to be the plan Rilla," Nyssa answered in a matter of fact tone. "The Rilla in the prophecy comes from a Paradise."

"Was it their plan for you to leave me there?" Her voice was almost a whisper.

"The plan was for you to live there."

It wasn't the answer Rilla was expecting. "They didn't ask you to leave me there?"

"No," Nyssa conceded. "But I couldn't live there. The rules they had, the ridiculous way of life. I just couldn't."

"So, you left me with Erton just because you didn't want to live in a Paradise. You abandoned me for no reason?"

"At least I let the dragons know where the Paradise was. They would be able to find you."

"Wait a minute." Shuut sat up straighter. "*You* told the dragons where the Paradise was?"

Nyssa nodded, confused by Shuut's reaction.

"That means *you're* the reason they were manipulating me. If you hadn't left Rilla, you could have taken her to Illaria yourself. But without you there, they couldn't be certain Erton would take her himself, so they made me look for her. It's all *your* fault!"

Rilla looked at her mother in shock. She barely remembered her, but in what memories she had, Nyssa had not been this sort of person. Rilla wasn't at all like Erton, so she had come to the conclusion that she must be like her mother. But she couldn't imagine letting the dragons manipulate her to such an extent that she would abandon one child, let alone two.

Nyssa started to explain, but Shuut walked off. Rilla quickly shook her hair forward to shield her face from her mother.

* * *

Plyke and Arishen returned to a tense camp. Nyssa was busy looking through the items in her rucksack. The others were finishing up the curing process. Shuut was missing.

"Where's Shuut?" Plyke asked as they placed the roots and apples they had found on the ground. No one answered. Rilla pointed away from the camp. Plyke left to find her.

He found her near a tiny stream, dangling her bare feet into the cool water. He knew something was wrong, knew better than to broach the subject himself. Taking his shoes off, Plyke sat beside her and lowered his feet into the water.

"What do I do now?" Shuut asked, sounding lost. "I was groomed for such a long time to find her – my half-sister. I didn't even know that's what she was. They hid so much from me and manipulated me into doing things for them, just like everyone said they would. But I never believed it because I'd lived with them for so long. They were my family. I ..." She shook her head, frustrated and angry. "I never thought they would do that to me. And now that I've found Rilla, and have my mother back, I don't know what to do.

"It should feel like all my dreams have come true, but now I have no goals and, worse than that, I've realised that my mother caused half of my problems without a second thought. I'm overjoyed to have her back but I can't believe she did all of that to me, and to Rilla."

Plyke looked at her sadly. Her feelings were overwhelming him without him even touching her.

"I know exactly how you feel. I was trained my entire life to hide who I was. I was meant to lie to my Partner our whole lives. Then suddenly, because of Rilla, because of you, all of that changed.

"It was like a dream come true. There was less of an immediate threat that I would be found out and killed. Eventually, I was found out, but I don't think anyone will kill me now. It's like I'm free now to do and be anything that I want and ... I don't know what to do. I don't know who I am without hiding in that shell.

"I have a Partner who knew about me and helped me keep my secret hidden without me knowing it. He's the perfect friend and when one of us dies, he'll discover that I've betrayed him because how can the Partner relationship work when one of the Partners isn't even human?

"I've found two cousins and an aunt which is more family than I ever dreamed of knowing and I feel more alone than ever. I don't know who I am. I can't face what I've done to Tika. So ... what do I do now?"

"Two cousins and an aunt? What are you talking about?" Shuut looked over at him enquiringly.

Plyke hadn't told Nyssa, but he trusted Shuut. "My mother is Nyssa's sister, Kora. I didn't say anything because they seem to be very ... different people."

"We're cousins?" A small smile crept over Shuut's face. "Fancy that."

"Please don't tell Nyssa." He was glad Shuut was taking the news well, but she was nothing like her mother.

"I won't tell her, Plyke," Shuut replied, almost bitterly. "No good can come of that. At best, she'd just find a way to ruin your life too."

Plyke didn't reply. He didn't know what to say. After a while, he looked at Shuut. She was crying. The banwep who had no friends or family, who felt nothing for anyone and treated almost everyone as an enemy or simply a nuisance, was crying. They now both had more family than they'd ever dreamed of. He shuffled closer to her and put his arm around her shoulder, taking in her fear and pain, sharing his own with her. For one brief moment, they knew each other completely and then it was over.

At the sound of a twig snapping, Plyke stood up and moved away. His eyes caught a movement within a thick clump of trees. He drew his axe as Shuut unsteadily drew her sword. They eyed the trees warily, looking for any movement. What they least expected was for Tika to walk out from behind them. He looked calm, but frustrated. Plyke realised he must have heard at least part of the conversation.

"Try having your dreams shattered instead. I'll bet you'll feel worse after that. I'm glad you can find solace in each other's baseless fears. It's more than I could ever do for my Partner. Once I'd served my purpose of keeping him safe in our Paradise, I was practically discarded without a word." Plyke made to reply, but Tika cut him off. "Eliséo says it's time to go. We need to get your entire precious family to Illaria before half of you die."

Plyke watched him go wordlessly. His relationship with Tika was only getting worse. It would probably be best for him to sever the Partnership before they got to Illaria. How could they possibly keep it going at this rate?

* * *

Tika returned looking furious. He handed over care of the horse to Arishen. Shuut and Plyke returned close on his heels, both avoiding Tika. Rilla could see that something was wrong. She didn't need Plyke's empathy to feel it. As much as she wanted to stay near Eliséo, especially knowing that he would soon leave her in Illaria, she felt that Tika needed her more. Rhanya's letter still preyed on her mind. He had entrusted the boys to her care and she would do everything in her power to make sure nothing bad happened to any of them.

She looked at Tika and nodded to the back of their group. He understood, and walked with her to keep up the rear. It was better that way. He didn't want to feel Plyke's eyes on his back. Rilla saw the anger and frustration in his eyes.

"What will you do once we reach Illaria?" she asked him suddenly. Tika turned to look at her in surprise.

"I don't know. Maybe see if I can work in their stables?" As an afterthought he added, "If they have stables."

"That's not really what I meant," Rilla said gently. "Eliséo said only lintep are allowed in Illaria. What if they don't let you in?"

"Well, I suppose that's when we'll find out what this Partnership means to him," Tika answered bitterly. "If he doesn't fight to keep me with him ..." He left the sentence unfinished. They both knew what that would mean. "I suppose I could go back to Turon or find my way to Silvaren again. The elves might take me in if Eliséo asked them to."

Rilla squeezed the letter from Rhanya tightly in her fist. How could she possibly keep Tika safe if he wasn't even in the same place? Would the lintep make an exception based on his Partnership with Plyke? Would they let Arishen in because of his seer abilities? She tried not to think of what would happen to the two of them if they weren't admitted into Illaria. Somehow, she would have to find a way to keep them close to her, at least until she was certain they could look after themselves in the Outworld.

* * *

It was late in the afternoon when Eliséo heard the Bramble River. His estimation had been right. They would reach it that night. As the sound of the river grew louder, the woods started to thin. Before they were out in the open, Eliséo found a place for them to make camp. He had no idea who might be waiting for them on the other side, but he didn't want to give them an entire night to plan for their arrival.

Once everything was set for the night, he paired up the Paradisians for their sparring practise. Tika had used his bow enough earlier in the day and needed to work on his dagger skills.

"Plyke with Tika, Rilla with Shadow, Arishen with me."

The only one who didn't mind the pairing was Arishen, but none of them voiced their irritation at the situation. The enemy could just as easily be a friend who had recently betrayed you and you wouldn't be able to just walk away.

Before they began, Eliséo gathered thickened the air around all of their blades. Each pair walked off to a separate part of the clearing, giving each other plenty of room to spar. They all began slowly and worked on the skills they knew they were lacking in.

Plyke was defending against a smaller and quicker weapon. Tika attacking with a significant disadvantage, having to dart in and out of any openings he could see. Rilla first worked with her short blade and then her long one, Shuut teaching her the difference between them and how to use them together. Arishen was being pushed to his limit by Eliséo, both physically and mentally. Eliséo was using every trick he knew to get Arishen's powers to work during a fight, but to no avail.

* * *

When they finally stopped, the Paradisians were exhausted and spotted with bruises. All they wanted to do was eat and lie down, but for Rilla and Plyke, there was more training that night. They each took an apple and went to sit with Nyssa. With a silent look, Eliséo made Rilla aware that he would not be watching their lesson. It would be too easy for her to accidentally use their link with Elessa again. Nyssa might have been fooled once, but it was doubtful she would stop questioning if she did anything else that a lintep shouldn't be able to do.

Nyssa pulled three white stones out of her pocket once more and placed one in front of each of them. "Today, I want you both to concentrate more on controlling your powers. Plyke, you'll need to work on bringing your power from behind your wall and controlling it yourself. Rilla, you'll need to only use as much power as is necessary for a particular task."

Much as she wasn't the ideal mistress, Nyssa had pinpointed their weaknesses. Plyke looked terrified.

"I won't let anything happen to you, Plyke," she told him gently. "I just want you to practise the same thing repeatedly tonight. Call on your power, encircle the stone and lift it before placing your power back inside your wall." She waited for Plyke to agree to her lesson plan before turning to Rilla. "You'll only get one stone tonight. If you lose it, your lesson is over and I will not allow you to use your powers until tomorrow night."

"You can't stop me," Rilla retorted.

"Actually, I can," Nyssa informed her coldly. "I'm sure you don't want a demonstration of that, so don't test me.

"All you need to do tonight is control the movements of that stone until you know exactly how much power you need to use for every action. Is that understood?"

Rilla nodded wordlessly. She was curious about how Nyssa could possibly stop her from using her powers, but not curious enough to force a demonstration. She spent the next few minutes moving the small white stone in varying ways, using as much or as little power as she thought she needed. At first, it was more difficult than she thought it would be but after moving the stone in every way she could think of without losing it, she found it easier and got bored.

Carefully, she placed the stone in front of her and turned her eyes to a nearby fallen branch. She studied it for a time, wondering how much power she would need to lift it up and move it to the side. She guided a tendril of her power out towards the branch and wrapped it around the middle. Slowly, she tried lifting it. It was a lot heavier than the stone, so she sent out two more tendrils and wrapped them around either end of the thin branch. Careful not to make any sudden movements, Rilla lifted the branch just a few inches above the ground. She reeled in her power and watched as the branch came closer, manoeuvring it around Nyssa and placing it in front of her. With a self-satisfied smile, she unwrapped the three tendrils of power and drew them back into her wall. Only then then did she notice the stormy look on Nyssa face.

"Didn't I tell you I would stop you from using your power if you didn't listen to me?"

"You said I shouldn't lose the stone," Rilla defended herself. "It's right there in front of you, beside your stone. I didn't lose it."

"I told you to learn how much power you needed to control the stone. That's all."

"I did that until I was bored half to death."

"I don't care if you get bored," Nyssa shouted at her. "You do exactly what I tell you to and nothing more. Is that quite understood?"

Eliséo walked over at the sound of raised voices.

"Is all well?" he inquired politely.

"No, it isn't," Nyssa replied hotly. "How am I meant to help Plyke learn to control his power by himself when I have to keep an eye on little miss know it all?"

"I didn't say I know it all," Rilla tried to defend herself. "But if you're going to pay all your attention to Plyke and none of it to me while only giving me one simple task, then you've got to assume that I'm going to get bored and try something different."

"I expect you to obey your teacher."

"In all fairness, Nyssa, you rarely obeyed your teachers." Eliséo pointed out calmly. "She is your daughter, after all. Just try to imagine what it would have been like for you if you had not used your power from a young age as you did. Imagine how much you would want to test your abilities if you had only found out a few weeks ago that you had any power at all."

Nyssa stopped and stared at Eliséo. Rilla was certain that she was going to yell at him too, but she didn't. She looked at him uncertainly before closing her eyes and smiling. Rilla risked a quick look at Eliséo's eyes. They were shining ever so softly. If she hadn't been looking for it, Rilla doubted she would have seen it at all. He was pushing those memories and alternatives on Nyssa without her realising. Before her mother reopened her eyes, the silver shine vanished from his eyes, returning them to a dull grey leaving no trace that he had just used his magic.

"Your lesson is over for tonight," Nyssa informed them abruptly. "I think we should do separate lessons tomorrow. That way I can focus on both of you properly."

Rilla was startled by the change in her. She glanced over to Plyke. He didn't seem to care one way or the other. Nyssa had been spending more time with him anyway, so it wouldn't really make a difference to how his lessons progressed.

Not wanting her mother's mood to turn against her again, Rilla quickly got up and walked to the other side of the campsite, positioning her sleeping mat next to Eliséo's.

* * *

Nyssa watched Rilla in silence. As Plyke and Eliséo made to set out their sleeping mats, she held the elf back by his wrist.

"Exactly what is your relationship with my daughter?"

"As the Ambassador of the Elves, I was ordered to see her safely to Illaria," Eliséo answered smoothly.

"I didn't ask what your position is." Nyssa didn't like being toyed with.

"My position and relationship with her are as one," he replied calmly. "Until we reach Illaria, I will do everything in my power to protect her in every way I can."

"Does that include protecting her from a mother she doesn't seem to want?"

"No." Eliséo shook his head. "But it does include protecting her from a teacher who never completed her training to become the mistress she could have been."

"How dare you!"

"Nyssa, there is no point getting angry over this." Eliséo lowered his voice almost to a whisper. "It was your choice and there is no secret about it. Everyone in Illaria knows you mastered things as quickly as you could so you could progress to the next without giving yourself the chance to remember everything you were being taught. It went in one ear, you performed the task, and it went out the other ear."

Nyssa was furious with Eliséo, mostly because he was right. It was yet another way that she and Kora were complete opposites. Kora may have been slightly less powerful than Nyssa, but she, like almost everyone else in Illaria, had worked harder to learn everything they could about their power. Nyssa had insisted on flying through her lessons in record time, passing tests with flying colours to then forget half of the skills and simply use her favourite ones.

* * *

Eliséo twisted his wrist from her grip. "You can have the first watch tonight with Shadow. Wake Arishen and Tika in a few hours."

He walked over to his sleeping mat, lay down and closed his eyes, instantly finding the comfort of Elessa's embrace waiting for him. With a sigh of relief, he opened his eyes and looked over at Rilla. Silent tears were streaming down her face. He cursed Nyssa for the rough handling of her daughter. He waited until Nyssa and Shadow had left to make their rounds before reaching out to wipe the tears from her cheeks. She opened her eyes at the touch, smiling sadly at him.

"What will I do without you in Illaria?" she asked him, with a quick glance at the boys to make sure they were all asleep.

"You survived well enough without me before you reached Silvaren. I am certain you will do just fine without me when I leave." When he saw her crestfallen expression, he wished he could take the words back. "You can talk to me every morning and every night. Distance really means nothing to our bond."

Eliséo put his arm around her shoulder. In a rare moment of weakness, Rilla collapsed into him, hugging him as tightly as she could, her hot tears soaking

304

his shirt. She shook uncontrollably. Eliséo knew she was terrified of him leaving her, especially in the hands of lintep who might be able to stop her from using her power, but there was nothing he could do. He needed to talk to Eléna and quickly. He held Rilla close, stroking her long red hair until she had cried herself out. Eventually, she calmed down, disentangled herself from him and lay down, eyes closed.

* * *

Nyssa returned to see Eliséo bend over and kiss her daughter's forehead. She stood still, not making a sound. She did not want the elf to know what she'd seen. He might wish to fool her, but she could see the truth with her own eyes. She would not let an elf have more influence over her daughter than she did. The dragons had forced Shuut under their influence for years. She wasn't going to make the same mistake again. It was her turn to be the most influential person in the lives of both her daughters.

Chapter Fifty-Five – River crossing

Eliséo walked down to the bank and looked out over the Bramble River. At least they were not at the widest point. It looked to be just under a mile to the other side. The Paradisians had learnt to swim in Silvaren, but none of them would be confident enough to swim that far. They would have to build a raft for the crossing.

He left Rilla to watch over their campsite and took Plyke with him back into the thicker part of the forest. As soon as he saw the types of branch he was looking for, he pointed them out to Plyke. They were long and strong but quite thin.

"We need seven of these. Find them and bring them back to camp." As an afterthought he added, "If you find any vines, bring those as well. We're going to need something to tie the raft together."

The easy part over, Eliséo walked the forest, placing his palm on a few of the trees until he found one that was suitable. He'd once forced Rilla to ask a tree for thin branches for Tika. This would be worse. He took a deep breath, placed both hands on the tree and closed his eyes. In his mind, he pictured a thin log ten feet long and asked the tree to detach it. A few moments later, the log came crashing down to the forest floor.

He did this over and over again, feeling the pain of the tree as it broke off log after log for him. The pain was almost too much to bear, but finally it was over. Eliséo looked at the logs scattered at his feet and bit back tears. He hated doing that to a lesser tree. They never deserved it, but at least some were more willing than others to help. He always tried to find a willing one if he could. It made things just that little bit less painful.

You could have asked Rilla to help you, Elessa suggested softly.

I promised I would never ask her to do this again, Eliséo replied firmly as he lifted the first of the logs over his shoulder and walked back to camp. By the time he returned, most of the others were awake. He called Arishen and Plyke to help him carry the rest of the logs over while Rilla and Tika broke camp.

Once all the logs were laid out side by side, Arishen and Eliséo placed six of the longer branches that Plyke had collected across them. They held them steady as Rilla, Tika and Plyke tied the vines around them. Nyssa and Shuut watched on inquisitively.

By mid-morning, they were ready. With three people on each side, and Shuut leading her horse, they carried the raft down to the riverbank. Eliséo pointed out the most gradual slope down to the water that he could find. Shuut waited up on the bank with the horse as the others carefully carried the raft down to the river.

Eliséo stepped on first, holding the raft steady by digging a long branch deep into the riverbed. Rilla stepped on lightly behind him, with Arishen close on her heels. Tika joined them, but as soon as he'd shifted his weight onto the raft, it began to sink. He quickly hopped back onto the bank.

"Looks like three at a time." Eliséo was disappointed not to be able to carry more of them across at once, but he could not bear to think about asking another tree for more logs and they did not have time to spend half a day finding them on the forest floor.

"I'll take Arishen and Rilla to the other side and then come back to get two more of you. Shadow, the horse cannot cross with us. If the dragons have trained him well enough, he will find his way back to them."

"Isn't there a better way to do this?" Shuut asked immediately. "What if someone attacks Rilla and Arishen while they're by themselves over there?"

Eliséo shrugged uncomfortably. "Besides you and me, Rilla is the most skilled with her weapons. You are still too weak to be of any use in a fight, and I need to stay with the raft."

Shuut and Nyssa looked ready to protest again, but it was Plyke who placated them. "You haven't seen Rilla and Arishen in a fight before. They're both really good. And if Arishen's powers come into play, like they did the day I was ambushed, then they'll have the advantage over any attackers."

Shuut and Nyssa slumped in defeat in an identical manner. Eliséo saw the sadness on Rilla's face as she watched them. He knew she doubted either of them would ever treat her with the familiarity they treated each other.

Eliséo pushed the raft out into the river. Arishen and Rilla settled themselves down on the raft, trying to move as little as possible. Eliséo found a strong, smooth rhythm using the pole to propel them across the river. The water was shallow enough at this part of the Bramble River that the pole should be able to push them across to the opposite bank.

It took a little less than an hour to reach the other side. Eliséo held the raft steady as the two Paradisians hopped off. He looked around warily. There was a narrow meadow of long grass before a dense forest blocked further view. An uneasy feeling settled in his stomach.

"Be careful," he told them. "Take cover near the forest and keep a constant watch until I return. If anyone attacks you, do not let them corner you in the trees. You both have long weapons, so the grass will be a better option for you. If you find yourselves outnumbered, fight back to back so that you only have to worry about the attackers in front of you. Most importantly, be open to your powers, both of you. It could mean the difference between life and death. Do you understand?"

* * *

Arishen and Rilla nodded, they could see he was worried. He didn't normally give them this much advice. But he didn't usually leave any of them on their own for almost two hours. They barely waited for him to push off from the bank before turning to the steep rocks in front of them. The jagged edges gave them plenty of foot and hand holds. Rilla peeked out over the top into the meadow beyond. It was all clear. She nodded silently at Arishen. They heaved themselves over the edge and ran as fast as they could to the cover of the trees.

Heart racing, Rilla ran until the trees thickened around her. Only then did she finally pause for breath. They positioned themselves so that one of them could keep an eye on the meadow and the other on the forest.

"Do you really think we're in danger?" Arishen asked in a whisper. Rilla only shrugged, not wanting to make any more sound than necessary. Eliséo had scared her. She looked past the meadow to see the raft on the water. He was less than a quarter of the way across the river. Even if the return crossing was faster because the raft was lighter, it would still be over an hour before he would reappear. For that whole time, they were on their own. With even a little bit of luck, they should be fine. No one on this side of the river could possibly know their movements and no one could be expecting them. It would only be by pure chance that anyone would come across them.

* * *

Is she open to you? Eliséo asked Elessa when he was certain Arishen and Rilla had reached the cover of the forest.

Yes. She understood your meaning perfectly, his tree replied warmly.

Don't contact her unless you need to. I don't want to distract her.

Elessa let the moment for a retort slip by. She knew Eliséo was worried about leaving Rilla alone and knew better than to chide him at such a time. For the first time that she could remember, Elessa felt a twinge of guilt.

Do you wish I hadn't bound her to me?

You are the one who taught me that wishing for something to be different is a waste of time and energy, Eliséo responded automatically. *Unless there is something you can do about it, there is no sense in thinking about how things could have been. Just keep an eye on her and tell me if something happens.*

* * *

Rilla could feel Elessa in her mind. Oddly, she found it comforting rather than annoying. In the Paradise, if anyone had tried to be as close to her as Eliséo and Elessa, she would have immediately been suspicious of them. However, in the Paradise, she only really had one friend. Rilla found herself clutching the note that Rhanya had written her, yet again. It was strange that he was still comforting her, even though he was dead.

Rilla shook her head to clear her thoughts, and froze. Someone was nearby. There was a shadow off to her left. As slowly as she could, she turned her eyes and then her head in that direction. Hidden in amongst the trees, less than twenty yards away, was another group of the massive men who had attacked them on this side of the river.

"Run!" she screamed. Startled by her cry, Arishen jumped involuntarily before turning to see the four men now running towards them. He followed Rilla out into the meadow, drawing his long daggers as he caught up with her. They turned to face their attackers. The men broke free of the trees, slowing to a walk when they spotted their prey.

Even though Rilla had only been sparring with one sword recently, she drew both. She doubted the strength of both hands on a sword would help her as much as speed. Terrified, she waited for the men to reach them. There was nothing else they could do. Running was out of the question and calling out for help was useless. Eliséo had to be at least half way across the river by now. Even if he turned around, he would not be in time to help them.

"Any bright ideas?" Arishen whispered through clenched teeth.

"Back to back." She remembered Eliséo's advice.

When the men were only a few feet away, they drew their weapons menacingly. Rilla had expected axes and swords, but their daggers were barely longer than Arishen's. That didn't make them any less deadly. They suddenly broke into a run, daggers brandished high above them.

308

Rilla took a chance and ran towards them, slashing at their bellies while their arms were still overhead. One crouched over in pain, the others surrounded her. She had just cut herself off from Arishen. It was a stupid decision and she knew it, but at least she had injured one of them. Scared half to death, she waved both swords around her to keep the others at a distance.

Arishen appeared near her, darting in and out of range of one of them men with his daggers, piercing and slashing at his skin over and over. The cuts weren't deep, but Arishen succeeded in distracting his attention from Rilla. As soon as he saw an opening, Arishen dodged around the man and through the gap that had been left open. In seconds, he was with Rilla. They turned back to back and finally had some sort of advantage.

The four men attacked relentlessly. Even the wounded one wasn't backing down. Rilla and Arishen were outnumbered and less skilled. All the attackers needed to do was tire them out and then kill them.

Attack, Rilla. Use your power. Elessa's voice broke through her terror. It was all the encouragement she needed. She pulled her power out of her tower and wrapped her swords. Instantly, she felt more confident. Blows still rained down on her, but she fought back more vigorously.

As best as she could, she defended against one man while attempting to attack the injured one. Taking advantage of every wince, every misstep, she finally began to gain ground. Defending herself against a blow from the injured man, she continued to move her blade in an arc coming down on his arm. She had intended to cut through his arm, but her aim was thrown off by the others. Instead, she cut through his bicep. Half of his arm fell to the ground beside him. The man clutched what was left of his arm and screamed in pain. The other three didn't even glance his way. There was no loyalty between them.

* * *

Arishen started losing ground, bumping into Rilla's back repeatedly. They were going to die unless one of them thought of something. His mind was racing as he defended himself. Why couldn't he think?

Thrust left, defend right.

He obeyed the thought immediately.

Defend left, defend right.

Finally, he understood what was happening. His powers were coming into play. He realised that he could see what the men were going to do a second before they did it. It was an advantage, even if a small one. At least he would be able to defend himself and occasionally even attack. But they couldn't keep this up for long. He tried to extend his vision to Rilla, but every time he did, all he could see was fire. A few more glimpses showed him what he needed to see.

Fireball.

"Shoot fire from your fingers!" he cried out.

"What?!" Rilla sounded frantic.

"Fire! Like Nyssa with the dragons. Now!"

* * *

309

It was a bad idea and Rilla knew it. But it was probably the only idea that would save them. She let her power take care of her swords. It knew what to do for at least a few seconds while she concentrated. She closed her eyes briefly, drawing her body heat towards her hands. Opening her eyes once more, she focussed on the man in front of her, dropped her swords and shot fire out of her fingers.

* * *

At the sound of the blood curdling scream and the smell of burning flesh, Arishen ducked. But Rilla wasn't moving. She was frozen in place. He turned and grabbed her shoulders, moving her around in a circle to stream fire at all four men. In moments, the mercenaries were rolling around on the grass, screaming and trying to put out the flames. Rilla was still shooting fire at them.

Without warning, the fire ceased and Rilla fell to the ground, her body shaking uncontrollably. Arishen knelt beside her, trying to stop her shivering. Her skin was ice cold. He looked at the burning bodies. They weren't a threat anymore, but fire on the dry grass soon would be. He picked up Rilla and carried her to the riverbank. The rocks from the river stretched a few yards before the grass started. He gently placed her on the rocks before running back to the forest to gather as much firewood as he could carry in one trip.

As he returned, he stopped at one of the bodies, trying not to gag on the smell of burning flesh as he lit one of his branches on fire. As soon as it was alight, he raced back to Rilla, arranging the remaining branches in a peak before igniting the whole lot. He went back to retrieve their weapons. Not knowing what else to do, he pulled his rucksack off his back, pulled out all his clothes and draped them over the shivering girl. When that didn't seem to make a difference, he took the cloak out of Rilla's rucksack and covered her with that too. He lay down behind her, chest pressed up against her back, and rubbed his hands up and down her arms trying to warm her.

* * *

Eliséo watched the attack through Rilla's eyes. Elessa had brought him into their link almost as soon as the fight began. He couldn't believe he'd left her unprotected. What if she'd been killed while he was still on the river?

She's not out of danger yet, Elessa warned him. *She's used most of her body heat. Arishen might not be able to save her with a fire and extra clothes. She needs Nyssa and she needs her now.*

She was right. Eliséo knew it, but he was barely listening to her. His most difficult task was coming up. Making sure that Nyssa got on the raft next and not letting anyone understand that he knew there was trouble on the other side of the river.

Just try to keep talking to her, he told Elessa. *Do not let her mind switch off or we might lose her.*

In a few more minutes he would be at the bank. He could already see Shuut, Nyssa, Tika and Plyke waiting for him. They were waving their hands frantically and pointing at him, behind him. He turned to see what they were pointing at. There was smoke coming from the other side of the river – a lot of it. The fire Rilla had started must have caught on the grass. It hadn't rained in days, maybe even

310

weeks. From what he had seen, Arishen had taken her onto the rocks. He hoped they would be safe from the fire there. Rilla needed heat, but not that much of it.

"I'm coming across next," Nyssa blurted in a panic as soon as the raft hit the rocks. "That smoke started too suddenly. Rilla must have done something stupid."

Thankful that he didn't have to convince her, Eliséo simply nodded his head.

"Plyke, you come with me in case I need your help," Nyssa instructed. The two of them clambered aboard the raft, giving Eliséo barely a moment to rest before starting the second journey to the opposite side.

* * *

Scared out of her mind, Nyssa couldn't stop talking and fidgeting. The closer they got, to the other side, the quieter she grew. At first, all she could see was smoke, then raging fire spreading across the narrow meadow. The trees had caught fire, and it was spreading through the dense forest. She could barely make out Arishen and Rilla through the smoke until they were just a few yards away from the rocks.

The two were huddled together beside a small bonfire, Rilla covered in a pile of clothing as Arishen desperately tried to warm her. Nyssa and Plyke climbed onto the rocks with Eliséo following after pulling the raft up out of the water.

"What happened?" Nyssa asked Arishen.

"It was my fault!" he instantly defended Rilla.

"I don't care whose fault it was." Nyssa spoke calmly, her heart beating wildly. "Just tell me what happened."

"We were attacked by four men and we were going to die. I told her to shoot fire at them, like we saw you do in the Drakos Mountains."

"You did what?! And she managed it? What were you thinking?" Nyssa flew into a rage. "How stupid could you both be? Don't you know how dangerous it is to do that without training?"

Eliséo placed a hand firmly on her shoulder. "Perhaps we can save the lectures until *after* you help Rilla. What do you need?"

"Heat," Nyssa replied quickly. "Lots of heat. More than I can give her. More than I can take from Plyke."

"More than you can take from the fire?" Plyke asked her. "Rilla used the fire in her torch to burn a karlik. Maybe we can use the heat of the fire somehow and spread it through her body so we don't burn her."

Nyssa turned and looked at him in surprise. Why hadn't she thought of that herself? She supposed she wasn't skilled enough to try it. Powerful enough, certainly, but she had skimmed through her lessons without actually mastering the skills she needed. Frightened to experiment on her daughter, she looked pleadingly at Eliséo.

"You cannot let your daughter die."

It was all she needed to hear. Nyssa sat down between Rilla and the fire, rubbing her hands together. If Rilla could improvise, so could she. Peeling back the layers of clothing Arishen had draped over her, Nyssa placed a hand on Rilla's stomach. From that central location, she should be able to spread the heat around her body.

Rilla's skin was ice cold to touch. Hesitantly, Nyssa reached her other hand towards the fire until it was so close that the heat was painful. She pulled that heat in a constant stream from one hand to the other, feeding it into Rilla slowly and carefully. To help her concentrate, she closed her eyes.

"Nyssa, that's enough," Eliséo called out. "You don't want to boil her blood." Nyssa's eyes snapped open and she saw Rilla dripping with sweat. She took her hand away from the fire and placed it on the rocks, draining the excess heat into them until Rilla stopped sweating. Finally, she took her hand from Rilla's warm skin and draped the clothes back around her.

"Why isn't she moving?" Arishen asked softly. "Why isn't she talking?"

Nyssa looked over at Eliséo, too afraid to answer.

* * *

Eliséo felt the fear cascading off Nyssa. "Rilla's body was starting to shut down from extreme cold. It will take a while for everything to start working again."

"This is all my fault." The seer buried his head in his hands, slumping to the rocks.

"It was a better idea than letting yourselves be killed by those men. Rilla wouldn't have done it if she could think of anything else." Eliséo attempted to reassure the boy. "I'm counting on you to keep her safe and warm while I bring Tika and Shuut to this side. Can you do that for me?"

Arishen nodded, raising his head and looking straight at Rilla. Eliséo took Nyssa and Plyke to one side.

"You should be safe for now. The men who attacked us before were always a few days apart from one another. Don't wander away from each other. And Nyssa?" The lintep looked up at him. "If Rilla starts talking, do not yell at her. I am certain she has learned her lesson already. If not for her actions, they would both be dead and the two of you would have been next if those men were smart about it."

Without giving Nyssa a chance to retort, he dragged the raft back into the water, picked up the pole and started back across the river to Tika and Shuut. The sun was starting to dip in the sky. He didn't want to still be on the water when night fell.

"What happened?" Shuut asked as soon as he reached them. Eliséo saw the horse was gone and a heap of fruit was laying on the grassy bank. They must have gathered all of it in an attempt to occupy themselves instead of worrying about something they could do nothing about.

"Arishen and Rilla were attacked by another pack of men. The only thing either of them could think of to stay alive was for Rilla to shoot fire from her fingers like Nyssa did in the Drakos Mountains." Eliséo grimaced at the thought. "They both knew that it was dangerous, but neither of them really understood what would happen."

"Are they alive?" Tika asked in a whisper.

"Yes, Tika. They are alive. A little the worse for wear, but alive." He shared a look with Shuut. She understood what that meant for Rilla. "Let's get that fruit over to the others and figure out how to get past the fire."

Along the way, the three of them thought of and discarded a handful of ideas to douse the fire. They didn't have any buckets and the fire was too big. Tika eventually came up with a plausible idea. They would need to ask Nyssa whether it would work. None of them were familiar enough with lintep magic to know. Eliséo suspected it was possible, but wasn't certain Nyssa would be able to douse the entire fire by herself.

312

"You want me to do what?" Nyssa asked incredulously when Tika explained his plan. She shook her head and crossed her arms. "Absolutely not. It's not possible. I cannot carry water."

"Why not?" Eliséo asked innocently. Rilla smiled to herself at his mockery.

"For one thing, water is liquid, not solid. Exactly how do you propose that I lift it up?" Nyssa asked angrily.

"I'm not an expert in lintep magic, that's *your* area of expertise," the elf replied cheekily.

"How heavy is water?" Rilla asked. All eyes turned to her. It was the first time she'd spoken since the attack.

"Rilla!" Nyssa breathed out a sigh of relief. "How do you feel?"

"I'm fine, really. Still feeling a little stiff, but I'll be over that soon. How heavy is water?" Rilla repeated.

"Why do you need to know that?" Nyssa asked her sceptically. "You're not thinking of experimenting with your powers again when your last attempt left you barely alive?"

"It sounds like a good idea," Rilla mumbled.

"I absolutely forbid you from trying it!"

Rilla glared at her angrily. "In case you hadn't noticed, we're being hunted. If you can think of a better way to douse the fire, then do it. Otherwise, I suggest the three of us pick up as much water as we can and try to clear a path through the fire for us."

"I hate to say it Nyssa, but Rilla's right." Shuut came to Rilla's defence before Nyssa could start yelling at her. "If Tika's idea is possible and you don't have any better ideas, then you need to try it. We're sitting ducks if we wait here until the fire burns itself out."

"Any attackers would have as much trouble getting through that fire without magic as we would," Nyssa protested.

"But they can travel up the river under the cover of darkness and catch us trapped on the rocks." Shuut had a point. Nyssa sighed.

"I don't think I'll be much help," Plyke ventured softly. "I can barely control my power enough to pick up a stone."

Rilla inwardly cursed herself for not thinking of that beforehand and saying that all three of them could do it. Of course, Plyke couldn't do it ... yet. She was certain that, with proper training, he would be able to do it too. From the bits and pieces, she'd seen, and the fact that he was Kora's son, she was certain his untapped power must be quite incredible.

"Of course you'll be able to help," Rilla answered him brightly. "With me and Nyssa busy with the water, neither of us will be paying attention to anything else. We'll be relying on you to make sure we aren't attacked with magic by the same person who attacked Shuut."

Tika caught her eye and thanked her. Rilla had just secured Plyke's position in their magical dealings in a way no one else had thought to do.

In a moment of hesitation, Rilla turned her head away from the others and closed her eyes. *What if we get half way through the fire before the water runs out and we're trapped? Will your dome of air be able to keep the fire away from us?*

I'm sure it would, Rilla, Eliséo answered her quickly. *But Nyssa knows the elves too well to not realise how much power it takes to do that. We cannot allow her to know who I am. It would be even more dangerous than anyone finding out that you are bound to Elessa.*

"So how are we going to do this?" Rilla opened her eyes and turned to a still smouldering Nyssa.

"You're the one with all the bright ideas," her mother retorted sarcastically. "Why don't you tell me?"

"Well, we're going to have to carry as much water as we can, because we won't be able to get back to the river once we start moving." Rilla generally thought out problems best if she spoke her way through them. "So, we'll need to use as little water as possible as we go along. I suppose if we can shape our power it might work. With the stones I used a tendril, but I suppose I can make any shape I want to. If I make something like a watering can and seal off the top so that I don't spill any accidentally? That could work. Then the water will come out of the spout like rain."

She tilted her head from side to side, giving the idea some thought until she noticed the incredulous look on Nyssa's face. Assuming her mother thought the plan wouldn't work, Rilla decided to experiment.

She concentrated on pulling as much of her power out of her tower as she thought was safe. Next, she imagined it was a ball of clay, like the potters back in the Paradise used to use. She shaped it with her mind into a large watering can and walked over to the river. Skimming the surface of the river, she allowed water to flow into the watering can until it was as heavy as she could handle.

Slowly, so as not to overbalance, she turned towards the small bonfire Arishen had made. She tilted the watering can until water poured out of it onto the fire. She smiled proudly at the result.

"I don't know if it'll be enough to get us through the fire but, with Nyssa's help, we just might do it."

Nyssa stepped back from her, pointing at the fire. "How did you do that?"

Rilla looked at her uncomprehendingly. Eliséo tried to smooth Nyssa's ruffled feathers. "One of the things we've noticed about Rilla and her powers is that because she didn't grow up around other lintep, she isn't bound by the same limitations and rules that you are. If she sees a problem, she simply works with her power to suit that circumstance and finds a solution, usually without being able to explain how."

"So, you're saying ..." Nyssa shook her head in disbelief.

"She thought that a watering can would be the solution, so she moulded her power into that exact shape to help her," Eliséo confirmed.

"She can't just manipulate her power like that." Nyssa refused to yield. "It shouldn't be listening to her commands at such an early stage. Not *those* sorts of commands anyway."

Rilla had been quietly listening to the conversation up until that point. It was clear to see that she didn't understand what the problem was. Eliséo tried to motion her to remain silent, but she wasn't looking at him anymore. She was looking curiously at Nyssa.

"I don't understand the problem. I thought of a watering can, and that's the shape my power turned into. What's wrong with that?"

"What's wrong with that?" Nyssa's voice rose to a higher pitch and turned wildly to Eliséo. "She knows nothing about magic and she manipulates her own power at such an early stage."

"Nyssa, calm down," Eliséo tried to reason with her. "We don't have time for this right now. She's obviously working well with her power so let's just forget that problem for a moment. The biggest question is whether *you* can work as well with *your* power."

"I can't do this." Nyssa crossed her arms.

Rilla was shocked by the admission. Nyssa had been so harsh with her and Plyke in their lessons. Rilla thought she must have been that way because she was so much more skilled than they were.

* * *

Eliséo roughly grabbed Nyssa by the arm, dragging her away from the others, before she could do any more damage.

"I can't do this." She repeated before he had a chance to open his mouth. "I wasn't trained for any of this in Illaria."

"You think that any of these children were *trained* for this?" Eliséo asked her harshly. "No. They were brought up in a Paradise that was meant to be peaceful and then flung out with a banwep who would have left them as soon as she could, had other people not forced her to stay with them.

"They have survived by strength of will alone and not one of them is yet sixteen years of age. Are you trying to tell me that they are any better equipped for this than you?"

"You don't understand." Nyssa tore her arm away from him. "I never thought I'd really be in any danger and I didn't bother to master the skills most lintep do. I can't do what Rilla is doing."

Eliséo shook his head angrily at her. "Then you need to swallow your pride and ask your daughter for help with her idea or find something else that works just as well for you. If we do not move before sunset, we will not survive the night."

He left Nyssa to think it over and rejoined the others. They all looked at him with questions in their eyes, but he gave them no answers. It would be difficult for Nyssa to admit the truth to them. He would not do it for her. She had made stupid decisions about the use of her powers long before any of them ever came into her life and she had to live with the consequences.

* * *

Rilla watched curiously as Nyssa walked up to her, chin lifted in the air.

"Would you please explain to me, in precise detail, how you managed to carry water with your power?"

Rilla's eyes widened. She fought the urge to look over at Eliséo or talk to him through Elessa.

"Um, of course I will. Just let me pour out the rest of the water because it's getting quite heavy."

Rilla climbed back up the rocks and drenched the grass surrounding them until all the water was gone. When she came back down, she found everyone but Nyssa had moved downstream a bit to give them some privacy.

Nervously, she sat down across from her mother. In as much detail as possible, she spent the next half hour explaining everything she had done to Nyssa, trying to give her as many demonstrations as possible. Nyssa tried and failed to mould her power into a watering can shape at least a dozen times before finally succeeding. Both let out a cheer when Nyssa finally managed to pour out some water. The others ran back to see what the commotion was about. Nyssa, looking quite pleased with herself, told them that she was ready.

Everyone shouldered their rucksacks and climbed up the rocks onto the wet grass. They stood there patiently for a few minutes as Nyssa and Rilla scooped up as much water as they could carry into their watering cans. Water hovered above their heads. No one voiced their fear of what might happen if that water wasn't enough.

Shuut and Eliséo quickly discussed their route. As neither of them had travelled this exact part of the Outworld before, they had no way of knowing how far and in which direction the forest spread. They agreed to head due east and hope for the best. It was more likely that the forest was spread further up and down the riverbank than perpendicular to it.

They walked towards the burning forest, Rilla standing to the front and on their left, Nyssa on the right and slightly behind. Between the two of them, they had agreed that Rilla would douse the fire ahead of them until her water ran out and Nyssa could keep watch in case the flames closed in behind them. Once Rilla ran out of water, it would be up to Nyssa to get them the rest of the way out. It was a good, if risky plan. If the fire closed in behind them, Nyssa might run out of water soon after she took the lead from Rilla.

Rilla looked over at Nyssa and nodded. There was no turning back now. She walked as confidently as she could towards the flames, pouring as little water as necessary in front of them in a wide arc so that the flames were well away from them on either side. Rilla was pleased to notice that her plan was working except for one detail.

"It's getting too hot!" Rilla shouted out over the roar of the fire around them. "I can't reach far enough out! Get Nyssa up here!"

Within seconds, Nyssa was by her side. "What do you need?" She yelled over the cracking and splintering of trees.

"You take that side. I'll take this side." She pointed to the right and then to the left. "It's getting too hot."

For the first time since they'd met, Nyssa didn't put up an argument. She simply did as she was told and helped Rilla. The heat died down to a bearable level within a few minutes. No one mentioned that the change in plans meant they wouldn't be able to get as far as they'd thought before their water ran out. No one had to. They were all thinking it.

They walked for well over an hour before the fire started to lose heat. At that point, Rilla stopped Nyssa from wasting any more water than they needed to. Once they had cleared the fire by a few yards, Rilla turned and dumped the rest of her water, soaking the mossy undergrowth of the forest in a long stretch across, making sure the fire wouldn't be able to simply jump across and follow them. The Paradisians looked at her in horror as she drained her watering can down to the last drop and pulled her power back into her tower.

"Keep your water just in case," she told Nyssa.

"What did you do that for?" Arishen asked in confusion. "The fire is still behind us."

Rilla looked over at Eliséo and Shuut. They were the only ones who understood what had to happen next.

"Now, we run," Eliséo told them. "As far as we can. Our only hope at this point is to get well clear of the forest and make sure we can stay clear of the fire."

Following close on each other's heels, they ran through the thinning forest. Shuut set the pace, as she was still the weakest in their group. Her lintep healing powers had done wonders, but she wasn't completely back to her full strength.

After twelve miles or so, the trees finally gave way to grasslands. Shuut slowed to a halt before they emerged from the relative shelter of the forest. She glanced back behind them. The smoke was still visible above the tree line, but the flames weren't high enough to see.

* * *

Eliséo stood behind Shuut and stared out over the grasslands. "The sun will set soon. We will wait here until then. There are no clouds, so we should be able to see well enough to climb the first hill. From there, we can see anyone approaching and keep an eye on the fire."

Shuut nodded her agreement breathlessly and slumped down to the ground, leaning back against a tree. Nyssa and the boys followed her example, exhausted by the exertion of the afternoon. From the corner of his eye, Eliséo saw Rilla begin to fidget with just a few moments of rest.

"Rilla and I will find something to eat. We'll be back by dusk."

Rilla readily followed him back into the forest. Careful not to stray too far from each other, they looked for any tell-tale orchids to show them where to dig for tubers. Rilla covered the contents of her rucksack with her cloak so they could fill the rest of it with the tubers and fruits they found. Aside from what Tika and Shuut had found on the other side of the Bramble River, they had no food left. They scavenged until sunset.

Eliséo set a brisk pace as they headed back towards their companions, but slowed when he noticed Rilla wasn't keeping up with him.

"What's the matter?" he asked as he turned to wait for her. "Is the rucksack too heavy?"

Rilla shook her head and stopped walking. "Are you as angry with me as Nyssa for burning those men?"

It was not a question he was prepared for. "It was a dangerous move."

"But was it the *right* one? Would you have done the same thing if you were in my position?"

"I saw the entire fight through Elessa," he confided in her. "If either of us had thought of something you could do to save yourselves any other way, we would have told you. Arishen suggested the fire and you started it before we could think of anything else."

"But you wouldn't have done it, would you?" She looked closely at his face. He kept his expression impassive. "You're not angry with me, but you think it was a bad idea."

"It was a dangerous idea – probably the only thing you could have done to save the two of you – and it came at an extremely high cost. What if Nyssa wasn't travelling with us? What if I didn't get her to you in time? Your healing powers would not have been able to save you. You would have died anyway."

"I would have saved Arishen," she whispered with tears in her eyes. Eliséo shook his head.

"I don't know how to put this to you any other way, Rilla, but no one would have cared that Arishen survived if you had died."

"Because I'm the prophecy child." She tilted her head to one side and looked at him almost angrily.

"Nyssa and Shuut would have thought that, yes," he conceded. "However, the boys would not have cared about the prophecy at all. Do you still not understand? They all know that you are the reason they are alive today and not just because you got them safely out of your Paradise. You mean more to all of them than anyone else in the world.

"I hate to sound like Nyssa and Ratchin, but you really do need to stop experimenting so much when you think there might be danger involved. You have had a lot of practise with healing now, but do not try anything new in that area. With everything else, just try to be careful. We are only about a week or so from Illaria. Let us try to get there without any more 'accidents' and figure out a way to get Tika and Arishen inside the lintep stronghold."

"Don't worry about that. I already have a way to get them in." Rilla told him confidently. When he pressed her for details, she refused to tell him. Eliséo kept his peace. Her plan would be revealed to him soon enough.

Dusk soon arrived. Everyone was rested and Nyssa had dumped the rest of her water into their water flasks. There was no point in wasting it on the ground if the fire was no longer a threat to them. Rilla split the tubers and fruit she and Eliséo had gathered into everyone's rucksack.

Eliséo led them through the grasslands. His elf vision was the best suited for this kind of travelling. Within a half hour, he had safely navigated them to the nearest hill. It wasn't much, but any sort of higher ground would be safest for them after the attack and Rilla's stunning display of magic. Plyke hadn't picked up on any magic nearby, but Eliséo did not take that as a sign that their pursuer had given up on them.

"I shall keep watch tonight," he informed them. "The rest of you can join me, but only one at a time. You will all need to be well rested by morning. These hills will not be safe for us if our pursuer is anywhere nearby. We will need to get away from here as fast as we can."

Nobody protested. Shuut offered to take the first shift with him. The others gratefully accepted and arranged their sleeping mats close to each other for warmth. Eliséo and Shuut positioned themselves back to back so that the banwep faced the forest where she'd be able to see better with the soft glow of the distant fire and together settled into the first shift of the night.

Chapter Fifty-Six – Separate ways

Eliséo woke everyone at dawn. He did not want to waste a moment of daylight. Sleeping mats had been packed away and shortly everyone was ready to move. Trying to accommodate Shuut's current state of fitness, Eliséo pushed the group as hard as he thought she could handle. They were passing through hilly grasslands, so on the downward slope he made them run and on the upward slope, he slowed to a steady walk.

The one person Eliséo hadn't taken into account was Nyssa. She was not a seasoned traveller. Mother and daughter tired as easily as each other. He could see the Paradisians were itching to move quickly, as was he, but there was nothing they could do. At their current pace, it would take them longer than the week he had estimated the night before. Throughout the day, they stopped twenty times just to allow Nyssa and Shuut a chance to catch their breath.

By dusk, they had covered a decent distance, perhaps thirty miles, but it was not as much as Eliséo had hoped for. Once again, they settled on a hilltop for the night. As they sat close together in the cool night air, Nyssa asked Eliséo whether she should continue the lessons with Rilla and Plyke. At the mention of her name, Rilla looked over to them. He glanced over at the two young lintep and noticed that Plyke was sitting, motionless, with his head in his hands.

"Plyke, are you well?"

He barely moved in response. Tika answered in a soft voice. "He's been complaining of headaches all afternoon. Looks like it's gotten quite bad."

Nyssa was instantly on the alert. "Have you been getting headaches too?" The question was directed at her daughter. Rilla shook her head, red curls swaying in the breeze.

"Is Plyke older than you?"

"I don't know, Nyssa," Rilla replied. "No one really keeps track of birthdays in our Paradise. We were just put in groups for the Choosing. The four of us were born in roughly the same year. That's really all we know."

Nyssa looked uneasily at Eliséo. Lintep on the cusp of their power peaking often suffered from headaches just before their power tried to escape them. The headaches varied in intensity depending on the strength of their power and their control over it. Plyke's headaches could have started before Rilla's either because he was more powerful or because he had less control over his power. Neither reason lessened the urgency of getting him to Illaria as quickly as possible.

"We need go separate ways in the morning." Eliséo shook his head.

Nyssa nodded sadly. Knowing her time with the two young lintep was now limited, she took three of the small white stones from her pocket and handed one to Plyke and two to Rilla.

"Rilla, this will apply to you too when your headaches start. Your power is part of you, but if you can't control it and work well with it, that's when it will leave you. The best chance you have of keeping your power until you reach Illaria is to practise your skills repeatedly, familiarising yourself with your power.

"As often as you have time to do so, practise the simple skill of moving the stone around. Rilla, I know you've already grown bored of that exercise, but I'm not a mistress and I don't have any other basic skills to teach you that you haven't already somehow picked up by yourself. All I can suggest is that you use your power to pick up both stones and move them in different directions until you could do the exercise half asleep."

* * *

Rilla took her two stones and immediately began to practise with them but stopped when she noticed Plyke had still not moved. She watched as Nyssa moved closer to him.

"Plyke, you're safe now," Nyssa told him softly, lifting his head out of his hands. "Let go of your power and I promise it won't leave you – not while I'm here."

Nyssa fell flat on her back.

"Rilla, wrap your power around me and Plyke, now!"

Rilla dropped her two stones and leapt into action. She sent out her power in a dome, closing slowly around Plyke and Nyssa until she felt a slight resistance.

"Tighter!"

Unsure of exactly what she was meant to be doing, Rilla made her dome smaller, pushing against what she now realised must be Nyssa's power. She could feel Plyke's power within that, striking out, trying to break free.

Not knowing if she would hurt either of them, she kept reducing the size of her dome, making the walls thicker as she did so. She only stopped when she saw Nyssa sit back up again.

"What happened?" Rilla was almost too scared to ask. "What did we just do?"

Nyssa held her breath for a long moment before answering. "Remember when I told you I could make certain you couldn't use your power without my approval? Well, this is how I would have ensured that."

"I don't understand." Rilla was certain that she did understand but wanted very much to be wrong.

"To make sure that Plyke's power didn't escape him, I surrounded him with my power just like I asked you to do with mine. In theory, if I wanted to stop him using his power altogether, all I'd have to do is fit my power around him like a body suit."

"In theory?" Plyke finally spoke. "Haven't you done this before?"

"Not really." Nyssa raised her eyebrows apologetically. "But it was the only way to stop your headaches when they were already so bad."

"So you didn't really know that I would be safe if I let go of my power?" It was more of a statement than a question. Nyssa shook her head slightly.

"But I thought Rilla would be able to help if we needed it and I was right."

"*Thought*?" Plyke's voice was dangerously low. "You *thought* Rilla would be able to help? You're the one who keeps telling her not to experiment and that's exactly what you just made her do, while holding my life in the balance."

"Nyssa did what she had to for your sake Plyke." Eliséo tried to reassure him. "Had she not taken the chance, your headaches would not have stopped and your power would have left your body the first chance it got. We know, now, that Rilla is capable of holding your power close to you too, so if it ever gets to that stage again, we know what to do."

The explanation did little to calm Plyke. "How do I make sure they don't get so bad in the future?" He refused to look Nyssa in the eye as he asked the question.

"Practise any and all skills you've learnt so far. Practise as often as you can, even if it's just for a minute each time you stop to catch your breath."

Plyke closed his eyes. Rilla watched as he fumbled with his power to lift the white stone Nyssa had given him.

At Nyssa's instruction, Rilla withdrew her power from around her mother. She was shocked by what she had just done. Nyssa had given her the key to controlling any other lintep who might be less skilled or less powerful than she was. The weight of that knowledge was debilitating.

"Is it really that simple for one lintep to control another?" she asked Nyssa in so quiet a voice that she nearly wasn't heard.

"In essence, yes," Nyssa admitted. "But that lintep would need to catch you unawares or know a lot more about how to use their power than you do."

"That doesn't sound very difficult at the moment. Both Plyke and I could easily be caught unaware and I'd say *most* lintep know more about using their power than we do."

"Plyke, perhaps. But you are a bit of an oddity. You don't know much about using your power in a conventional way, but you are able to do things just by thinking them. I don't think any but the most skilled lintep would have any luck trying to control you."

Then you wouldn't really have been able to stop me using my power, Rilla thought to herself. Not wanting to think about it any further, she returned to her sleeping mat and curled up on it, closing her eyes tightly.

We'd better get to Illaria sooner rather than later. She voiced her fears to Eliséo. *I don't know if I can do that again without Nyssa. And I know that Plyke won't be able to do it for me.*

We will go our separate ways tomorrow, Eliséo reassured her. *If we go at full speed and travel part of the night, we might make it in a few days, but I do not know if the boys will be able to keep up that pace. Sleep now, we will sort it out tomorrow.*

Rilla slept beside Eliséo that night. Shuut had insisted he not keep watch that night so that he would be able to last without any sleep, if necessary, until they reached Illaria.

* * *

Plyke had been plagued by dreams half the night of whether he should tell to Nyssa that he was her nephew or not. He reasoned that, at this point, it couldn't hurt. They were about to go their separate ways. The next time they would see each other, he would already be under the tuition of lintep masters and mistresses and of her reach. He walked over to her, trying to move as far from the others as possible.

"Nyssa, I don't quite know how to say this, and I don't know if it will make a difference to you anyway," he mumbled the last half of the sentence. "But I'm your nephew. I'm Kora's son." He looked at her for some kind of positive reaction, but all he got was a shocked face.

"Kora's son? Why didn't you tell me? That means she was living in that same Paradise when I arrived ..." Nyssa looked panic stricken. "Was she one of the people that Erton...took care of?"

Plyke looked to Arishen, eyebrows raised.

"Not while we were there," the seer answered awkwardly. "I had a dream that she escaped when they tried to kill her. I don't know where she went, but she left the Paradise."

321

"How long ago was that?" Nyssa asked immediately.

"I don't know," Arishen shrugged. "At least a few weeks ago."

"Have you dreamt about her since? Do you know if she's still alive or where she was going? Anything to help me find her?"

"Sorry, no. It doesn't really work like that. My dreams don't follow people. They just show me bits and pieces of what they want me to see."

Plyke moved away from Nyssa. Consumed by the thought of Kora, she was completely ignoring him. It wasn't quite the reaction he had hoped for. Shuut tugged his shirt.

"Don't take it personally. She's always had a strong streak of selfishness." Plyke's hand accidentally brushed against Shuut's arm as he turned towards her. He saw flashes of memories where Shuut was dragged wherever Nyssa wanted to go with no care of what was best for her daughter.

"Well, she doesn't really owe me anything. We only just met after all. Maybe we'll get to know each other in Illaria."

"If she doesn't get it in her head to look for her sister instead. That's what half of our travels through the Outworld were all about – looking for Aunt Kora." Shuut shifted her weight restlessly at the memory. "Well not this time. She's getting me to Illaria first. I've finally got used to the four of you, I'm not letting you out of my sight for longer than I need to. Not now that I know you're my cousin and Rilla is my sister."

* * *

At the mention of her name, Rilla looked over to Shuut and Plyke. A stab of envy shot through her once more. Shuut motioned her over while Nyssa was cross examining Arishen about his dreams. Plyke joined Tika, giving them some privacy.

"I know you think I must hate you for everything, but I don't really. It wasn't your fault that the dragons lied to us. It was Nyssa's fault for letting them manipulate her and then me.

"As for the Paradise, I *did* owe you a life debt and you were right to hold me to it. You were just doing what you needed to do to save your friends ... well, fellow Paradisians anyhow."

Rilla was surprised by the admission. "But you kept trying to leave us and were so angry any time I forced your hand to keep us with you."

"Call it a banwep's curse." Shuut shrugged and held out her hand. Rilla shook it warily before being pulled into a hug. Shuut whispered in her ear. "You're my sister and that makes a difference to me. Look after the boys but don't forget to look after yourself as well. I know Eliséo would risk his life for you, but try not to put him in that position, okay? We'll get to Illaria as soon as we can."

Before she realised what was happening, Rilla was standing by herself. To say she was stunned by Shuut's farewell was an understatement. Despite her misgivings about the separation, she smiled. Under no other circumstances that she could think of would Shuut have revealed that to her. She was startled out of her musings by Eliséo's voice.

"The sun's rising. We need to go."

Hands waved in farewell. Nyssa came to give Rilla a hug, but said nothing. Rilla half-heartedly returned the embrace. She still wasn't sure how she felt about her

322

mother. There would be plenty of time to get to know her, to understand her reasons for abandoning her, when they were both in Illaria.

* * *

"Be safe and we'll see you soon." Eliséo shouldered his rucksack and started off down the hill. Only once he was certain the Paradisians were behind him did he pick up the pace. They easily kept up with him. There was no need to push them too hard. As long as they kept up a good pace all day with minimal stops, they would make good time.

They ran for no more than two hours at a time. Even though he could have easily run all day and all night without stopping, he didn't want to tire out the others. During their breaks, he made certain that both Rilla and Plyke practised using their power as Nyssa had instructed. Plyke struggled with his stone, that it kept him occupied for the entirety of each of their breaks. Rilla was less consumed by hers. She practised the skills Nyssa had taught her, but by their third break, she was well and truly bored by the task.

"Perhaps try a combination of things," Eliséo suggested to her. "It was only really done in the more advanced lessons in Illaria, but it might at least pose a challenge to you."

"What kind of combination?" Rilla asked, intrigued by the notion.

"What is the first thing you would do if we are attacked again?"

"Pull out my swords," she answered automatically.

"Assume that is not possible."

"Go invisible," Tika piped up. "If I was Rilla, I'd go invisible and then use my powers to throw something at the attackers. They wouldn't be able to see where she was to attack her or to know where the next stone would come from."

"Very good, Tika." Eliséo smiled. The small boy blushed at the praise. "You would have made a fine lintep."

"Try that next time we stop. Go invisible and then move your stone around. You can even try moving other objects. I am not certain how difficult it would be, but you could attempt to throw the objects rather than just move them gently. If you think you can manage it, you can go invisible even while we are running."

* * *

For the next two hours, Rilla concentrated on trying to go invisible while running. She found it more difficult than she had thought it would be. It was good to have something to challenge her.

If she had understood Nyssa correctly, her power would try to escape her if she didn't learn to control it. Control was never something she had considered doing with her power. Working with it, asking it to work with her, yes. But controlling it, no. Somehow, the concept felt wrong. It just seemed like it would be a constant struggle if she tried to control something that wild and powerful.

Maybe that's where Plyke ran into trouble. From what she had seen, he held onto his power with an iron grip and forced it to do as he wanted. Maybe it was because he grew up in the Paradise knowing it could kill him. Maybe it was because that was what Kora taught him. Whatever the reason, it was making things more difficult for him.

323

Rilla made sure no one was looking at her before risking a daytime conversation with Elessa. *Do you think if I explained to Plyke that he could try working with his power rather than struggle to control it, that it might make things easier for him?*

It's not a bad idea, but it could be too late for him to try that now without a master or mistress lintep around in case things go wrong. Elessa replied quickly and then cut their connection.

Daylight only lasted for ten hours. The days had been getting shorter with the cool change in weather. Even so, they had travelled close to fifty miles that day. Eliséo had told them if they managed to keep that pace going, it would only take another four days to reach Illaria.

As the others set up camp, Rilla walked over to her cousin, hoping that he would take her suggestion. Any time her skill had been a topic of conversation, he seemed to become angry with her and she still wasn't exactly sure why.

"I've been thinking about what Nyssa told us yesterday." Plyke looked up as she sat down beside him. "She said our power will try to leave us if we can't learn to control it."

"I remember," Plyke answered, a hint of anger in his voice.

"Well, I just wonder whether she's wrong about that. I mean, from what you've told us, Kora and Nyssa have very different ideas about how and when to use your powers. Maybe there are different ways for lintep to not lose their power."

"What do you mean?" Despite his annoyance, she'd managed to arouse his curiosity. Hoping that was all she needed, Rilla ploughed ahead.

"Please don't get angry when I say this, but it always looks like you're fighting with your power. You make it look like a struggle and if you lose that struggle, then your power tries to get away from you."

"Of course that's how it looks," Plyke told her moodily. "That's exactly what happens."

"Well, what I'm trying to say is, maybe that's not what *has* to happen. That's not what happens with me, anyhow."

The others had finished setting up camp and were now sitting around the two of them. Tika was listening closely to the conversation.

"What happens with you?" Tika asked, before Plyke could snap at her.

"I just think of what I want to happen and if it doesn't happen automatically, like going invisible, I ask my power to do whatever it is I need. Like with the fire and the water. I asked my power to help me carry water and it let me mould it into a watering can."

"So, you ask your power to work with you?" Tika laboured the point. "You don't try to force it at all."

Rilla shook her head, distastefully. "I don't think I'd *want* to try forcing it. It wouldn't feel right."

Plyke crossed his arms. "What if I try what you're suggesting and it still tries to get away from me?"

Rilla shrugged, munching on an apple she'd taken out of her rucksack. At this point, it was up to Plyke whether he tried it her way or not. It was probably a dangerous move, but she thought it was worth a shot.

"I'll take the second shift," Rilla told Eliséo before going to lie down in her sleeping mat. It had been a long day and she knew the next few days would be just as long.

* * *

"You could at least try," Tika pleaded with his Partner. "What's the worst that can happen?"

"Are you serious?" Plyke thundered. "The worst that can happen is my power leaves me and I die."

"If you stop being so stubborn, maybe you could try asking Rilla for some help so that doesn't happen. She could always surround you with her power, just in case, so that your power can't escape anyway."

"That's easy for you to suggest. It's not *your* life hanging in the balance."

"No, it's my Partner's life and I'm asking you to try everything you can to save yourself. Rilla's just trying to help." Tika finally lost his temper with Plyke. "Just because you're jealous that she effortlessly works so well with her power when you've struggled with yours all your life is no reason to be mean to her. In fact, it's more of a reason to listen to her – she doesn't look like she's in danger of losing her power at all."

"Tika," Eliséo interceded. "I know it looks like Rilla is safe from her power, but that is not the case. Her power hasn't started to peak yet. You are correct that she is handling it better than Plyke, but sooner or later, things will get much more difficult for her."

"So, you're saying that Plyke shouldn't try her way?" Tika stared at the elf in disbelief.

"No, I do not think that at all. Plyke should certainly try Rilla's way, but at most it would only buy him an extra few days, a week at the most."

"Well, that's something at least. It's up to you Plyke. How badly do you want to stay alive?" Tika left his Partner and went to lie down next to Rilla.

"I'll take the last shift," Arishen told Eliséo as he went to join Rilla and Tika.

* * *

Plyke huffed grumpily. "I guess that leaves me with the first shift." He saw Eliséo's near imperceptible shake of the head. "You think I'm being an idiot, don't you?"

"It is not my place to judge you, Plyke. I am only here to see you and Rilla safely to Illaria." Ever the diplomat, Eliséo deftly avoided his question.

"Don't you mean just Rilla?"

"No," he shook his head firmly. "Lady Eléna was quite specific about keeping you safe as well. I did not know she already knew who you were when we left Silvaren, but it makes sense now. She was good friends with your great-grandmother. She feels it is her duty to watch out for her family as much as possible. That means Rilla *and* you."

Plyke was stunned. He'd assumed, like everyone else, that Eliséo was only there for Rilla because of the prophecy. It hadn't even occurred to him that he was being protected too.

"But ... you're always so watchful over Rilla, not me."

"Do you think that may be because she has a knack of getting herself into trouble?" Eliséo raised an eyebrow at Plyke. "It has been easier to keep you safe because no one else knew who you were until just before we reached Goraburg.

325

By that time, Shuut was unconscious and we were more concerned about keeping Rilla's identity from Nyssa and the crystal dragons. They did not have any immediate interest in you, though if they had known you were Kora's son, that would have changed. In fact, if Nyssa had not been quite so shocked to hear about Kora, she would have taken a keen interest in you herself."

"Oh." Plyke had the decency to feel ashamed of his behaviour. "I didn't realise."

"There are a lot of things you do not realise, Plyke." Eliséo looked at him carefully. "That's why you should try to take some advice every now and then."

* * *

Eliséo was careful not to push the point too far. Plyke was fickle. One misplaced word and he would change his mind about something instantly. This would be so much easier if he could use his own magic to help Plyke through this stage. How bad could it possibly be to let Plyke see how much power he truly commanded?

Don't even think about it! Eliséo's eyes glowed softly as Elessa warned him off his train of thought. *He might not realise what it means if you help him, but it's certain to come up at some point in Illaria. You're already lucky he didn't mention that one time to Nyssa. If anyone even suspects that you're Eléna's son, Liessa's life will be rather short lived and your freedom will be taken away from you.*

Eliséo knew she was right, but he wished for the millionth time that it wasn't the case. If only Liessa had more power than he did, then there would be no problem at all, but she barely had any power to rightfully call her own. Without the crown to help her, she would have no more power than any other elf. Things would only get worse if she didn't have a powerful child of her own. He pushed the thoughts aside. There was no point worry about something that might never come to pass. For now, all he had to do was get Rilla and Plyke safely to Illaria so he could return to Silvaren.

* * *

Shuut missed her companions sharply. *Who would have thought a banwep could come to miss anyone, let alone four teenagers and an elf?* she thought to herself. She shouldn't be missing them at all since being reunited with Nyssa, but things were not going smoothly with her mother.

They had argued for a good hour about going to find Aunt Kora – again! Shuut had finally won the argument for two reasons. They had no idea where Kora had gone after leaving the Paradise and they had promised to meet everyone in Illaria. Nyssa had grudgingly given in. Since then, it had been two days of walking over the grassy hills.

Shuut was healing quickly and was well accustomed to travelling long distances. Already, she was outstripping her mother in stamina. If she knew the way to Illaria herself, she doubted whether she would have slowed down for Nyssa.

"You should guard your thoughts more closely," Nyssa said, with some disappointment.

"Not everyone pries into other peoples' minds," Shuut retorted hotly.

"Even *you* used to do that. What changed?" Nyssa was genuinely surprised.

"Maybe I don't want to be that person anymore. Rilla and Plyke could have tried to read my mind at any time and neither of them ever did."

"That's just because they haven't been trained to do it properly."

Shuut was already shaking her head before Nyssa finished speaking. "No, they didn't do it because they respected my privacy. Rilla only did it once by accident and refused to try it ever again and all Plyke ever had to do was touch my skin to know everything he wanted. They both knew they could do it to me and anyone else they met and they never did."

"Well, we know Plyke's excuse is because he was taught by Kora. She was so powerful and so much more skilled at everything than me. And one day she stopped using her powers. Just decided it was wrong. We had the biggest fight over that." Nyssa's anger died with that memory.

"And yet you still dragged me over half the Outworld looking for her."

"She's my sister." Nyssa shrugged helplessly. "I would do anything for her. Even if we didn't agree on everything, she still knew me better than anyone else and was always there for me. And I lost all of that with a stupid fight."

Shuut bit back a cutting reply as an image of Rilla drifted in front of her. She smiled at the thought that she had a sister now too. And a cousin. She'd only known them a few months but she knew they would always be there for her. They'd already saved her life a number of times. They had fought plenty of times and somehow always gotten over it. So why hadn't Nyssa and Kora?

"What happened in the end, to make Kora leave?" Nyssa had never told Shuut the whole story.

Nyssa sighed and closed her eyes for a moment. "Everyone knew that Princess Rilla had fought the humans who hated magic. She didn't want humans and lintep to be enemies. Some of her more controversial ideas were that lintep shouldn't use their powers on humans, particularly their ability to read and manipulate thoughts.

"Well, most of the younger lintep in Illaria disagreed with that notion. It was really only the older generation who still thought it was an interesting idea. The end result was that I disagreed with Princess Rilla's ideas and Kora didn't. She believed in Rilla's ideas so strongly that she grew angry with our assumption that we should because we could.

"Towards the end of her days in Illaria, she spent a lot of time in the library. I didn't make any effort to talk to her those days. Then one day, she was gone. I should have gone after her straight away, but I ... just let her go."

Shuut listened quietly, finally piecing together everything that had happened since. Nyssa had taught Shuut what she believed and Kora had taught Plyke what she believed. Rilla hadn't been taught by either of them, but instinctively sided with Kora and Plyke. It hadn't taken very long in their company for Shuut to second guess what she'd been taught by Nyssa.

"The younger lintep in Illaria, had they ever been in the Outworld before?" Nyssa shook her head. "Had you and Kora?"

"Yes, but only once. Our parents took us all to see Queen Eléna in Silvaren." Nyssa smiled at the memory.

"Us all? Are there more of you?" Shuut was stunned at the idea that she had more family out there.

"I really didn't tell you very much, did I?" Nyssa grimaced. "We had two brothers and a little sister but they were all killed by humans."

"What? Why?"

"For the same old reason. We are lintep and they were afraid of magic and didn't want to give us a chance to use our powers on them." Nyssa walked ahead of a stunned Shuut.

"How could that happen? Didn't your parents try to heal them, like Rilla can?"

"I don't want to talk about it, Shuut. Not now."

Nyssa shut down. Try as she might, Shuut couldn't get another word out of her for days. At least she now understood why Kora and Nyssa had such strong opinions about Princess Rilla's ideas, but somehow, they had chosen opposite sides and it had driven them apart.

Chapter Fifty-Seven – Life or death

It had been three days since they had parted ways with Nyssa and Shuut. The hills had continued, but they were now spotted with trees. Eliséo knew this area well. They were less than forty miles from Illaria, but it was still too far.

Plyke's headaches had continually grown worse. He had agreed to try Rilla's method of working with his power rather than trying to control it, but he couldn't manage it. Any time he came close to doing it, he would panic and pull it back in. Eliséo was pleased he had not been forced to contain the boy's power.

Rilla's headaches hadn't started yet, but Eliséo had been watching her closely. She was tiring more easily than usual. Any time he asked after her, she dismissed his worries with a wave of her hand. It wasn't until late on the fourth day that he understood what was happening.

They had slowed to a walk by midday. Plyke's headaches had gotten infinitely worse. Tika had taken to gently holding his elbow to guide him in the right direction. Rilla had stopped using her powers to blend into the background.

"We can't keep going like this," Arishen whispered to Eliséo. "Even I can tell you're getting worried. How far away are we now?"

"By now, probably thirty miles." Eliséo tried to hide the dismay from his voice, but he knew Arishen could hear it.

"Isn't there some way we can let the lintep know that we're coming and we need their help?"

"Short of Rilla or Plyke knowing how to communicate with the lintep whistle and hoping that there is someone to hear it, no."

"There might be." Tika had been straining to listen to the conversation. "If there are any fringa around and I call for them, they said they would come to help us."

"I doubt the birds can help us, Tika," Eliséo answered him. "However, you can try if you like. Anything is worth a try at this point. You will probably have to whistle a few times throughout the day. They are unlikely to hear you if you only do it once."

Tika nodded. He whistled the tune under his breath a few times before whistling it as loudly as he could. Every few minutes, he whistled again. Eliséo shared his hope that help would come, but was resigned to the reality that they were on their own.

It was late in the afternoon when they heard a crash behind them. Eliséo turned, sword already half drawn, to find Rilla had collapsed. He ran to her, falling to his knees. He checked for her breathing and a pulse. She was alive, but unconscious.

"Plyke, do you feel any bad magic?" Eliséo called out. When the boy didn't respond, Tika went over to ask him again. Plyke looked at him, completely unfocused. Eventually, he shook his head. At least they could rule out an attack on Rilla but the alternative was almost worse.

Eliséo picked her up and started walking towards Illaria again. "We have to get there as quickly as we can. Rilla isn't going to last long now without a lintep master or mistress."

"What's happening?" Arishen asked, as he shouldered Rilla's rucksack and helped Tika pull Plyke along.

"She is worse than Plyke now," Eliséo replied through gritted teeth.

"But how can that even be possible?" Tika asked in confusion. "She hasn't had a single headache."

"Headaches are the most common symptom," Eliséo told them. "Mostly because a lot of lintep fight with their power so it begins to struggle against them earlier. There are very few who react like Rilla. It only happens to those who work with their power instead of against it. Their power is not as desperate to escape their clutches until just before their power peaks. It is much more dangerous because you have less warning."

"Less warning?" Arishen asked in a frightened voice.

Eliséo swallowed a lump in his throat. "It means we need to reach Illaria tonight. Even tomorrow morning might be too late."

They all knew they couldn't possibly get there in that quickly. They quickened their pace as much as possible. Tika desperately whistled the fringa's tune every few seconds.

* * *

Nyssa's stamina had finally started to increase. She wasn't as fit as Shuut, but at least she wasn't holding them up anywhere near as much anymore. They'd barely spoken since Shuut had last asked her about Kora and the rest of her family. It was the most Nyssa had ever told her about them. It was a painful memory – not one she liked to dwell on.

"Did you hear that?" Shuut stopped suddenly, turning to look all around them.

"I don't hear anything," Nyssa half whispered before she felt a weight crushing in all around her. She grunted, pushing her power out to defend herself. That was when she realised what was happening. She was trapped. She turned to scream at Shuut.

"Run!"

It was already too late. Shuut was pushed up against a tree, struggling to free herself from something she couldn't see.

"How long has it been, Nyssa?" A cruel voice called out as a lean, tanned woman stepped out from behind a tree, inspecting her fingernails.

"No, no, no. Not you," Nyssa sobbed.

"Is that any way to greet your oldest friend?" The woman looked up from her fingers and fixed Nyssa with her impossibly pale blue eyes.

"What do you want, Lishe?" Nyssa asked in a trembling voice. "You already have more power than you ever dreamed of."

"Yes, but then, I was only ever envious of *your* power. Remember?" She absentmindedly twirled a strand of black hair between her fingers as she walked closer to Nyssa. "The power that you apparently still haven't mastered. Your gift always was wasted on you. The masters were so disappointed.

"And then what did you do? Disappeared to find Kora. Weak, stupid Kora. But that's not all you did, is it? No, you had to find a way to placate her, so you went and gave the crystal dragons their prophecy child, thinking that would bring the two of you together. After all, if the prophecy comes to pass, there will be even more people to rally around Kora's cause, won't there? Even if you still don't quite agree."

"Please, Lishe, let us go." Nyssa's legs would have given way under her if she wasn't being held in place by Lishe's power.

"Now why would I do that?" Lishe smiled viciously, glancing at Shuut. "I don't think I'll be needing you when I have this one. She's the one I've been tracking. I know the crystal dragons trained her to find the prophecy child and she did, didn't she? Now she's going to help me find her."

"So, you had groups of men roaming the Outworld, looking for us?" Shuut asked hollowly.

Lishe pinned Shuut with a calculating stare. "I followed you from the Drakos Mountains to that Paradise. Once you disappeared, I realised you'd found it. But that little brat tricked both of us by changing her name to Karinya." Shuut drew in her breath sharply. "Oh yes, I was close enough to hear all of that. But I followed you anyway. It wasn't until you left Silvaren that I realised what had happened, but by then you had the elf with you and those damn children were given weapons."

"So, you backed off and hired mercenaries to do your dirty work for you. Well, they failed miserably," Shuut replied smugly.

Lishe's mouth twisted into a smile. "No, they didn't. They weakened and frightened you. Every time you killed them, I knew your position. I don't know how and where you disappeared to for so long after I managed to ensnare your mind, but I knew exactly when you returned when the next group were killed.

"Stunning display that. You know the fire has only just started to burn itself out? It took me quite a while to track you through all of that. Who was responsible for that? Nyssa or little Rilla?" She looked from one to the other. "Now which of you is going to tell me all about her?"

Shuut kept her mouth shut. Nyssa panicked.

"We'll tell you anything. Just don't kill us."

"I won't kill this one, not yet." Lishe looked over at Shuut. "Her power isn't worth stealing. She'll be much more valuable to me alive. She's going to help me get Rilla on her own."

"And how do you propose to do that?" Shuut asked.

"Travelling together for such a long time, I'm sure there is some sort of loyalty between the two of you. When she realises I have you, she'll come quietly to save your life. Of course, that will mean that I get to kill both of you at the same time."

Nyssa frantically pushed her power out, struggling to free herself from Lishe but she was too panicked to do anything.

Calm blue ocean. Calm blue ocean. Calm blue ocean. She chanted the verse the masters had taught her to clear her mind before attempting anything difficult with her power. Taking a leaf out of Rilla's book, she experimented with her power. Nyssa gathered as much heat as she thought she could spare in her mouth. Ready as she ever would be, she spat flames out of her mouth towards Lishe. To her horror, the flames stopped inches from Lishe's head. Nyssa watched as Lishe turned to face her and the flames slowly travelled back towards her.

"Now, you're going to tell me exactly where I can find Rilla." Flames danced along Nyssa's left arm, searing her skin. Shuut called out for Lishe to stop, but Nyssa could barely hear over her own screams.

"Tell me who is with her and where she is or this will only last longer." Lishe watched in fascination as she dragged the little ball of fire over Nyssa's arms and legs, waiting for her to give in. "I can do this all day if you don't tell me. I need the practise anyway."

Nyssa howled in pain, refusing to tell Lishe anything now that she knew her plan. She would die to save the daughters she had abandoned. She just had to hope she could do one last thing to help them. Lishe laughed cruelly at Nyssa's cries and Shuut's desperate pleas.

"Tell me where to find little Rilla. Is the elf still with her? Is she on her way to Illaria or did you find a master to teach her outside the stronghold?"

Nyssa remained tight lipped and closed her eyes as she inwardly chanted. *Calm blue ocean. Calm blue ocean. Calm blue ocean.* She knew what she had to do and only hoped that it would work. It would give Shuut just that little bit more protection from Lishe. Nyssa tried to block out the pain of the fire dancing all over her skin as she pulled all of her power into her mouth. It was the only part of her she was certain wasn't held fast by Lishe's power – she could still talk.

She opened her eyes and held her power in her mouth, waiting for Lishe to move just another inch to the side. Timing would be everything. She looked at her daughter with tears in her eyes. Shuut was screaming uncontrollably and struggling against Lishe's power. Nyssa waited patiently for Lishe to turn her attention to Shuut. As soon as she did, Nyssa took her opportunity. She shaped her power into a spear and hurled it from her mouth straight at Shuut, making sure that it went into her open mouth.

* * *

The banwep instantly stopped screaming and gagged. She looked down in confusion. Lishe followed her eyes, taking a moment to understand what had happened. She turned to see Nyssa's lifeless eyes. She'd killed herself by giving her power to this banwep. She'd managed to keep her power out of Lishe's clutches for a little while longer. Lishe cursed in frustration, focussing all of her attention on the banwep as she allowed Nyssa to fall lifeless to the floor.

"Stupid, stupid Nyssa," Lishe muttered angrily, as she fitted her power around the banwep like a body suit, making sure to cover her entire head as well. "If she thinks giving her power to you will save you for very long, then she's sorely mistaken. I *will* have her power, just as soon as you help me kill Rilla."

* * *

Hours after Rilla had collapsed, Tika was still whistling his tune. His lips had dried to the point of cracking, but he kept whistling. If there was even the slightest chance that the fringa would come to help them, he wouldn't stop. Plyke was becoming more unsteady on his feet. Tika and Arishen were practically carrying him between them. Rilla's head was slumped on Eliséo's shoulder as he continued to carry her over the unending hills. The three boys walked into the elf when he stopped dead in his tracks.

"Up against the trees, now!" His tone of voice warned them off questioning him. They helped him set Rilla down next to Plyke and pulled out their weapons, scanning the forest for any sign of movement. When he saw nothing, Tika began to relax until he noticed Eliséo was still on the alert.

Minutes later, he finally heard what Eliséo heard – a crashing sound like a herd of animals charging towards them. If Rilla and Plyke had been able, all five of them would have been up in the tree branches. As it was, they were crowded as close to the trunks and out of the rough pathway as possible. They held their weapons at the ready as a group of kryti came crashing through the trees with a flock of fringa surrounding them. One of the little purple birds started whistling a high-pitched tune that the others quickly took up. The effect was immediate. The five kryti stopped in their tracks, spreading out to make sure their birds weren't in any danger.

"Tika?" The first purple bird flew over and landed on the boy's shoulder. "What happened to Rilla? Did she experiment too much?"

Tika, shook his head, crying in relief. "No, her power is peaking. We need to get her and Plyke to Illaria now. Can you help us?"

"Why do you think I rallied so many flocks around me? Just for the fun of it?"

"Thank you." Tika gently hugged the tiny bird and kissed his glossy black beak. "Eliséo can show us the way."

* * *

Eliséo watched warily. He hadn't been with them when Rilla and Tika had saved the fringa and the kryti. He wasn't convinced that the kryti wouldn't rip the heads of all five of them, as they were wont to do with their prey. It took every bit of his self-control not to attack when the nearest one bent over to pick up Rilla. The fringa noticed his uneasiness and hopped over to his shoulder.

"Rilla saved my kryti's life. Even though his debt to her is paid, as it is to Tika who helped her, he would never hurt either of them or any they travel with. They are very loyal creatures with long memories."

"Why did more than just your kryti come?" he asked curiously, still not at his ease.

"Some of my fellow fringa heard Tika whistling, they flew in to take a look at the situation. When the message reached me that two of the travellers looked quite ill, I thought it best to bring extra help. Of course, I expected the banwep to be the fifth person, not an elf."

"She's a few days behind us. We needed to get to Illaria as quickly as possible so we split up," Tika quickly explained. "I'll explain on the way."

Another of the kryti bent over to pick up Plyke. Eliséo, Arishen and Tika climbed up onto the backs of the other three. As soon as they were secure, the kryti leapt into action, the one carrying Eliséo taking the lead.

They ran at a steady pace, not even slowing as night fell. Eliséo guided his kryti through the thickening woods. He glanced back towards his companions as they travelled and grew increasingly concerned as he saw Plyke fall in and out of consciousness. Eventually they came to a tall hedge that ran for miles in either direction, blocking their way entirely. The kryti tried to blunder through the hedge with no luck.

"What now?" Tika asked. "How do we get in?"

"This is the most difficult part," Eliséo answered, evading his eyes. "As Ambassador of the Elves, I can enter any time I choose. Rilla and Plyke would also be able to pass through the barrier without trouble."

"But we're not lintep." Tika pieced together the problem.

"Exactly. By law, they won't let humans enter."

333

"What if we just try walking in with you?" Arishen suggested. Eliséo motioned for him to try. The seer parted the branches and tried to walk through to the grassy field beyond but could not proceed.

"We're not going to be separated now," he said angrily. "Not after everything we've been through."

Tika pointed to Plyke and Rilla's arms. Goosebumps. The lintep were whistling to each other. Eliséo thought of and discarded a number of scenarios to get them all in. Eventually he settled on the only one he thought might work. Rilla had told him earlier that she had a plan to get Tika and Arishen into Illaria. She was the key.

"Hide Rilla and Plyke," he told the kryti. "Don't let the lintep see them until I've spoken to them first." The huge beasts moved to do his bidding and not a moment too soon. Within minutes, one elderly lintep, accompanied by two much younger ones, had emerged from the bush. Eliséo smiled in recognition.

"Well met, Master Aurelius." Eliséo bowed ever so slightly to the old man.

"Well met, Ambassador Eliséo." Master Aurelius returned the bow, taking in the sight of the two humans, five kryti and the flock of fringa behind the elf. "What brings you to Illaria with such *diverse* company?"

"These kryti came to help us bring you two lintep," Eliséo explained. "I was escorting them to Illaria myself, but we've been beset by a few challenges and now they have now both been unconscious for hours. Can you bring them back to us, or is it already too late?"

"Marilisa, Tommaso, this will be good practise for you." Aurelius motioned the two younger lintep forward as the kryti stepped aside to reveal Rilla and Plyke lying unconscious on the ground. Eliséo thanked his lucky stars that they had agreed to help before taking them into Illaria. "Don't be too forceful, but guide their power safely back into them."

Tika stood protectively over Plyke as Marilisa knelt beside him. He watched as she placed a hand on his forehead and closed her eyes in concentration. Sweat beaded on her forehead.

"This power is too wild and strong," she panted. "I can't do it."

Aurelius instantly took her place by Plyke's side, likewise placing his hand on the boy's forehead and closing his eyes. In less than a minute, Plyke's eyelids began to flutter. Tika hugged him as soon as his eyes focused on him. For the first time in weeks, Plyke did not hesitate to show some affection for his Partner, hugging him back tightly.

"Master Aurelius?" Everyone turned at the sound of Tommaso's voice. "I've gathered her power all around her, but she isn't waking up."

Eliséo fought down the panic inside him. *Can you wake her?* His eyes glowed a soft silver as he reached out to Elessa.

Not while another lintep is touching her, Elessa replied immediately. *It's too dangerous. They'll easily feel my presence.*

Tommaso moved away from Rilla, giving Aurelius room to kneel beside her. The old lintep placed his hand gently on Rilla's forehead but only for a few moments. He took his hand away and looked up at Eliséo in confusion.

Elessa took the opportunity to make a connection with Rilla. She found all of her power, milling around outside her impressive tower, apparently lost without Rilla's mind to guide it. Without losing another moment, she dived into Rilla's tower, calling out as loudly as she could to the girl. Eliséo, seeing how dangerously silent

Rilla was, followed Elessa into the tower. Together, they managed to wake her mind and bring her slowly out of unconsciousness. They pulled out of her tower and away from her mind just as she began to open her eyes. Only the faintest glow emanated from her green eyes. Eliséo hoped that the others hadn't been watching her too closely.

"Did we make it?" she asked in too quiet a voice. Eliséo breathed a sigh of relief at the sound.

"Not without some help from us." The little purple fringa flew down and landed on her shoulder. Rilla reached up, smiling, to stroke its chest with her finger.

"Does this put me in your debt?" she asked weakly. "Or are we really even now?"

"We were already even, but you scratched my back once so now I'm scratching yours. You'll all be safe here."

The lintep had all been looking on curiously, but at that point, Aurelius spoke up. "I fear that we cannot allow the humans to enter Illaria. It is against our law."

"But we've travelled all this way together," Arishen complained. "We're not splitting up now."

"You don't have a choice in the matter, young one," Aurelius explained. "If your friends choose to enter Illaria, they will do so without you."

"No, we won't." Rilla's strength was returning. She stood up, helping Plyke to his feet, to face the older lintep. "We will refuse to enter Illaria without Arishen and Tika."

Eliséo hid his surprise. It was a bold move, if it worked.

"We don't particularly care what you do," Marilisa replied coolly. "If you want to die or lose your power to stay with your friends, then that's your decision. Let's go." She turned to walk off, Tommaso hesitantly following her. Only Aurelius stayed behind, looking between the two young lintep and then back to Eliséo.

"Ambassador, why would you bring these lintep here in the knowledge that they would refuse to enter without their human friends? It's possible they will both die because their power is so great."

"You'll forgive me, Master Aurelius, but perhaps you should look a little closer." Eliséo prompted him. "I don't think you'll want either of them to die, especially not the girl."

Marilisa and Tommaso turned back around as Aurelius took a step closer to Rilla, examining her closely. He turned his attention briefly to Plyke, but came back around to Rilla. Eliséo knew he'd already guessed who she might be, but the lintep wanted to be certain.

"What is your name, child?"

"I am Rilla, daughter of Nyssa." There was a sharp intake of break from the three lintep. "And this is Plyke, son of Kora. From what we've been told, the four of us are the last remaining descendants of Princess Rilla."

Aurelius sighed deeply. "And even with that knowledge, you would rather die than be separated from your human companions?"

"They're not just our companions," Plyke finally spoke up. "Tika is my Partner and Arishen is a close friend and a seer."

Tommaso looked at Arishen in excitement. "A human seer? Surely the law will make an exception for such a rarity."

"The law will make no such exception," Marilisa answered hotly. "I don't care who they are, they aren't bringing humans into Illaria."

"Are *you* going to answer to Lord Aaron if Rilla's great-grandchildren die because of you?" Eliséo asked her.

* * *

Sparks shot out of Marilisa's eyes towards Eliséo. Rilla reacted instantly, hurling part of her power out to intercept the flames, driving them down into the dirt and extinguishing them.

"I count Ambassador Eliséo as one of my friends and will protect him as aggressively as I will all my friends. Either you grant the five of us entry to Illaria or you send us away, but don't you dare attack us." Rilla stood defensively in front of her companions with the five kryti growling lowly behind them.

"Marilisa, stand down," Aurelius told the girl sternly. "You may be a training guardian of the border, but that does not give you the right to attack Ambassador Eliséo or any lintep requesting entry to Illaria."

Marilisa bit down a retort and stormed off past the border of Illaria. Once she was out of sight, Aurelius exchanged a quick word with Tommaso and sent him to follow her.

"My apologies, Ambassador. Marilisa is one of our more hot-tempered trainees with strong views against humans." Turning to Rilla and Plyke, he continued. "It stands to reason that the descendants of Princess Rilla are so attached to humans. These are very unusual circumstances, but please accept my invitation to the five of you to enter Illaria."

Rilla relaxed slightly. She brought her finger up to her shoulder and brought the fringa around to face her. Gently, she stroked his chest and kissed his glossy black beak before bringing him over to the kryti she had once saved. The kryti took Rilla up in one arm and Tika in the other, once more shouting out gutturally in respectful farewell. Once they were safely back on the ground, all five kryti and their flock of fringa took to the woods.

"For the humans to enter, we will all need to hold hands. The barrier won't let them in otherwise."

Aurelius held out his left hand. To make sure Tika and Arishen weren't accidentally left behind, Rilla and Eliséo went through last, with Aurelius and Plyke in the lead. Rilla was relieved when Tika and Arishen both got through the border, but her enthusiasm ended when she came through herself and saw Arishen writhing and screaming on the ground, eyes firmly shut. She immediately looked for Tika to make sure it wasn't a reaction of the barrier on humans, but he was staring at Arishen in just as much shock as everyone else.

"What's happening?" Aurelius was the one to ask the question on everyone's lips.

"It must be a vision, but even the worst ones in our Paradise didn't do this to him," Rilla answered in a hushed voice. "I'm not going to try to wake him up from it. Last time I did that, I ended up with a broken nose and a black eye."

They all watched the seer anxiously through his screams until he finally fell silent. Once she was certain his dream was over, Rilla shook his shoulder, leaning as far back from him as possible. He instantly opened his eyes, looking wildly around him. He locked onto Rilla.

"Nyssa's dead."

"What?" Rilla shook her head in disbelief. "What are you talking about? Shuut is with her. She'll protect her."

"No." Arishen lost control and started sobbing. "Nyssa was tortured and now she's dead. Shuut has been captured and can't get away. She's in danger. She's going to die. We have to go back and save her!"

Rilla looked helplessly at the others. She had no idea what to do. Eliséo recovered first.

"Did you see their faces?" the elf asked.

"No, I never do, but it was Nyssa and Shuut. I'm sure of it."

"Do you know where they were?"

"No." Arishen slumped his shoulders.

"Do you know if it has already happened or is going to happen?"

"No, but I think it has happened."

"Can you be sure of that?"

"No, but please believe me. Whether it's happened or not, whether Nyssa is alive or dead, Shuut is in trouble."

Rilla looked at Eliséo in concern. Aurelius alone kept staring at the seer.

"Have any of your visions ever come to pass?" the old lintep asked him.

"Yes," Arishen answered eagerly.

"Have any of them *not* come to pass?"

"Yes," he admitted. "But the ones that didn't come to pass were because we changed the circumstances before they could. We can't change these circumstances because we aren't there. Nyssa is dead and Shuut needs our help."

"But Arishen, we don't even know where to find them," Rilla pointed out.

"Don't you care that your mother is dead and your sister is in danger?" Arishen practically screamed at her. Rilla backed off immediately. She'd never seen Arishen so angry before.

"That is not fair, Arishen," Eliséo stepped in. "Rilla is right. You cannot leave Illaria now. Both she and Plyke will die if they do not remain here and you and Tika would never survive out there on your own not to mention the lintep probably would never let you back in here if you left."

"But you could go," Arishen suggested. "All you would have to do is follow the path we took all the way back to them. They can't be more than a few days behind us."

"If your vision has come to pass, by the time I get there, they will no longer be there. Unless whoever captured Shuut continues on to Illaria along the same track, then I have little chance of finding them."

"I can't believe you're just going to let Shuut die."

Rilla knew the accusation wasn't directed solely at her, but she couldn't help feeling responsible for that decision. She racked her brain, trying to find some solution to the problem.

"Master Aurelius, does Nyssa have any friends left in Illaria?"

The old lintep thought for a moment before slowly nodding.

"Do you think any of them would be willing to search for her? And for Shuut? Eliséo could tell them where we came from and perhaps they could spread out from there ..."

"I wouldn't be able to force any of them to do so, but if they agree after hearing the seer's vision, they would be free to help you." Master Aurelius spread his hands out.

Rilla looked to Arishen. He breathed a sigh of relief and nodded gratefully to her. She had to look away from his eyes before she broke down. Just by looking at him, she could see his vision floating in front of her. It was horrific. She could only hope that it wasn't a true vision, that something had or would happen to change it.

The sun had risen by the time Aurelius led them away from the barrier. The Paradisians walked with heavy hearts into their new home. Rilla alone knew that Eliséo would not be staying with them. She would feel more alone than ever before. First, she had lost Rhanya, now Nyssa and possibly Shuut. She didn't know how she would manage being away from Eliséo.

Take heart, Rilla. Elessa risked a short conversation with her. *We'll always be there for you, even if you can't see us.* She smiled at the thought and moved ever so slightly closer to Eliséo as they followed Master Aurelius to the lintep stronghold.

www.ingramcontent.com/pod-product-compliance
Lightning Source LLC
Chambersburg PA
CBHW072203130726
47910CB00011B/1793